Ankita Verma Datta is an Economics graduate from Mumbai University and is trained in advertising communication and marketing at the Xavier Institute of Management/ Communication. She has spent more than a decade in the advertising industry, handling a wide range of clients from finance, insurance, education, food industry, and also government sector and political campaigns, before starting her own communications consultancy in 2003. Apart from marketing and advertising, she has interests in various other fields, including curating antique Portugal houses in Goa and 'hobby-breeding' the exotic dog breed of Tibetan Mastiffs. An ardent nature and animal lover, she spends her time between Mumbai, Lonavala and Goa.

Trust Me Not is her debut fiction novel and she intends to continue writing socio-political thrillers with current relevance in future too. She writes to evoke and entertain.

She can be reached at:

Facebook: www.facebook.com/ankitavermadatta/

Twitter: @ankita_reflects

Website: www.ankitavermadatta.com

TRUST ME NOT

ANKITA VERMA DATTA

JAICO PUBLISHING HOUSE
Ahmedabad Bangalore Bhopal Bhubaneswar Chennai
Delhi Hyderabad Kolkata Lucknow Mumbai

DISCLAIMER

This is a work of fiction. Names, characters, businesses, places, events and incidents are either the products of the author's imagination or used in a fictitious manner. Any resemblance to actual persons, living or dead, or actual events, is purely coincidental.

Published by Jaico Publishing House
A-2 Jash Chambers, 7-A Sir Phirozshah Mehta Road
Fort, Mumbai - 400 001
jaicopub@jaicobooks.com
www.jaicobooks.com

TRUST ME NOT
ISBN 978-93-86348-94-4

First Jaico Impression: 2017

Page design and layout: Special Effects, Mumbai

Printed by
Gopsons Papers Limited
A-2 & 3, Sector 64
Noida - 201 301 (U.P.)

CHAPTER 1

"Damn!" exclaimed Reeva as she paced restlessly in her cabin. She wanted to let out a scream. Under normal circumstances, she absolutely loved doing what she did, but today was just not that day. Her large, brown eyes smouldered as she took a deep breath to calm herself.

"Tell me, what did he say? In his exact words."

"He said that he didn't expect this… um… shit from our agency." Reeva's assistant looked around uncomfortably. "And that you should be fired." She had almost mumbled the last word.

"Fired?" Reeva was furious.

The assistant nodded, avoiding eye contact.

"Oh yeah, of course… fired." Reeva chewed the words, "Because apparently, I don't know how to do my job." She sank into her chair and the assistant scurried away at the first opportunity.

Reeva couldn't believe that the jerk from the pricey McPherson & Solly had not only completely trashed her perfectly analyzed and balanced advertising pitch, but even called her boss to explain elaborately why he did it. Reeva's secretary had informed her that Mr. Ajay Sehgal's temperature was high enough to contribute to global warming. She sighed. *Honestly, people are beginning to have very petty and narrow mindsets. Especially those around me.*

In no mood to talk to anyone, her temper hit the danger mark when she saw Buddy, her bonsai cactus, lying dry and lifeless on the sill. "Hari Prasad… why haven't you watered Buddy?" Reeva screamed at the peon.

Harry appeared sheepishly, hands clasped, knowing that the use of his full name spelled trouble. "Madam, the office electrician says the water will seep through the back and short-circuit the wiring."

"How often have I told you? This is not a fish; it's a bonsai cactus that needs just a *little* sprinkling."

"Okay madam," Harry looked down, tactfully pretending to decipher the tile pattern on the floor.

He shuffled away quickly, reminding Reeva of a tortoise retreating into its shell on the slightest provocation. For Reeva, retreating wasn't an option. She still had to work through the rest of the evening and placate her tenacious though fair boss. Ajay Sehgal, her long-time boss, could be most accommodating and yet unmovable as a rock once he decided to dig in his heels. She knew her current mood vibrated off her cabin, as colleagues gingerly walked past her door, avoiding her eye. She mentally kicked herself for being so loud.

Harry reappeared at her cabin door, "Madam your tea, strong and with Splenda." Harry knew, a light and aromatic Earl Grey wouldn't work now.

"Thank you Harry," her tone softened.

"Never mind madam... but please call me anything, *anything* but Hari Prasad."

She peacefully sipped her hot tea, but her short-lived tranquility was shattered with her intercom's loud ringing. "Hello?" She barked into the phone.

"Can you come in?" commanded her pissed off boss.

Here it comes, she thought, *a long lecture on realigning the presentation, with generous advice on client management thrown in*. She knocked and entered the cabin. Mr. Sehgal was on a call and waved for her to sit. Reeva had always fancied herself being in his position – of someone who was exceedingly busy without being self-conscious of it. Finally, he hung up and eyed her sceptically. He well knew that Reeva's bursts of creative energy were often offset by her bouts of inertia. She wasn't lazy, but often procrastinated for that better strategic idea which seemed to lurk just around the corner. And, once it struck her, nobody could make her let go of it. She was like a dog with a bone. In the past, this had caused many storms in teacups, especially Reeva's.

Mr. Sehgal played with his limited edition Mont Blanc. "Mr. K from M&S called."

"I know, sir."

"He said today's presentation lacked the glamour and grandeur the product's profile demands." His tone was flat, which was a dangerous sign.

"I reserve my own views on that, sir," Reeva matched his tone.

"Hmm. He also said you haven't taken his calls for the past three hours. He wanted to discuss key changes before he leaves for his trip."

The colour drained from Reeva's face. So, the persistent ringing every fifteen minutes wasn't some pesky guy offering her a credit card, but Mr. K himself. She hadn't listed him in her contacts, yet. She would be damned. Deciding offence was her best defence, she presented her case.

"Well... I believe Mr. K has a narrow vision and does not understand the scope of our presentation. After all, he is from banking and not marketing. We need to look at long-term objectives..."

Mr. Sehgal cut in, "Reeva, Mr. K's an important client. You will execute his campaign the way he wants, and by this Friday, before he leaves for Havana to attend a cigar conference."

"But it's already Tuesday!"

"Good. You have two full days. Use them well." He turned to his documents, clearly unwilling to negotiate.

"But Mr. Sehgal..."

"Reeva, next time, please don't avoid a client's call. I'll send the re-brief right away. Get your team started now." His eyes didn't leave the files.

She returned to her desk, muttering, "Mr. K is leaving for Havana to attend a cigar conference, is he!" Her circumstances had deteriorated considerably in the last fifteen minutes. To top it off, the social scenario at home was going to make her life difficult over the next two days as she struggled with her new presentation.

Reeva loved driving her passion-red Beetle. But parking was a battle she faced on a regular basis. She drove into her complex and as expected, found her parking spot taken. Too tired to get into an argument with the guard on duty, she parked in the last available vacant spot. All she wanted was to change into her old, grey T-shirt, grab dinner while watching her favourite TV show and finally curl up with a book.

She exited the lift and saw that the front door of the house was slightly ajar. She groaned, *Oh no, another visit from Mrs. Mehta.* She wasn't looking forward to company, especially from a self-proclaimed, nosy, agony aunt.

As she entered, a fancy envelope flew at her face. "What the heck?" She instinctively struggled to catch it, while balancing the files in her arms. A grinning seventeen-year-old stood before her. This unique male specimen was her younger brother Apps, short for Apoorva. Apps was a nickname earned because of the many applications he downloaded on his phone. But their mom had insisted on calling him Appy, and Reeva loved it just because it irritated him.

"Aha… the corporate princess arrives. Where did you park the royal carriage your highness?" teased Apps. He knew that parking issues irked her.

"Stop it Apps... What's in the envelope?"

"That wedding invitation, which Mom has declared we have to attend."

"But I thought we were to ditch it." Her head furiously calculated the new time limits for the presentation, for which Mr. Sehgal had already issued a grade-five tornado warning.

"Not any more… we're going and you're driving us. Can you manage that without causing a pile up on the freeway? Final Destination style?" Apps wore the grin she always found infuriating.

"But I can't go. Work commitments. I'll talk to Mom."

"Not possible. I've already said yes and Dad is cutting his trip short to meet us there." He performed a little shimmy-and-shake move.

Ignoring him was in her best interest for the moment, so she moved in looking for Mom instead. She had clearly informed her last week about her tight schedules.

Reeva walked into the living room to witness Mrs. Mehta delivering a monologue of the calibre that would put any proclaimed godman or guru to shame. Mrs. Rai sat transfixed on the chair opposite her – concrete evidence that hypnotism was a real art. Reeva always felt her mom was way too benign, soft and tractable.

Reeva tapped her mom lightly on the shoulder. Both women snapped out of their trance but Mrs. Mehta was the first to react.

"Reeva, there you are! I haven't seen you around much lately."

"Yes Mrs. Mehta, work has kept me a bit busy."

Mrs. Rai raised her brows with slight disapproval. She preferred Reeva to address all elders with a relationship tag, not by their names.

"Oh, come on sweetie, a girl like you should have some fun. You aren't getting any younger."

Mrs. Mehta was known to hit below the belt. At the Rai residence, Reeva's marriageable age was discussed as if it were a matter of national emergency. Reeva had time and again failed to explain that at twenty seven, she still had a long way to go – personally and professionally.

"Mrs. Mehta, how's Sunaina doing by the way? She hasn't visited in a long time." Reeva decided to counter with genuine interest. Sunaina was Mrs. Mehta's elder daughter whom she had wed off at a young age of twenty. She often landed up on her mother's doorstep after an episode of marital discord, as she struggled to adjust with her new family and an equally young and immature husband. But Mrs. Mehta was a pro at the 'war of the words'. She causally brushed off Reeva's tangential attack and shifted the focus back on her with vigour.

"Oh, she will be visiting soon," she said, dismissively. "By the way Mrs. Rai, I have an excellent catch for Reeva."

"Really?" Mrs. Rai almost moved towards her on the sofa.

"Yes, yes. A respected family from Bangalore, looking for a matured, dusky bride."

She continued, "The boy is an IAS officer. He too, like Reeva, forgot about his passing age while building his career. In his late thirties, he has a thing against fair skin. I don't understand his attitude. I mean which man wouldn't like a fair bride?" She squealed with laughter.

Right that moment, something snapped in Reeva and she felt like a Spanish rodeo bull with Mrs. Mehta as the red flag.

"Mrs. Mehta, I think it's getting rather late. I'm convinced that saving your daughter's failing marriage should be your priority rather than finding me a match. I don't think she'll go back to her husband if she lands at your place one more time. Don't you think?" She smiled and fluttered her eyes.

"Reeva!" Mrs. Rai admonished her, but she couldn't care less. She was tired, stressed out and ravenous.

Mrs. Mehta got up with a jerk, toppling the crystal glasses

on the table and creating a mess. She left in a huff without a word, even though Mrs. Rai called after her. Reeva plopped on the sofa and closed her eyes. Mrs. Rai returned and sat next to her.

Reeva began, "Mom..." she wanted to explain. But she saw that her mom's eyes shone with tears. It was an unexpected turn and if it was going to be emotional blackmail, Reeva already knew it would work.

"Why do you get so angry Reeva? Do you think we're your enemies?" Her voice quivered.

"No Mom. I just don't want advice from walking-talking chandeliers that don't matter to me."

"We just want to see you happy and settled. The way you're going, it will only turn you into a lonely woman. Look at your temper and manners!"

"Look Mom, I'm sorry, but I like my life the way it is."

"You will understand the need of a partner only when you're on the wrong side of your thirties."

"Mom, I never said that I won't *ever* get married."

Mrs. Rai was at it instantly. "Well then it's settled. Coming Friday, give yourself a chance to check out some of the most eligible bachelors at the Jaiswal wedding."

"Yeah Mom, that's what I wanted to discuss. I told you I wouldn't be able to come. You forgot."

She didn't respond, but only looked down again. Her brows creased. Afraid of another barrage of tears, Reeva gave in immediately.

"Alright Mom, I'll come. But no hard-selling, okay?"

Elated at the prospect, her mom hugged her briefly, but as she walked to the kitchen, she declared, "You better wear something nice for the wedding."

Reeva sighed in exasperation. The wedding issue was settled, though not to her liking. Mrs. Rai had unwittingly managed to push her into a corner.

After dinner, Reeva decided to select her ensemble for the wedding. She checked herself in the mirror while fretting that it was a day-long event. This meant she needed at least two outfits. She found dressing up very cumbersome, but had to concede this time. Reeva knew that she was attractive, in a way that she could turn heads in any room. With average height, shoulder-length hair, wheatish complexion, and a small face with an olive chin, she was delicately elvish. But the highlight was her large and dark brown eyes, which could flash every emotion with equal honesty, and that made it easier for people to read her, much to her disadvantage. Her high metabolism rate was her trump card – it kept her enviously slim despite her healthy appetite.

To her dismay, Reeva realized she only had a black evening gown, which was completely inappropriate for the day event. Panicking, she decided it was time to call the only fashion saviour she knew. She speed-dialled her dearest friend Kinsy, short for Kinnari.

Kinsy took her time answering the phone. She was notorious for leaving her phone on silent mode, making her inaccessible at the most urgent times. "Hey Reevs, I was just about to call you!"

"Why? What happened now?"

"You won't believe... I picked up a Louis Vuitton tote today at a massive discount, like, almost thirty per cent!" She sounded excited enough to need a sedative.

Reeva sighed. She knew how crazy Kinsy was about brands. "Listen Kinsy, I need something to wear for that wedding I have to attend on Friday."

"But, I thought you weren't going."

"I know. Change of plans. Mom is insisting on showcasing me."

"Oh wow, then we gotta dress you up." Reeva could imagine Kinsy jumping with glee.

"Nothing fancy, okay? Something light-coloured. Elegant but not dressy," she warned her friend, who tended to go overboard.

"Don't worry, I have just the outfit for you," said Kinsy.

"Okay, I'll come see you tomorrow after work." Reeva smiled, for they both wore the same size.

"Sure. We could catch dinner afterwards." Kinsy sounded excited.

Unsure of her work scenario, Reeva mumbled something between a yes and a no and ended the call with a sense of accomplishment. Kinsy had once again come to Reeva's rescue with her enviable wardrobe. Finally, she glanced at the clock and groaned. It was close to midnight and she had a challenging day tomorrow, starting early morning. Taking a deep breath, she sank into her bed. As soon as her head touched the pillow, she drifted into a dreamless sleep.

CHAPTER 2

The following morning was a breeze. Reeva rushed out of the house even before the house help Asha could get her bearings. As she brushed past Asha *tai*, she immediately asked, "*Beta*, you're leaving so early today. Did you eat?" Asha *tai* had been with them for almost a decade and considered it a privilege to fuss over everyone in the family.

"No *tai*; tell Mom I'll be late tonight. I'm going to Kinnari's place after work."

"*Beta*, do you want me to pack a sandwich?" she called after her, but the lift door was already closing. Reeva wasn't a breakfast person. Contrary to all fitness and diet experts, she felt carbohydrates in the morning made her sluggish.

That day, however, she had mentally conditioned herself to approach the day as if in a boot camp – arrive at office, organize the desk in minutes, work for four hours straight, re-strategize on the presentation, and have a working lunch at 12:30pm. She had also reserved an early afternoon slot for a brainstorming session with the creative team. She wanted to be ready with the modified strategy by 5pm. This would give the team an entire Thursday to realign the creative pitch to the new strategy, since she was off for the wedding on Friday.

If all went well, she could be out by latest 6:30pm. Then it struck her. If she was not there on Friday then who would present the fresh pitch? She could not afford Mr. K throwing another temper tantrum. She would have to discuss this urgent matter with Nihaal, the moment she reached office.

As Reeva drove into the commercial complex that housed her office, she felt a new sense of purpose. She parked her car, looked up at the tall, imposing modern structure made of glass and steel, and took a deep breath. Working for Creative AdZone Inc. had always given her a high. It was not the biggest advertising agency in the market and her paycheque was not the fattest, but it gave her a sense of ownership. She was fairly well known within the industry with few successful projects under her belt. Feeling elated, she smiled to herself. The morning sun was bright and everything felt achievable, however difficult or unapproachable.

Reeva sat across Nihaal Kapoor, the agency's top-notch and highly talented creative director, and no less than a budding celebrity in the advertising industry. Her exasperation was growing by the minute. They had been at it for the past twenty minutes but Nihaal was vehemently refusing her proposal.

"Reeva, you don't understand. It's a big pitch and that too in the final stages. It's not a good idea for me to lead the presentation alone. Besides, you know it won't look professional. You are the client servicing director; this is your job." Nihaal folded his arms.

"Nihaal please, you will do just fine. You've done it in the past," persisted Reeva.

"But you know I prefer to cover only creative aspects. Besides, I wouldn't want to handle a query pertaining to marketing or media." Nihaal was very particular about job roles. "Why not let someone else from your own department cover for you?"

"Nihaal, there's not enough time to orient someone new into this pitch. And don't worry, Rajani will cover the marketing and media details."

"It's not about covering the other aspects. You know I can do it. But even if I agree, what makes you think Mr. Sehgal will let you go through with this?" He narrowed his eyes.

"I'll manage that part Nihaal. But look–"

"I'm not convinced it will work."

"Nihaal, c'mon. You know I wouldn't ask you if it weren't an emergency. If you do this, I will owe you one." Reeva was now panicking.

Nihaal was quiet for a beat. Finally, with just a mumbled 'okay', he sighed and looked away. The abruptness of it completely threw Reeva off.

"Great, see you later for the fresh briefing," she said, recovering from his unexpected response. She was dazed. After a long tirade about everything that could go wrong, he had agreed with a single word – 'okay'.

Reeva could never understand her relationship with him, even after four years of working together. At office, they often shared coffee breaks in the canteen, worked until late and discussed moot issues passionately. But that's where it ended. Nihaal was the brooding kind. He had a certain mysterious, masculine appeal, which Reeva knew that few female junior artists in the creative department found irresistible. He had those earthy good looks with a touch of sensitivity and perceptive intelligence. She found working with him effortless as he was always full of bright ideas and could quickly deduce and interpret ideas. In any strategy presentation, he was a smooth operator, anticipating the client's questions and expectations. He was not much of a people's person, but then the creative nature of his work allowed him the luxury of being incommunicado. Most importantly, he never lost his cool. Reeva knew that she could rely on him anytime.

With Mr. K's presentation taken care of, the day went by rather smoothly. As always, Nihaal was thorough during the creative briefing. With all doubts put to rest Reeva finally felt that her life was *not* turning into an episode of *24*.

Reeva left office with just a fifteen-minute delay, which wasn't too bad. She planned to reach Kinsy's house by 8pm latest and decided that after the fitting, she would even take up the offer of dinner, depending on whether Kinsy would turn a single dress trial into a full-blown fashion event.

But things proceeded faster than expected, as for once, they agreed on a pretty peach-coloured, Indo-western, fusion dress, with cream and gold embroidery. It was exquisitely feminine without being typical and with Kinsy's expert touches, the entire effect was magnificent. Afterwards, they decided to take the short walk to Becky's, a neighbourhood deli.

Even though Reeva was enjoying her outing with Kinsy that evening, she intermittently brooded over the coming weekend. She was still unhappy about how her mom had emotionally blackmailed her into attending the wedding. But Kinsy had a rather interesting take. She felt Reeva should date those eligible bachelors for an entire year, before taking a call. An outwardly reasonable approach until it became apparent that she wanted Reeva to date them all simultaneously. They had a series of gut-splitting laughs over the various possible, funnily tragic outcomes. After dinner, Reeva walked Kinsy to her apartment, picked up her car from the driveway and drove back home, tired but relaxed.

The following day passed smoothly too as she convinced Mr. Sehgal that Nihaal was a better person to present the second round to Mr. K for two reasons. First, it was a creative-driven pitch which Nihaal could handle better. Second, in case Mr. K was still cross with her, it was best for their agency that he did not see her again, at least not right away. Mr. Sehgal agreed after giving her a long, hard stare. Well, one could not question logic.

And then finally, she was ready for the day that was going to recast her life, in a way she would have never expected.

The wedding was an all-day crème-de-la-crème affair, with religious ceremonies scheduled for the morning and afternoon, followed by lunch. Mrs. Rai alleged that the evening was going to be filled with Bollywood-style singing and dancing.

Rumours of a celebrity visit were rife wherein Mrs. Rai too contributed. And dinner was going to be an exclusive seven-course sit-down affair with exclusive butler service. Reeva could sense that delivering this information was her mom's ploy to make her stay until evening, without any protest.

They were supposed to leave home by 8am, as it was a two-hour drive and Mrs. Rai wanted to be in time before the rituals began. Reeva was dreading the afternoon's harsh heat which would contribute to some awkward pictures of her that would eventually find its way to Facebook and other social media sites.

With Reeva on the wheels, the drive was smooth. Apps was still sleepy and her mom was pre-occupied with the upcoming event. She was left alone to listen to her favourite tracks right through the journey. As the family's black sedan glided smoothly towards its destination, Reeva desperately hoped for an open parking space at the end of the journey.

But the mood lasted only until they made an entry at the venue. It was a huge, sprawling, palm-lined banquet ground with a large open area in front, decorated in a heavenly dream sequence theme with an impressive white colonial lookalike structure at the far end. Reeva's brow immediately knitted in worry, as only the VVIPs had valet parking. She had to now find suitable parking spot. As Reeva snaked the car through the maze of several other vehicles and a humongous crowd, Mrs. Rai spotted her close friend Mrs. Patel and decided to get off with Apps, leaving her alone with her parking woes.

At the next turn, the parking manager signalled her towards a slot between a BMW and a Mercedes. Reeva figured it to be a little tight, but she did not want to go around in circles, especially after witnessing the long queue of cars behind. Much to the risk of damaging both the fancy cars, she decided to attempt parking her sedan between them. As she took the left turn to squeeze between the two cars, it immediately became obvious that she was stuck at a strange angle. Reversing would scratch the BMW on the right and if she turned in completely her car would scrape the Mercedes on the left. She cursed the length of her car and frantically reversed to make a second attempt, in vain.

Without a doubt, she was stuck in between. She panicked as the people behind her resorted to impatient honking. Her hands and forehead were clammy with sweat even with the air conditioner.

At that moment, there was a knock on her window, jolting her with surprise. In her anxious state, she registered the perfectly shaped strong hand, and the next moment its owner filled her vision. An attractive face sporting a charming smile, alit with light brown eyes that crinkled with humour, was looking at her. It was difficult to miss his aquiline nose, strong jawline and cleft chin. He gestured her to roll down the window. The car was instantly filled with the sounds of incessant honking.

Before she could explain her situation, he spoke in a calm manner, but with an impish grin, "Come out and hand me the car key." His voice was deep and sexy.

"What?" she was confused as he did not look anything like a valet.

"Give me the key… I think you need help parking this monster." An amused yet indulgent smile took over his lips but he sounded as if he was used to being in control.

"Huh, yeah okay." Reeva stepped out of the car and handed him the keys.

He deftly manoeuvred the car to fit into the parking lot. Reeva could not take her eyes off him. In less than a minute, he was out of the car and threw the key towards her, which she caught clumsily.

Her mind numbed with the relief and his irresistible charm, she could only manage a mumbled "Thanks" in response.

"No need," he smiled.

He walked towards his car, a BMW SUV, got behind the wheel and started the engine. As he drove past her, their eyes met and he winked with that same boyish smile and a mesmerizing charm that was hard to miss. Reeva was still rooted to her spot as he took another turn and vanished out of sight.

With a vague sense of déjà vu, she dialled her mom and walked towards the main building.

The family's suite on the first floor was reserved in her dad's name. Her face lit up when she saw him standing before the mirror, wearing a sherwani.

"Hey sweetheart, there you are." He turned and hugged her.

"Dad, you're early. I thought you were reaching later." She hugged him back. It was like finding an ally in enemy territory.

"Well, I couldn't upset your mom," he smiled.

Her dad, Rajeev Rai, was the most anchored person Reeva had ever known. He was never affected by his environment or people present in it, and easily attracted respect for his grace, quick wit and profound knowledge. He never formed quick opinions, but once he came to a conclusion it was difficult to change his mind. Reeva, at times, wondered if she was anything like him.

Mrs. Rai was almost ready and Apps was casually sprawled out of the sofa in a traditional kurta, which he had adamantly, and much to her chagrin, worn over his Levis. Reeva dressed quickly, mentally blowing kisses to Kinsy for coordinating everything, from shoes to accessories. She stepped out of the bathroom feeling beautiful and was received by Dad's gushing compliments and Mom's proud approval. Then, the Rai family proceeded to the lawns where the morning rituals were to be held.

White and cream was the theme of the event, just like a wedding scene from a Hollywood movie. From the hand-woven tablecloth to the butler's dress, and from flower arrangements to the garden umbrellas overhead, everything belonged to a picture-perfect fairytale setting from heaven. Even the bride and groom, and their families were dressed in shades of cream and white, with matching pearls and diamonds. As Reeva sipped a perfectly mixed Mojito, she made a note to get the contact of the event managers for future reference.

As soon as Mr. and Mrs. Rai busied themselves with socializing, Apps too pulled a vanishing act, leaving Reeva alone. She gazed around idly, indulging in her favourite hobby of 'watching people'. And then, she almost choked on her drink as she spotted Mr. Cool-Parking guy. He was having an animated discussion with a group and from the laughter and smiles, she figured that they were really enjoying his company, specially the women. Reeva, once again, rounded off how good looking he was, but could not shake off the feeling that she had seen him somewhere. As she feasted her eyes, he turned suddenly and looked straight at her. Instinctively, Reeva looked away quickly even though she knew he had caught her and in the process, spilled some Mojito on her borrowed ensemble. Reeva struggled with the napkin to get rid of the cocktail stains from her dress. To salvage some of her self-respect, she looked back at him, defiantly. This time, he smiled widely and waved. She managed an awkward smile in return and was relieved to see her mom walking towards her.

But it turned out, her mom had an agenda. She wanted to introduce her to some 'very important' people. Translated, it meant people who had sons of marriageable age. Reeva managed to plaster a smile on her face as she was showcased before a number of people.

Just as she was beginning to get impatient with the social drill, she spotted him again, walking straight towards her. He looked every inch a model in his beige sherwani and was accompanied by a tall, elegant-looking lady, who seemed to be in her early fifties, with porcelain skin and chin held high. She was holding on to his arm.

Suddenly, Reeva heard her mom muttering in her ear.

"There comes Mrs. Kabi." Mrs. Rai made a face.

"You know her?" Reeva was surprised.

"Of course, I do. The famous Mrs. Kabi and her pricey son Kunaal. She only wants a diva for her boy."

Reeva tensed immediately. Kunaal Kabi? Of course! He

was featured on the front page of *CEO Vision*'s last month's issue. At thirty three, he was the youngest executive to have headed the maximum number of media corporates. Currently, he was on the board of more than three global media and communication giants. An Ivy League graduate, he was touted as the man with the Midas touch within the industry.

By then, the mother-son duo was standing next to them and Kunaal gave Reeva a nod of recognition. Mrs. Kabi hesitated for a second and greeted Mrs. Rai politely.

"Oh! Hello Mrs. Rai, good to see you here." Mrs. Kabi was courtesy personified.

"Yes, Mrs. Kabi, nice to see you too," Mrs. Rai replied with a nervous smile.

"Is this pretty young lady here your daughter?" her tone was soft and benign.

"Oh yes, this is my daughter Reeva. She's feeling a bit out of sorts, you know… the midday sun doesn't suit her." Mrs. Rai passed on a fancy napkin from a nearby table, gesturing at Reeva to dab her face, embarrassing her sufficiently.

"On the contrary, I think she's quite a resourceful person," said Kunaal.

"You two have met already?" Mrs. Kabi was puzzled.

"I was witness to Miss Reeva's expert parking skills today." Kunaal gazed at her. Reeva felt hot and uneasy.

"Anyway, Mrs. Rai, this is my son Kunaal, of course, you must have heard about him." Mrs. Kabi dismissed the entire situation and Kunaal greeted her. "Well, we shall be seeing you around later then, Mrs. Rai," said Mrs. Kabi, before walking away.

Kunaal looked deep into Reeva's eyes and said, "I'll be

seeing *you* around, for sure." Somehow, these absolutely innocuous words thrilled her. But, as soon as they were out of hearing distance, Mrs. Rai was at it already.

"What do they think? That every girl is just dying to be Mrs. Kunaal Kabi?" She grumbled irritably.

Somehow, the statement failed to dampen Reeva's spirit. She was turning over Kunaal's statement in her head and her mom's disapproval of Mrs. Kabi's patronizing attitude did not matter. Excitement bubbled within her accompanied by a nervous flutter in her stomach. Yet, she felt on top of the world. The promise of being courted by one of the most eligible bachelors was exciting and dangerously thrilling. But Reeva felt confident; after all, she wasn't a sixteen-year-old. Plus, he was gorgeous. There had to be something more to her chance meeting with this handsome bachelor.

The day proceeded uneventfully as Reeva kept looking out for Kunaal. But he was nowhere to be seen. She felt dejected thinking he had already left, to attend to something important. Her spirits only lifted in the late afternoon when she spotted Mrs. Kabi walking across the corridor, although alone. Reeva's only hope was that he could not have gone away leaving his mother behind.

As the evening fell, typical to any hill station, the temperature dropped and Reeva's mood bettered. It was her kind of weather. She smiled as she changed into a black, off-shoulder, fitted cocktail dress and black pumps with stonework.

The large reception area was decorated exquisitely in

matte-gold and shades of deep red, and looked much like a Bollywood set. Having spent the afternoon with her mom, she decided to stick with her dad for the evening.

They were seated at a pre-allocated table for six, with her dad and his four other associates. And as expected, the discussion soon enough veered towards business, politics and economics.

Her mind wandered off to Kunaal, wondering if he would come. Her enthusiasm was beginning to deflate but she was putting up a good pretence of being interested in the conversation around her.

"Mr. Patel, what do you think of the Jaiswal-Thapar alliance?" Mr. Das threw up a bone in the air, hoping to witness a dog-fight. Nothing was better than a controversial topic for idle talk.

"I think it's a match made in business heaven." Mr. Patel was already comfortable with his crystal glass, which held the sparkling, amber liquid.

"Yeah, I guess in these tough times, it makes sense to consolidate. With the construction industry facing such a slowdown, it only makes sense the Jaiswals and Thapars pool their strengths. A marriage between the families is the perfect answer," quipped Mr. Sharma.

"The question is why has economic slowdown become a reason for marriage alliances today, rather than the couple's compatibility?" Her dad, Mr. Rai, got to the crux of the matter quickly.

"What do you think Rajeev?" All eyes were on him.

"I think today, everything comes with a price tag, even things which shouldn't, including happiness and peace of mind," he smiled ruefully as everyone on the table mumbled in agreement. The men went on to discuss politics, corruption, red-tapism and bureaucratic delays in business projects, and finally the discussion veered towards the inevitable hot topic of how criminals were being given party tickets.

Reeva, who had been a mute spectator until now, spoke on an impulse, "Political parties give tickets to criminals because they know they will get elected with a large voter base. As long as they keep getting votes, they will keep holding the positions. And because it doesn't matter to people like us, the voting pattern won't change." Her own impassioned response surprised her. Then, she was flummoxed further by a voice that had gotten into a habit of catching her off-guard.

"Wow! Gentlemen, can I join you at the table?" Kunaal asked, adjusting his tie. He looked sharp in a well cut and obviously designer, black jacket.

Reeva felt adrenaline rush through her body.

"Oh yes, Kunaal, please sit," Mr. Das was quick to respond. Kunaal thanked him and took the only vacant chair.

"Pardon me for overhearing Mr. Rai, but I have had the pleasure of being introduced to your lovely daughter earlier today and now I'm impressed by her clarity on the subject of politics," said Kunaal, who was met by a one-word response from Mr. Rai, "Really?" accompanied with an amused smile.

Kunaal responded by extending his hand, "By the way sir, I'm Kunaal Kabi."

Impressed? Really? thought Reeva. She hadn't formed one complete sentence properly before him until now and he was impressed already. Either this guy was cheesy or else he was not as intelligent as people thought he was. Or was she missing something? With Kunaal at the table, conversation took a definite turn towards politics and corruption, and

Reeva realized that he did have some real world views on those matters. As he clearly led the conversation, her dad watched him with detached amusement. Finally, Kunaal turned to him again.

"Mr. Rai, would you mind if I requested your lovely daughter to accompany me to welcome a rather important guest of the evening?"

"Sure young man, but remember, it's at your own risk." He patted Kunaal's arm lightly, then winked at Reeva and whispered, "Don't kill him, he seems nice."

"Dad!" she admonished him, reeling with nervousness.

She took Kunaal's hand and followed him. He held her hand very delicately and draped it on his arm, and they moved towards the VIP guest entry.

"So Reeva, what do you do?"

"I work for Creative AdZone... I head the client management department." She tried sounding serious, but it came out as self-important. *Not very classy Reeva*, she mentally chided herself.

"Hmm, Creative Adzone... Mr. Ajay Sehgal, right?"

"You know him?"

"Yeah, I've met him a couple of times at various symposiums."

"Oh." Reeva wasn't surprised, considering that 'media and advertising' was a small world. Then, she added, "But I guess I need not ask anything about Mr. Kunaal Kabi. Of course, the world knows about him." Reeva didn't realize that she had sounded sarcastic, but he merely raised his eyebrows and spoke almost earnestly.

"You're free to ask me anything you want Reeva, but right now I think your question should be, 'Who are we going to welcome'?"

His phone rang and he answered urgently. "I'm almost there." He held her hand and they moved towards the VIP entry.

"Reeva, we're here to receive Mr. Rishi Uttur. You know him, right?"

Reeva nodded. Of course, she knew Mr. Rishi Uttur. He was a man of power, a former Union Home Minister and President of Jagrut Bharat Party, the formidable opposition party in the spotlight. But there were reasons she personally admired the man. He was probably one of the few politicians who was media savvy, yet did not hesitate in speaking his mind. This left him explaining plenty of his public statements to the media and social flag bearers, who took his statements quite literally. She liked him even more for this, because here was a man who was not willing to compromise on his beliefs in the name of diplomacy. He was polished and not prone to cheap political tricks. For his intelligence and open-mindedness, he was one of her favourite public figures. Lastly, he dressed well and could very well be put into the category of well-groomed and suave politicians. This was a very short list.

Reeva stood next to Kunaal, as they received Mr. Uttur and the politico's unpresuming attitude immediately impressed her. Ramcharan Jaiswal, the groom's father, led the welcome party. A religiously devout person in his mid-fifties, he had singlehandedly built Jaiswal Construction conglomerate from scratch. He was a traditional man, personally and professionally.

In contrast, Dindayal Thapar was a man born into wealth. Construction being the family business for decades, he operated like a hard-core capitalist, doing what worked best in *his* interest. He was a tall, strong man with a grave personality. He wore his thick, black hair, though dyed, swept back on his forehead and sported a well-trimmed thick moustache. He never mixed morality with business and the world knew it. No wonder, many eyebrows were raised when the marriage alliance between the culturally different clans like Jaiswal and Thapar was declared.

Many camera flashes and enthusiastic conversations later, the hullabaloo settled. Kunaal managed everything with panache, constantly sticking by the politician's side. The moment they were away from the crowd, Mr. Uttur turned to Kunaal, "So, how have you been Kunaal? Haven't seen you much lately."

"Mr. Uttur, you're the one at the political hub of Delhi. I'm very much around here, just like today."

"Why don't you join me at the dinner table now Kunaal? We could chat," proposed the politico.

Just as she was beginning to feel uncomfortable standing next to Kunaal, Mr. Uttur turned towards her, "Reeva, right?" She was amazed that he had remembered her name even in the crowds. She nodded politely, as he continued "Kunaal is a very dear friend Reeva; I wouldn't want him to leave his friends behind." And then, with a smile, instructed, "Kunaal, why don't you ask her to join us at the dinner table?"

"Sure, Mr. Uttur. We will see you at the table," Kunaal smiled consciously but brightened to see Reeva nod in acceptance.

The security whisked Mr. Uttur away to bless the young married couple and join the exclusive dinner table, which now had two seats reserved for them. This was too much luck, too quickly. First, to be the fancy of a handsome, eligible guy, for whom women were willing to kill. Then, to be asked by an influential political leader to join him at the dinner table.

Working within the media industry, this itself was a fantastic opportunity for her to build further roads for future references. But Reeva was suddenly worried about her parents. As if reading her mind, Kunaal quickly took her dad's number from her and informed him about their new dinner arrangement.

The thirty-seat, exclusive dining table was set with silver cutlery and expensive glasses. Reeva was surprised that Kunaal and she were to be seated next to Mr. Uttur. The dinner progressed pleasantly and they chatted about Delhi, global politics and upcoming projects, while steering clear of controversial subjects. Mr. Uttur was polite, paid attention to whatever was being said and even complimented good ideas. This included the one he paid to Kunaal on the last game of golf they had played together. By the end of it all, she was glad the evening had panned out differently than expected, and also wondered if that last glass of wine had been a bit too much.

As the dinner was concluded and Mr. Uttur departed, the crowd started thinning. Reeva too felt drained – maybe it was all the excitement or maybe it was the wine. She sat exhausted, as Kunaal walked back to her, his jacket off and casually flung over his shoulder.

"Are you up for a little walk?" Kunaal's query was more a plea.

"Yeah, okay," she smiled.

They walked towards an artificial pond, which was

flanked by wrought iron benches. Kunaal did not attempt to hold her hand like before.

"It's been a long time since I've done this," Kunaal sighed, as he sank into the bench, stretching his legs.

"What, moon watching?"

"No, relaxing like this. Not wanting to do anything... anymore," he gave her a beseeching look.

"Yeah, I get that feeling very often, almost every morning," she rolled her eyes.

"Reeva, do you ever let your guard down?" Kunaal smiled, as his eyes bore into Reeva's.

"Why do you ask this?" She didn't want to be scrutinized.

"Because, I can't ever let *my* guard down. And we both... we're very much alike." Kunaal looked at her, but in the dark, it was difficult for Reeva to make out his expression.

"Why? Are you worried about getting hurt?" she asked, not knowing where this conversation was going.

"No, I'm worried about hurting others." His gaze was fixed at the moon's reflection on the pond's tranquil water.

Her phone vibrated in her purse. Knowing that it was time to leave, she looked at him trying to process what he had just said.

"It wouldn't feel right to me, to hurt anyone," she said.

"Oh Reeva, not everything is about what is right." A pained look covered his face. "I think you should get going. It's quite late now. I'll be in touch," he said abruptly, looking away.

Reeva didn't like being dismissed and protested, "I wonder if you intend to use telepathy to get in touch as you don't have my phone number."

Kunaal sighed. He fished out a card from his jacket pocket

and waved it with an almost sad smile. She then remembered giving it to him at the dinner table. She smiled back.

Just then, as she prepared to leave, Kunaal gripped her arm, with the pressure of his hand bordering on painful. He lightly pulled Reeva towards him, bringing his face dangerously close to hers. She caught a whiff of his perfume and the sexual tension in the moment sent her heart racing F1 style.

He whispered, "Hope to see you very soon, sweet Reeva."

Not knowing how to react, she placed a quick peck on his cheek and felt his light stubble graze her lips – a sensation that would linger for a long time. She stood up and with one final look into his eyes that were distraught with emotions, slowly walked away. At the last bend, she turned and saw him still on the bench, but this time, he was looking up at the moon.

CHAPTER 3

Every single day, for the past three weeks, Reeva had been expecting Kunaal's call, message or even email. But there was an eerie silence from his end. She often chided herself for such immature juvenile behaviour. She even tried convincing herself of all the valid reasons for why he couldn't have gotten in touch. Maybe he was busy or travelling abroad or worse, he was unwell. Her pride prevented her from digging up his contact details, which would have been far easier than going through the agony of not knowing. But as always, Reeva's practical side had prevailed.

Yet the question lingered, "Why did he do it?" After all that attention, tenderness, meeting with the politician, making her feel special and the promise to be in touch, he had simply vanished. It wasn't as if she was having a nervous breakdown, but Kunaal's detachment was deeply upsetting. Her mood had markedly worsened in last few days.

"Here you go angel," her dad placed her morning cup of hot Earl Grey tea on the breakfast table and Reeva was back to the present. He then turned the newspaper in Reeva's direction and tapped on an article, "Interesting piece of news for you, here."

She sipped the hot tea and felt the bulbs in her brain pop alive. She saw that the entire bottom part of the business section of the *Times* featured an alliance between the Jaiswal and Thapar construction groups to form J&T Infra Developers Ltd. The PR feature carried details of this corporate entity and nature of projects the company would undertake, with a photograph of Jaiswal and Thapar shaking hands and happily looking into the camera.

"Dad, I knew this was coming, but it's quicker than expected."

"If I know Thapar even a little, I'm not surprised. That man can smell an opportunity from a mile away. Together they're capable of influencing many 'influential' people."

"You mean the forming of J&T is a front for something else?"

"Oh, I don't know really. But I know that nothing motivates those two more than profit."

"Well that goes for most construction companies. Look at the realty rates in the city. Skyscrapers after skyscrapers with unoccupied flats from top to bottom, yet a common man struggles to buy a small apartment. Or he probably spends a lifetime paying off the loan. Where is the basic principle of demand and supply?"

"Reeva, this is just the tip of the iceberg. The construction industry is large enough to be one of the key economic indicators, besides the political interest that gets invested in it." Her dad was an established and respected architect with a keen and even a dark insight of the industry.

After some quiet comfortable time, Reeva's dad whispered conspiratorially, "Hey, by the way, why such a long face?"

Reeva was uncomfortable, not wanting to lie. She stood up, stretched a bit, and announced that she needed a hot bath. She needed privacy to lick her wounds. Mr. Rai narrowed his eyes before disappearing once again behind the newspaper.

After a lazy weekend, the following week too began on a slow note. Monday was uncharacteristically quiet – hushed tones, everyone pre-occupied, eyes glued to computer screens. By midday, Reeva was already wishing that the day gets over. She had an insane amount of market research data needing assimilation but by early evening she had waded through most of it. And now, her brain felt jammed up.

As Reeva looked at the reddish hue of the setting sun through the side window of her decently sized cabin, exhaustion gripped her completely. She pressed her palms on her tired eyes and massaged them, enjoying the feeling. With a deep sigh, she opened her eyes only to see Nihaal leaning casually on her cabin door, arms crossed, patiently gazing at her. He was wearing khaki baggy pants, a black tee, a hoodie jacket, and looked ready to hit the gym.

"Nihaal? I'm sorry I had no idea you were here."

"It's alright." He smiled.

"So, what's up? Any news on the McPherson & Solly account?" Reeva recovered quickly.

"Yeah, Mr. Seth is taking the approved presentation with him to Havana to share it with the European counterparts. But that's not why I'm here."

"You're not? So you've more grief for me!" joked Reeva.

"Hey, don't shoot the messenger," Nihaal shrugged. "Mr. Sehgal wants us to attend a briefing session with J&T Infra Developers tomorrow. Apparently, someone new from our office is also supposed to join us at the meeting."

"Someone new? Who? And J&T? Isn't it a bit early for them to start talking to ad agencies?"

"Wow! You could go easy with the questions. I have no idea about anything Reeva. Just that the meeting is scheduled for post lunch, around 3pm. But Mr. Sehgal mentioned we have a great chance to bag the J&T account. And it's a meaty one for sure, I can tell from his enthusiasm."

"Well, tomorrow is another day," Reeva stared at her computer screen wearily.

"Reeva... a word of advice from me?"

"Yeah?"

"I think you should call it a day... for today, at least."

She had detected something in Nihaal's voice. Was it just professional concern or genuine compassion? But Reeva had no energy left in her to ponder over it any further, so she simply responded with a nod. Nihaal was promptly gone and she started clearing up her desk.

As the cabin lights in the aircraft were switched on, the flight's captain declared their descent into Indira Gandhi International Airport. Kunaal straightened his business class seat into an upright position and looked at Jaiswal and Thapar seated in the adjoining row. Jaiswal, taking advantage of the two-hour flight, had dozed off as soon as the plane was airborne and was now waking up only after a politely gentle nudge by the flight attendant.

Kunaal envied people who could sleep anywhere, a quality he could use. But his wound-up personality did not allow him the luxury. He often spent sleepless nights even in the most comfortable, yet unfamiliar beds of five-star hotels, preferring to take day trips if the distance allowed. Thapar was another story. For the last hour and half, he had been on his iPad, diligently skimming through the data presentation on upcoming polls, compiled meticulously by his executive assistant. Kunaal was sure that the content of the presentation would be discussed in detail during the one-hour drive to Ashoka Road, the residence of Rishi Uttur.

As soon as the flight landed and the seat belt sign was off, Kunaal unbuckled it and removed his laptop from the overhead bin. The pretty flight attendant flashed a special smile at him. Although he was used to regular female attention, Kunaal never allowed his male ego to inflate beyond a point. Suddenly, he did a double take. The flight attendant's identity tag read 'Reeva'. As she had passed ahead, he had to bend sideways to read the name, which was actually 'Reena'. The attendant raised her eyebrows, thinking he was flirting with her. Kunaal apologized with an embarrassed smile. Much to his chagrin, this name played on his mind more than he would have liked to admit.

They were out of the airport within minutes as they only had hand baggage. A uniformed Jaiswal Constructions' driver holding a placard, quickly guided them to the waiting Mercedes. Finally, as they relaxed in the car's luxurious confines, the conversation turned to the inevitable subject.

As expected, Thapar initiated, "So Kunaal, have you been

through Daily News Survey on the upcoming polls for the next year? It seems as if Jagrut Bharat Party is all set for a clean sweep. Rishi Uttur must be a happy man."

"Yes, I read that report. I think JBP will retain most of its states and unseat National Progress Party in at least five more states. There will be plenty of anti-incumbency votes," Kunaal's response was measured.

Kunaal knew the dicey agenda for the meeting with Rishi Uttur and was unsure whether it would end up being favourable. He knew Uttur personally, and that he had only agreed to this meeting for Kunaal's sake.

"Yeah, you're right. When conditions are unfavourable for the common man, then the general trend is to uproot the current government. The wave is decidedly against NPP in Maharashtra and specially in Mumbai, thanks to Sathya Raj Mane's foolish and incompetent governance as a CM. But Uttur can easily sort out this land issue for us once JBP is in power. Then, our game will move to an international scale," said Jaiswal, while obsessively wiping his glasses with a soft tissue.

Kunaal knew this was Jaiswal's nervous tick.

"Well, state is an added advantage, but if JBP makes it to the centre, then it will smoothen out many other issues for us. And, I guess Kunaal has Rishi Uttur eating out of his hands," Thapar smiled.

"Mr. Thapar, I haven't been able to present your issues to him. This was a bit sudden and he's been busy. I have no idea how he'll react to your proposal." Kunaal was a bit non-committal. Any other politician, and he would be placing bets in favour of a successful deal going through, but he knew Uttur.

"He is our best bet in the current political scenario. JBP is a tsunami waiting to hit NPP. If he's willing to play along, then his party and everybody involved benefits. I'm not talking small money here, as you're aware Kunaal," smirked Thapar.

"Yeah, anything's better than that Sathya Raj Mane. He could have governed better as Chief Minister, if he didn't drag his feet on most issues. He should at least now work towards retaining Maharashtra, which is one of the highest tax paying states of the country," added Jaiswal.

"Ramcharan, come on, you know it's people like us who decide about who retains power, when and where," Thapar patted Jaiswal lightly on his shoulder.

"We should be there soon," observed Kunaal, noticing the roads getting wider and cleaner, devoid of any slums and roadside shops that marked all the countries' large metropolitan cities. But this was the capital, the nation's seat of power. He felt that power surge through the air, as the car entered Ashoka Road, which was marked by a beautifully maintained garden-island roundabouts and straight roads lined with tall, flaming red Gulmohar trees.

Finally, the car pulled up outside a large yet nondescript white bungalow with high walls and a tall, wide wooden gate. The white marble nameplate on the gate column had 'Rishi Uttur, 17, Ashoka Road' etched in gold font. That no one from outside could peek inside the bungalow signified importance and exclusivity. Since they were expected, the gate swung open, the car moved in and deposited its passengers on the main porch. As they climbed up the wide stairs leading to Uttur's office, Thapar became serious with anticipation and Jaiswal completely dull and expressionless;

Kunaal felt the power once again. Uttur's secretary guided them to the meeting room, "Please wait here; sir will be with you in ten minutes. I'll order some refreshments." The room was large and airy with wide French windows overlooking the garden. Thapar chose to settle comfortably in the sofa meant for informal chats, tactfully avoiding Uttur's huge and antique formal table with guest chairs.

Rishi Uttur breezed in five minutes later.

"There you are my friend," he beamed and shook Kunaal's hand.

"Hello sir, looks as if you've been busy."

"Oh you know, with elections less than a year away, it's a bit of a race." Uttur turned towards the other two men. "Mr. Jaiswal... Mr. Thapar... good to see you again. If I were to believe the media reports, then J&T collectively is now a fifteen-thousand-crore company. Hope you're having fun managing it."

"Uttur sahab, if you're with us then this figure can easily become more than double," Thapar's smile was somewhere between sly and sheepish. His guile amazed Kunaal.

"Mr. Thapar, I'm supportive of every single entrepreneur, after all growth in business means progress for the country. And please don't call me *sahab*. It makes me feel old and outdated. I mean, this isn't the British Raj anymore."

"Oh sure, sure! No offence was meant, please. I was just hoping that you were a bit more selective about the so-called entrepreneurs."

"What do you mean?" Uttur's eyebrows narrowed, just as a butler entered with a tray of refreshments. Kunaal mentally thanked him for the distraction.

"Mr. Uttur, let me update you about our latest

developments." Jaiswal took over and Kunaal relaxed. Jaiswal was the more tactful one.

"Yeah sure," Uttur nibbled on a biscuit.

"We've received an expression of interest from Galactic Studios to bring their franchise into India. They have earmarked a $300 million investment for a joint venture with J&T to build, manage and operate Galactic Studios in India."

"Galactic Studios from the U.S.? One with a franchise in Singapore, Hong Kong and Sun City? That's very good news. Please let me know if I can be of any help. If all goes well, we'll be in office by the time your project gets going. I'll do everything I can to fast-track all clearances for you." Uttur was beaming, finally able to unravel the mystery behind the request for this meeting.

Thapar took over again, "Well Mr. Uttur, I'm glad you understand the importance of this for us. But we're not here for clearances. That comes in at phase two. We're currently trying to finalize a land package of about hundred acres for Galactic Studio's site."

"Alright, so tell me, where's the problem with that?" Uttur enquired with genuine interest and Kunaal tensed.

"You see, Galactic Studios' site-research team has finally shortlisted Dharampur as a strategically suitable location for the site; equi-distant from a megapolis like Mumbai and the fairly large city Pune. Their investment is conditional to our ability to acquire that land and build it there."

"So, what now? Come on Mr. Thapar, you've a budget of three hundred million dollars at your disposal. You can get any land you want."

"There's just one little problem. We checked the state

records. That land is earmarked for Garib Griha Pravesh Yojana." Thapar paused for effect and then continued, "Mr. Uttur, if we receive commitment of future support in this matter from your end, then I can assure you that there will be generous financial support in return from J&T, for the upcoming elections. We know you can easily get that land released for us." Thapar looked at Kunaal, who wasn't sure if he imagined it, but Uttur's face darkened for a moment. A heavy, palpable silence descended.

Only after ten seconds of complete silence, Uttur spoke in a flat tone, "Mr. Thapar, I laud your guts in approaching me with such a corrupt proposal. Or should I be amazed at your complete lack of understanding politics and political leaders?" Rishi Uttur's voice was strained with anger. "If I hear one more word from you about this, I'll ensure that your company is never able to execute any international project. And, I warn you against approaching any political leader for this. Now, the only reason I'll leave you guys courteously to finish your tea and not take action against you or publicly shame you is because Kunaal is a friend and you're in my house. Gentlemen, feel free to leave at your will. This meeting is over." Uttur looked sternly at Kunaal and stormed out of the room. Jaiswal and Thapar sat in silence even after Uttur had already exited the room.

Kunaal was stunned but immediately followed Uttur, realizing his mistake in organizing this meeting. The country's most dynamic leader, at the edge of a historic turnaround of power, could have never entertained such a proposal. Kunaal felt blindsided by the duo. Trying to unethically grab the land earmarked for Garib Griha Pravesh Yojana, that too a housing scheme for the poor and homeless, to build a commercial enterprise for personal gain, was the lowest form of corruption. Kunaal knew he had to come out in the clear on his stand about this with Uttur right away.

He gingerly entered Uttur's room hoping to pacify him and do some damage control, if possible. Uttur looked up from a file he was holding. "Really, Kunaal? Is this what you've come to now?"

"Let me explain," he spoke urgently, "I didn't know about all this. Those two never gave me any idea about the land's status. If I knew, I would have never brought them," Kunaal decided a little white lie wouldn't hurt. He had only been aware that the land was controversial. He had never known that the land was earmarked for state welfare and that the duo was expecting corrupt action from Uttur.

"Listen Kunaal, I have to leave now. Let's take this up when I visit Mumbai next month." Kunaal was relieved that Uttur was still willing to meet him. He stepped out of the room wondering about Thapar and Jaiswals angry state of minds. But that was of lesser importance because right then, he had just dodged a high-speed trailer by only a few inches.

CHAPTER 4

Moving from Kolkata to Mumbai had been a major adjustment for Shalini Ray. She had always known that the lifestyle and work culture in the two cities were vastly different, but experiencing it first hand was something else. Somehow, she was never able to overcome the alienation she felt in Mumbai. She found the city too fast and impersonal, even mean at times. After spending four years in Mumbai working a variety of public relations jobs, she felt she didn't fit in. This was a real setback, knowing that she was never returning to Kolkata.

That was the city where her roots were and where her single mother still lived. But she had wanted to get out of Kolkata badly, after losing her younger sister Malini to an untimely mishap. Her absence was like a gaping wound for Shalini. Everything about the city reminded her of her sister. The crowded roads, old trams, puchkaas at Goriahaat, and Howrah Bridge were all silent witnesses to a happy childhood spent together as inseparable sisters. An escape from the city had sounded like a good idea back then, but as they say, you can run from everything except yourself. The harder she tried to forget Malini, the deeper she sank into her memories. And so, Shalini's grief had shadowed her very core and tainted the fabric of her life. Yet, she hid it well, disguising it under a tough personality and pretty starched sarees.

With a honeyed complexion, tall height and lithe body, Shalini Ray was an exotic beauty. She had black kohl-lined eyes and long, dark hair. But she lived in an unapproachable mental fortress. This was her own creation and also why, at thirty, she was still single. Although many men tried to woo her, their attempts had invariably crashed like sea waves against dark foreboding rocks. Her bitterness made her socially aloof, but she tried to cover this by being supremely efficient and an invaluable asset to her employers. However, she had zero tolerance for two things – unethical practices and stupidity.

Today was her first day at Creative AdZone. The chairman, Ajay Sehgal, sounded like a reasonable man and had promised that soon, she would handle important PR projects. Currently, she was to get the feel of the place as she would be setting up a new subdivision. The director of the client management department, Reeva Rai, would brief her and a meeting was scheduled with J&T. As Shalini walked into the office, the receptionist greeted her cheerfully, and guided her into the cabin.

Shalini's cabin was functional, well organized and had its own tea and coffee amenities. This, she appreciated. She set up her laptop and powered it up, wanting to get going as quickly as possible. As she slipped CAZ's corporate profile

DVD into the drive, there was a light tap on her glass door. A young, attractive girl stood leaning against the door, smiling. Shalini gestured her to come in.

"Hi, I'm Reeva. You must be Shalini."

Shalini shook her hand, with momentary hesitation, which Reeva noticed.

"Yes," she said without smiling.

"So, how do you like our office? Hope you're comfortable. Is there anything you need?" Reeva spoke warmly even though there was a certain reticence from Shalini.

"Well, thanks. But I'm just getting started. I'll ask the relevant department if I need help."

Reeva was thrown off by her lack of appreciation or courtesy. Her smile froze and then melted away. She wanted to retaliate with an equally icy response, but merely said, "Okay then, here's the J&T file. I believe you're to lead from the PR front. Their office is a forty five-minute drive, so we leave at 2pm." Reeva left as Shalini busied herself with the J&T file not bothering to respond with any courtesy. But both women had realized that this was a rocky start.

Jaiswal and Thapar were in the plush boardroom on the twenty first floor of their building. The soft light of the late morning sun was lighting up parts of the wooden floor, creating a dramatic shadow play. The boardroom had floor-to-ceiling glass on two sides; one side offered the view of the city's vast green racecourse and the open skies. The other showed J&T's huge interior office space, housing over one-hundred-and-fifty personnel, and done up in absolutely modern design using steel, glass and black marble. The effect was astonishing as everything was polished to perfection.

The J&T conference room was charged with tension. Jaiswal, deep in thought, massaged his forehead as if he had a headache. Thapar paced languidly like a caged lion.

"It was a big mistake. This is not what I expected. I didn't expect Kunaal to fail," mumbled Jaiswal.

"It's not Kunaal's fault; we should have done a better background check. Kunaal will always be an asset, especially when we need heavy duty media PR and image building for J&T. It's that high-handed Rishi Uttur I'm pissed off with. Does he think he's the only honest politician being offered a bribe? This is how things have always worked in this country and he knows it. How dare he insult us?" Thapar's seething anger was peppered with bitterness.

"Yes, you're right about Kunaal. He is an opinion leader in the market. As for Uttur, I'm happy the matter didn't escalate," Jaiswal conceded.

"Uttur is an issue I'll tackle another time. Right now, we need to set things back on track, and quickly. We cannot proceed without that land. Galactic Studios needs to know our response within three months. There has to be another way."

"I don't know Dindayal. JBP is all set to win Maharashtra state elections. Your own poll analysis predicts that. Now with Uttur knowing our plans, he'll do everything in his power to ensure we don't get the Dharampur land."

"What about Sathya Raj Mane? Do you think he can help?"

"That man is not much use even now. After he loses office, he won't be able to enter his own party's office, so helping us is a far cry. His position and power is valid only until elections. Any decisions that he takes now can, and will be, revoked by the next government."

"But what if we can make him stay in the CM's office for another term? He can sure help then." Thapar smiled slowly.

"I don't understand."

"Ramcharan, have you heard about the Fixer?"

"Oh come on Dindayal, are we discussing mythical creatures now? Everybody's just heard about him; nobody has met or seen him. From what I've heard, he works like a CIA operative in a B-grade Hollywood movie. You don't expect ghosts to solve our problems now, do you?"

"No Ramcharan, I know he's for real… and as good as gold."

"How can you be so sure?" Jaiswal was getting uncomfortable.

"Because I know how to reach him, my friend." Thapar turned towards Jaiswal; his eyes filled with manic determination, the wheels of evil already turning in his mind.

Reeva was in her cabin, setting her notes and questions for the J&T meeting when the intercom rang. The beep jarred her already raw nerves, post her encounter with Shalini. "Reeva? If you're not too busy, can I see you for a bit?" said her boss. He sounded uncharacteristically relaxed. She sighed, picked up her organizer and briskly walked over to his office which was just across the corridor from her own. She knocked on the door.

"Reeva, come sit," Mr. Sehgal said casually, "So, did you

meet Shalini?"

"Yes, I did," Reeva's curt response made him smile.

"Hmm... So what do you think?"

"Mr. Sehgal, if what I thought mattered we would be having this discussion before she joined."

He nodded, "Well, you do have a point there. And precisely why now's a good time to update you about a few developments." Reeva sat on the edge of the chair in rapt attention. New developments excited her and right now she needed some serious distraction.

He continued, "You see, recently, I've been thinking of a business extension into Public Relations. With a few potential clients ready to join in and elections round the corner, the timing can never be better than now."

"Yes I'm aware of J&T's interest, but are we expected to handle any big ticket political campaigns too?"

"That's a definite possibility, yes. But we'll know for sure in a fortnight. Meanwhile, the sub-division will be known as Media Vision PR. MVPR for short. This brings me back to Shalini Ray and the purpose of her joining us. Her experience in PR is commendable. She will be assisting you in setting up this new division, within the next month."

"Assisting me? In setting up MVPR? I don't understand," Reeva stared at him.

"Reeva, as of now, I'm asking you to take over MVPR as Assistant Vice President, with a thirty five per cent pay hike, company-maintained luxury car and category-I company benefits. I can assure you this move will be beneficial in the long term for your career."

Reeva was stunned. "But sir, my experience in PR is limited to a couple of projects, and heading a PR firm would be preposterous," Reeva sensed a weight settling on her shoulders.

"Well, your presence in MVPR is more about your business acumen and ability to take strategic decisions. Shalini will take care of operations. Reeva, don't undersell yourself. All you need is a day's orientation and you'll be good to go. Plus don't forget, Creative AdZone will always have a place reserved for you."

"Who will I be reporting to?" Though this question confirmed her acceptance of the offer, it was of crucial concern. She was used to working in a certain style and changing it now would prove to be a pain, and in the wrong place. Also, the word 'assistant' in her designation signified the presence of a vice president above her.

His doubts put to rest Mr. Sehgal eased back in his chair and played with an expensive crystal paper weight.

"Your reporting might be dual. To me... and of course directly to the vice president. You will be meeting that person soon, by the way. So shall we consider it settled?"

Reeva nodded. She knew this would be a challenge, but then she wasn't going to pass it up.

"Okay then, I'll ask Jacob from HR to update you about your new package. And Reeva... Congratulations!" he smiled brightly.

Reeva stepped out feeling elated and nervous simultaneously. *Okay, Shalini Ray, let's roll now*, she smiled, and almost bumped into Nihaal.

"Hey, hey, hey... somebody's happy," Nihaal found her smile infectious.

"Well, there's been a development. I might leave this company." Reeva felt good and wicked doing this to Nihaal.

"What?" Nihaal's voice was low and his face turned ashen. At the sight of his expression Reeva immediately backtracked, feeling sheepish. "I mean Boss has just asked me to move to the company's new sub-division."

"You mean Media Vision PR?" This was Nihaal's turn to enjoy stumping Reeva. "Mr. Sehgal just asked me to supervise all creative design inputs, for all MVPR clients in future. So, unfortunately you're not getting rid of me that easily." Being a tall guy, Nihaal crouched slightly to look into her eyes with a wink and a meaningful expression.

"Alright Mr. Smarty Pants, let's get going for the J&T meeting. I'll see you in the car park. And, if you don't mind, please bring along Miss High and Mighty too."

"You mean Shalini Ray?" Nihaal let out a throaty laugh.

"Is that what they're calling her these days?" Reeva winked and walked towards the media department. She briefed the team, and realized that she'd lost more time than expected. She rushed towards the exit when her vibrating phone displayed Nihaal's name. "Yes, yes, I'm coming; give me two minutes," she replied, sounding harried.

Rushing past the reception, she overheard the operator. "Sure Mr. Kabi, he's available; I'll put you through."

Reeva stopped dead in her tracks, turned on her heels and approached the cheerful receptionist, "Was that Mr. Kunaal Kabi?"

The receptionist replied sweetly, "Yes ma'am, it was. He was asking for Mr. Sehgal. Would you like me to patch you through later?"

"Oh no, it's okay," Reeva was disappointed. So, he wasn't ill, away or busy. He had simply been avoiding her. He had not bothered to check on her, even out of sheer courtesy. Her disappointment turned into indignation.

Reeva had never admitted, even to herself, that her expectations were possibly unreasonable. Or maybe she had misread the signals from Kunaal. She told herself that it was time to stop obsessing about him. Yet, the sense of losing something that could have been incredible was too much to handle, more so because she had never been impressed by or attracted to someone easily. *You've been such an idiot, Reeva*, she thought.

She was quiet throughout the drive to J&T's office. Nihaal and Shalini discussed the agenda of the upcoming meeting. While getting out of the car, Nihaal looked at her questioningly and Reeva responded with her brightest smile, hoping to mislead him.

At the J&T office, they were guided to the plush waiting area outside Thapar's cabin. A selection of cookies with an exotic range of teas and coffees had been laid out. Reeva was not in the mood for anything and denied politely. Shalini and Nihaal settled for a dark brew of Ethiopian roast coffee.

Soon they were called in and Reeva was surprised to see only Thapar in the office. She had expected a joint briefing with Jaiswal. Thapar began the briefing without any fuss coming straight to the point.

"Hope it's alright for me to assume that you have had the opportunity to read the background material on J&T." There were nods and mumbled affirmations as he continued, "From my limited understanding of the advertising and PR world, I know you guys will be playing a crucial role in helping J&T achieve its business objectives." Reeva immediately got the impression that this was going to be a one-sided briefing session and not an open Q&A format of meeting, which they were used to.

"We at J&T want people to believe in us, and our capability to bring international scale and levels of advance development to our country. We want to be seen as a highly professional construction group and that our projects are managed using state of the art technology."

"Mr. Thapar, we're curious, which construction project will your company be undertaking as your flagship project?" Shalini was the first to interrupt Thapar and Reeva agreed with her tack. "After all, a construction company is only known by its projects."

"Well Miss Ray, we'll soon be announcing the project and you'll be the first to know. Meanwhile, I can only tell you that it will be an international venture in the entertainment industry. Your job is to get the media and public completely focused on the scale of the project and how it will claim a glamorous tourist spot for India on the world map. This project will be worth close to three hundred million dollars." Thapar had a self-satisfied grin.

"Of course, Mr. Thapar. Rest assured, our campaign will be aimed towards generating both market and investor goodwill," added Reeva.

"Sure… but that's a done deal. But I'm interested in the strength of your PR SOS."

"Pardon sir?"

"Oh, come on, you're not expecting me to hold your hand through this, are you? In a project as large as the one we're discussing, negative publicity is common. We all have our enemies in competition or politically motivated campaigners and even over-zealous social groups. Any of them is entitled to make a mountain out of a mole hill. How good is your team in firefighting?"

"Our team will be fully equipped in managing things to the extent that ethical code of conduct allows us to Mr. Thapar. This I can assure you of," Shalini crossed her arms defiantly, sending a clear signal to Thapar that the operational lines won't be crossed. Thapar went rigid for a beat but then chose to ignore the oblique remark.

The rest of the meeting was regular discussion on company ethics and philosophy, which was nothing but a fancy way of making the company's commercial objective sound unselfish. Nihaal had been the silent spectator throughout the meeting, but he was the first to speak as the three exited J&T office. "Want to know my gut feeling? When a business owner wants the public to believe something so badly, there's always something not worth believing in it."

Shalini was stern-faced and not very talkative. Reeva had a splitting headache, with a dry and itchy throat. The post-meeting discussion between them was hence, rudimentary at best. Reeva politely refused Nihaal's offer to drop her home, as she stayed in the opposite direction. Nihaal hailed a cab for her and waited until she got in.

He leaned on the window and looked at her intently, "You better take care. You don't look too good."

CHAPTER 5

Manek Vir was in his late forties, but his fitness level belonged to a much younger generation. Being ex-military, a daily workout regime was built into his mental programming and he could still run twenty four kilometres without losing breath. He was a relatively short, squat man with thick shoulders and large hands, which gave him the appearance of a professional boxer. Years of rigorous field work had toughened his muscles and his body had not suffered any age-related sagging. He walked fast and talked slow.

His personal mantra was 'logic above all else'. Manek Vir assisted the Fixer in everything, who never met anyone personally. Those who knew the Fixer's identity could be counted on one hand and he had his own stringent codes and fail-safes for all circumstances. To reach him, one had to go through Vir and his thorough checks. Vir had been with him for a decade and they had an excellent working relationship, as both did not believe in investing personal emotions into jobs. Everything was about achieving objectives. There was no rejoicing when a project was well executed or remorse if a project got botched up. Together, they were like a well-oiled machine.

Almost everyone who approached the Fixer were very powerful people with stakes large enough to require his attention. Most cases did not require any form of violence or direct breach of law, but it wasn't completely ruled out either.

Over his years with the Fixer, Vir had experienced a variety of low-life creatures. Some with next-to-nil moral foundation and some with extraordinarily vicious agendas. All wanted power and riches. A few wanted vendetta. But right then, as he sat in front of Thapar, at a rather mundane looking coffee shop, Vir thought of him as a new species, something like a snake: sleek and dangerous. He sensed trouble when Thapar insisted on meeting the Fixer right away. Most wanted the job to be over and done with quickly, maintaining as little direct involvement as possible. They all knew subconsciously that though the job would be done, there was always a price to pay, sooner or later. But not this one. Vir's instinct was to show Thapar the door. However, his job was to take the cases to the Fixer, not shortlist them. What Thapar was asking for was achievable, although its effect was going to be far and wide.

"So, how does this work? I mean, the case is complicated and requires detailed briefing. And our name cannot get exposed, under any circumstances."

"We only need a single line instruction. Rest we will work out. This is not your corporate presentation, Mr. Thapar. Secrecy is the core principle we work with," said Vir, almost impatiently.

"So it can be done? Will you need our support?"

"Yes, it can be done. All we would want from you... is to stay out of the way," Vir almost growled.

"Okay, so what next?"

"I'll get in touch once I have set up a teleconference with the Fixer. Be ready with your financial offer." Vir stood up, collected his possessions and walked out, ignoring Thapar's mumbled goodbyes. He had protocol to follow before he presented the case to the Fixer.

Reeva was thankful it was a Saturday as the fever had left her feeling weak and disoriented. Since she got back from the J&T meeting the previous day, she felt exhausted and her head hurt. When her mom had brought her soup, the sight of it made her want to throw up and she could only manage a few spoonfuls. Worst of all, her weakness made it difficult to read or even watch TV.

She had switched off her phone and her laptop since Friday afternoon, breaking a record of being off-grid for twenty four hours. Yet, every time her mom answered the landline and explained her condition to the caller, she deliriously thought it was Kunaal. Then, she would realize he didn't have her number. On Sunday, when Kinsy visited, they had an unavoidable discussion about Kunaal. "How are you feeling now?" Kinsy's cheerful voice was laced with tenderness.

"I feel as if I've been tumble-dried in a top loading washing machine."

"Well, look at it as a much-needed forced rest. No office for you anytime soon," declared Kinsy.

"But, I'll have to. I didn't get a chance to tell you. I just got offered a post of Assistant Vice President at my office, with full Category-I benefits and a chauffeur-driven car," she proudly announced, hurriedly adding, "You know, I have to start work on setting up of the new sub-division as soon as possible…"

"Stop it Reeva!" Kinsy's sharply cut Reeva off.

"What?"

"Reeva, get real. Stop being such a mule. If you go on like this, you'll end up hurting yourself."

"Kinsy… I can't be taking it easy at such a crucial time in office."

"I'm not talking about work."

"Then get to the point."

"Okay. Why don't we discuss Kunaal then?"

"Kunaal has nothing to do with this."

"Really? Then how come the most level-headed person I know has suddenly turned into an emotional wreck? Hiding behind the façade of a busy work schedule. You seriously want to convince me that this has nothing to do with Kunaal Kabi?"

"Seriously Kinsy, I am under a lot of work pressure. Besides, I already told you, Kunaal was just a passing fancy and I've moved on."

"Good. Now that you've said it for my benefit… do it."

"Oh Kinsy!" Reeva was exasperated by her continual nagging, yet her voice came out low and tired.

"Okay… okay, I give up. Congratulations on the promotion, we have to party as soon as you're good to go." She smiled happily. "Just, one more thing… Now that you've given up on that handsome devil, you don't mind if I make an attempt on him, do you?" winked Kinsy, and flashed a wicked smile.

"Alright Kinsy...now you've done it." Reeva picked up her pillow and threw it at her.

Settled in with his favourite evening companion, a glass of limited edition single malt scotch, Vir felt simultaneously comfortable and focused. He loved the late evening breeze and the sound of waves that reached his seaside apartment terrace. A lone seagull flew by, calling out to a companion and Vir exhaled deeply.

The past three days had been very busy for Manek Vir as he had called upon many of his connections, both new and old, to verify the J&T case. A thorough man, he hated any surprises. That's why he always cross-checked all available information, personally. Within seventy two hours of meeting Thapar, he knew the entire background of J&T, its employees and promoters and even the upcoming international project with Galactic Studios. He even knew of their 'failed' meeting with Rishi Uttur, and after that, coming to a logical deduction was a simple task. Thapar and J&T needed them badly.

It was clear that turning the political tide against JBP was as good, or bad, as trying to stop a freight train with failed brakes. Retaining Sathya Raj Mane as the state's CM would be a resultant occurrence, even though the NPP was up against an anti-government wave.

For JBP to lose hold in the state, it would need to make some really big mistakes. But Vir knew that Rishi Uttur always took measured steps and would not do stupid things. Also, he was an honest politician, which complicated matters. He had already dispatched a detailed report on the case to be physically delivered by someone at a pre-fixed secret location for the Fixer, as the protocol prohibited use of any form of electronic media. Vir was completely comfortable with this arrangement, as his years of training and covert operations experience had sharpened his instincts.

He was now itching to discuss the case with the Fixer and was willing to bet that this case would not be accepted on grounds of its complexity and far-reaching ripples it might create. In the past, only one case was rejected by him. But, that case was of a personal nature and Fixer had a strict rule about not meddling in people's personal affairs or matters of the heart.

Today was the designated day to speak him. There were pre-fixed dates when they connected, irrespective of whether there was an active project or not. Sometimes, their exchange comprised just few words like "All Good?" and "Yes" as a means of checking in on each other. Their jobs were well defined and compartmentalized. The Fixer operated at higher levels and Vir was an on-ground field operative gathering data and information apart from being on the front line. But it was the Fixer who always defined and dictated the strategic moves. Their projects always had plenty of money involved which was a good motivator but Vir secretly believed that Fixer already had enough money and that there were other mysterious factors that drove him to such clandestine operations. He often wondered if it was a deep-seated psychological desire to control things that did it for him.

Vir dialled his number at midnight, which was answered on the third ring.

The familiar voice did not wait for pleasantries, "I've read your report. It's comprehensive. Is there anything new you need to add?"

"No. That's about it." Vir sensed the compliment hidden in the statement and felt proud. The Fixer never made ornamental statements.

"Okay. Accept the job. Thirty million dollars should be deposited in a foreign account."

"What in case of negotiations?"

"They won't negotiate. Tell them we may need media support from time to time." This was the first time that he had asked for any client support which puzzled Vir. Normally, they operated as far away as possible from the media.

The call was disconnected. Deep in thought, Vir twirled the ice cubes in his drink. The game had begun.

Kunaal was nervous – actually clueless – about how to handle Rishi Uttur, if he started discussing the fiasco that took place at his residence. He truly valued their friendship. He had personally come to receive him at the airport as they were to travel together to the party head office. Kunaal, being influential, had access to the airport interiors. He finally saw Uttur emerge from the far end of the arrivals hall at Mumbai airport, surrounded by a small group.

Uttur too spotted Kunaal early, moved swiftly and greeted him with a firm handshake and a pat on the shoulder, then issued instructions to his fellow party members. Both exited quickly and boarded the car in the VIP parking area. In the car, Uttur was all business and despite Kunaal's fears, did not revisit the J&T issue. He had other things on mind.

"Kunaal, it's good you could meet me here. There's plenty I need to update you about." Kunaal listened silently. "I don't know if you're aware, we just received the election dates from the Election Commission yesterday. It's in April next year and that's just seven months away."

"Yes, I was expecting them to be held in the first quarter."

"I need your help, Kunaal," Uttur looked directly at him.

"Oh come on sir; just tell me what needs to be done."

"We've selected Shri Pramod Saran as our chief ministerial candidate for the elections in Maharashtra. I want you to handle his entire public relations campaign and media exposure at state level."

"Of course, you needn't worry. I will ensure that the best professional team handles it." Kunaal knew that Uttur wouldn't trust anyone else with this job. Maharashtra was an important fort for JBP and he would do everything to topple NPP over. "That's the point Kunaal, I'm asking for more than your professionalism. I'm asking for your personal involvement. Can you commit this much? This is very important for my party and... even personally."

Kunaal registered the urgency in the voice of this man he respected so much, and smiled, "You have my word; I'll look into this personally." Uttur visibly relaxed. The car glided through Mumbai, towards its southern-most end, which housed the political hub of the state. Kunaal knew Pramod Saran as a political veteran from JBP, who had been with the party for as long as he could remember. He had risen through the ranks, coming from a modest background. He had worked hard at grassroots and had a good following among the masses since the days when he had been a mere corporator. Pramod Saran's direct involvement with the common man had earned him a good reputation. But as he rose, his former positions were filled by people he thought were undeserving of the seat.

His need to implement changes at policy levels required that he worked at higher levels. But the more he moved away from the ground, the more his policies and philosophies were diluted by those who worked below him. He had realized that it was harder to explain his belief system to others than to practice it. Often, he was left red-faced by the rabid conduct of people who under the name of party ideology inconvenienced the public.

Govindrao, Pramod Saran's right-hand man, was one of those party hardliners, who did not believe in drawing any lines. Kunaal knew that for the benefit of Pramod Saran's campaign, he would need to keep an eye on this overzealous, livewire party worker who was high on power.

Despite continual protests from her parents, Reeva made it to office on Monday morning. She planned to spend the day in office catching up on all the pending paperwork, so she could keep to herself. She had promised herself that she would not think about Kunaal and was mostly succeeding.

Lost in thoughts, she mechanically went about pressing lift buttons, opening doors and greeting people till she reached her cabin. As she opened the blinds and let the natural light flood in, she realized Buddy was missing and panicked. She called Harry who entered with her morning tea. His sense of timing pertaining to her needs was always impeccable.

She asked him, "Harry, where's Buddy?"

"Madam, I didn't move your plant," he said, looking around the room, "I'll check around the office now, madam." Having sent Harry away to look for Buddy, Reeva powered up her laptop after almost three days and expected a barrage of emails. Even from her crowded inbox panel, one sender's name sent her mind and heart reeling out of control. There sitting in her inbox were, not one, but two emails from Kunaal Kabi, sent on last Friday and Saturday.

Her hands felt unsteady as she clicked on one. Her heart leapt and was disappointed at the same time, by the simply worded message that held a note of urgency and also a tinge of desperation as it was sent twice. The message simply read: *Reeva, I've been trying to reach you. Where are you? Please contact me.*

Reeva was instantaneously filled with a righteous rage. *How dare he? First, he ignores me as if I'm nobody and then expects me to be available at his beck and call.*

But her heart chimed in, *So he was thinking of you, when you were in bed, unwell. That seems like a karmic connection.*

Immediately, her determined mind cut in, making a valid point. *Not a chance. Merely writing a one-line email, that too after such a long gap, doesn't qualify for any kind of leniency.*

Lost in a churning sea of emotions and startled by a sudden knock on her door, Reeva spilled the tea on herself. Nihaal was already by her side with a wad of tissues and a forehead creased with concern. She took the tissues and wiped her arm, while smiling sheepishly at him.

But then she brightened to see Buddy looking bright and

healthy in his hand. "Where did you find it?" She asked as he kept it on her table.

"Well, this little friend of yours desperately needed some sunshine. I was in early and left it out on the terrace for a bit. But don't worry; this wasn't a case of unlawful abduction. I had all intentions of returning this prized possession to its lawful owner," he teased.

"There... a smile looks a lot better on you than me." He still had a thoughtful look. His humour was always dry, so that made her wonder whether he was joking or serious.

"Nihaal, thank you," said Reeva. Her intercom rang. Nihaal silently mouthed 'bye' and Reeva picked up the receiver.

"Reeva, do you have anything important scheduled for today?" Mr. Sehgal had no idea of her sick weekend.

"Not much, Mr. Sehgal, I'm in office all day today," Reeva was guarded as she wasn't up to taking up any excessive work or meetings today but she wasn't going to shirk from work on grounds of being unwell.

"Good. It's time to meet the Media Vision PR's Vice President. You ready?"

"When will that be?" Reeva had already begun preparing herself mentally for the meeting. Though a bit weak and tired, there was no way she was letting go of the opportunity to meet her future boss and the mystery person who would lead MVPR.

"This evening 6pm, at the Taj coffee shop. We'll drive down together." Reeva was excited and then immediately worried. She had not dressed for a formal meeting, and even though she looked sharp with a khaki cargo and black T-shirt, she would have preferred a business suit for the first meeting with the MVPR head. She pulled up her working files on the desktop, thinking about Kunaal. She had decided not to respond to his email with steely determination. If he was repenting then he needed some more punishment and if he wasn't, then it would be pointless to respond anyway.

The day passed quickly and around 5pm, Mr. Sehgal's secretary reminded her that they had to leave for the meeting in ten minutes. Reeva quickly brushed her hair and applied some light makeup. The drive to Taj was uneventful, with Mr. Sehgal busy on his phone.

She stealthily caught her reflection in a mirror she walked through the hotel's lobby. She looked presentable enough and felt confident. Finally, they settled around an antique coffee table, next to the French windows. She faced her boss, leaving the middle chair empty for the guest. The view of the quiet sea with numerous yachts on the lapping waves was mesmerizing and soothing. With sun almost setting, the sea had a shimmering orange hue to it. The sun itself looked delicious, almost edible, like a big, round orange candy. As soon as they settled, Mr. Sehgal started to update her.

"Reeva, today's meeting is not just about introducing you two. You remember me mentioning a political campaign? We're expected to get some confirmed news on that as well today."

"Is the new vice president a reason for us getting this campaign?" Reeva was trying to connect the dots.

"You see Reeva… you may have heard of this person…" Then he abruptly stopped speaking, his focus shifting to the entrance as he spotted their guest. "Aah… there he is," his face broke into a courteous smile.

Reeva turned around and spotted him immediately. Her

heart leapt to her mouth as she watched Kunaal walking coolly towards them. He smiled broadly as he shook hands with Mr. Sehgal.

"Kunaal?" Reeva managed in a barely audible whisper, her face drained of all expressions.

"Reeva… meet the future Vice President of MVPR… Mr. Kunaal Kabi. You must have heard of him. Kunaal… this is Reeva Rai. She's one of my best human resource assets, mind you," said Mr. Sehgal, smiling proudly.

"I don't know of Miss Rai's view of me, but I've been fortunate to meet her earlier. I'm honoured by your generosity in extending such quality managerial support, Mr. Sehgal." Kunaal extended a hand towards Reeva; she stood there, numb, and all sights and sounds receded to the background.

A seething righteous anger engulfed her. His audacity irked her but she maintained a deadpan expression and took Kunaal's extended hand, which he held tightly for just a tad longer than what sensibilities dictated.

"Really… you two have met?" Mr. Sehgal was surprised, but for different reasons.

"Oh nothing sir, we were just briefly introduced at a social function. I'm surprised that Mr. Kabi even remembers," Reeva said icily, and they settled down. Kunaal had not reacted to her comment.

"So Kunaal, what are our timelines and when do you think we can get started?"

"Mr. Sehgal, we may need to speed up the Media Vision setup. There's news for you… we have already bagged JBP's state level account, including the PR and media campaign for their chief ministerial candidate Mr. Pramod Saran. Activities need to begin as soon as possible."

"That's great. I think we can gear up for that. What do you think Reeva?"

"Yes sure, we can start strategizing too. We'll need to set up a meeting with JBP party officials and Mr. Pramod Saran to get a first-hand brief." Reeva was all business. If she was to work with Kunaal, she wasn't making herself an easy prey.

"Of course, I'll get that lined up. Mr. Uttur has asked me to look into this campaign personally."

"So Kunaal, when can you come on board? Your cabin will be ready in a week."

"Don't worry Mr. Sehgal. Irrespective of the cabin, I intend to start soon, probably early next month. Meanwhile, I'll co-ordinate with Reeva, during the setup and for other meetings and discussions."

"Hope you don't mind me calling you Reeva," he looked intently at Reeva.

"You can call me anything Mr. Kabi; we're here to work together, so what name we address each other, does not change our *professional equation*." Her emphasis on the last two words made Kunaal bristle in his seat. If Mr. Sehgal noticed any undercurrent in the exchanges between them, he didn't make it apparent.

The meeting concluded and they walked towards the exit. Kunaal tangentially hinted at dropping Reeva home, which she religiously ignored. Since Mr. Sehgal lived in South Mumbai, he could not drop her. Earlier, during their conversation, it became known that Kunaal's route overlapped with Reeva's.

"Kunaal, could you drop Reeva off? She drove with me to the meeting and has no ride," suggested Sehgal. Kunaal was waiting for this opportunity.

"Of course, Mr. Sehgal; no sweat at all," Kunaal said smoothly and Reeva couldn't protest without coming across as rude or unwilling to play as a team.

"Okay then, look forward to seeing you in office soon, Kunaal." Mr. Sehgal's Mercedes arrived and he was gone. Once again, Reeva and Kunaal were left alone, just like at the end of the wedding. But this time, Reeva was guarded. As the valet brought Kunaal's SUV, he opened the passenger door for her to get in, tipped the valet and got behind the wheel. Reeva inhaled a heady mix of polished leather upholstery and Kunaal's expensive Issey Miyake. Soon, the car glided through the beautifully lit, seaside stretch of Marine Drive. Since this was still late evening, traffic had backed up as the late workers were now trudging home, stuck in bumper-to-bumper traffic. The thirty-minute drive to Bandra, where Reeva lived, was going to take at least an hour.

They were quiet for a while; Reeva not wanting to talk and Kunaal not knowing where to begin. He switched on the car's audio system and Beethoven's familiar symphony surrounded them. Reeva had been stealing glances at him at intervals, fascinated by his amazing profile and strong, muscular arms and hands as they maneuvered the steering wheel. But she was still angry and not willing to relent even an inch. Kunaal was the first to break the ice.

"Listen Reeva, I understand you're upset. But I tried to get in touch with you before today's meeting." In response, Reeva gave him an unflinching, icy stare.

"Okay, okay... a bit late though. I agree I should have shared these developments with you earlier and I apologize for that. I was really caught up." Reeva's silent treatment continued.

"Oh come on Reeva, don't be such a child." Now, Reeva was offended and Kunaal realized his mistake the moment he mouthed those words. He hit the steering wheel hard with his open palm in frustration, "Damn."

"Mr. Kabi, don't worry. I will not allow any past misunderstanding to get in the way of my professionalism," said Reeva, without a trace of emotion.

The next moment, she felt a sudden jerk and grasped the door handle as Kunaal hit the brake and sharply turned the car to the left and brought it to a halt at the curb. Reeva was breathless by the sudden manoeuvre, but Kunaal turned to face her coolly. He was quiet for a few seconds, and then spoke with a firm voice, emphasizing every single word. "Reeva... if you feel... for even one moment... that I didn't think of you in the past month, then you couldn't be more wrong. I thought of you... every single day. I just didn't know what to do about it." He rubbed his eyes and sighed tiredly, looking completely lost.

She looked away, towards the sea.

"Look now... Can we arrive at a few working rules for the future? You'll have to forgive me for the past. In return, I promise you that I'll never hurt you, intentionally or unintentionally. Is that a fair deal?"

A reluctant smile appeared on her face as her anger assuaged and she nodded.

"A quick coffee for a peace deal?" he asked and she smiled in agreement. They decided on a newly opened seaside café, at Bandra Bandstand, near her home. The atmosphere was lively, as scores of young couples sat canoodling and held hands, dreamily looking into each other's eyes. Reeva felt a little out of place. She knew Kunaal was enjoying her discomfort as she caught one of his sideward glances. After placing the order for both of them, he finally said, “Reeva, we’re supposed to be working together and I’m incredibly attracted towards you. You do know that this complicates matters for me?”

Reeva was truly enjoying the attention, but didn’t know how to respond to this peculiar question.

“You’ll have to promise me that you won’t make it any more difficult.”

“How so? By growing a beard and a moustache?”

“Forget it... you’re no good,” said Kunaal impatiently. Then with narrowed, thoughtful eyes, he added, “On second thoughts, you may look very cute with those two additions.” They laughed and chatted for a while as time flew quickly. And then, abruptly, Kunaal checked his watched and signalled for the bill. “Got to get going now,” he announced, as if he had belatedly remembered an important appointment.

On the way out, Kunaal held her hand and opened the door for her to get into the car. He dropped her outside her building and waited until she disappeared into it before speeding off. Reeva was almost dream-walking. Between her and Kunaal that evening, a lot was said. But what was left unsaid, was even more delicious.

CHAPTER 6

Sathya Raj Mane, the acting chief minister for the state, even with the Category Z security, was a very insecure man. Through the heavily packed schedules, he often deeply contemplated what had caused such an irreversible downward slide of his state regime. The last message from the party's high command was loud and clear, 'Shape up or ship out'. He knew after the approaching elections, he was a doomed man. His delayed decisions, delegation of projects to ineffective people and mostly his apparent lack of vision clubbed with downright greed had all finally added up.

Like every self-respecting politico with an ounce of ego, he dreaded being sent into an anonymous political retirement. But the power in politics lasted only as long as one occupied the chair of office. Especially for those who never bothered about the needs of the common man and society. Of this, Sathya Raj Mane was truly and fully guilty. He was now a desperate man ready to trade his soul. But in his current standing, there were no takers even for that.

Every morning, Mane found it unbearable to attend office, go through stacked files asking for his urgent attention and hold meaningless meetings. That he may not be occupying this chair and office by the first quarter of the next year made him reluctant towards all state level initiatives. Hence, the request from the J&T promoters for a personal meeting failed to excite him. But Thapar and Jaiswal had been one of the major contributors to NPP funds in the past and he did not wish to ruffle any more feathers, unnecessarily.

Both men now awaited him in the VIP waiting room of his luxurious bungalow in Malabar Hill, the exclusive residential area of South Mumbai, which held both his office and residence. After making the duo wait for the customary twenty minutes, despite not being busy, he entered the visitor's lounge and asked his secretary to leave them alone. Whatever they had to say, he preferred to hear it alone.

"Hello Mr. Thapar and Mr. Jaiswal. How are you? Heard about the J&T launch… Congratulations!" Mane kept his tone formal and to the point.

"Thank you for your wishes. How's the government running these days? I mean election dates are set already and campaign work must begin soon." Thapar was at his best courteous behaviour. He didn't intend letting Mane know that he considered him a weak political candidate and a sure shot loser after the coming elections.

"Come on Thapar sahab, you're a media savvy person. I'm sure you've seen the poll analysis… and the media is out to kill NPP even before the elections are held. If left to them, JBP would form the government tomorrow," Mane chuckled, with cynicism.

"No, no... no Maneji, it isn't so simple. Media after all

runs on TRPs. Dog biting a man is not news, but man biting a dog definitely is," Thapar smiled broadly at his analogy.

"What do you mean Thapar sahab? I'm a little confused about who's the man and who's the dog. Was there anything specific you wanted to discuss in today's meeting?" Mane was business-like again.

"Well, I meant that the world of media is far removed from the practical world and its ground realities. And, yes there's something very specific we wanted to discuss, but first I've a question for you. Did you wonder why we called for this meeting at your residence and not Mantralaya?" Thapar's smugness was beginning to irritate Mane, who shook his head slowly.

"So that our meeting appears to the public and media as a courtesy visit. Nothing more," added Jaiswal enthusiastically and continued, "You see, we've some plans for J&T and may need your help."

"Help?" Mane was fully attentive now, "How can I be of help?"

"No Maneji, the correct question is can we help you?" corrected Thapar.

"I don't understand."

"Maneji, we all know your days in this position are numbered. Let's face it; you can be of no help to us or anyone, if you're not sitting in this office and on that chair." Thapar got straight to the point and Mane instantly felt his temper flare. He growled, "What do you mean?"

"We don't mean to be rude Maneji," Jaiswal cut in. "Our flagship project will need some important land clearances by early next year. You could do that easily for us. Provided... you are still the CM."

This time Mane did not react immediately, choosing to see the game unfold to its full extent. "Which land are we talking here?" he asked, weighing the situation.

"We need a hundred-acre plot at Dharampur, for a commercial entertainment project," continued Jaiswal.

"But there are no commercial construction zones in Dharampur. Ninety per cent of it is mostly agricultural or housing projects for homeless or low income groups." Mane tapped his fingers on the table and arrived at some quick deductions.

"We're talking about the land earmarked for Garib Griha Niwaas Yojana," Jaiswal concluded and waited for this to sink in.

"Hmm... that's complicated. It will need corrections at policy levels and will involve top level bureaucrats, local Dharampur MLAs, and couple of other officers in Secretariat, if we're to release that land. How badly do you need it?" Mane's corrupt instincts were kicking in.

"Only as badly as you need to stay in power, Maneji," said Thapar smiling slyly and continued. "How does it work if we resort to the oldest form of trade? A barter. We help you retain the CM's chair and you give us that piece of land. Sound like a fair deal?"

"Your offer sounds tempting, but equally farfetched and overambitious from where I see it." Mane was definitely interested, but also sceptical. What did these two know of politics and voter's mindset?

"Then you need to change your perspective as this game will be played very high up. Right now, you just need to start the process of releasing the Dharampur land for us. Once you give us a green signal, we can formally inform

Galactic Studios that the land acquisition is in process. The paperwork can be concluded early next year when you continue your office as the CM." Thapar waited for impact. "By the way… there won't be contributions from J&T into the NPP election fund this time. We can't afford to get tied together."

Contribution to the party fund was hardly an issue to be deliberated upon now for Mane. If what Thapar and Jaiswal were offering materialized, it would mean a new lease of life to his political career. Anyway, Mane did not see a better option on the horizon. Winning elections on his goodwill and the voters' trust was out of the way. These white-collared businessmen were his only hope and right now he was ready to cut a deal with the devil himself. Besides, he had nothing to lose, they did.

Setting up of Media Vision PR was all-consuming, backbreaking work for Reeva, as they were on a crazy deadline. Everything was supposed to be up and running within a fortnight. The only respite was that MVPR was located on the same floor as Creative AdZone, in the extended area not utilized by the company. So, for her, the move to the new subdivision was smooth. Shalini Ray, though not friendly, was a thorough professional and a great help. Reeva often got the impression that Shalini did not generally like many people and she especially did not like Kunaal. She often noticed Shalini changing her schedules to ensure she avoided Kunaal.

But what was driving Reeva with superhuman energy was

Kunaal's regular presence in her life. They spoke regularly, but only to discuss work, yet these phone calls thrilled her. He often dropped by her office to discuss probable clients, strategies and supervise paperwork. Unfortunately, this cancelled out any possibilities of leisurely café visits and they were restricted to Harry's pantry tea and coffee, often joined by Shalini, Nihaal or Mr. Sehgal. Reeva was eagerly waiting for Kunaal to join officially, hoping to see him for longer periods. She also knew that Kunaal was cautiously trying to maintain a safe distance from her. But she often caught him gazing at her, when no one was watching.

Workwise, they were fairly on track with the company stationary scheduled for printing the next day. The logo designs had to be finalized that day. Reeva had worked with Nihaal on these and was proud of the final outcome. She believed that Nihaal easily belonged to the list of top ten talented people in the country, and that the lead agencies would have been honoured to have him work for them. But his work-on-my-own-terms attitude made him un-employable by the same agencies. Nihaal earned an enviable pay package already and yet Reeva felt he was underpaid.

As always, Reeva's face lit up when Kunaal entered her office. "Hey, what's up? Are we good on the corporate stationary?" he asked breezily.

"Yeah, we're all set. Design needs one final look. See you in the conference room," replied Reeva.

"Alright, I'll have a quick word with Shalini meanwhile. I think she should join in too." Kunaal's casual reference to Shalini somehow pinched Reeva.

Soon they were all seated in the conference room going over the designs. Nihaal's work was flawless, so the designs were finalized quickly. Kunaal suggested they give the final touches in the design studio to save time. Nihaal was more than glad to take them to his kingdom. Being restricted to strategizing and supervising due to ever-increasing responsibilities, he hardly every got a chance to actually sit before the screen and feel the keyboard and mouse.

Once at the studio, Kunaal briefed Nihaal in his brusque and streamlined manner. Reeva was mesmerized by both men's expertise, equally talented and yet so diverse in personalities. As Nihaal quickly executed the changes on the computer screen, Kunaal asked Reeva, "So, what do you think?"

Reeva stooped low towards the screen, wanting to look at the design closely and casually placed her hand on Nihaal's shoulder. She knew this gesture would have conveyed intimate comfort to any observer. She felt Nihaal's muscles ripple and tense under her fingers. "I think we could do away with the lines." She spoke without moving her hand, appearing engrossed in the design. Reeva was very protective of her personal physical space. Moreover, she had never before touched Nihaal, apart from formal handshakes, and this new intimacy left him confused, surprised and nervous at the same time.

For a few seconds, Nihaal's senses were fully consumed by her touch. But he was a perceptive guy. He sensed that Reeva's sudden physical contact had a purpose and so he played along. He promptly executed the changes with a smile playing on his lips. At first, Kunaal felt strangely awkward at the sudden display of comfort level between his colleagues. Then he felt a frustration as hot as lava rise within him. He snapped, "Okay Nihaal, I think you can wind this up as Reeva says. I need to get going," he said curtly and was out without offering any greetings to Reeva. *Bull's eye*, she thought.

She returned to her cabin and attacked the paperwork waiting for her. Before she knew, it was dark outside and she had to switch on her cabin lights. As most of the staff had already left, a certain calm descended over the office. Reeva loved such rare quiet times, when things slowed down and she could hear her thoughts. She was very happy about the effect her manoeuvre with Nihaal had had on Kunaal. He had gone ballistic. Yet, something was nagging her. *Had that been fair towards Nihaal?* She could only hope that Nihaal didn't read too much into the hand-on-shoulder gesture, but then he was a sharp guy.

While she was busy sorting out this mess in her head, she spotted Nihaal coming towards her cabin and immediately tensed with guilt.

"May I?" he smiled.

"Come on in. When did you get so formal?"

Nihaal smiled broadly and put down the steaming Earl Grey tea.

"And when did you start drinking tea?" She knew Nihaal drank black coffee.

"This one's for you... I was running by the pantry anyway," he shrugged.

"Thanks," responded Reeva tentatively.

"No worries... just wanted to run the final stuff by you before things proceed for printing today."

Reeva was relieved to get the discussion back to work. What she had done with Nihaal was apparently harmless and minor, but she knew what her intentions had been and this was eating away at her. Once they went over the designs and approved them, Nihaal relaxed in his chair and extended his legs, crossing his feet at the ankles. Reeva knew this was his contemplative posture and waited for what was coming next.

"So, what do you think of Kunaal?"

"What do you mean?" As soon as the words were out of her mouth, Reeva mentally kicked herself for sounding defensive.

"I meant to ask if he's good to work with. What did you think?" Nihaal stared at her.

"Yeah, he's a dedicated professional – intelligent and motivated."

"So was Hitler. How is he as a person?"

"Oh, he's alright," she said non-committedly.

"Okay, that's good. Don't want our star performer to be stumped by a stranger. You know, I'm rooting for you." He smiled and winked.

Reeva was relieved to be back in the neutral zone, but was left wondering if Nihaal was seeking certain answers. "Thanks Nihaal, you're a great support," she smiled.

"Yes, remember you can always count on me." Nihaal gathered his stuff. "See you tomorrow at the great political circus." The entire team, including Kunaal, were going to congregate at Pramod Saran's office early tomorrow morning.

Punctual and always wanting to have a head start, Shalini reached Pramod Saran's office first, at 9am, thirty minutes earlier than the appointed time. She decided to go through her line of questioning for him, once again. This new job was becoming far more challenging and demanding than she had expected. But that was not what worried her. A more serious issue had cropped up. She hated Kunaal.

Worse still, her presence had not deterred or upset him and he had gone about the business around her coolly, under the guise of professionalism. *How could he be so nonchalant with her, after what happened between him and Malini, her beautiful younger sister, her baby?* She felt the bitterness consume her again as she contemplated ways to avoid Kunaal permanently. Luckily, Nihaal interrupted her chain of thought as he entered the waiting room and settled down opposite her.

"All set?" Nihaal knew in this meeting his job was that of a silent spectator and he had to merely soak in whatever was being discussed. "Yup... I'm wondering if they are," Shalini smiled wryly. She knew political briefings often turned out to be one-sided, monotonous declarations of what the political party believed it could achieve. To her surprise though, the promises always worked, especially if people were fed up with the current government. People voted based on emotions and not rational decisions.

Soon, Kunaal and Reeva joined them, as they came in separately. Shalini sensed a spark between them. She knew Reeva was playing with fire and wanted to warn her, but despite her good intentions, she ended up rubbing Reeva the wrong way. Something about Reeva threw her off.

Ultimately, they were ushered into the conference room that seated twenty people. Their team took one end of the table, leaving the other for the politicos. Shortly after, Pramod Saran and Govindrao entered the conference room, followed by Rishi Uttur, who first smiled at Kunaal and then greeted Reeva by her first name. This surprised the others and Nihaal raised his eyebrows.

Reeva was genuinely pleased to see the politico.

The discussion began with party's PR campaign as Uttur settled back giving centre stage to Saran. Clad in a cream kurta, Saran was a neat and meticulous man. He began with the party manifesto and what the JBP campaign needed to convey.

"We want to focus on the plans we have for the state's large-scale development with special emphasis on interiors and villages. JBP should come across as a positive group with a broadminded and progressive approach."

Govindrao, who until then had been watching the discussion like a game of lawn tennis, spoke abruptly, "I think we should also remind people of the inefficiencies and mistakes of the current NPP government. They should be exposed. We need to truly drag them down once and for all, giving them no chance to recover." He spoke sharply, his voice loud and hoarse.

"But Govind, we shouldn't come across as petty and narrow-minded. Only those who are low on agenda resort to such tactics. Besides, NPP is at the bottom of the opinion polls anyway. I think we should concentrate on what we can offer to the common man," Saran calmly countered him.

"But the party workers are all charged up, they want to tie NPP to the back of a horse and drag it around the ground. They expect aggression from their party. We can't afford to lose."

Rishi Uttur who was quiet until now finally intervened "Rest assured Govind... we will not lose. I agree with your point about keeping the party workers charged up, but at the same time, there's no point kicking your opponent boxer who's already on the ring floor." He smiled patiently at Govind Rao. "You need to gather all your manpower and channelize it towards creating more awareness about the development projects for the state and people's welfare..." Uttur looked intently at Govind and added, "...and only you can do it Govind. Don't forget, you represent the common man." Govindrao visibly relaxed after that. His humungous number of loyal followers was the only reason he had a seat at the table. Reeva smiled inwardly at Uttur's natural knack for leadership.

"Oh sir, by the way, we also want to personally extend an invitation to the MVPR launch party next week. It would be really nice if you all could attend," Kunaal deftly used the pause in discussion to invite the JBP heads.

"I'm not sure if I'm in town. Besides, you know how I feel about the media parties. But let's see. Saranji and Govind will make it I think, if schedules permit," answered Uttur.

"Oh, I have heard of Kunaal sahab's parties. They are out of the world." Govindrao's voice had a quality of chalk scraping on board, when excited. A representative of the masses, he hardly ever had a chance to taste the company of classes. Kunaal eyed him keenly. He had a hunch that Govindrao was going to be a liability.

Reeva held the phone two inches from her ear and could still hear the speaker's shrieks loud and clear.

She winced as Kinsy ranted on, "What the hell did you say? Kunaal Kabi likes you... he's also your boss... and you had coffee with him?" Kinsy's voice was a delirious mix of wonder and confusion. Reeva tried to sound as level as possible, while struggling to suppress the laughter bubbling inside her, "Yes Kinsy, he's my boss now and it was just an unplanned coffee break on the way to drop me home."

Kinsy jumped on this, "Oh, so now he even drops you home." She sounded sarcastic.

Reeva took a deep breath, "Kinsy, when I accepted the Assistant Vice President's position, unfortunately I didn't get to choose the Vice President. Kunaal and I are colleagues, nothing more. The lines are clearly drawn."

"Like hell they're drawn," Kinsy muttered, still unconvinced. "I don't understand why you're so hell bent on boarding a bus that has no brakes." This put a smile back on Reeva's lips as Kinsy continued, "I only know this much... that man... around you... is nothing but clear and present danger."

"Kinsy, I sure am not boarding any bus."

"Reevs, I've seen how he affects you. What if he makes a move on you?" Kinsy spoke rapidly.

"Well, I don't have to worry about that... not for now at least. Anyway, got to go."

She disconnected the phone and was instantly lost in her thoughts. She knew that Kinsy's concern was not totally unjustified.

However, Kunaal always kept her at arm's length. But she couldn't complain. She had been forewarned by Kunaal's promise of 'I will never hurt you intentionally or unintentionally'. Though these words had sounded like music to her ears then, they were the reason why he was keeping a distance from her now. He was effectively negating any possibility of further emotional involvement. This too could have worked, if Reeva didn't have to go through the torture of seeing him daily. Somehow, she dangerously liked the idea of getting hurt better than the cold distance between them, often overcome by a strong desire to take Kunaal by the shoulders and shake him.

Suddenly, her intercom beeped. Mr. Sehgal asked her to see him in his office immediately in a strained voice. As she knocked and peeked in, she was surprised to see Shalini Ray already seated across him. She sensed palpable tension in the room. Shalini was expressionless and stared straight ahead, refusing to even acknowledge her.

"Reeva, Shalini has proposed that before MVPR's official launch party is held and announcements are made, she should resign from MVPR... effective now." He spoke unemotionally.

Reeva was thrown off by this.

"The reason being?"

"Kunaal." The staccato, one-word answer hit Reeva like some physical impact.

"I don't understand. We are professionals and I believe any decision should be grounded on professional reasons alone." Reeva was surprised by her own composure, despite her anger.

"Hmm... well, she believes Kunaal has very strong media connections and is thus prone to be biased in his conduct, while handling MVPR clients. She has also accused him of unethical conduct in using his media contacts to wrongly misguide the general public in the past."

"Strong media connections are always an advantage for any PR company. And 'misguiding people' is a very serious allegation. I do believe Kunaal should also be called in for this meeting," Reeva forced herself to maintain a professional decorum.

"I agree with what you have to say Reeva, but Shalini is entitled to her views as a professional. In my experience, this is one of the most unique situations that I've ever faced. Yes, we will be getting Kunaal on board with this, but not before we've sorted this out."

Mr. Sehgal then addressed Shalini directly, "Shalini, since you've very clearly expressed your inability to work with Kunaal, I have a suggestion. I think you could work as a freelance consultant until we finish the on-going projects. And you could coordinate singularly with Reeva. Is that acceptable to you?"

"Thank you Mr. Sehgal," Shalini said, without missing a beat, as if she had already anticipated his proposal. "I understand my professional responsibilities and I don't wish to jeopardize your project. However, it is subject to a condition that any MVPR official I'm working with is not being influenced into any form of unethical conduct." She decidedly looked straight into his eyes.

Reeva was infuriated with Shalini's open insinuation that she could be influenced into unethical practices. But before she could speak, Mr. Sehgal lightly raised his palm in her direction.

"Shalini, you have my word. MVPR will never ever indulge in any unethical practices. Is that good enough for you?"

"Yes, it is."

"Okay then, I'll also speak with Kunaal in this matter and I make a personal appeal to the professional in both of you that you will make this transition smooth and without any hitch. Reeva, please make the necessary adjustments."

Both women exited the cabin simultaneously and walked away in opposite directions. Shalini walked purposely towards her cabin and Reeva felt deflated as she reached hers. She sat and stared at Buddy for a long time. What if these allegations were actually true? An ugly thought crossed her mind and she quickly squashed it, determined not to let it find its roots.

Reeva had always believed that Shalini was a bitter soul but this had gone too far. She decided now was the time to settle it all by talking to Kunaal and hearing his side of the story. She knew that Kunaal was capable of many things, but not of lying to her. She immediately walked towards his office.

But as Reeva approached Kunaal's glass paned office she stopped dead in her tracks as she faced a deeply disturbing scene. Shalini was already in Kunaal's office and they were engaged in an intense discussion.

Kunaal sat back in his chair, his chin resting on his hand as if in deep contemplation. In contrast, Shalini stood leaning slightly across Kunaal's desk with both hands firmly planted on the surface. She spoke forcefully and every now and then, her hand came off the desk jabbing a finger in the air, aggressively towards him.

Reeva couldn't hear what was being spoken in the cabin, but could guess that Shalini was barging Kunaal with accusations. Kunaal was speaking minimally and still being cut off by Shalini every time. And then, he suddenly banged his fist on his desk sending the pen stand flying off. He stood up abruptly and spoke briefly but aggressively. Reeva's breath was caught in her throat, as he moved swiftly towards Shalini but then at the last moment, moved past her and opened the door. He held it wide open and with his other hand gestured for her to leave his cabin. Shalini threw a venomous look at him and exited the cabin, banging the door behind her.

As Shalini turned towards the corridor, she faced Reeva. Their eyes met and both women stood still for a few seconds. Then Shalini walked away abruptly and Reeva sensed Kunaal's presence at his cabin door. He simply stared at her with empty eyes. With great effort, she turned and slowly walked away. And Kunaal did not call after her.

Reeva walked out of the office building with only her handbag and phone, leaving behind even her laptop in the office. She needed to be somewhere alone and was relieved to find her favourite spot, a secluded stone bench under the Gulmohar Tree, vacant. With all clutter receding into the background, she was forced to face the inevitable questions. What was Shalini accusing Kunaal of? What circumstances had forced Shalini to resign? Why was Kunaal so angry? And, why didn't he stop her outside his cabin to explain things? She knew that there were no mundane, run-of-the-mill answers to these questions. And, the only available explanations would be dark and sinister.

Suddenly, she sensed a presence next to her and instinctively jerked her head sideways to see Nihaal gently sit down next to her. He didn't look at her but merely extended a paper tea cup towards her as he sipped his own coffee. Reeva held it gingerly with both hands. They sat there for a few minutes – Reeva concentrating on her tea and Nihaal looking straight ahead, sipping his coffee. The companionable silence between them had an embalming effect on her frayed nerves and Reeva found herself relaxing. After a little while, she strangely found that it was far easier to talk to Nihaal than she had anticipated.

"How did you know where to find me?"

"That was easy. If you didn't already know, stalking is another creative pursuit I regularly indulge in."

"So, you were stalking me?" She felt a smile tug at the corner of her lips.

"Yeah. If following a zombie can be defined as stalking..."

Reeva shook her head and decided to play along. She knew he sensed her pain.

"How come you're here sharing your precious coffee time with me... don't you want to beat the rush hour and get home?" This was first time Reeva had asked Nihaal a personal question.

"Nope... no rush for me. I'm sure my housemates don't miss me so much."

"You share your accommodation with housemates?" She couldn't picture him sharing his living space with anyone.

"Yup, Sir Couch and Mr. TV are excellent housemates. Very accommodating and... talkative only when I want them to be," Nihaal smiled.

"What about your family?" Reeva was happy to have the focus away from herself.

"Mom and Dad are in Delhi." Nihaal's answer was cryptic.

"What compelled you to shift to Mumbai, leaving them behind?"

"A difference of opinion between my dad and I. He believed that I wasn't good enough for the construction business. And that I wasn't taking the right decisions."

"And you didn't believe him," stated Reeva, just to keep Nihaal going.

"On the contrary, I fully believed in his opinion." There was a sarcastic smile playing on his lips. "Guess I'm not good enough to compromise on my beliefs and principles in the name of cut-throat business practices."

"So, you left your dad's well-set construction business to be on your own… wow!" whispered Reeva with awe.

"Well, it was close to a decade ago. I was twenty two then… and my dad's construction company was one of the biggest in Delhi. You must have heard of Gibraltar Constructions Ltd."

"I don't believe it. Your dad owns GCL, and you live this life of a recluse, away from the business!"

"No Reeva, I live my life. That business, along with all its moral liabilities, belongs to my father."

"But don't you miss your mom?"

"Yes, I do. She's my only connect with the life I left behind. I meet her every time I'm in Delhi or she's in Mumbai… and we regularly talk over phone and emails."

He continued, "She was my anchor when I decided to move away. Even now, she emotionally blackmails me into accepting gifts from her so that she can make my life easier, for example – a car. I only do it to make her happy." He chuckled softly.

Reeva now understood why Nihaal never used the expensive sedan idling in his garage. As she searched his face, she couldn't find even a fraction of remorse about the decision he took so many years ago. She admired him for it. Somehow, he had uncomplicated things for her and she had the clarity she needed.

"Have you heard about Shalini quitting? What do you think?" asked Reeva.

"Yes, I know. She has her own reasons and I think we better not delve into them. Plus, even as a freelancer she's a good deal. My bigger concern is the current leadership of MVPR and whether it lies in right hands."

"Well, it's a matter of free will and choice. Shalini chose to quit, I wouldn't have. I still believe it's a professional setup and the decisions should also be so. Her personal equation with Kunaal should be kept out."

Reeva had spoken self-righteously and in response, Nihaal looked at her intently as if wanting to see deep within her. He spoke after a long pause with a conviction of a man with experience.

"Reeva, I just wanted to say something." He paused, to have her full attention. "Whether you like it or not, every single choice you make defines you for the rest of your life. Many choices come to you. The question is whether you're able to select the right one for yourself. Finally, all that matters, is following your heart." She felt something frozen deep within her beginning to melt rapidly and tears stung her eyes. Instantly, Nihaal's hand was over her shoulder. They stayed like that for a few minutes and Reeva was the first to emerge from the reverie. Nothing more was needed to be said. As she quickly blinked away the tears, Nihaal gave her a rueful smile and they walked together towards Reeva's car like good old friends, an invisible bond enveloping them.

CHAPTER 7

The following days at MVPR were hectic as the entire team worked towards the launch party. It had been scheduled for a weekend to ensure full attendance. The venue was located centrally at a seven-star banquet hall, which could accommodate five hundred people. But Kunaal handpicked the guest list of only two hundred, including few celebrities and politicos.

Even though every single day was a race against time, Kunaal felt the spark within him diminish rapidly. After the head-on collision with Shalini, Reeva's cool, aloof business-like approach cut through him every time their paths crossed. He no longer felt as confident and content as he used to, frequently asking himself the question, *What's the point of all this if it does not make me happy?*

The sight of Reeva quietly walking away from his cabin, as he watched helplessly, filled his vision every now and then. He had wanted to explain everything to her, but his feelings for her had complicated the situation. He had no clue what he would have said to her had he approached Reeva that day. His emotions towards her were becoming increasingly difficult to handle. Kunaal had therefore totally immersed himself in the preparations for the MVPR launch party, with the hope of distracting himself. But as the days passed, his sense of unease only grew.

On the day of the event as he was going over the final check-list and the probable questions from the media representatives, there was a knock at his door. He was disappointed to see his driver enter, hoping it would be Reeva. Lost in his thoughts, Kunaal listlessly watched him immaculately hang his evening jacket on the coat hanger and leave discreetly.

He sighed and looked at his watch. The invites had gone out for 8pm and he wanted to be there at least half an hour in advance. Closing the file, he ran his hand through his hair. He picked up the jacket and walked towards the washroom across the lobby. Most of the staff had already left for the day to go home and change.

Just as he reached the washroom, he saw Reeva emerge from the women's bathroom. She was wearing a simple, wine-coloured, knee-length dress. The off-shoulder dress showed off her pretty collarbones and her radiant, delicate skin was enhanced by the elegant diamond-and-red-stone necklace. He had never noticed Reeva using any lip colour, but today her lips were fuller with a deep red matte lipstick. Kunaal was speechless. They stared at each other for a few seconds before Reeva broke the spell.

"Hi… you're still here?"

"Yeah. I'll be leaving as soon as I'm ready," Kunaal pointed towards the suit he held in his other hand. His mouth felt dry. "What about you? How come you didn't go home to change?"

"I had anticipated the delay, so carried the change with me." Reeva's nervousness was making her speak too fast.

"You look beautiful," Kunaal gushed and saw her cheeks flush. "How are you getting to the venue? Are you driving there?" he added quickly.

"No... I guess... a taxi."

"Let's go together. I'll be ready in ten minutes."

"No thanks, I'll figure something out." Reeva didn't want to go with Kunaal even though her heart was jumping like a child who had seen her favourite candy.

"Oh, come on Reeva, you don't want to take a taxi dressed like this."

Reeva was at a loss of words, but then she saw Nihaal emerge from the other end of the hall. Even for one of the most glamorous parties being held in the town this evening, Nihaal was dressed in classic blue jeans, a fitting tan T-shirt and a smart black jacket flung over it. He looked sharp and handsome. He walked towards her as she frantically waved at him. She said, "I'll go with Nihaal... I mean, we're going together. See you later," Reeva said nervously, refusing to look Kunaal in the eye. Nihaal was surprised as Reeva took his arm and almost dragged him away. He turned just in time to wave at Kunaal and manage a "Hey".

Kunaal shrugged and proceeded to the washroom. Reeva had openly avoided going with him and this left him edgy. What was even more unsettling was the ease with which her hand had slipped through Nihaal's arm. *This evening is going to be sheer torture*, he thought as he looked into the mirror and shook his head in dismay.

The night was crackling with electricity as the guests started arriving. The party was no less than a red-carpet event. One luxury car after another lined up to deliver their celebrated occupant at the doorstep, causing a mini-traffic situation. But it was only adding to the glamour and hype as every disembarking personality was being subjected to incessant camera flashes. Even the bouncers were dressed in sharp suits and ties, looking more like a team of alert Black Cat commandos on duty.

Reeva and Nihaal reached the venue before time and it looked like a full house as no journalist was willing to let go this opportunity. Moreover, the guest list had already been leaked to relevant people, which was a good enough incentive. All in all, it was a perfectly staged media jamboree. As a seasoned player, Kunaal knew how and where to play his cards.

Busy discussing the flow of the event with a colleague, Reeva noticed a small cheer go up in the air. She turned towards the entrance expecting to see a major celebrity, but instead saw Kunaal enter the venue along with Mr. Sehgal. Undoubtedly, these two men were the heroes of MVPR and Creative AdZone. Kunaal was at his charming best, returning every single greeting, shaking hands and being what came naturally to him – an irresistible and handsome man. She could see some young female trainees swoon in a corner virtually salivating over him. Suddenly, she felt a jab of irrational jealousy. She wanted to avoid Kunaal, but there he was in full glory, in her face.

As Reeva saw him walking towards her, she quickly dialled Nihaal's mobile to trace him but spotted him at the far corner talking to the organizer. He obviously couldn't hear his cell-phone ring over all the noise.

"I guess a proper compliment is due," said Kunaal and before she could react, he took her hand and kissed the back of it lightly. "You look beautiful Reeva," he murmured softly. Reeva could see the two junior female interns gasp and ready to faint in the background. She politely pulled her hand back, though she could still sense a smouldering feeling at the place where his lips had touched her skin. "Thanks," she said with a tight, artificial smile.

"Reeva, can we be good friends just for the evening?"

"With a little bit of luck, we can be good colleagues at the most." Reeva's tone was flat.

"Reeva... you have to stop being so difficult."

"I'm being difficult? Why don't you target easier prey then, Mr. Kabi?" Reeva turned around and saw Nihaal patiently leaning on a nearby table, waiting for her. Apparently, he had seen her missed call and come looking for her. She smiled, took his arm and they walked away from Kunaal.

Kunaal stood affixed; he realized that she thought of him as a cheap, egotistical womanizer. So *this* was the problem that needed to be fixed. With a clear objective in sight, he felt elated for the first time in many days. He now knew what he had to do.

Apart from Kunaal, the evening was panning out pleasantly for Reeva. She decided not to leave Nihaal's side, just in case Kunaal decided to accost her again. Although, he had gotten busy with the evening's guests and did not bother her again, she doubted that he would use the first opportunity to close the conversation she had left open. He was just not the type to let things be or quietly retreat when presented with a challenge. Deep down, she knew how similar they were – drawn by new challenges.

The evening was in full swing with a vast majority of guests already present, light music playing in the background and exotic hors d'oeuvres being served continually. Reeva saw Rishi Uttur enter with Pramod Saran and Govindrao and walked towards them.

Kunaal and Mr. Sehgal were already welcoming the group. Kunaal was standing next to Uttur as she greeted him. Uttur seemed delighted to see her and immediately placed his hand on her head and said, "You look like an angel my dear, god bless," he smiled and looked meaningfully at Kunaal.

They all turned towards the stage as the emcee invited Mr. Sehgal, Kunaal and the politicos to the dais. The media representatives were more than eager to get a bite out of Uttur regarding JBP's general political agendas, but he politely stuck to announcing that MVPR would be handling JBP's campaign. The other questions pertaining to business objectives and clients were deftly handled by Kunaal. Soon, to everyone's relief, it was time to end the press conference and the official part of the evening. Most staffers were looking forward to it. Kunaal took the mic and spoke effortlessly. His perfect diction and lovely voice had everyone spellbound, including Reeva.

"Friends, colleagues and my partners in the media industry, I once again thank you all for your presence, support and cooperation as this lovely evening unfolds. However, before we close this session, I would like to personally thank one special person, without whom all this would have been impossible." Kunaal's declaration sent a wave of murmurs among the guests. After a dramatic pause, he continued, "I would like to invite Miss. Reeva Rai, Assistant Vice President, on stage."

Reeva froze in her seat and only got up after a nudge from Nihaal. Feeling the adrenaline rush through her nerves, she walked up to Kunaal and stood next to him as he shook her hand. "Dear friends, Miss Rai here is the sole reason I'm here. Without her hard work, perseverance and professionalism, we wouldn't have been able achieve what we have in such a short time."

He continued, "As a special recognition, I'm here by appointing her Strategic Business Advisor the board which will make her at par with me in all decisions that we make."

This hit Reeva like a jolt; she looked at Kunaal with questioning eyes and he nodded. She looked towards Mr. Sehgal, who was smiling. There was a deafening roar of claps as Reeva managed a smile and addressed the crowd. "Thank you Mr. Kabi for your generous appreciation, but it was a team effort. I hope I will be able to live up to everyone's expectations." She nodded at everyone and walked back to her seat. *What's his game?* She looked at Nihaal who elaborately bowed before her.

They laughed and walked to the bar. As the evening progressed, she was able to put Kunaal out of her head and relax with the help of some gin and tonic. Having Nihaal by her side, Reeva felt taken care of. With a firm no to Reeva's request for a third drink, Nihaal excused himself to meet a few ex-colleagues he had spotted earlier.

After the political party including Uttur left the venue, Kunaal relaxed. But he kept a weather eye on the party, which was only beginning to peak, with the DJ belting out the current hits. As the crowd descended on to the dance floor, he spotted Reeva, alone, at a far corner table. And when he saw her order another drink, he decided to intervene. He approached the waiter and asked him to hand him her drink instead. The waiter relented easily seeing it was Kunaal Kabi. He walked to her table but she failed to notice his presence as she gently swayed to the music.

"Reeva... I think you shouldn't drink anymore," said Kunaal, nevertheless placing the drink before her.

Reeva immediately sat up. She looked around and did not see Nihaal anywhere.

"Looking for your boy toy? He isn't here. My advice... Spare the poor guy," Kunaal chuckled.

"Why are you here? I'm sure it's not to impose moral policing on people's drinking habits."

"First, you're not just people. Second, you're a senior official of MVPR. It's not good for your image."

"I don't need lessons on conduct from anyone, especially you."

"Okay... I concede. Care to dance with me?" He extended a hand towards her. Emboldened by the effect of gin, she was tempted to take his hand and she almost did. But suddenly Nihaal breezed in.

"Sorry Reeva, got stuck for a bit longer," he said pulling a chair. "So, how about that dance now?" he said and then suddenly noticed Kunaal's extended hand and Reeva's discomfort.

"Oh... sorry Kunaal, the lady is my date for the evening." Nihaal looked at Kunaal and flashed a disarming smile. Kunaal smiled at him, "No worries, Nihaal," and briskly walked away. Astonished, Reeva looked at Nihaal and asked, "What was that? You don't dance. But nice save anyway," she winked.

Nihaal suddenly turned serious. "This is not a game Reeva. But if he's going to play, then he has to play fair."

Reeva knew that he was trying to tell her something, but she wasn't sure. Yet, deep down at some primal level, she felt that from here on, the three of them were unwittingly a part of a dangerous dance, to the music of life.

The early afternoon sun was harsh on Manek Vir's back as he worked on his rose bushes, pruning them deftly and readying them for the next blooming season. He paused and looked up at the sun, squinting at it, as the sweat trickled into his eyes. His hands were muddy because he preferred working without gloves. He inhaled the earthy smell as he loosened the soil around the roots. These simple acts always made him feel connected to nature and relaxed him.

He had driven down to his farmhouse late last night on an impulse and didn't regret it one bit. He needed this break. This was the first time that Vir felt wired up about a case. The inactivity was unnerving him. Ever since they had taken up the J&T case, he hadn't received any clear instructions from the Fixer about how they intended to proceed, which was unprecedented. His instructions were always decisive, firm and quick. But this time, every scheduled call that Vir made to him was terminated by the Fixer, with an instruction to wait until the next.

Pressure was mounting on Vir; Thapar was becoming

increasingly impatient and a possible liability. After the first fifty per cent of their fee had already been deposited in the account, it was becoming a nerve-wrecking experience to hold off Thapar.

Though he implicitly trusted the Fixer's sense of precise timing and flawless execution, the unusual long gap of inaction was beginning to trigger an alarm in Vir's head. He was a man of instinct and now his instincts were telling him to return the money and close the case. But in his world, things didn't work that way. The arrow was already out of the bow and any return journey was out of question. Besides, it was not his decision to make. His extensive military training had ingrained him with an almost unshakable respect for the chain of command. As long as every soldier executed his part without any errors or deviation, they would come out victorious.

Vir took a swig of iced lemonade from the big glass tumbler and relished the cool liquid inside him. Suddenly, his Blackberry vibrated. He held the phone with the tips of his muddy fingers and squinted at the screen. The screen flashed an unknown number with which Vir had become too familiar over the years. It was an unscheduled call from the Fixer and another first in his experience with him. The voice on the other end spoke without any greetings.

"We need to activate the case now."

"Yes." Vir had programmed himself over the years to speak less and listen more. This habit had always paid him good dividends, especially in his dealings with the Fixer. "Get in touch with Inspector Nagpal from Navi Mumbai police station." His voice was neutral. *Why the police?* wondered Vir.

The Fixer spoke for a few more seconds. In measured

words, he explained the role of the policeman in their plan. As the bigger picture emerged before Vir's eyes, he smiled. For an opening shot, this was a master stroke. Although, the ingenious plan depended upon how the human psychology played out, yet Vir knew he could rely on the inherent flaws in human behaviour.

"Remember to emphasize to the inspector that his timing and correct positioning will be crucial. We will have limited strike possibilities. Remind the clients about the media support we'll need." The line went dead and Vir felt relieved now that he had a task at hand, still disliking the presence of external elements in the plan.

Instead of going back to the rose bushes, Vir decided in favour of a nap. He needed all his strength to execute the first strike. He walked into the cool, living room, settled comfortably on the couch and drifted off to sleep.

With the MVPR launch party being a bigger success than what was imagined, the atmosphere at the office was jubilant. However, once the dust settled, the heads were back to the grind with the pressures of campaign planning.

Reeva had worked non-stop for the last two months and the launch party was the denouement. But it was only the beginning. There was a long list of events to be coordinated and organized, interviews to be fixed and appearances to be planned every week. And much of it involved government systems, which was the real challenge. Shalini had been very upfront about the huge work-culture gap that existed between the corporate and political worlds. As a rule, they were to add a considerable delay period to every commitment they received pertaining to availability of any person, information or feedback from JBP.

"So, are we ready to roll from next week?" Reeva's tone held an element of finality. The unison of eagerly affirmative nods around the conference table satisfied her.

"Okay, so I think we should kick off with the lowest rung and work our way upwards closer to the elections," said Kunaal. "We'll start with Govindrao making appearances at charity events and social cause activities. We'll later shift focus on to Saran and during the last and final lap, we'll bring in Uttur. Okay?" Kunaal's question was thrown up in the air, but Reeva knew it was for her.

"Yeah. I think this works. This way we start soft and build up the hype closer to elections. I guess there's an inauguration scheduled for next week. What's the event Revathy?" Reeva turned to her assistant.

"It's the inauguration of an orphanage in Navi Mumbai. It was promoted by the local JBP MLA and partly funded by Sharan's share of party fund."

"In that case, it makes sense for Govindrao to inaugurate it. I guess JBP too would suggest that. But who will be accompanying him from MVPR?" Although Govindrao had been respectful and well behaved with her, the guy still gave Reeva the creeps. She didn't want to accompany him. He had a temperament akin to that of an aggressive pit bull. "Maybe I should ask Shalini," stated Reeva as an afterthought. She was more hands-on compared to her, with better knack for on-ground management.

"I can go," said Kunaal, his tone suggestive. Reeva was surprised because she had the distinct feeling that Kunaal did not like Govindrao either. Suddenly, it dawned on her; he was going for the same reason why she wasn't. He didn't trust him. Like her, he too suspected that Govindrao was too volatile to be left alone to interact with the media. He needed a tight leash and Kunaal was best suited for the job. She nodded.

"Okay then guys... see you all again for the next weekly meeting. Let's get going." Kunaal clapped his hands as if to break them out of their reverie. As the team quickly dispersed, Reeva and Kunaal were left alone in the conference room. Suddenly, the atmosphere became awkward. As she noticed Kunaal, she picked up a glass of water and sipped, even though she wasn't thirsty. Deciding retreat as the only wise option, she gathered her papers from the table.

"Reeva... we need to talk." His voice was calm, yet the underlying urgency was unmistakable.

"Yeah?" Reeva continued collecting her belongings.

"Not here. Can we meet for dinner somewhere?"

"Kunaal, you know that's not possible." Reeva knew the situation could easily escalate out of control and she instinctively glanced at the door. "Why, Reeva? Can't we give us a chance?" A faint whiff of desperation crept into his voice.

"Chances are given only if one's willing to take them. And you Kunaal... only know to manipulate. You don't take chances."

"I understand that I've given you enough reasons to not like me, but I can explain."

"You don't owe me any explanations... believe me you don't."

"Yes Reeva, I do... listen I didn't mean to..." Before

Kunaal could finish, he was cut off sharply by Reeva.

"That's the problem Kunaal, you never mean anything." With that, she walked out of the conference room, leaving him alone.

He sat there numb for a few minutes mindlessly and unseeingly scrolling through his phone screen, waiting for the sudden wave of turmoil inside him to subside. Then he slowly gathered his stuff and walked out. The more he felt convinced that he was at a dead end with Reeva, the more helpless he felt. And that was an alien emotion for him.

Reeva had not slept well the previous night and felt a headache building at her temples. Her encounters with Kunaal always left her in an emotional turmoil. Yesterday's meeting in the conference room was no exception.

She dialled the pantry for a cup of tea but heard only a steady ring. She disconnected; frustration bubbled inside her. She stepped out of her office but could not find Revathy or anybody else to send to the pantry.

She walked to the pantry, which was located at the far end of the hall, beyond the cluster of the work stations.

She pushed open the pantry door. The temperature inside the small room was a few degrees higher than the rest of the air-conditioned office. A mixed aroma of tea, coffee and boiled milk filled the air. Harry sat on his plastic bucket chair, staring blankly at the wall. Up close, she noticed that the creases on his face appeared deeper and his hair had more than a tinge of grey in them.

"Harry?" Although she had wanted to instruct him quickly

and leave, maybe even reprimand him for not answering the phone, something about the way he sat, changed her mind.

"Huh... madam?" He was clearly surprised to see her, confirming that he hadn't heard the phone ring. Very few people in the office knew that he had left his family behind in a small village in Uttar Pradesh after a particularly bad year of failed crop and huge debts or even that his full name was Hari Prasad. Her knowing this little fact about Harry was the basis of their human bond and why she felt responsible towards him.

"What happened, Harry? Are you okay?" she asked, her headache worsening by the minute.

"It's nothing madam, I'm okay. You could've called me," he pointed towards the phone.

"Never mind... is something wrong?" She asked tenderly and he turned his face away from her as a single heart-wrenching sob escaped him.

Reeva was aghast. "Harry... what happened?" Her words were forceful, but her tone was soft. Harry looked at her and quickly wiped his eyes with a handkerchief. He sniffed and stuffed the handkerchief back into his pocket.

"Madam... my home..." Harry's voice quivered.

"What happened to your home, Harry?"

"They're going to demolish it. They say that the building is too weak for us to live in. I have lived there forever now. I cannot go back to my village in UP. I have debts to pay. I'll be on the roads. My life is there and I have nowhere to go. How will I keep my job?"

Reeva placed a hand on Harry's shoulder and said slowly, "Slow down. No one can just break down your home Harry. Who said this to you? Did they do any tests to check the building for stability?"

"Nothing, madam. Just a sahab from the municipality office had come to our building. He said it was weak and needs to be broken down and we have to leave. We can't live there."

"Don't worry. They can't break down your building just like that. Have any of the residents complained against this decision?"

"We don't know who to go to, but Nandita didi is talking to officers from our side."

"Nandita didi?" Reeva never trusted social workers who offered to help the less fortunate. She felt that these people were the worst kind of ambulance-chasers, always wanting to get something out of the situation.

"Madam, she's the local social worker and Janmanch NGO's activist. She's a very kind lady."

"Harry, can I meet her?" Reeva knew she owed him this much.

"Yes madam, sure, sure. Please come. She will be happy to see you. She lives nearby in Sunder Nagar only," Harry's face lit up with gratitude.

"Okay Harry. How about coming Sunday?"

"Yes, yes. I'll tell her you're coming. You'll really come, madam?"

"Yes, I will Harry," assured Reeva, "Now cheer up. And please, can I have some tea now?"

"Yes madam, right away." Harry busied himself immediately. Reeva was amazed by his naïve ability to trust and hope so quickly.

Realizing that she urgently needed to fish out that absconding strip of Aspirin from her bag, she walked back to her cabin. As she passed Nihaal's cabin, she saw him deeply engrossed in some design artworks he held on his lap. She was tempted to stop by, but continued to walk, her head throbbing. But as soon as she passed his cabin, Nihaal called after her.

"Hey Reeva... just a minute." He was standing at his door, blocking it from closing. Thankfully, his stance told her clearly that he wasn't expecting her to come in or have any elaborate discussion.

"Yeah?"

"Looks as if our Harry is into some kind of a spot, regarding his house. I don't know if I can help him, but I sure can look into it. Maybe put my construction experience to some good use. I'm planning to visit him this weekend. Are you game?"

"Really? I just told him that I'll be visiting him coming Saturday. Did he give you any details?" she was surprised and relieved at the prospect of company.

"Nothing actually. Apart from a Godzilla visiting him and threatening to break down his house. We need to look into this. Saturday it is then. I'll call you." He ducked back into his cabin. Again, Reeva was left wondering whether Nihaal was more emotional or practical. Maybe he was a rare case of a practical *and* emotional being; she smiled to herself.

Inspector Nagpal reported half an hour late for his 8am shift on Friday morning, at Navi Mumbai police station. But this was only one of the minor benefits of being the Inspector of Police. Anyway, it would have been impossible to pass up the delicious paranthas with homemade butter his wife had prepared for him. He stifled an imminent burp and settled at his desk. Inspector Nagpal eyed his kingdom once again and barked his first order of the day.

"Shinde, get me the complaint register. Now." A typical start to a typical day, but with a little difference. Along with the delicious breakfast, his beautiful but bossy wife of twenty years had also served him an ultimatum – to organize the dowry amount to wed off their only daughter to an IPS cadre boy, within the next six months. He was badly in need of a long weekend and this one would have been ideal, if not for that phone call he had received two days ago.

The caller's instructions had been precise and Nagpal had cross-referenced his credibility through a reliable source. But it was the voice that had caught his attention. It sounded like the man was used to authority. Plus, the money was good for a seemingly easy task. But he had to give up his weekend holiday plan.

Instead, he had dedicated this Friday to be present at the orphanage, to be inaugurated by Govindrao, as his special duty. He smiled menacingly as he thought of him. This was going to be fun. In the past, he had loved beating and rounding up his men from impromptu rallies. Now, he wanted to bring him down hard, once and for all. The man was nothing but the rabid pet dog of the JBP. He drummed his fingers on the desk. Finally, he checked his watch once again and stood up. It was time to make Govind Rao pay for all the transfers and punishment postings he had meted out to him.

As the political cavalcade of cars entered the orphanage's campus, it raised a cloud of dust from the unpaved road. Clearly, the home was still to receive its finishing touches and piles of construction debris lay around in ugly patches. The designated playground for children still looked barren and harsh.

A flurry of activity ensued as the cars stopped before the main building. Kunaal could see a crowd beginning to converge upon them. A group of JBP political supporters brandished party flags, a large bunch of media representatives ready to aim their mics and cameras and finally, the apologetic looking staff of the orphanage accompanied by few kids aged five to twelve years, holding small welcome bouquets, eager to please the arriving party.

Getting out of the car, Kunaal didn't miss the inconspicuously positioned policemen afar, ready to swing into action at a moment's notice. As he stepped onto the road, he saw a layer of dust already settled on his Ferragamo shoes and was momentarily distracted. When he looked up, he saw an inspector smiling at him. "Welcome Mr. Kabi, I'm Inspector Nagpal, Navi Mumbai Police Station, on special duty here today," he extended his hand, which Kunaal received unsurely.

Govindrao's bulky frame, almost stumbled out of the car, his hands folded in a greeting mainly intended for a good photo op. He barely managed to hold on to his three cell phones. His eyes narrowed as he saw Kunaal and Nagpal shaking hands. Kunaal noticed a fleeting expression of distrust and hatred cross his face. He sensed a dark hostility between the two men, which could only come from many battles and unsettled scores.

The trio walked towards the main building as media representatives crowded them like a swarm of bees. JBP workers hailed a number of party slogans in the background.

Suddenly, the expression on Govind's face was menacing, almost predatory. He growled, "What the hell are you doing here Nagpal? I had asked Shinde to be here today."

"Shinde is on some other duty, and by the way, he reports to me." Inspector Nagpal was unaffected by the derogatory tone.

"How come today you've found time from licking the prized NPP ass? Or have they kicked yours?" Govind laughed boisterously.

"You tell me Govindraoji... is licking an ass better or being one better? At least, I don't have to bend over for anyone," Nagpal smiled mockingly. Govind's reaction was instant and sharp. He would have been at Nagpal's throat had Kunaal not body-blocked him.

"What are you doing, Rao? Please think of the party. You cannot get into a fight with a law keeper before the media. Control yourself," Kunaal hissed. Nagpal smirked visibly for Govindrao's benefit, who was panting with anger, his nostrils flared.

"By the way, Mr. Kabi, who is our chief guest for today?" asked Inspector Nagpal innocently. Both Kunaal and Govind turned towards him, confused.

"What do you mean?" Kunaal was the first to recover.

"I mean I didn't receive the official order detailing today's event and the chief guest's name."

"Of course, of course. Mr. Govindrao is the chief guest for today's inauguration," said Kunaal, as if to clarify a minor misunderstanding, still trying to mentally process the lapse that had caused Nagpal to ask such a question. Rao's jaw dropped.

"But, I'm sorry sir; I cannot let the function begin or Govindraoji to preside over it, unless I get the clearance from above. This building is public property."

"Watch out Nagpal. You're crossing your limits." Rao's voice had that high-pitched trait of a broken saxophone. Few party workers had already moved in, sensing some kind of tension. Kunaal could see a few media reps getting ready as if waiting for an impending drama scene.

"On the contrary, I know my limits as a police officer; it's only the dogs that need to be taught theirs."

"Nagpal, I warn you... stop it," he roared. Kunaal panicked, knowing that his worst fears were coming true. By now, almost a dozen party workers were standing behind Rao. The media reps had already prepared their cameras. This was a reporter's jackpot – a face-off between a politico and a police inspector.

"No, Mr. Rao, I warn you to stop now and go back. Or else I can, and will have you arrested for disturbing a public event and insulting a police officer."

Kunaal wasn't sure if it was the statement that did it or whether Govindrao, as usual, was high on the power of his supporters, for he lunged at Nagpal and before Kunaal could intervene, slapped Nagpal hard across his face while shouting, "You worthless bastard, you will get me arrested? How dare you? Don't you know who I am?" Govind was frothing at the mouth.

For a few seconds, Inspector Nagpal was dazed along with everybody, as Rao shook him by his collar. Kunaal was in shock too as he separated the two men. A slight trickle of blood appeared on Nagpal's upper lip where Rao's hand had connected squarely. Kunaal quickly offered his handkerchief to the police officer hoping to reason with him. Nagpal accepted it, which instantly turned bloodied as he dabbed his lips. Then, still staggering from the assault, he looked hard at the handkerchief, gestured towards his team policemen and spat, "Arrest him."

The two words initiated a full-blown fight between the party workers and the policemen. There was no way Rao's followers were going to let the police arrest him. The simple event had turned into a warzone with police resorting to lathi charge to curb the mob. The orphanage's staff, along with the kids, had quickly retreated into the safety of the building. Kunaal stood aside and watched hopelessly. The media reps were recording the fight on-camera and some were making frantic calls to their offices asking for an OB van. He was contemplating the PR damage this was going to cause, when his eyes spotted the senior media executive Arunabh Roy, an established name in the media industry. He smiled, gave a thumps-up to Kunaal and walked away, leaving him to wonder what a senior executive was doing here in the first place; this was a low-profile event.

Exasperated, Kunaal pulled out his phone and started making the requisite damage-control calls, while constantly thinking about how he was going to explain this to Rishi Uttur. This fiasco was going to be covered on all news channels within the next hour. And it was going to cause some irreparable damage to JBP's image.

CHAPTER 8

Reeva stared at the TV in horror as the clip of Govindrao slapping Inspector Nagpal played on loop, in slow motion, on Arunabh Roy's channel. Already, speculations were being made by political analysts about JBP's credibility as a balanced party and the probable cause of such high-handed behaviour from one of its prominent workers. Senior police officers were making a statement about their inability to serve the public due to interferences from politicians. Slant remarks were being made about JBP's cocky attitude post favourable exit polls. All in all, it was an earth-shattering PR disaster for the party.

She was joined in the conference room by Mr. Sehgal, Shalini, Nihaal and finally Kunaal, who had walked in looking tensed and edgy. He hated losing control and by now, Reeva knew this well. The mood was grim and Shalini was the first to break the silence.

"We should get a statement issued by a senior JBP leader at the earliest. Silence can be dangerous in the given circumstances."

"How does one defend such an act of blatant hooliganism and disregard for the system? I mean you don't go around slapping a uniformed police officer. And definitely not when you're a politician, for God's sake," said Ajay Sehgal.

"But taking a silent position is not an option now when the elections are near and JBP is a front runner," said Reeva.

"You are right. We need to issue a statement and it has to come from Govindrao," said Kunaal.

"And how do you think that's going to happen?" asked Ajay Sehgal.

"Tactically – that's the best approach. The issue needs to be squashed at this level itself. If senior JBP leaders come in now, it will attract further undue attention." For once, Shalini agreed with Kunaal.

"It will have to be done. Govindrao has to come around. This was... and will be projected as a personal issue between him and Nagpal." Kunaal was firm. Silence descended as everybody knew that what was done could be undone by Rao alone. Kunaal's phone rang and seeing the caller's name, he quickly excused himself.

Uttur's voice was uncharacteristically tight on the phone, "Kunaal, how the hell did things get so much out of control?"

Kunaal said quickly, "Don't worry sir, we'll fix it. We're already working towards minimizing media exposure."

For once Uttur was impatient and cut Kunaal off midway. "I've already instructed Govindrao to issue an unconditional apology. Please ensure it gets maximum coverage." Kunaal sighed inwardly to hear this, "Thank you sir, this will help greatly..."

Uttur continued, "No, it won't Kunaal. I've already received a threat of abandonment from our state level coalition party. Now, we may not need them for numbers, but they're important for our goodwill in Vidhaan Sabha."

"I understand sir."

"Kunaal, we cannot afford anymore of such drawbacks. It's a tightrope walk from here to the elections. I want you to keep your eyes and ears open." Uttur disconnected the call with a perfunctory greeting. After all, he had handed over this large and prestigious campaign to him without any questions just because he didn't expect Kunaal to make any mistakes.

And although Kunaal wasn't used to his competency being judged or questioned, this was different. He was beginning to distinctly feel that this campaign was not going to be as easy to execute as he had anticipated.

It was a beautiful Saturday morning. The receding monsoons had left everything looking fresh and clean. Recent tight work schedules made Reeva truly appreciate such days. She had to visit Harry's home today. She stood waiting for Nihaal on the curb of the main road with little or no traffic, and deeply inhaled the fresh air.

Suddenly, the silence was filled with the deep backfire of a heavy-duty motorbike, possibly a Harley Davidson. Fascinated, Reeva watched the helmet-clad biker. She sensed the biker slowing down, his movement almost predatory.

As he neared her, she tensed; her brain was already processing various possible retaliations with a thumb poised over the call button of her phone. The biker halted before her and pulled off his helmet to reveal a familiar face.

"Nihaal?" Reeva sighed in relief and a smile broke onto her face. "Wow! Is this yours? Impressive! I never knew you rode a bike!" She walked around the bike.

"Why, you think I'm too boring for something like this? He smiled, "I almost missed you because I have never seen you in a skirt before." Reeva was wearing a long, ankle-length, printed skirt with a fitted singlet, accessorized with a chunky necklace and a pretty, paisley scarf. Now, seeing the bike, she wished she had worn jeans.

"By the way, have you ever been on a bike before?" asked Nihaal.

"Yeah, a few times, but not for long distance."

"No worries, I'm not taking you to the Bahamas on this. Hop on and let's go pay Harry a visit." Reeva adjusted herself onto the back seat clutching onto Nihaal's shoulder as the bike surged ahead powerfully.

"Hold on tight," shouted Nihaal, lifting the visor of his helmet halfway as he sped off. Reeva's pretty scarf kept flowing into the air, but she couldn't care less. This day promised to only get better.

As expected, Reeva and Nihaal's journey was akin to a hurdle race once they entered the dense locality of Sunder Nagar.

Harry's building cluster, Navdeep Complex, lay smack in the middle of the glamorous city of Mumbai, surrounded by high-rise, seven-star buildings. As a remnant of the booming era of textile mills that employed thousands of people there, the area was now ridden with shoddy and dilapidated double-storeyed housing clusters. The roads were narrow and lined with equally squalid kiosks selling everything, from potatoes to cheap candy, and from household supplies to stationery.

Nihaal stopped at a tea stall to ask for directions. Harry's building was just round the corner, but the road was blocked and the bike could not go any further.

"Okay, here we are. I guess, from here on, we're foot soldiers." Nihaal removed his helmet and locked his bike.

"Come on princess," he led the way. Reeva's senses were assaulted on all fronts, especially her nose as she picked up mixed aromas of fish cooking in bad oil, burning waste and urine mixed with that typical stale, salty smell of the sea in low tide, unique to an overcrowded, coastal city. Navdeep Complex was a U-shaped building cluster with a small open space in the centre and was consistent with the general unkempt and dishevelled look of Sunder Nagar. But it did not lack in life or activity.

The complex housed close to a one-hundred-and-twenty families, which Reeva registered on her first cursory look. Every floor had a common gallery and toilets shared by the inhabitants of the floor. Privacy was clearly not much of an issue for the inhabitants as they sat around in bunches, on benches placed in the open space in the central courtyard. Some were even enjoying their afternoon siestas in hallways and galleries.

Women gossiped in small groups, while they attended to their household chores like cleaning grains or cutting vegetables. Men read newspapers, played cards or cleaned their autorickshaws. As Nihaal was about to enquire about Harry's room, they heard a familiar cheerful voice call out to them.

"Madam… sir!" Harry was ecstatic as he ran towards them. He was still buttoning his shirt. This was the first time Reeva had seen Harry outside his office uniform. He looked older, more vulnerable. He eagerly offered to serve them tea, but they politely denied with a promise to revisit soon. Reeva was keen to get to the bottom of the issue as soon as possible.

Harry enthusiastically led them through a maze of alleyways to meet Nandita Sahay, the social activist. Her modest, stand-alone, one-room, brick-and-mortar structure was old but neat, like it belonged to a progressive village and not the ugly underbelly of a big metropolitan city. The kitchen had neat rows of hanging pots and pans. The terracotta lamps hanging on the front added to its quaint charm.

As they entered, Nandita looked up from the book she was reading, eyes dazed for a second before she snapped back into reality and then her face broke into the purest of smiles. Nandita belied stereotypical activists. She looked only a few years older to Reeva and was dressed in loose, black pants and a khaki shirt with folded sleeves, and a thin, dark blue stole hung carelessly around her shoulders. Her thick dark hair was tied into a knot. And her open friendly manner was instantly endearing.

"Harry bhai, you're finally here and that too with a bunch of advocates?" She teased Harry while smiling warmly at Reeva and Nihaal. She gestured towards the cot, but Nihaal chose to perch himself on the bare kitchen counter, allowing both women to settle onto the couch, as Harry settled comfortably on the floor.

"Nandita didi, please don't say that. Just like you, Reeva madam and Nihaal sir want to help me."

"Hello Nandita, I heard about the municipality officer's visit to Navdeep Complex. Are they really threatening to pull down the building?" asked Reeva pointedly.

"They don't care to threaten; they just send notices, once they have completed the required paperwork, Reeva," she smiled ruefully. "For them, these people are like insects, to be fumigated. But first, let me offer you some lemonade." The sincerity in her voice prevented anyone from protesting. As she pulled out a jug from the battered, barely functioning fridge, her sleeve pulled up revealing a deep, long scar on her forearm. Reeva noticed it, but thought it would be too personal to ask. Their eyes met and Nandita saw the awkwardness on her face.

"Don't worry about this," she said, pointing towards the scar. "When you're in a war, battle scars are inevitable."

"What battle? What scars?" Contrary to his withdrawn manner, Nihaal was clearly cued in.

"Oh nothing. I participated in a protest against the allotment of a petrol pump to a businessman." She paused; sighed and continued in response to the quizzical looks. "It was to be rightfully allotted to a war widow. The businessman bribed his way through, trying to get it for himself. I applied for RTI and was threatened by his men to withdraw my application. When I refused, they attacked me. The good thing is that his petrol pump dream vanished, but the scar remained," she said nonchalantly.

They admirably stared at Nandita.

"Anyway, coming back to the Navdeep Complex case, Harry's home for twenty years, I think we're up against corruption at levels beyond comprehension," she said.

"Yes, of course! Bulldozing an entire building would

open up a prime piece of land for development, to someone's profit. The question is whose?" Reeva realized that any construction company could benefit hugely of it.

"It's all a bit complicated until they're able to throw the long-term residents out of their homes. After that, it's a cakewalk for them. It's only a matter of tweaking a few policies," Nandita said thoughtfully while sipping her lemonade.

"It surely can't be that easy for the municipality," said Nihaal.

"Oh, it's damn simple. Do you know that the municipality still uses visual inspection methods to categorize the state of the building? There are proposals to introduce more scientific methods in future. But, until then, all it needs is an officer willing to sign a statement based on visual inspection that Navdeep Complex falls under category C1, meaning it's dilapidated and in need of urgent demolition. And poof! Navdeep Complex is gone," she snapped her fingers. Her voice was calm, but her face looked worried.

"So, what can be done?" Reeva felt the heaviness in the small, crowded room.

Nihaal spoke decisively, "We need to question the right people. I'll get opinions from a few expert structural engineers so I know about the actual status of Navdeep Complex. Maybe someone can sniff around at the municipal office about this." He looked at Nandita meaningfully and she nodded.

"Reeva, could you use your political connections to probe deeper? We need a failsafe option available, if anything goes wrong." Nihaal was analytical and objective, ready with an action plan.

As they talked for a while, Reeva started developing a certain respect for Nandita and her unconscious selflessness. Nandita had a true desire to work for good causes without feeling like a martyr or wallowing in self-pity. There was no larger-than-life, self-righteous drama about her. She was just an ordinary person who sincerely wanted to make the world a better place. And this was a rare quality.

By afternoon, as Nihaal and Reeva left Navdeep Complex, the sun was already harsh. Suddenly, Nihaal slowed and brought the bike to halt at the curb.

"What happened?" Reeva screamed to be heard over the din of the Harley's idling engine. Nihaal removed his helmet and winced exaggeratedly at her voice. She giggled.

"I know a nice place to eat nearby. Want to grab some lunch? I don't know about you, but I'm famished," he said.

"Great, let's go." She didn't mind spending more time with him.

Nihaal drove into a pretty, gravel pitted compound surrounded by thick, shady trees with artificially created waterfalls and ponds. It looked like an oasis in the middle of a commercial desert. The restaurant was set at the far end of the compound with the glorious Arabian Sea in high-tide as the backdrop. They ordered an enormous lunch. Reeva questioned their decision to order a heavy and spicy meal on a hot afternoon, but then the sun suddenly weakened and gusts of cool wind picked up.

"Looks like we still have some residual monsoon clouds hanging around." Nihaal glanced at the now choppy sea.

"I'm not complaining," she smiled.

"Oh yes... you will be. When we're hit by sudden rains and you think of our ride." Nihaal had a teasing smile on.

Reeva remembered they had a bike and not a four-wheeler. But she was enjoying too much to let Nihaal play the wet blanket. "We shall take it as it comes," she announced.

"Oh, I'm impressed by this new spirit of adventure." He winked. After they finished their meal and ordered some tea, the conversation turned to office and work.

"So, do you think we can help Harry and Navdeep Complex?" she asked, enjoying the breeze on her face.

"It depends on how deep or how high this case runs. But I think a political push will definitely help. I think Kunaal can help. JBP will know to pull the right strings." His voice was level. But Kunaal's name created a brief awkward moment. Reeva nodded.

Then, as if on cue, rainfall descended rapidly on the fibre rooftop. Soon, a chaotic roar surrounded them. Their bill was already on the table and Nihaal grabbed it before Reeva could even move.

"It's my treat."

"You're old fashioned," Reeva teased him.

"Nope, I'm not. You can pay next time we are out on work."

"Old. Fashioned." She emphasized each word and stood up, amused. The rain fell steadily and they were forced to hang around until it slowed to a drizzle.

"Okay, let's hit the road while the rain gods still allow us. Looks like it was a bad day to bring out the bike." Reeva laughed at Nihaal's rueful voice and tied her scarf around her head. They trotted towards the bike and took off. But within a few minutes, the rain picked up and Nihaal had to stop under a bridge. Although just late afternoon, the overcast sky gave a feeling of dusk..

"Listen, can we go to my place to wait for the weather to change before I drop you home? It is closer and we can reach there in ten minutes tops," he said.

"Okay. But I'll take a cab back home," she looked up, sounding resolute.

"Deal." Nihaal was in a hurry to get out of this situation. They rode quickly, hunched against the falling rain. Reeva felt the chill in the wind as the bike sped and found the warmth emanating from Nihaal's body oddly comforting. As promised, they were at Nihaal's apartment building in ten minutes. He stopped the bike at the front.

"Top floor, 701. The key is under the copper pot by the door. Go on up; I'll park and be there soon," said Nihaal, half-lifting his visor and drove off. Reeva considered waiting for him but not wanting to come across as unsure, took the elevator to the seventh floor alone. What Reeva hadn't anticipated was that she would find company in Nihaal's apartment, waiting for her.

The door to his apartment was ajar. She lightly pushed the door further open. Right across the fairly large and elegantly decorated hall was a floor-to-ceiling bookshelf and facing it with her back towards the door stood a very elegant woman of medium height. Her elegance exuded not merely out of the cream and gold tissue silk saree, but also from her posture and luxurious thick shiny hair. Then suddenly, as if sensing Reeva's arrival, she turned and looked straight at her standing at the door.

Reeva was instantly besotted by the open and warm

beauty on the face that stared back at her. Strangely, Reeva felt scrutinized and appreciated at the same time.

"Oh, hello! Come on in. You must be Nihaal's friend. I'm his mother." She smiled, "My son isn't very social but you are too pretty to be a thief or a murderer." Her voice could easily belong to a news channel presenter – tinkling, clear and perfectly pitched. She too exhibited Nihaal's trademark sense of humour.

"Hello ma'am... I'm Reeva." She managed to croak, feeling awkward and out of place. She was dripping wet and standing in the middle of a bachelor pad, facing a mother.

"Please call me Mrs. Kapoor or just Nilanjana. Sit down and let me fetch you some towels. I assume my son isn't far behind, parking that black monster?" The question was rhetoric, but her voice and smile were kind. Then she turned and vanished into a room. As Reeva struggled to shake off the excess water from her hair, Nihaal entered through the open door taking off his wet jacket. Then he stopped in his tracks, his jaw dropping as he saw his mother entering the hall, holding the towels in her hand.

"Mom?" His voice filled with surprise and pleasure. "Why didn't you tell me you were coming? I would have picked you up from the airport."

"Hello dear, actually it was supposed to be a day trip, just in and out," she said casually, hugging him. "I thought it was pointless dragging you out on your precious weekend. Now, due to bad weather my flight is cancelled and rescheduled for early morning tomorrow." There was unadulterated adoration in her eyes. "Besides, had I told you I wouldn't have gotten the opportunity to meet the pretty Reeva."

"Oh no, no Mom... Reeva is just a colleague," Nihaal blushed.

Mrs. Kapoor paused and then smiled, "Oh yeah, sure. Let me get something hot to drink for the both of you." She walked into the kitchen.

Nihaal slumped into the sofa and Reeva sat on the edge of a wooden settee, careful not to get it wet. As she dried herself with the towel, she was sharply aware that he was watching her and that his eyes were enchanted.

Mrs. Kapoor returned with a tray of hot chocolate and almond biscotti. They talked about Reeva's family, her work and general anecdotes from the cities of Mumbai and Delhi. She felt welcome, appreciated and revered. In that easy, companionable atmosphere, time flew quickly and soon, dusk approached.

"I think I should be leaving now. It's late," said Reeva, realizing it was getting dark and still raining.

"Oh dear! Why don't you stay for dinner? Nihaal will drop you then."

"Actually ma'am... er... Mrs. Kapoor, I was supposed to be home by lunch time," said Reeva.

"I understand, my dear. In that case, you should really get going."

"Okay, let me get you an Uber," said Nihaal. As he left the hall looking for his cell phone, Reeva was left alone with Mrs. Kapoor.

"Reeva, my dear," said Mrs. Kapoor, looking intently at Reeva. "I don't know if he has told you, but my son likes you a lot. I know this because I know him," she smiled kindly. "You're the first girl he has introduced me to – although unknowingly. But I sincerely hope there's more to it than what both of you know or acknowledge." She touched Reeva's shoulder lightly. "God bless you," she smiled and sat back. Reeva didn't know how to respond to this revelation, apart from fidgeting nervously and murmuring thanks. She didn't know whether it was proper to thank her or whether she should have corrected Mrs. Kapoor's erroneous perception.

Nihaal returned, and Reeva quickly picked up her now dry scarf and purse, bidding farewell to Mrs. Kapoor.

In the lobby, Nihaal said, "I'm sorry about Mom, she tends to get a bit carried away." He scratched the back of his head, "Not that I regret it," he added smiling boyishly, his head cocked to a side.

"Then don't," she said meaningfully, "Your mom is a lovely woman. Besides I had a great day today." She stood on her toes and pecked his cheek murmuring, "Thank you" and got into the cab. She glanced back as she exited the gate. Nihaal was still standing where she had left him, wet wind lashing at his light rain jacket.

She settled back into the seat, and thought about what Nihaal's mother had said and the unmistakable pull she felt toward him. Soon, she needed to look within and face some important questions that had been nagging her for a while. Was it possible to be attracted towards two men at the same time? And, what was the emotion that set apart the possibilities of loving someone and being *in love* with someone?

A well-dressed butler expertly poured the vintage Dom Perignon in the three exclusive champagne flutes. Thapar nodded approvingly and dismissed him. Jaiswal wiped his spectacles and put them on to signal the commencement of their clandestine meeting. Manek Vir, who preferred obscure locations for such meetings, was clearly uncomfortable about the two making a big deal out of the Govindrao incident by holding a meeting in a five-star presidential suite. He seriously hoped they were not trying to impress him because nothing but a cool and disciplined mind earned his respect.

"Cheers... to the first JBP stumble." Thapar drank the champagne with a look of glee and Jaiswal followed suit. Vir took a small sip out of politeness, hating its citrusy, fizzy taste. He was a scotch person, but he hadn't protested when they ordered champagne because he hadn't intended to drink anyway. As a rule, he never mixed alcohol with work and never drank during the day. He immediately decided to steer the topic towards work.

"I agree that the anti-JBP coverage in the media has created a dent in their image. But this is not enough. We're still very far from our objective which is to make JBP fall. We'll need to hit harder," Vir said quietly, placing his glass on the shiny, Italian marble table.

"Yes, yes we will. But I loved watching that media-savvy Uttur shy away from the cameras and only responding with 'no comments'," sneered Thapar.

"I'm impressed with Arunabh Roy's work. He made sure every bloody channel and newspaper had something to say about it. And I have also heard that JBP and Rudra Dal are breaking their alliance," guffawed Jaiswal, clapping his hands. The JBP-Rudra Dal alliance was a matter of technicality alone but the rumours had left JBP red-faced.

"Gentlemen, please remember that this was just one event. Govindrao has already issued a public apology and people have short memory. It will take a lot more than this for JBP to lose their reputation," said Vir, hoping to bring the practicality back into their discussion.

"Oh come on Manekji, you're such a spoilsport. We must enjoy every achievement, however small. I'm just disheartened that Kunaal has sided with JBP. He would've been an asset to us." Thapar was remorseful. "Anyway, what's next now?" Vir knew that Thapar wanted to reach the Fixer directly but till now Vir had effectively stonewalled him.

"I'm awaiting further instructions. Meanwhile, I need a full background on Arunabh Roy. Is he trustworthy? Obviously by now, he must have more or less guessed our game. We need to keep an eye on him."

"Oh don't you worry Manekji. He's been completely bought over, lock stock and barrel," laughed Thapar.

"I don't like taking chances Mr. Thapar. Never. Ever." Vir sounded irritated, "Next strike will be more intense. I believe you must be aware of all upcoming big ticket projects planned within the construction industry?"

"Yes, we mostly are. What information are you looking for?" Jaiswal leaned in with curiosity.

"I need a list of all on-going and upcoming construction projects. From that list, I want you to shortlist only those companies and projects that have direct or indirect investors from JBP." Vir folded his arms. Thapar and Jaiswal exchanged smiles.

"It will be done. Anything else?" Jaiswal asked in a conspiratorial tone. "By when do you need it?"

"I need it as soon as possible. Let me know when you have it." Vir got up, collected his possessions from the table and left, ignoring his barely touched champagne glass, now sweaty with tiny water beads. He knew that he could've gotten this information through his sources within twenty-four hours. But he wanted to keep these idiots busy and out of his way. Arunabh Roy, however, was an element who didn't fit in. Although, for the first time the Fixer had given the client freedom to use their own resources. Vir was never comfortable with loose ends and Arunabh Roy had unwittingly become one such loose-end. If he knew too much, he could easily turn into a liability.

The air in Vir's penthouse smelled musty from the receding sea in low tide. He switched on the lights and walked across the hall, noticing that the French windows onto his balcony were open. He walked out and breathed in the sea-scented air that was still a bit warm from the hot October day.

As dusk fell, he decided it was a bit too early for his customary glass of scotch on the rocks. Deciding in favour of a healthy snack, he grabbed a tray of freshly cut fruits from the fridge. He switched on the TV and settled down on his favourite couch. Most news channels were still covering the 'Slapping Gate Event' finding new angles to keep the story alive. Finally, he stopped on News Today with Arunabh Roy's face, talking animatedly on a panel discussion about JBP's political maturity. There wasn't an iota of doubt in Vir's mind that Roy was a politically savvy, highly intelligent and perceptive man. But he also seemed cocky and too sure of himself, confident in the belief that he could make or break people's careers. This made him a subject of concern, if not a threat. He made a mental note to bring this up with the Fixer.

As the thought still lingered in his mind, the phone rang at its designated time. The voice breathed into his ears, curt and confident as ever.

"We need to plan the next move before they recover."

"Yes, I know. Things are already underway. We'll have the information shortly." Vir referred to the upcoming construction project with JBP involvement matter.

"Okay. Also, work on the list of all corrupt officers working in the administrations of currently JBP-ruled states."

"Okay," responded Vir.

"Stand by for further instructions," said the Fixer, and Vir knew the call was about to be terminated.

"Need to discuss our client's asset Arunabh Roy," he spoke a bit too fast and was met with a pause from the other end. Just when Vir was beginning to kick himself for bringing up something that wasn't on the agenda, the Fixer responded.

"Don't worry. It will be taken care of at the right time." As usual, the response had no language frills. The line was disconnected and Vir let out the breath he was unconsciously holding in. He always felt uneasy with the deathly cold indifference in the Fixer's voice.

He moved to his well-stocked bar. The next day being a national holiday, he decided to have an extra drink. He turned on his favourite Blues 'N' Jazz album and took a quick cold shower before finally hitting the bed.

The alarm rang loudly and awoke Reeva abruptly. She shut it off and squinted around, still disoriented. Groaning, she plopped back into her pillow realizing it was a holiday. She burrowed deeper into the pillow but once awake, she could never go back to sleep. Finally, she got up and padded with the efficiency of a penguin towards the bathroom.

As Reeva emerged from her bedroom, the house was filled with the aroma of delicious breakfast. She stepped into the main hall and saw her dad sitting on the floor, tinkering with his old antique gramophone, which worked perfectly well, much to the chagrin of her mom. Reeva smiled at the scene. Numerous LP records strewn on the floor surrounded him. Her dad always cleaned his gramophone with a special micro-fibre cloth every week and travelled to the other end of the city just to get it serviced.

"Hey Dad," she mumbled. Still feeling lazy, she slumped onto the couch.

"Good morning princess, you're up early." He threw a distracted yet cheerful glance; then busied himself with delicately placing the needle onto the record. As it touched the record, an extremely nasal and plaintive male voice from a forgotten era filled the room.

"K.L. Sehgal," he announced proudly to her. Reeva always found the whole needle on black rotating disk fascinating to watch.

Her dad sat on the low settee next to the gramophone with his coffee and swayed his head to the music. Apps entered and plopped himself on the couch. He stuffed his ears with large wads of cotton as if protesting to the music and Reeva giggled. Apps was an engineering student and the constant company of twenty-pound books had lately made him moody and withdrawn.

"Hey Apps... very busy nowadays?" Reeva knew this question irritated him. But surprisingly, he answered almost politely, pulling out the cotton wad from one of his ears.

"Yup, next term starts soon. I've still got plenty to cover. How's your work? Did you get that top floor cabin with floor-to-ceiling glass?" Reeva was surprised that he asked.

"Yes, I did get the new office." Reeva raised her brows, "You should drop by sometime."

"Yeah sure, if you find time off from your dates," Apps winked. The doorbell rang simultaneously. "I'll get that," he quickly added. As expected, his friend Bala stood at the door. Finding a perfect excuse to bail, Apps quickly disappeared into his room with him.

Suddenly, her dad looked at her directly and said, "Come on. Go ahead."

"Huh?" Reeva was a bit startled, "What?"

"Yeah, go ahead. You want to talk about something," her dad smiled kindly.

Reeva looked at him, embarrassed, "Am I that obvious?" she chuckled, "Actually, it's about somebody I want to help in my office. The municipal corporation wants to bring the poor guy's building down, and he has nowhere to go."

"Hmmm... poor guy's building," he repeated, deep in thought, "You said it Reeva, it's the story of all the poor in this city. Has it been categorized as C1 already?"

"No... not officially. But residents have been informed verbally."

"But, what do *you* want to do about it?" he asked.

"Don't know Dad," Reeva sighed, "I met up with a social worker along with a colleague. It smells like a case of money-motivated action. Let's see if we can get to the bottom of it."

"Reeva, be careful. These things run very, very deep. You're way out of your depth here," he paused to see her disappointment and added in a resigned manner, "Okay, anyway, leave me a note on the complex's exact location and other details. Maybe I can fish out some information for you." He smiled as Reeva brightened.

Soon, Mrs. Rai breezed into the hall, mumbling about an upcoming kitty party. But before Reeva and her dad could make any sense of it, her phone rang. She stared at the screen of her phone with widened eyes and then answered it with a cautious 'Hello'. Both of them listened, alert as she answered in mere "yes, yes" and "of course, sure" at regular intervals, her surprise ultimately breaking into a happy smile.

"Oh no, no, you don't have to mention that please... we will be there Mrs. Kabi." Reeva's attention was now completely directed at her.

"Mom, what's happening?" Reeva's brow was knitted at the last sentence.

Mrs. Rai sat down next to her. "Can you believe it? That was Mrs. Kabi. She's hosting a champagne brunch at her house next month. It's in honour of some top-notch Harvard faculty member visiting Mumbai. She wants us to attend. She almost pleaded and said Kunaal would love to have Reeva there." She clapped her hands, but Reeva's cold, unhappy demeanour stopped her

"What happened, Reeva? Aren't you happy?"

"Mom, you should have asked me before saying yes," Reeva said rather sharply and walked towards the French window. She stared outside, clearly sulking. Her mom threw a helpless glance at her dad, but he too shrugged his shoulders in confusion.

"Come on Reeva, what's wrong with you?" She approached her.

"Mom, for once stop being a matchmaker and stop interfering in my life," Reeva spoke and then immediately regretted it. But before she could make amends, Mrs. Rai stomped out of the room, teary eyed.

"Hey princess, what was that about?" Her dad asked, gently but firmly demanding an explanation.

"I know Dad. I shouldn't have acted like that."

"What's bothering you?"

"Don't know. Dad, what does one do when your brain and heart are telling you two different things?'

"Hmm. It's a tough call. But remember, the use of the brain and the heart is always mutually exclusive. Don't try using them together," he smiled and Reeva nodded.

Deciding to give her mom some space before approaching her again, she thought of the only person she wanted to talk to right then.

Reeva stared at Kinsy's eager face on her computer screen. While Reeva was on her work desk, Kinsy sat cross-legged on her bed holding a pillow.

"Hey Reevs, how are you doing? Sorry for ditching our chat last time; this client is a real pain in the wrong place," rattled Kinsy.

"It's okay Kinsy, but you look pretty settled in for a hotel room," laughed Reeva.

"Forget about me. I'm waiting for some juicy news of your love triangle. How are the two men treating you? You know, I feel like one of those girls from Sex and the City discussing this with you." She grinned, and then added, "Or have you closed the gates to your heart for one of them? In that case, send the banished prince to me," she winked.

Reeva sighed, "Actually I don't know Kinsy. I'm attracted to both of them. They have their own set of qualities. I don't know if I love both of them or if it's just an infatuation."

"You do know you can't have them both, right?" Kinsy narrowed her eyes.

Reeva smiled wearily, "I know; it's just that they're both so different, yet so appealing. And if I choose one, then how do I know I won't miss the other? It's a mess." Reeva planted her hands on her temples.

"I must remind you of the devious ways of a certain Kunaal Kabi. Reevs, he's a manipulator. How are you so sure about him? In my verdict, Mr. Good Guy, aka, Nihaal is totally in love with you, and he seems much more sensitive than Kunaal. Why would you ever consider a scary, rollercoaster ride instead of a walk in the flowery park?" Kinsy had chosen her words carefully. She still needed to know her friend's mind.

"Kunaal's mother called Mom; she has invited us to a house party she's hosting next month. She said Kunaal absolutely wants me to attend."

"What? That's real low even by Kunaal's standards, using his mom to bait you."

"Come on, I also met Nihaal's mom a few days back. She's a lovely lady."

"What? Grrrreat! Now that's my girl. You know what? Forget the men; choose the right mom-in-law. How charmingly medieval is that?" Kinsy laughed.

"Listen Kinsy, I know there are parts of Kunaal's personality that I don't understand. But shouldn't I at least try to understand? Or do I just let it linger forever unresolved in my life?" The fog in her mind was clearing. Why was she keeping Kunaal at arm's length? He genuinely wanted to be with her and had made serious attempts to that effect. Was there something that she was subconsciously worried about finding out?

Kinsy took a deep breath, "Hmmm… you're right sweetie. Go ahead. But promise me you'll back off before you hurt yourself." Reeva nodded, looking into the intense eyes of her friend on the chat-screen.

"What about Nihaal?" Kinsy asked next and Reeva sighed. She knew that in discovering Kunaal she might end up losing Nihaal – even as a friend. But the fact that she was willing to take that chance told her that she was attracted to Kunaal in a very basic primal way.

CHAPTER 9

Nandita was thirsty, very thirsty. The crowded corridor of the city's municipal corporation office was insufferable. The air smelled of sweat and urine emanating from the nearby lavatory. Like any government office it was teeming with all kinds of people including the 'land sharks' and 'power-brokers'. A bored female janitor was making a show of sweeping the floor, only causing the old accumulated dust to rise up.

She had been sitting huddled along with a small group of Navdeep residents, on a wooden bench outside the Town Planning Officer's cabin for over an hour. Nandita hadn't wanted to leave even to grab a drink for fear of missing her appointment with the officer. He had agreed to meet with them only after a persistent follow up.

Finally, Nandita's face lit up to see the officer's secretary approaching, "You've been called. Make it quick; sahab has to leave immediately."

They entered his office as a group, their nerves in a knot

of anxiety. The office was well organized and extremely cold. It had been freshly sprayed with room freshener. The environment of the room was in complete contrast to what lay outside beyond its doors. After hesitating for a beat, Nandita stepped up and said, "Excuse me, sir."

The chief officer looked up through his glasses, surprised as if he wasn't expecting anyone in the room. "Yes?"

"Sir, we're here regarding Navdeep Complex of Sunder Nagar."

"Oh yes, yes, Miss Nandita Sahay, right? Please sit down. "But, why so many of you? I'm an administrative officer, not a politician to be impressed by a large gathering." His tone was brusque and dismissive. "Now, please get to the point."

Nandita was irked by his attitude, but decided to stick to the agenda. They couldn't afford any deviations at this stage.

"Sir, the occupants of Navdeep Complex have been informed that they will need to vacate the premises as it will be soon demolished. We need to know the reasons and also what will happen to the future of its occupants."

"Hmmm... let me see." The officer picked up a file from the top of a pile of documents and studied it for a full minute, turning few pages back and forth. "Here it says that the building is not safe for occupation and is a hazard for the lives of the residents," he said, his tone emotionless.

"But sir, the building is a strong, old structure. And these people have been living here for the last two... three generations. Is there any plan to relocate these people?"

"Listen madam, we have an experienced team of civil engineers and their full-time job is to analyze the life of a building. If they believe it is a hazard, then it's a hazard. As far as the relocating goes, it's not the department's concern."

"What do you mean it's not the department's concern? How can you say that?"

"I'm stating facts. As per the records, Navdeep Complex is an unauthorized structure built in 1973 on government land that has been earmarked since 1970 as a green zone and children's park. The rehabilitation and relocation schemes are applicable only for slum-dwellers not for unauthorized constructions. The official evacuation notice will be served to the occupants within forty five to sixty days." The words were delivered like a hard blow.

Nandita's face was ashen and the group around her shrunk in fear. "But what happens to these people?" The urgent panic in her voice softened the officer a bit, "Miss Nandita, I'm just an administrative officer here. I don't make policies. Please understand that you can't help these people."

"But they've lived for decades in Navdeep Complex..."

"Which is an unauthorized construction." The officer cut her off. He continued, "Are you aware that fifty four per cent of the people in this city live in slums and another twenty five to thirty per cent in chawls and on footpaths? Very soon, this city will become the slum capital of the world. Even if the government wants to help these people, where's the space?"

"And now the remaining ten to fifteen per cent, already living in plush, high-rise apartments need more space, am I right?" she asked bitterly.

The officer looked at her and nodded, "Yes, unfortunately." His tone was dejected and helpless. "I suggest you ask your people to start looking for an alternate accommodation." The officer sat back in his chair. Nandita collected her things, mumbled 'thank you' and gestured at her group to leave. As she was about to step out of the room, the officer called out.

"Uh… Miss Nandita, can I make a suggestion, strictly off the record?" He gazed at her thoughtfully. "Every government land has a purpose and status. Maybe you can put up an RTI on whether there's any proposal to review the status of the land Navdeep Complex is built on. If you're looking for a motive behind why this is happening…" he paused and then continued, "You'll come to know," he smiled nervously and resumed his work. Nandita smiled. She hadn't lost yet.

Reeva frantically searched for the black pumps that she had planned to wear to office. She checked her watch and cursed herself for oversleeping and finally wore a new pair of black platform sandals. They didn't compliment her formal grey skirt suit perfectly, but she decided to sacrifice fashion for the sake of punctuality.

She was already running late. Searching for her car keys, she remembered that the car was at the service centre. Hurriedly grabbing a muffin from the table, and her handbag, she rushed downstairs to get a taxi. As she sat in the cab, she didn't want to eat that muffin anymore. She was already craving a hot cup of tea and a warm mushroom quiche from her favourite patisserie near the office. But there were internal meetings scheduled for the morning. Finally, she gave in to an impulse in her, urging her to break the monotony and drudgery.

She dialled her assistant's number and instructed her to cancel her first meeting and asked the cab driver to stop at the patisserie.

At the French-themed café, she was cheerily welcomed by

the curly-haired attendant. "Good morning Reeva, will it be your regular today?" Reeva smiled and nodded.

As the attendant busied herself with Reeva's order, she started walking towards her favourite seat in the café. The next moment, she had stopped in her tracks as an inexplicable panic rose within her. Right across from her, at a corner table outside the café, sat Kunaal. He was reading something intently on his Mac, with a half-eaten croissant and an espresso cup by his side. She turned back to the attendant nervously, "Actually Steffi, make that to go." The attendant's expression was quizzical, but she started packing the quiche in a brown bag and poured her tea in a takeaway paper cup. Reeva quickly paid her and made to leave.

As she looked at Kunaal, she noted he hadn't once looked up from his laptop. A group of teenaged, giggling girls barged through the door of the patisserie and Reeva stepped aside to let them enter. Their careless, exuberant attitude made Reeva smile.

Suddenly, Kunaal threw a somewhat preoccupied gaze in her direction and then resumed reading. Reeva saw the breeze play with the hair on his forehead, just the way it had the first time she had seen him. In a formal black jacket with an open collared white shirt, sitting there alone, somewhat lost, he looked absolutely gorgeous. At that moment, something shifted in her and the decision was made. She decidedly walked up to his table, her heart thumping.

Kunaal didn't look up until Reeva stood across his table.

"Good morning, I see you're busy," said Reeva, setting down her breakfast and taking the seat opposite him. She flashed her most charming smile. Kunaal's face lit up even as he shook his head in mock dismay with a lop-sided smile. He eased back in his chair, but still didn't say anything.

"Are you normally this talkative or is today special?" Reeva quipped mischievously.

Finally, Kunaal chuckled, "Oh yes, today is special. Someone very gorgeous decided to share the table with me today."

Reeva smiled, "Friends?" She extended her hand.

"Just friends… really?" Kunaal paused as if thinking, "Okay. Not good enough, but will do for starters," he kissed the back of her hand.

"So, what brings you here? I mean… what are the chances of us meeting here?" He grudgingly let go of her hand.

"Actually, I intended to sneak out of here without letting you know," she smiled.

"You mean you were going to avoid me deliberately? Wow!" Kunaal exhaled, "Reeva, you know what, I've never played Russian roulette in my life."

"Meaning?"

"Meaning that I now know what it feels like to bet the game on a number and see the dice roll onto that very number as the roulette spins. I just feel lucky," he smiled.

"Hmmm… that's a deep analogy," Reeva pouted. Suddenly, Kunaal covered her hand with his, "Don't do that!" He whispered urgently.

"What?"

"That thing you just did with your lips. It drives me crazy." An awkward silence followed. She retrieved her hand deciding to retreat to the safe zone.

"Actually Kunaal, I was going to ask for your help regarding our office boy Harry. The Municipal Corporation is going to demolish his building. He and all other occupants have lived there for decades. But now they say it's unauthorized and hazardous. These people have nowhere to go, Kunaal."

"Hmm... Normally that's not how it works. But let me look into it. Just send me the details. I'll figure out the deal here." He continued with a smile, "I'll do whatever needs to be done… I promise." His assuring tone made her smile too.

They took the short, pleasant walk across the park to the office together.

In the building, as the elevator door was closing, Reeva realized that a strap of her left shoe was awkwardly twisted. "Damn," muttered Reeva, looking down. She didn't want to bend down in her fitted skirt.

Kunaal immediately extended his hand, "Here, hold on to me. You don't want to twist your ankle." As the elevator arrived on their floor Reeva stood awkwardly, balancing on one foot while clutching on to Kunaal's arm, and adjusted her shoe strap. The doors opened and Shalini Ray stood before them. There was a loaded pause as nobody moved or said anything. Something as innocent as her hand on Kunaal's arm could easily seem intimate in the confines of an elevator, especially between colleagues.

Then Shalini stepped aside with a deliberate movement, waiting for the duo to exit. Reeva put her foot down and Kunaal shifted his laptop to the other hand, pressing the button to hold the lift open for Shalini. Formal greetings were exchanged, and Shalini stepped into the elevator, unsmiling. As they walked away, Reeva was flustered by Shalini's coldness, but they both let it slide, not wanting to delve into the subject.

While parting, Kunaal said, "Let's catch up soon?" He

searched her eyes. Reeva smiled in return. As she walked through the office, she found the colours around her brighter, the sounds of perfunctory greetings pleasant and her colleagues more beautiful. She smiled back at every person. She felt good, in fact – great!

Manek Vir parked his jeep on the empty road and impatiently got out. Not a soul was in sight. All he could hear was the rustling of the leaves from the bamboo tree cluster, as the wind picked up.

He checked the map on his iPad once again to confirm if he was headed in the right direction. Until now, he had meticulously followed the roadmap given by Thapar, which was supposed to lead him to the secluded farmhouse, jointly owned by Jaiswal and him. Vir had almost been off-roading; at times even taking a road that he strongly felt would lead to a dead end. But eventually, that road always connected to another one of the same kind. He was getting nowhere. As someone who was punctual and never lost his way, this was getting irksome.

He decided to drive for some more time before calling Thapar. Luckily, within two kilometres he recognized faint signs of habitation – an abandoned tea stall, dried tyre marks and general sense of human presence by way of litter. Soon he arrived outside a tall iron gate with high stone walls extending on both sides. His trained eyes spotted the CCTV camera perched high on one of the walls instantly. A call button with a one-way intercom was hidden behind the creepers and vines. He pressed the button. The response was immediate and the iron gates slid open. He drove further inside for about half a kilometre on a gravel driveway.

At the end of the drive, sat a massive villa, with a Bentley and a Rolls Royce parked outside. A fountain in the middle of the circular driveway reminded him of Piazza Navona in Italy. He tossed the car key to the valet and walked up to the main entrance. A nondescript, safari-clad attendant received him.

Stepping into the large hall, Vir spotted Thapar on the huge mahogany table at the far end of the room. He was reading *The New York Times* and *Financial Times'* lay by the side. He guessed they had been specially flown in.

"Welcome, welcome Manekji, I hope you didn't have much trouble finding this place," Thapar stood up.

Vir eyed the newspapers sceptically, choosing to ignore the pointless question. The use of his first name irked him. Thapar followed his gaze and apologized, "What to do, we're old timers. We're still used to holding the newspaper in our hands. Somehow, online news from the computer doesn't feel believable. But we still have to keep an eye out you know," he guffawed and invited Vir to sit down.

Jaiswal made a hurried entry, profusely apologizing for the delay and invited him to join them at the brunch table. Vir was impressed by the layout on the table. It had everything, from juices and croissants to pastries and imported salamis. The spread was huge and utterly excessive for three people. Ignoring this and without any formalities, he served himself. He was famished and defiant. The industrialist duo, after exchanging a surprised glance, hurriedly joined in.

"I have a tip off on JBP," Vir finally looked up from his plate, "It's about the exposé of a senior civil services official with JBP government, in a southern state," he spoke flatly.

"Oh... already? That was fast," Thapar sounded impressed. "Do you have the details with you now?" Vir stopped eating and wiped the corners of his mouth with a napkin. Casually fishing out a small envelope from his pocket, he pushed it across the table. "Here it is. The memory drive in it has everything you will need." He continued eating as he spoke, "When this information goes public, JBP will suffer a knockout blow."

Thapar's eyes went wide. He finished his juice in a single swig and wiped his hands on the napkin. Taking the small black memory stick, he moved towards his laptop.

Jaiswal too had lost all interest in the food and was about to get up when Vir spoke again. "Don't bother. It is password protected. There's no chance in hell you can open it, unless you give me the full background on your asset," he said coolly, looking at them.

Thapar looked confused but Jaiswal enlightened him, "Dindayal, he's referring to Arunabh Roy."

"Of course, Manekji. Arunabh has been our associate for many years, and has aided us many times... especially whenever we needed to use media to manipulate or influence public opinion, you see," grinned Thapar.

"Does he work for the money?" Vir asked flatly.

"Who doesn't work for money, Manekji?"

"I mean, does he work *only* for the money?" There was a pause as Vir searched their faces. "Because trust me, there's plenty of money floating out there for him, Mr. Thapar. Shit loads of money, actually! Sooner or later, someone will be willing to offer him more than you. Hope you understand this." He wiped his hands.

"So, what makes you so sure of his loyalty?" He continued

to observe them. Suddenly, Jaiswal who had been a silent spectator of this conversation, got up and brought out his Bottega briefcase. He unlocked it and fished out a slim folder. Waving it at Vir, he said, "Here's the proof of Roy's involvement in each of our projects. This alone, is enough to not only destroy his career, but also lock him up for good. So, no, he will never mess with us. And, we're businessmen. We're not politicians with a limited term. We're here to stay," he smiled confidently.

Vir relaxed in his chair. Thapar looked at him expectantly, "Can we have the password now?" Vir folded his arms. "There's no password. You can access it now. Just make sure it gets the maximum of exposure." Both men didn't seem to have taken his tricky manoeuvre kindly, but Vir didn't care. He didn't work for them, but it was his job to ensure that they had their backs covered, for the sake of the operation.

Vir stood up and decided that his job for the day was done. His instructions from the Fixer had been concise. Spend as little time with Thapar and Jaiswal as possible and speak even less. Their principle was not to use online communication, as leaving an online trail was always risky. That's why Vir had had to travel to deliver the information.

Pointing at the memory stick Thapar was still holding, he said, "Most of the stuff in there is about exposing the deliberate loopholes in policies, created by the senior administrators to suit the ruling JBP government. But there's enough material for your media source to have a field day with JBP's image." Vir picked up his belongings, "I'll be in touch about the next step. Good luck." He shook hands with the mildly offended men and exited the hall. The duo sank into the sofa, warily eyeing Vir until he was out of their sight.

"So, what do you think?" sighed Thapar. "This is a dangerous game we're playing Dindayal." Jaiswal was in a contemplative mood.

"True. But, don't forget our end game Ramcharan. The Galactic Studios. If we crack that, we may never need to play again. The game will come to us. But for that, JBP has to fall, at least at the state level."

"Don't you think we should have discussed the Navdeep Complex case with Vir?"

"Oh, come on, Ramcharan. We are the ones paying them to achieve our objective. We don't need their permission to act. We know the business and the game. This is not the first time. And Navdeep Complex is just an additional nail in JBP's coffin," Thapar smiled. He had already switched on his laptop. Rubbing his hands in anticipation, he inserted the memory stick.

"Yes, of course. I just hope nothing backfires," said Jaiswal. "I mean involving Sathya Raj Mane and playing our own game on the side..." his voice trailed off.

"Don't worry. There's no direct involvement of Mane. He's just going to play a limited role. He doesn't need to know much." Thapar eyed Jaiswal meaningfully, "Navdeep Complex is just a cover for whatever happens to the people associated with it. It will leave JBP searching for a place to hide its face. Rest Arunabh Roy will take care of," he smirked, "and Mane simply needs to earn his keep, after all, he gets to keep the chair."

"What exactly is going to happen to the people associated with Navdeep Complex?" he asked, not looking in Thapar's direction.

"Time will tell, my dear friend. Time will tell." He laughed mirthlessly and turned his eyes to the laptop and all the files on the memory stick. Jaiswal moved closer for a better look. After a while of browsing, they exchanged triumphant looks.

"Bingo! This calls for an urgent meeting with Roy," Thapar announced and Jaiswal nodded enthusiastically. "Let me fix it for tomorrow."

The wheels were beginning to turn. They had their next moves worked out. Or at least, they believed so. Little did they know that a single unexpected move from the other end could upset their game. Big time.

Little Sia looked up at Nandita from her notebook, her eyes wet. "What happened Sia? Are you okay?" asked Nandita. Other students of the tuition class eyed Sia curiously.

"Thank you Nandita didi, if you weren't there, I would have never learnt to write English."

"No Sia, you would have. If not me, somebody else would have taught you."

"But I want to learn only from you didi." Sia hugged Nandita tightly and mumbled into her hair.

Nandita sighed and looked around at all the kids, "Come on, come on, pack your bags and get out of here," she chided them gently, "And remember the essay test tomorrow!" They responded with a collective protest but she hushed them down.

With the kids gone, Nandita contemplated the long day ahead of her. She was scheduled to meet Reeva today. There was a lot she needed to update her about as they were on a very tight schedule.

She stepped out of the house, and immediately ducked to avoid a flying cricket ball. A chorus of "Sorry Didi" went up in the air. She giggled. Nandita loved Sunder Nagar. She knew she wouldn't have wanted to be anywhere else. Sunder Nagar made her come alive. It was her home, a safe haven for a girl on a mission.

She walked briskly towards the bus stop, hoping to catch the next bus. But she had to make a quick stop at the stationery shop to buy few pens and a notebook. As she left the shop, she noticed a man walking casually behind her on the mostly empty road. Her defensive instincts kicked in. *Wasn't he standing next to me at the shop?* She asked herself. Seeing the bus arrive, Nandita broke into a trot but the man behind her continued in his casual saunter, showing no intention of catching the bus. She scolded herself for being paranoid and boarded the bus, somewhat out of breath.

As Nandita searched for an empty seat, she saw that man again. He was standing on the steps of the bus, looking cool and disinterested.

She could no longer ignore him. Nandita looked at him properly for the first time. He was a regular looking guy, dressed in an oversized dark green shirt and blue jeans. But it was his mean, cold eyes that gave him away. His eyes never stopped at anything, they were constantly moving. When her stop arrived, she stood up and glanced around, but couldn't see him. Sighing with relief, she got off and brisk-walked to the train station. She didn't see the man again.

Nandita bought the ticket and waited for her local train, which was running late by ten minutes. She engrossed herself in a book but within minutes her instincts kicked in again, telling her that she was being stared at. She looked up just in time to notice a sudden movement in her peripheral vision. Carefully scanning the crowd, she did a double take when she saw the same man again, leaning against the refreshment stall sipping tea from a small cup, trying to look inconspicuous. Blood rushed through Nandita's head.

A single bead of sweat traversed across her temple and dropped onto the open page in her lap. It was a warm day, but wasn't hot enough to sweat. The train halted in front of her and she got on with several other women. Sinking back into her seat, she thought of calling Reeva but knew that she was too far away to help. Then she spotted the female railway guard, at the corner of the compartment and pushed her way through the crowd.

"I need help," Nandita was breathless and had to repeat thrice before she could be heard over the noise.

"What happened?" asked the guard, almost uninterested.

"Somebody is following me," she shouted over the din.

"In here?" The guard asked giving her a strange look.

"No, he's been following me since I left home."

"Oh! Which station do you get off?"

"Lower Parel," answered Nandita.

The guard shouted in her ears, "When you get off, go to the stationmaster's office. Better still, straight to the police station. You can recognize this man, right? I'll come with you if you wish." Nandita nodded but it didn't make her feel any better.

She got off at Lower Parel. Reeva's office wasn't too far from the station and Nandita knew that if she stayed with the crowds, she would be safe. Yet, she sensibly decided to take a cab instead of walking.

Before she entered Creative Adzone's building, she noticed

her stalker once again, across the road, staring at her. Then suddenly, he walked decisively in Nandita's direction.

Nandita turned and moved quickly inside the building complex, almost panicking now. In her overwhelmed state of mind, she had to ask for directions twice. Clutching her bag closer to her chest, she stepped into the elevator. Finally, even as she sat in Adzone's reception area, her legs shivered from the rush of adrenaline. And her face betrayed her relief when she saw Reeva walking towards her.

"Hello Nandita," Reeva hugged her, "Come, let's talk in my cabin." She could sense that Nandita was not her normal self. Once inside, Nandita sank into the chair and hid her face in her hands with a deep breath. Reeva walked to her side, touched her shoulder and asked gently, "What's wrong Nandita?"

Just then, Nihaal peeked in, "Hey Reevs, what time is Nandita..." His voice trailed off as he saw the two women. He entered the cabin and shut the door behind him.

"I think I was being followed today," declared Nandita.

"What do you mean? Where? When?" asked Reeva.

"On my way here, today."

"Nandita, are you sure? I mean, could this be your imagination?"

But Nihaal cut in, "Nandita, did you see the guy properly? Would you be able to recognize him?"

"Yes, of course. I remember him very clearly. He followed me from Sunder Nagar," she shivered.

"Hmmm... When did you file for the RTI on the Navdeep Complex Land?" Nihaal's brow was creased.

"Just last week." Nandita's lips quivered, "Something's not right. I've faced threats before. I've been manhandled and attacked. And I know when I see a dangerous situation. Somebody is not happy with my digging around."

"What do you mean Nandita? Nihaal, do you think this has something to do with her filing the RTI petition?" Reeva's voice was urgent.

"I don't know Reeva. But I had said earlier that we don't know how high or how deep this runs. Nandita met the officer and immediately filed for an RTI. This is enough to wake the sleeping wolves."

"Nihaal, I'm worried. We will have a very small window to operate if we need to take any action. The information from the Public Information Officer would take anywhere between thirty to forty five days. And, the officer had warned me about the evacuation notice in forty five to sixty days."

"There's something very fishy about this case. My friend Aditi runs an architecture firm. She sent a team of civil engineers to check the structure. According to her, it's rock-solid sturdy and can last another decade or more before it requires any re-evaluation," said Nihaal.

"Shouldn't we first inform the police about someone following Nandita today? Are you guys not bothered about it?"

"No point. Police won't take action on Nandita's statement. Not until the guy makes any real move. Only celebrities and VIPs are entitled to that luxury," scoffed Nihaal.

"He's right. Don't worry Reeva, I'll be careful. I promise." She smiled.

"You set your eyes on that man again, even once, you call me right away. Put me on your speed dial now," insisted Reeva.

"Also, if you have any friendly neighbours it would be nice if you kept them informed of your whereabouts all the time," added Nihaal. "I'm headed towards your side for a meeting in a little while. I'll drop you."

Nandita nodded, grateful for Nihaal's company.

"Let me call in for some refreshments... maybe some sandwiches? It's almost lunchtime." Reeva picked up the phone to call the pantry as the atmosphere in the room lightened slightly.

They were chatting companionably when suddenly Reeva's cabin door opened without a knock and Kunaal stood there smiling. He held a silver-coloured invite in his hands.

"Hey, I see you guys are having a nice time... good." He smiled, looking pointedly at Nihaal. "Reeva, here's the invite for the champagne brunch at home next week. Thought I should hand it over personally." Kunaal handed her the invite without sitting down, and after quick greetings, he was out of the cabin within seconds.

Suddenly, the room was filled with silence as Nihaal quietly munched on his sandwich and Reeva smiled awkwardly at Nandita who had sensed the unmistakable undercurrents among the trio.

Finally, Nihaal got up and said, "I'll be ready to leave in half an hour, Nandita. Please wait, if you don't mind." He glanced at Reeva, opened his mouth as if to say something, but changed his mind. He mumbled, "Never mind."

Reeva felt as if her heart had been squeezed dry. She wanted to explain the situation to Nihaal, but decided against it. *What in the hell are you going to explain to him anyway? What's there to explain? You already made a choice. Are you ready to tell him that?*

Half the clothes from Reeva's wardrobe were either spread out on her bed or lying bunched up on the settee. She had decided to wear a semi-formal cream skirt and blouse to the brunch but had forgotten that she had lost too much weight. The damn skirt was now loose and refused to stay put on her waist. Reeva sat down on the edge of the bed, her face in her hands. She hated dressing up but this particular day was important. They were due to leave for the brunch at Kunaal's place in an hour.

She decided to talk to her mom about her situation when the doorbell rang and her mom called out to her, "Reeva sweetie, can you get the door please? I'm still dressing up." Exasperated, Reeva answered the door. A man holding a large grey package stood outside. He smiled at her, "Ma'am, package for Miss Reeva Rai."

"Yeah, that's me. Who's it from?" The guy turned the slip and said, "The consignee is Mr. Kunaal Kabi. Could you please sign here?" He flashed his polished and rehearsed to perfection smile.

Claiming the surprisingly light box, Reeva returned to her room. She ripped off the tape securing the lid and stood transfixed. There lay a Christian Dior, powder blue-coloured dress with a pretty sapphire brooch on the left shoulder. It was utterly feminine with an off-shoulder neckline and a layered handkerchief hemline ending around the knees. The dress was worth a few thousand dollars. *Why has he sent me such an expensive gift?* She fumed. Just then, Reeva's mobile rang and she saw Kunaal's name on the screen.

"Kunaal?" She breathed into the phone, "What the hell is this?"

He paused before speaking, "So, you finally received the

package! It should have reached you last evening, actually." He chuckled, "I swear I would have got that store manager fired if it hadn't arrived today."

"Kunaal, I cannot accept it."

"Why?"

"Because, it's too damn expensive and it's not like we're dating," she said and immediately regretted the words.

After a beat, Kunaal said calmly, "Reeva, when I saw this dress, all I could think of was you wearing it. Without you, it's just a piece of cloth." Kunaal hesitated and then spoke silkily. "And… about us not dating – that can be changed easily. If that's okay with you."

There was heavy silence on the phone. The words were out. Reeva lost her voice to nervousness as colour rose to her cheeks. Finally, Kunaal said, "So, I take that as a yes." He continued with cheeky authority, "Now, wear that dress!" He whispered, "I want to see you soon, very soon." Then he added as an afterthought, "And Reeva, please don't drive. I won't be there to park your car this time. My car will be there soon to pick you and your mom."

While Reeva was still recovering from the phone call, her mom entered and slowly approached the dress spread out on her bed. "Christian Dior? From Kunaal?" she gasped, checking the label and tag. She hugged Reeva tightly. "Oh! my dear baby… I'm so happy for you. You've grown into such a fine young lady. You deserve no less," she added proudly.

Reeva finally managed to send away her mom after some gentle chiding. She got dressed, feeling lucky to have found the right accessories to match the outfit. She pinned the sapphire brooch just above her heart, and felt cherished and secure in Kunaal's love. Her face glowed with happiness. She hardly knew that it was just the beginning of a very tricky journey.

The Kabi residence formed the entire twenty-first floor of the plush, seven-star, high-rise building. Embellished with antique chandeliers and lamps, it spoke of expensive taste. It was a six-bedroom apartment with a large hall that could easily accommodate fifty people. It also had a sea-facing terrace. Reeva and her mother were received at the door by a formally dressed young girl, who handed them an event card, with details of the brunch.

As they stepped into the hall, Reeva spotted a few Bollywood starlets and other small-time celebrities but not Kunaal. Reeva's mom tugged at her arm and whispered, "I hope I'm not underdressed for this." Reeva smiled, "Mom, you look perfect, don't worry." They stood unsurely at one end of the hall not knowing anyone around. Reeva spotted Mrs. Kabi at the far end of the hall talking with some foreign dignitaries. In a peach linen pantsuit she looked classy. Her long hair was sleek and shiny and moved like silk on her shoulders.

Then, the girl who had received them at the lobby approached Mrs. Kabi and whispered to her. She looked discreetly in their direction. Mrs. Kabi's gaze followed hers, spotting Reeva and her mother instantly. She smiled, and politely excused herself from the group. On her way to Reeva and her mom, she collected a couple of her socialite friends.

"Well, hello Mrs. Rai." Mrs. Kabi greeted her mom with

warm enthusiasm hugging her sideways, while she blew out a kiss in the air. "Good to see that you could make it," Mrs. Rai responded brightly, matching Mrs. Kabi's enthusiasm.

Mrs. Kabi looked Reeva up and down and gushed, "My gosh Reeva, you look stunning. That's a Christian Dior you're wearing? It looks bespoke, not off the rack. I'm impressed. My son's good taste is rubbing off on you." She laughed and continued, addressing her friends, "Ladies, meet Mrs. Rai and her lovely daughter Reeva. She's a very close friend of Kunaal," smiled Mrs. Kabi meaningfully.

Slowly growing impatient and uncomfortable, Mrs. Rai was about to excuse herself when Mrs. Kabi held the edge of her saree, observing it carefully. "Mmmm... lovely, is this an Anamika Khanna creation Mrs. Rai?" she asked enthusiastically. Mrs. Rai had a confused look on her face, but then she added hurriedly, "Oh no Mrs. Kabi, this is from the designer range at the Paridhaan; you know they also have an outlet in South Mumbai," she offered excitedly.

Mrs. Kabi frowned for a second and then smiled, "Oh, you mean the shop Paridhaan?" she smiled demurely, "Still buying stuff from the stores, are we? How very quaint!"

Reeva intervened, "Mrs. Kabi, I don't see Kunaal anywhere. Is he around?"

Mrs. Kabi said, "Well, he hasn't arrived yet. Normally, he sticks to his schedule. And today of all the days, he had another reason to be on time." She threw an off-hand jibe at Reeva, smiling sweetly. She then politely excused herself and left, her elite brigade in tow.

Reeva had been impatiently checking her watch for the past hour. Her mom had managed to find a few friends and was chatting away happily. But, there was still no sign of

Kunaal and she felt edgy. She decided to go find the restroom, happy to be away from the suffocating crowd.

After mistakenly opening doors to personal rooms twice, Reeva decided to return to the hall when she noticed a door with *KK* inscribed on it in brass letters. Ignoring the warnings in her mind, she put her hand on the ornate brass handle and turned it. She entered the room and was instantly stupefied.

The room was a dedication to Kunaal, resplendent in memories from all phases of his life. There were pictures of him winning trophies, swimming, hiking, even skate-boarding from school days. There were shelves completely adorned with trophies, medals and certificates for his successes in academics and extra-curricular activities. Everything was absolutely well kept and neat in the room, including the bed, which looked like it had never been slept in.

The impeccable room gave Reeva the impression of a museum, with things on display. But there were no personal touches. Although, she felt like she was peeking into Kunaal's life for the first time, something didn't feel right to her. She then came across Kunaal's graduation picture from Harvard. She ran her fingers across the frame and was momentarily lost in the picture. It was closest to the Kunaal she knew. A sudden sound at the door startled her, and she turned around to see Mrs. Kabi staring back at her, displeasure etched on her face.

"Oh, there you are. So, you finally managed to reach my son's room." Her tone was caustic.

"Oh no Mrs. Kabi, I was just passing by..." Reeva fumbled, as Mrs. Kabi held her hand up to interrupt her.

"It's alright." She softened a bit. "You're the first girl to, although I didn't think you would make the cut. Honestly,

I'm impressed." She added, "So, what do you think?" She waved a hand around the room.

"It's really nice," managed Reeva sheepishly.

"I decorated it all by myself," said Mrs. Kabi, getting nostalgic and then noticed Reeva's surprise. "Yes Reeva, Kunaal has visited this room only once, that too after it was fully done," she sighed.

"I don't understand Mrs. Kabi."

"Reeva, now that you intend to date my son, you also need to understand that he's been through a lot. He has had too much of everything, from bad luck to unlimited riches. He lost his father at an early age and never had a father figure to look up to. I raised him alone." She sighed, "This is probably the reason he has turned into a very private person. He needs his privacy to the extent that he does not live here in this house with me." She looked away, "And, he loves his personal space so much that nobody is allowed anywhere near. Think you can live with that?" Mrs. Kabi fixed her with a stare.

This revelation of Kunaal's personality perplexed Reeva. She knew he was borderline eccentric, but this was surprising. She didn't know what to say to the mother of the one guy she was hopelessly attracted to. Mrs. Kabi broke the spell by announcing, "Oh come on, girl. You have all the time in the world to think, but later. Let's get back to the hall for the charity auction now." This broke Reeva's reverie and they moved out of the room. She absolutely had to see Kunaal, in flesh, to ascertain that whatever transpired between them this morning wasn't a figment of her imagination.

Kunaal's car came to a screeching halt outside his mother's apartment building. He was driving his midnight-blue, low seating sports car. Hopping out, he tossed the keys at the valet and strode towards the elevator. He was very late for his mom's brunch and more importantly, he was late for Reeva. As he waited impatiently for the elevator, he tried to work out a defence for his delay, but came up with zilch. Kunaal decided to approach the situation with his usual cool panache and take-it-as-it-comes attitude.

He nodded at the besotted, starry-eyed receptionist as he exited the elevator. Entering the hall, he was dismayed to see that the charity auction was about to begin. Kunaal was supposed to conduct the auction today, but in his absence, Mrs. Kabi had been forced to replace him with their long-term family friend and physician Dr. Harsh Wardhaan. Although Dr. Wardhaan was older by almost a decade, Kunaal and he were close friends, and often spent time together. Kunaal entered and was promptly led to an exclusive seating area reserved for the chief guest and hosts. He eyes kept scanning the hall for Reeva. Dr. Wardhaan smiled at him from the dais and raised his glass. He sipped his champagne and shrugged his shoulders to indicate his helplessness in replacing Kunaal.

Mrs. Kabi stood behind the auction table. Kunaal watched as his mother explained the rules of auction. She finally looked at Kunaal, with cool aloofness and he mouthed a 'sorry'. She looked away.

Finally having found the elusive washroom, Reeva reurned to the hall and spotted Kunaal instantly. He sat up in his chair as their eyes met. Kunaal could feel the magnetic pull, even from across the hall. Just as he had imagined, she looked absolutely gorgeous in the dress and carried it with elegance. His heart jumped as she took a seat next to her mom. He almost got up to go across, but the auction had begun. Reeva fixed him with a steely gaze, looking every inch like an ice princess. She was obviously mad at him for being late. He felt restless and impatient.

Mrs. Kabi urged the ladies to put up something of theirs on auction and women started to place things like a scarf, clutch and even a pen on the auction table. Kunaal continued to gaze longingly at Reeva.

Suddenly, she stood up and threw a defiant look at Kunaal. She then walked to the auction desk, removed the sapphire brooch from her dress and placed it on the table. Mrs. Kabi raised her eyebrows and smiled, while Dr. Wardhaan handed her the numbered card. Kunaal shook his head in dismay. He had never bid at any of his mom's auctions till date, but now he was left with no option. His problem was with the rule that the bid-winner was entitled to have the first dance with the owner of the item. There wasn't a chance that he was going to allow that. Not today. Maybe never.

As Reeva took her seat, Kunaal walked up to Dr. Wardhaan to register himself as a bidder. His friend exclaimed meaningfully, "Kunaal! You're bidding? For whom?" He asked teasingly but Kunaal chose to simply walk back to his seat with a smile. Curiously, Dr. Wardhaan glanced across the hall, trying to figure out Kunaal's interest.

The auction began and soon the competition intensified. Mrs. Kabi smiled proudly as the bid values escalated quickly. Every year, she liked to exceed the amount of the previous year's donations, collected out of the annual charity-bidding event. This year was looking particularly good already. With every article that went up for auction Dr. Wardhaan glanced at

Kunaal expectantly and was met with a lazy, laid-back smile.

Finally, Reeva's Christian Dior brooch was announced. Kunaal sat up instantly and raised a hand, ready to bid. Reeva stood up and demurely approached the desk. Knowing that his friend was going to bid, Dr. Wardhaan deliberately announced the starting bid at two lakh rupees, more than double the value of most items auctioned that day. Kunaal narrowed his eyes at him and Dr. Wardhaan shrugged nonchalantly. Just as Kunaal readied himself to bid at a higher price, a voice went up from the other corner of the hall. It belonged to a leading real estate baron, Niranjan Shah, who stood up slowly and started at two and a half lakhs. Kunaal was thrown off momentarily, but he eyed his competition and raised his hand coolly indicating a counter bid. Reeva eyed Kunaal with a mischievous smile, but received no response. Niranjan Shah put up his hand again to raise the bid. Kunaal shot an icy look at his co-bidder, who seemed to be innocently enjoying the thrills of being in the spotlight.

Reeva was beginning to feel uncomfortable. Kunaal had already spent a fortune on the dress and now she was making him spend more, her only consolation being that the money would go to a charity. It took only a few more raised hands by the two men to escalate the value to eight lakhs. True to herself, Mrs. Kabi was cheering both men to raise the bids even though one of them was her own son.

Finally, Kunaal moved in for the kill. He held up two fingers, indicating an increase of two lakhs. Niranjan Shah shot a surprised look at him and burst out laughing, shaking his head in disbelief. He quickly gestured his withdrawal from the bidding. He bowed politely at Reeva and sat back.

A bout of cheers and claps went up in the air as Kunaal claimed the brooch at the final bid value of ten lakhs and secured it in his breast pocket. Reeva gushed at Kunaal, who gave her a lop-sided grin.

Soon the honorary dance was announced and the hall was filled with light music. Kunaal approached Reeva as she glanced at him nervously. He kissed her hand delicately before pulling her onto the dance floor.

As they swayed gently to the music, he whispered, "Finally."

She looked up at him, "Finally what?"

He smirked, "This dance. I've waited a long time for it. Since the day of MVPR's launch party."

Reeva gasped and looked into his eyes, remembering her denial on that day. "You're still holding onto that?"

Kunaal looked into her eyes deeply and took her hand from his shoulder and kissed her palm, "I do have a tendency to hold onto things Reeva, you will know soon." He smiled his trademark smile, "Come, let's go out on the balcony. We need to talk, alone." He glanced around the hall, and saw Dr. Wardhaan walk towards them.

"Hello, Kunaal, won't you do me the honour of introducing me to the beautiful lady here?"

Kunaal sighed, "Reeva, meet Dr. Harsh Wardhaan, our family doctor and also a close friend of mine." Dr. Harsh enthusiastically shook Reeva's hand. Before any conversation could ensue, Kunaal interrupted, "Hey listen Harsh, if you don't mind can I catch up with you later? I need to talk to Reeva, alone."

"By all means bro, go right ahead. You've officially earned it," he laughed.

Kunaal took Reeva away from the crowd, to the charming open deck that extended to a small, personal infinity pool. He led them to a shady spot under a garden umbrella. They sat down and an awkward silence ensued. Suddenly, Kunaal blurted out, "Reeva, next week I'm planning to visit Davos for three days to attend a business convention." He paused and added beseechingly, "Would you come with me?"

Switzerland had always been a dream destination for Reeva. But there were so many things to consider, both personally and professionally. She couldn't just get up and go. Before she could think of a response, her mobile rang and Kunaal frowned. She was surprised to see it was Mr. Sehgal calling.

She could sense the tension in his voice. "Reeva, have you seen the breaking news today?"

"No, I'm out actually." Reeva mouthed 'Boss' to Kunaal. He pulled out his own mobile which was off-ringer and was surprised to see a barrage of missed calls from Ajay Sehgal and also one from Uttur's personal number.

"Reeva, I need you to come to office immediately," he sounded urgent, "I'm not able to get through to Kunaal. Please ask him to come as well, if you can reach him." He disconnected.

Kunaal quietly asked Reeva to follow him to the TV room. They had to wade through the throng of guests, politely greeting everyone, before they could reach the library-cum-TV room. Kunaal tuned into a news channel. What they witnessed shocked them into a stunned silence.

"Let's reach office. I'll arrange for your mom to be dropped back home." His voice was devoid of any emotion.

They left the event with hurried excuses. Reeva was left

wondering if this was going to be the pace for the rest of the life she was intending to share with Kunaal. She was too overwhelmed to think clearly and they were both quiet throughout the drive. Kunaal had a tendency to be withdrawn and cold whenever he sensed a threat. Reeva realized that while she could expect anything in this world from him, she could never expect him to share his innermost trials and tribulations with her. She felt dark, foreboding thoughts clouding her mind and her heart tightening with an unexplained fear.

CHAPTER 10

Creative AdZone and MVPR's office complex bore an abandoned, deserted look over the weekends. Its solemn mood matched Reeva and Kunaal's, as they rode up the elevator to their office. They quickly walked into Mr. Sehgal's cabin and Reeva could sense the tension in the air.

Mr. Sehgal was perched on the edge of his table, his eyes glued to the TV. Reeva noticed his white golf shoes. He had probably been pulled out from the middle of a game. Shalini sat at the corner of the sofa absent-mindedly rubbing her forehead with the back of a pen. Mr. Sehgal nodded at them and pointed the remote at the TV to mute it and they took seats.

"This doesn't sound good Kunaal, not good at all." He shook his head.

"Any idea who exposed the story?" Kunaal asked evenly, although it was evident that he was struggling to control himself.

"Don't know for sure, but apparently, Arunabh Roy is

leading the media brigade. He's also doing a special segment on *News Today* about this exposé, along with experts' comments shortly. He claims that he wants to discuss the case threadbare for the common man's benefit and understanding," Sehgal smirked.

"That's not true. He's simply going for the kill. Somehow, he wants to cause maximum damage to JBP. It's not for the common man's benefit. It's for his and his benefit alone." Kunaal's hand was curled into a tight fist under his chin.

"What do you mean?"

"Roy has exposed the chief secretary of the state Mr. Shyam Mohanty, no less. That's a top IAS cadre bureaucrat we're talking about. I'm sure you're aware of the symbiosis between politicians and IAS officers, Mr. Sehgal. This information has come from someone sitting high, very high up. And, it makes me think, who's his source?"

"Actually, you're right. The main allegations against the chief secretary are fabrication of false grounds and pre-dating certain approvals for the benefit of the ruling party's minister, which happens to be of JBP."

Mr. Sehgal rubbed his eyes. "But it's far from proven yet. He hasn't presented any concrete evidence to the authorities."

"Nothing needs to be proven. These allegations are enough to taint JBP. Don't forget that the chief secretary directly controls all administrative matters of the state, whether it is public policies, execution or expenditure. It will be seen as if the JBP minister influenced him for his personal benefit." Kunaal sat on the edge of the seat. "The damage is already done, as far as public's perception is concerned."

"So, what should be our next steps?" Reeva looked expectantly at the two men.

"Reeva, I'll soon have a brief ready for the statement JBP needs to issue in a press conference, which should be scheduled for no later than tomorrow. You and Shalini will need to prep the JBP spokesperson to handle media questions," said Kunaal. Shalini nodded as he continued, "But, first I need to speak with Uttur." Then, as if on cue, Kunaal's phone rang. It was Uttur himself. Kunaal lifted a finger to excuse himself. He stepped out into the corridor. Taking a deep breath, he pressed the call button.

"Kunaal? I've been trying to reach you." There was a nervous urgency in the leader's voice.

"Yes, I know. Sorry for not getting back earlier. But, I have seen the drama on TV already. We're planning counter measures now," Kunaal said.

"Kunaal, this is a clear case of systematic targeting, with an aim to undermine JBP's chances of winning the elections. Come on, every political party has its own working equation with the bureaucracy for the sake of smooth functioning. Somebody wants to paint a bad picture of us."

"Yeah, that's obvious. Mohanty has a clean track record and so does the home minister."

"The facts have been twisted to make it sound like a case of corruption. In fact, the home minister had given enough autonomy to the chief secretary to operate in the best interest of the state. His only error was approving the purchases of construction material for the state's housing development corporation without a tender. Because, as per the market trends, the prices were to rise immediately by twenty per cent. Tender process would have delayed the purchase and it would have cost the state exchequer." Uttur paused to hear Kunaal's response.

"Right! There it is. That's our angle." Kunaal brightened for the first time. "We gave full autonomy to the bureaucracy to operate. That's our defence." Kunaal continued, "JBP's only fault is its fairness towards the highly qualified and intelligent civil servants of the country. The party's only operational error is that it relied upon the good judgment of its administrative officer." He finally allowed himself a triumphant smile.

"Yes, we could work with that. We can even prove it through the sequence of events." Uttur was regaining his composure by the minute.

"No point in trying to prove anything. The state where it happened has your government. Media and opposition will claim that all the evidence is fabricated by JBP, using its power," said Kunaal softly, not wanting to deflate Uttur's enthusiasm.

"Hmmm... You're right. I'll ask our official spokesperson to be in touch with you right away. Kunaal, please go ahead with what you think is right. Just make sure you turn it around." Uttur disconnected, leaving Kunaal to feel the added burden of the leader's implicit faith.

Kunaal re-entered Sehgal's cabin as Arnunabh Roy was making his closing statement on the JBP-Chief Secretary exposé. He sat down passively in his chair, watching Roy challenging the viewers with his well-formed thoughts and arguments, as he looked right into the camera. The camera zoomed into his face as he continued to speak forcefully, "Does the JBP believe that they can manipulate our country's administrative machinery to suit themselves? Are the systems meant to be flouted by them? Has corruption become a part of their system now? We owe these answers to this nation.

Our country needs to know. Are we, as true countrymen, ready for the answers? I urge you, here on News Today, with full responsibility, to seek the truth."

Kunaal sat back and smiled, impressed by the sheer energy of Roy's discourse. He would be questioning his own loyalty for JBP if he didn't know better. Finally, he addressed the other three professionals in the room.

"Reeva, you will receive my media brief in an hour. You will prep the JBP spokesperson. Shalini, please start working on your list of media contacts. I don't want a very large group. Just go with your trusted lot of media reps. All calls are to be made personally and nobody outside should know of this press conference. Nobody, and I mean nobody, should know until we actually hold it. And Shalini, please take Reeva's help if need be."

Shalini ignored Kunaal and addressed Mr. Sehgal instead, "Mr. Sehgal, I think I'm fine handling this by myself. I can set up the press conference for lunch tomorrow," she said curtly. Ajay Sehgal waited for a few seconds before nodding. Reeva bristled at being rebuffed so unceremoniously and Kunaal sighed inwardly. Shalini was refusing to play as a team member. But she was still needed on their side. Especially now, when she had an important part to execute. This was an all-hands-on-deck scenario.

The compact but well-equipped conference room of JBP's Mumbai headquarters was packed to capacity. The hand-picked journalists and channel representatives were busy adjusting their mics and camera angles, the urgency and importance of the occasion reflected on their faces. It had been a unanimous strategic decision supported by JBP's top members to hold the press conference in Mumbai, instead of Delhi, for the sake of secrecy and control. And judging by the crowd in the room, Shalini had made good on her word.

As Pramod Saran entered and approached the dais, the activity in the room increased with people taking their places amidst apprehensive murmurs. Reeva and Shalini found theirs too.

Kunaal got up to receive the senior minister, set to become the future chief minister of the state and whispered, "Thank you for letting us hold this press conference here."

"What? Let it happen in Delhi and run the risk of our press conference being hijacked by some anti-JBP zealots?" The politico smiled, giving a fine impression to media, of everything being good and under control. "We do have that much PR sense Mr. Kabi." To the people watching it would appear as if the duo were recounting a happy occassion. Kunaal took a deep breath and said, "You ready?" Saran replied without looking in his direction, "Always. Must say your team did a good job at the briefing." He nodded in Reeva's direction as his eyes met hers.

Kunaal got up to announce the press conference's agenda, "Gentlemen, as you are aware this press conference is being held to issue a statement in response to the baseless allegations levelled against JBP. I request you to please stick to the agenda of today's meet. Mr. Pramod Saran will make an official statement on behalf of JBP. There will be half an hour of a Q&A session following that, in which you are once again requested to adhere to today's issue. Mr. Pramod Saran, please," he sat down and gave the space to the minister.

Saran cleared his throat and leaned into the mic, his hands firmly clasped before him on the table. He glanced through the room, "My dear friends, I'm aware that you all represent a very powerful force called the media. And, it's a force which I respect. But you hold in your hand a weapon so strong that it needs to be used responsibly. My appeal today is for you to use your better judgment. So, before I come to the topic of allegations against our esteemed party, let me state some obvious facts." He paused for effect before continuing, "Friends, our country takes pride in a fine team of civil servants or IAS officers, who assist the political office bearers in all matters of policy formation and implementation, with their knowledge, experience and sharp minds. Each year, these minds are selected by a year-long examination process. Over five lakh people apply for UPSC examinations, out of which only one-hundred-and-fifty to hundred-and-seventy-five candidates make it to IAS ranks, to work closely with the people at the political helm of the country. Chief Secretary Mr. Shyam Mohanty is one such IAS officer with a clean track record, who topped the 1987 batch. And so dear friends, I'm not here to defend JBP," paused Saran. Silence had descended on the room. "I'm here to defend this honourable IAS officer." He finally delivered the knockout punch, slowly releasing the words.

Kunaal looked around the room and was satisfied to see the response. The media reps were silent and unsure, but definitely flummoxed. And that's all their PR team and JBP needed – a sliver of doubt in their armour of belief. JBP had used an emotional bluff, knowing it could easily backfire. For now, it seemed to work, but they waited with bated breath. He knew they were not out of the woods yet.

Saran spoke again, gathering momentum. "Without resorting to any political diplomacy, I would like to ask a candid question. What would you rather have? A minister who listens to the advice of an expert and gives him complete freedom to operate in the best interest of the state? Or should a home minister, in a bid to maintain his egoistic supremacy, undermine the thoughts and efforts of an experienced IAS officer? Mr. Shyam Mohanty solely acted in the benefit of the state and the home minister supported his decision to surpass the tender process, because he knew it was going to save a lot of money for the state."

The paparazzi were listening in rapt attention. Saran looked around intensely, slightly out of breath. "If you're out to penalize a civil servant for acting in the interest of the state and to save the tax payer's hard-earned money, then you can forget about any more like him, ever coming out to put their jobs on the line for the common man. So, we can all play safe, stick to procedures and be mired in our own limitations. But remember, if we don't let a thought grow, we shall stop growing as a society." Saran could now see the heads nodding in approval and he pushed on, "Not for the sake of JBP, but for the sake of a respectable IAS officer Mr. Shyam Mohanty, I urge you to minutely pay attention to the sequence of events that led to the supply contract. I can assure you that there was no foul-play and if ever any such discrepancy is found upon investigation, all existing supply contracts in the state will be cancelled and re-allotted." He continued, "Now, if you have any questions..." A barrage of mostly benign questions rose from the audience, which were handled smoothly by Saran. The press conference had gone better than expected and they hoped it would help assuage the public sentiment largely.

Ensuring that everything was in control, Kunaal walked towards Reeva, "Hey, can you hold the fort for me? I need to be somewhere."

Reeva sat up, "What? Now? You're leaving?"

"Yes." His tone was abrupt.

"Okay." Reeva sullenly watched him walk out of the door with quick, long strides.

As the crowd dispersed after the press conference, Reeva suddenly noticed something glittering on the table. It was her sapphire brooch. She picked it up and wondered if Kunaal was upset with her about something. His mood swings unsettled her.

"Left you out in the cold, has he?" Shalini's bitter voice startled her. "Well, this isn't the first time he has done it," she smirked.

"What? What do you mean?" Reeva almost growled.

"You know what I mean. Girls like you are an easy prey for him, because you make it so."

"Stop it, Shalini. I've had enough." Reeva's voice had an edge.

"What have you had enough of? His money, his good looks or his attitude? He treats you like you're nothing." Shalini snarled, slamming the files she held in her arms on the table. That did it for Reeva, who was ready to explode with anger.

"What is it to you? Did he dump you? Or do you think nobody is good enough for him, apart from you? Or are you simply jealous?"

In response, Shalini went cold and sank into the seat opposite Reeva. "So, he hasn't told you? I thought so." Her face changed and she seemed distant.

Reeva asked quietly, "What are you talking about? What hasn't Kunaal told me?"

"My little sister, my baby, my beautiful Malini," Shalini said as a single tear escaped her eye. "He killed her."

The taste of bitter gourd juice sliced through Vir's taste buds and he winced, almost wanting to spit it out. Instead, he gulped down the vile green liquid and paid the vendor. He had just finished his morning run and felt pleasantly exhausted. He ran every day, despite rain or sunshine. He had always been faithful towards his fitness regime and he intended to continue that way.

He sat down on a bench near his car and relaxed to the sound of waves crashing onto the tetrapod-shaped rocks. Suddenly, his phone vibrated. Nobody ever called him during his morning runs. If he was unsettled to sense the vibration of his phone, he was unnerved to see the caller's ID. The Fixer never called him unscheduled or unexpectedly, so it had to be urgent. He quickly got into his car, turned on the engine and air-conditioning and answered the call on the fourth ring.

"Hello," he said, sounding alert.

"How do you rate the latest JBP-Chief Secretary exposé?" For the first time, the Fixer had sought his opinion. Vir was flustered, but recovered quickly to cover the key issues, "I think we managed to plant reasonable amount of doubt in the minds of the common people about JBP's philosophy and functioning style. Although, they did come up with a good defence. But the public knows that rules were broken. So, I think we hit the target. The earlier 'slap-gate' event has already labelled them as a party with no respect towards law and order. They are now being viewed as a political party with flaws in its core philosophy. Even their popularity ratings have dropped."

"I don't trust the ratings conducted by a small group of people with vested interests. And, even reasonable doubt is just doubt. That's not good enough. We need more."

"Yes, we're ready to go ahead with our next plan. I'm waiting for your green signal."

"We need something bigger. We need to unfold a controversy so big that it will take down JBP, and we only have a few months. Tell the client that our plans are in place. The media will continue to play its role."

"Can we discuss the client and their media asset?" Vir added quickly, sensing the call was about to end.

"Speak."

"I suspect the client is acting without consulting us. They're also prone to taking unnecessary and dangerous risks."

"And this suspicion is based on?"

"It's a hunch, a bad feeling. They're very powerful and don't play by the rules."

"Look for the proof to substantiate this hunch. Call me when you have it." This was enough for Vir to go on.

Even though Vir was now a civilian, he was still ex-military. He had a set of rules that came from the mud and blood of the defence's front line, not from a paper-pushing office. He wanted to be sure he was not being played by Thapar and Jaiswal. They definitely had another agenda on the side but the Fixer needed proof. And for that, Vir had to dig deeper.

Reeva was on her second day of binge-watching Boston Legal and Dexter. She had spent a good part of the past three days in her room, only eating microwaved popcorn and her mom's special meals, which she made sure that Reeva ate, fussing over her sudden loss of appetite. Mrs. Rai thought her daughter was only taking a break. Of course, she believed everything between her daughter and Kunaal was fine. Kunaal had messaged Reeva that he was due to leave for Davos shortly. But she was at a point where she felt emotionally numb. In fact, she felt nothing, no anger, no sorrow or sadness.

Shalini's story had left a chink in her heart.

Kunaal had met Malini, Shalini's pretty, younger sister in Kolkata, at a child-welfare event organized by Shalini. He was the chief guest at the event. Malini had met him there and instantly fallen in love. They had decided to get engaged and Shalini had been very supportive. Those were the happiest days for the two sisters and their single mother. Three days before their engagement dinner, Malini had jumped off from her balcony. That Kunaal had driven Malini to her suicide by abandoning her mentally and emotionally was Shalini's cross to bear.

Reeva had expected to be sad, or even depressed, after hearing about Malini. But instead, she went home, looked up her collection of to-watch DVDs and locked herself in her bedroom. That was two days ago. Now, she felt sore and stiff from lack of movement. Her eyes hurt and she felt physically weak. Instead of getting up, she found it easier to give in and stay. And finally, after almost forty eight hours, she allowed sleep to take over.

She did not know for how long she was asleep, but it felt as if it was only seconds that she heard someone calling her from a distance.

"Reeva... Reeva? Are you okay sweetheart?" Her dad touched her forehead. Reeva flinched and moaned. Slowly, his face swam into her vision and she squinted as if trying to recognize him.

"Dad?" She sounded groggy.

"Yes, sweetie. You alright?" He asked.

"Why? I was just trying to sleep." She mumbled.

"Reeva, you've slept for straight eighteen hours! It's afternoon now," he said, "You need to wake up. Your phone has been ringing constantly. Some girl called Nandita is trying to get in touch with you. She already called twice. It sounds urgent."

Reeva sat up and looked at the clock in disbelief. She took her phone from her dad's hand and scrolled through the missed calls and messages, several of them were from Kunaal too.

"All good? You need to talk about something?" He looked concerned.

"No dad, I'm fine. Just needed to rest."

"Hmmm. You watch TV for two days non-stop and then sleep for a full day. I have never seen you rest like that. Or am I missing something here?" His tone was wistful, "Anyway, it's time for you to get up."

"Yeah, I'll just freshen up." Reeva walked to her bathroom.

"Uh… Reeva, please tell me this has nothing to do with Kunaal." He looked at her, his arms folded.

Reeva turned and faced him, "No dad," she said flatly.

She wasn't yet ready to discuss Kunaal with him. He nodded and left her room. Sighing inwardly, she immediately dialled Nandita.

To her relief, Nandita answered instantly.

"Hello Reeva? Are you out of town?" Nandita's voice was a mix of excitement and uncertainty.

"No, I'm here. What happened?"

"I've been trying to reach you since yesterday. Need your help about something, urgently."

"Is everything okay Nandita? Hope nobody tried to…" and Nandita's laughter stopped Reeva mid-sentence.

"No, no. I'm fine, everything is good. Actually, I want you to help me take a decision," she said.

"Of course, tell me."

"Can you come to Sunder Nagar this evening?" asked Nandita.

Reeva hesitated only for a second before saying yes. It was still late afternoon, and she could definitely do with some fresh air and distraction in the evening. Besides, Nandita needed her. Deciding to tackle Kunaal's messages later, she chose to get ready instead.

Approaching Nandita's house, she saw a small gathering of people inside, their footwear piled up outside the door. Reeva peeked in and spotted Nandita sitting on the cot surrounded by some men and women, some of whom she recognized as locals. Opposite Nandita sat a large swarthy man clad in white. The group seemed to be in midst of sorting out a minor disagreement. Nandita's face lit up as she saw Reeva and got up to receive her.

"Bhaleraoji, this is my friend Reeva. She's helping us with the case." She addressed the man and he bobbed his head, greeting Reeva respectfully. "I'll be back in a minute." She ushered Reeva out of the room and they walked away from the crowd.

"What's happening Nandita?"

"Reeva, you've got to help me. That man, Bhalerao Kadam, is Sunder Nagar's corporator for the past two terms. The people with him are small *and* big businessmen, influential shop owners and a few activists from our local area."

"Okay… but why have they decided to hold a tea party at your house?"

"Because… they want me to stand for assembly elections as an MLA candidate," said Nandita.

"Really? Wow!" Reeva was elated but then immediately sceptical about the demands of a political career.

"I don't know, Reeva. I mean I don't know what to tell them. I don't want to associate myself with any political party and then feel obligated towards it. That's not what I've worked for. That's not what I want," sighed Nandita, and focused on a dirty, stray puppy playing nearby.

"Which party are they asking you to join?"

"Bhalerao Kadam is a long-time JBP member. Any guesses?" she smirked.

"That's another matter Nandita, but are you prepared for this? You do know that if you agree, the situation around you will change immensely,"

"I know. I've thought about it. I do have a better chance of changing the system if I'm a part of it. But you know it's not that simple. Once you become a cog in the wheel, you have to roll with it."

"Well, there's a way around it. Why not go independent?" Reeva looked at Nandita, her expression defiant.

"What?"

"Yeah, why not? You go in there and tell those people that you agree, but on one condition. You will contest as an independent candidate. I don't know about the JBP corporator, but I'm sure that everyone from Sunder Nagar would agree. They know you and your work, and they see you as the right candidate to represent them. Come on, you can do wonders." She continued, "Let's go and talk to them. Either they take up your offer or they can forget about it." Reeva sounded resolute and Nandita had to smile at her conviction.

Bhalerao Kadam stood up as the two women entered the room. Nandita took her position on the cot and Reeva leaned against the wall next to her.

"Bhaleraoji, I've decided." Nandita looked composed as she spoke, not wanting to rush in. "I thank you for your party's offer, but I cannot accept it. It would be against my principles to allow myself to be influenced by the political structure." Murmurs of protest by the Sunder Nagar representatives came thick and heavy. She raised her hand to pacify the group. "But I understand the feelings of Sunder Nagar residents and I respect their faith in me."

She paused and looked at the expectant faces in the room. "So, I'm ready to do this with your support, but I'll do it as an independent candidate." With that announcement, a little cheer went up in the air and the corporator's face fell, his recruitment attempt a failure.

Sunder Nagar's residents, who were the true stakeholders in this were elated and congratulated Nandita. Some of them were quick enough to offer her space to hold meetings and dedicated staff for campaigning. Some even started discussing the urgent matter of the election symbol, which needed to be registered with the Election Commission, right away. The group was charged up and looked committed.

Reeva knew it was too big a task to be achieved in such a limited time, but as Nandita flashed a confident smile at her, she felt hopeful. Slowly, the crowd dispersed after further meeting schedules were set and finally, they were left alone. Nandita sighed and sat on the cot pulling up her feet, "I can't believe I'm doing this!"

Just then Reeva's phone rang and her face clouded as she saw the name. This was Kunaal's fifth call since morning. He had been calling for the past three days. As she put the phone on the silent mode, it once again vibrated with a text alert. It was from him: "Leaving for Davos now. Back next week. Where are you? Call me."

Reeva hurriedly pocketed her phone, but not before Nandita had noticed that awkward manoeuvre.

"What is it Reeva? You seem distant."

Reeva smiled, "Nothing that demands the attention of a future MLA."

"How's Nihaal?" Nandita ignored her weak attempt at humour.

"He's fine, just busy." By then, Reeva's heart was so full that one more question would have brought tears to her eyes.

Sensing the risk of breaking down, she changed the subject. "How about we visit that local food joint you mentioned last time, that serves yummy pav bhaji? I'm starving."

Nandita realized that Reeva was tip-toeing around certain issues, but she let it slip, not wanting to blindly poke around Reeva's emotions.

Mane eyed Thapar sceptically. What he was suggesting was extreme and risky. But if it worked, it would mean a decent money cache for him in case of his early retirement from politics. Jaiswal and Thapar had landed up unannounced at his office for an urgent discussion. Mane had simply obliged considering his own stakes. With passing time, pressure was mounting. NPP's High Command was unflinching about the ultimatum to him. If he lost this election, he was out of the game. But Mane's political prospects seemed to fall further, even as his blood pressure rose. Especially after his wife threatened to move in with their son and his family in California.

"Oh come on, Mane sahab, it's fairly simple. Just ask your administration to change the status of Navdeep Complex land from Green Zone to Commercial. It's just paperwork." Thapar grinned.

"What's in it for you? More importantly, what's in it for me?" Mane eyed them shrewdly.

This time, Jaiswal wiped his glasses and said, "Well, first, you have nothing to lose. That land is super prime. If it goes commercial and our subsidiary company develops it into a world-class residential-cum-commercial complex, then your share in it will be fair. And you know, it's a lot of money. If you stay in power, it will be easy to further camouflage the paperwork. And if you don't, well then, you'll anyway need this money." With that closure, Jaiswal sat back.

"Hmmm... but why such interest in that particular land? There are so many other lands available for development that are easier to manage too."

"You needn't worry about it Mane sahab. That land is as good as it gets for us." Thapar was getting impatient, "Let's just say some personal scores need to be settled," he smiled as Mane raised his eyebrows.

"Okay, that's for you to figure. I'll call for the file today. Let me see what I can do. But remember, whatever game you're planning, you better play safe."

"Oh yes of course, don't worry Mane sahab. The game is simple. We get Navdeep Complex demolished because it's built on a green-zone land and once the land is open, we get the green-zone status changed to commercial for our project. All you have to do is to get that land's green status revoked and make sure our subsidiary gets to develop it."

"Once the status is changed, awarding the land to your company at half the market's price index is an easy procedure." Mane shrugged nonchalantly, "But why a subsidiary? Won't J&T Infrastructure handle the project?" he asked suspiciously.

"Oh, it's just a technical issue. Taxation and such things, you see." Thapar was quick to add and Mane nodded slowly, as he sipped his lukewarm green tea, in compensation for an unhealthy lifestyle. He then excused himself for his next meeting.

Jaiswal and Thapar climbed into the waiting Jaguar outside the chief minister's residence. Thapar sighed and sat back.

"Dindayal, what exactly are your plans about Navdeep Complex land?" asked Jaiswal tentatively, giving him a sideways glance.

"What do you think?" Thapar laughed, "Don't worry Ramcharan, don't you worry." He patted Jaiswal's knee evading his direct question. "Nothing would be done without your knowledge. After all, our children are married to each other."

Jaiswal looked out at the vast expanse of the Arabian sea as the car sailed on Marine Drive. He never questioned his partner's methods as Thapar was a better businessman. But what personal scores did he want to settle? What was his specific interest in Navdeep Complex?

"I am just waiting to witness the humiliating defeat of JBP in Maharashtra. That will be a day to celebrate," sneered Thapar.

"Yeah, we can then get the land released within time for our dream project; Galactic Studios and the country will watch us in pride."

"Huh?" Thapar looked confused. Then, recovering quickly, he said, "Oh, yes, yes. No doubt, Galactic Studios will make us proud," he added with an over-enthusiastic smile.

Jaiswal's brow creased with concern as he removed his glasses and wiped them obsessively. He was worried. He knew that smile on Thapar's face. It wasn't a genuine one.

"What about the next strike?" asked Jaiswal.

"It's scheduled for over the weekend, for maximum media reach. The more people watch, the more it will be discussed," he said. "But Vir will confirm a day before." He sounded disinterested.

"But I must admit, this guy is impressive even though he's

a solo operative." Jaiswal wanted to draw Thapar out.

"Oh, yeah he is, but even he needs our help," he said smugly.

"You mean the media presence, right?"

"Not just that. He was falling short of manpower. I sent one of my men with a special brief," Thapar winked.

"What special brief?" Jaiswal tensed.

"Nothing much. I simply asked him to make sure that the news is well worthy of national coverage, at any cost."

"What have you done Dindayal? You know Vir. He won't like it if things go wrong. Besides, we hired an outsider only because we didn't want to get our own hands dirty. Why get involved directly now?" Jaiswal's face was ashen. Thapar was taking too many risks. Their involvement, if proven, would finish them off professionally.

"Relax Ramcharan. You worry too much." Thapar casually dismissed his friend. "Remember, there's a man above Vir who is running the show. And that man knows which side his bread is buttered. Things will be handled as we want."

Jaiswal was quiet. He wanted to remind Thapar, that all they wanted was to acquire a land for Galactic Studios. But now, it was slowly turning into something else. For the first time in his long association with Thapar, both professional and personal, Ramcharan Jaiswal was worried. He was worried for his honour, his family and even his life. Galactic Studios was their dream no doubt, but not if it needed blood.

The more the technician struggled with the overhead projector, the more impatient and agitated Reeva became. It needed to be up and running soon for the team to review the media clips. She glared at the already nervous Revathy, who was responsible for such technicalities.

They were working on the quarterly review report due for submission to JBP. The PR setbacks from the previous months had not helped. The wave of negative publicity created by the slap-gate and Chief Secretary exposé had become a tsunami, damaging the JBP's PR castle.

Personally, Reeva was thankful that Kunaal was travelling and that she did not have to face him yet. The technician finally managed to fix the projector and disappeared inconspicuously.

Just then, Shalini entered the room carrying a bunch of DVDs for them to view, accompanied with a peon carrying files containing the press coverage from print media. She smiled tenderly at Reeva, placing the DVDs next to her. This was the first time Reeva had come face to face with her after they had talked about Malini. This again was not a prospect she was looking forward to, but Shalini's smile somehow eased her frayed nerves.

"Hey Reeva, I've compiled all the television clippings date wise on these DVDs. It will be easier to refer. Also got extra copies made for the client." Shalini's tone was something Reeva was not used to. She wondered if Shalini was being kind or diplomatic. Before she could respond, Mr. Sehgal entered the conference room, accompanied by Nihaal, who refused to meet Reeva's eyes. The atmosphere in the room turned brusque. Reeva was the first to speak.

"Well, we have all the data we require right now, both

positive and negative. To be honest, the scenario is bordering on bleak for JBP and us."

"Hmmm... What are the opinion polls saying? Anything hopeful there?" Mr. Sehgal had never imagined such a scenario would unfold when they signed JBP as a client. He desperately needed Kunaal to work up some magic, but he was in Davos, not expected until the end of the week.

"Nope, situation is bad. People's sentiments are hurt. They hate the idea of politicians slapping policemen. It's the worst kind of image association for JBP." Shalini shook her head in dismay and continued, "Then came the case of Chief Secretary's rule-bending to suit JBP administration. Although it was a good save by Kunaal's strategy but corruption is a word that sticks."

"So, what do you think should be the way forward?" Sehgal looked around expectantly at his team.

"In the current circumstances, all we can do is generate more news about JBP," said Nihaal finally. "Bad PR for JBP is like a dead body we need to bury. But for that we need the sand of positive news. Good news and positive PR have the power to bury any bad news," he paused, then continued, "Of course, we pray that no more dead bodies surface," Nihaal spoke calmly and everybody's head bobbed in agreement.

"That sounds like a plan. Let's get going with it. Reeva please fix up a meeting with the party's honcho. Shalini, please back it up with media-scheduling. We need to quickly list down what good PR opportunities they can provide us. From now on, even if a grass-root level JBP worker feeds a stray dog, I want it to become reported news."

As the group got busy discussing the action plan, Mr. Sehgal noticed Reeva's changed demeanour. Her passive participation in the discussion had made it obvious that she wasn't being herself.

"What's happened Reeva? You don't seem convinced with what we're discussing. If you have a different point of view, now's the time to speak up."

"Oh, nothing Mr. Sehgal, it's just that I've been feeling a bit under the weather lately. I think I'm coming down with flu." Reeva's words did not sound convincing even to her own ears. For the first time in the day, Nihaal looked at her as if trying to scrutinize her.

"If so, take the day off. You can work from home if you wish. Just don't fall sick for heaven's sake." Reeva could see that he was relying on her and felt horrible about it as a professional. Then, realization struck her. Her attraction for Kunaal, wherever it was going on a personal front, was definitely fatal for her professional work. She would eventually end up making mistakes at work. It was time to speak up.

"Mr. Sehgal..." paused Reeva, and then spoke as if pushing the words out of her in a hurry before she changed her mind, "I request you to transfer me back to my earlier position at Creative AdZone. That's possible right?" She looked hopefully at the faces around her, which registered an array of emotions from mild shock to surprise. Nihaal sat up and placed both his elbows on the table, focusing openly on Reeva. Shalini looked shocked. She started to say something but stopped. There was a moment of heavy silence round the table before Ajay Sehgal spoke.

"What? Now? In the middle of all this? I mean, what's wrong with you women?" He chuckled sarcastically and looked at both Shalini and Reeva. "One or the other of you is always wanting to quit." He shook his head, immediately regretting the comment but continued, "To answer your question Reeva, yes you know you can go back to Creative AdZone anytime you like. You are an asset for us. But this is where I need you now." Ajay tapped his index finger on the table. "So sure go back, but I would rather have you fulfil your professional obligation here before you do." He added, "But, I'll leave the final decision to you. Think it over and get back to me on this by the weekend please."

He excused himself from the table and walked out of the room. Shalini walked over to Reeva and gently touched her shoulder. Reeva looked up and Shalini slowly shook her head as if asking her to stay. As she left too, Reeva was left alone in the room with Nihaal.

After what seemed like an eternity, Reeva slowly moved to rest her forehead on the table, her hair curtaining her face and hands clenched together on her lap. Nihaal slowly got up from his chair and took the seat next to hers.

"Hey," he said.

Reeva neither looked up, nor responded. The cool surface of the table felt good against her skin.

"Hey, Reeva." He wanted to reach out and tuck her hair behind her ears, to see her face.

"Nihaal, please go away." She did not lift her head from the table.

"Why?" He had no plans of leaving her side so easily.

"Because, I want to be alone."

"Really? You want me to go away because you want to be alone? Or do you want me to go away because you *believe* you screwed up and I'm still here, as a friend?" Nihaal sat back and crossed his arms. Reeva lifted her face to look at him and slowly sat up. "Why are you still here Nihaal?" Her voice was weak.

"Because, friendships are never by accident. There's a reason why people come into your life. Sometimes, we don't realize the purpose right away, but eventually we do. So, I'm going to be here, whether you like it or not." His voice was soothing as he made a conscious effort to avoid the 'I told you so' tone.

"Nihaal I don't know..." She started, but trailed off as he cut in quickly.

"Hey, don't explain anything to me. You don't need to."

"What if I'm trapped Nihaal? What if I don't know whether the next turn will get me out of the maze or push me deeper?"

"Then go ahead and take that turn. And keep moving. You just don't give up. Trust me Reeva; you're not trapped until you yourself choose to believe so."

Reeva looked at him forlornly, as she wrestled with her emotions. To her, Nihaal represented all that was nice and good, in direct contrast to her current circumstances.

"Nihaal, I feel as if I'm in a very dark place."

"I understand. First, you have to become your own best friend Reeva and then life will be easier. Start from within. Think about yourself." He smiled ruefully. "Remember, I told you that life will always present you with many choices. You have to choose carefully because you won't get a second chance. But sometimes you have to work for the choice you made. Never give up in a hurry. You understand me?"

Reeva smiled as she understood what he was trying to tell her and she adored him for it. To Nihaal, the whole room seemed to light up with her smile. He responded with one of his own. "Besides, I am always around." He winked and Reeva's smile was fuller.

"By the way, Nandita is contesting in assembly elections for the MLA seat. That too, as an independent candidate." The sound of her own clear voice surprised her.

"Yeah, she called. She was quite upset that I didn't visit her for the meeting with Bhalerao and other residents."

"What? She called and you didn't go?" In response, Nihaal looked away uncomfortably and realization dawned on Reeva. By not coming that day, he wasn't ignoring Nandita, he was avoiding Reeva.

"Actually, I'm a bit worried, you know. Nandita is too simple for this dirty game of politics. And we're nowhere close to figuring out who was following her the other day." He said, shifting gear quickly.

"I know. Yet, when I look at her I get an impression she's a tough cookie."

"She may be tough, but she stands no chance against the political mercenaries. It could get dangerous for her. And, she has a habit of rubbing people the wrong way, especially the ones in power."

"You think she cares? She's made a battle out of her life." Reeva shook her head in exasperation.

"Yeah, that's also true. Let's look at the bright side. If she becomes an MLA then I'll be able to claim with confidence that I know at least one true, honest politician, personally." Nihaal chuckled.

"Oh, come on. Don't be sceptical. We have our share of good politicians," protested Reeva.

"You know Reeva, that's what I like about you. You're

a believer. You dream and you hope. We need more of your kind around." He was smiling again, but this time Reeva saw a light in his eyes that warmed her heart.

CHAPTER 11

Madhukar Gowli floored the accelerator of the Scorpio-XUV and grinned spitefully. His vehicle now levelled with the luxury sedan that had overtaken him just moments ago. Gowli often found reckless driving a gratifying means to express his anger. On the road, he hated every rich kid who drove an expensive car. So, it had been a blow to his ego when the young couple had overtaken his vehicle from the wrong side. As his new yet beat-up, dented car now drove parallel to the sparkling new sedan, Gowli looked sideways baring his paan stained teeth at the driver, who was a young boy, still in his teens. The boy flashed his middle finger at him, speeding up, and the girl sitting next to him giggled carelessly.

Gowli gritted his teeth as mad anger replaced malice. He sped up to level with the car once again and sharply turned the steering wheel towards it. The sedan was forced to make an abrupt right for the save, but not before it bumped sideways and continued to scrape at the concrete divider for a few yards before coming to a stop, its driver's side badly damaged.

Inside the Scorpio, Gowli sniggered as he banged his fist on the steering wheel, speeding away. The other three occupants in his car exchanged worried glances. Finally, the senior most in rank, Rajat, took charge.

"What the hell do you think you're doing?" growled Rajat.

"What did I do? I just taught that rich son of a bitch a lesson," Gowli said bitterly, spitting every word out.

"Don't be an idiot. We're lucky there were no cops around. And that nobody was filming it. Or your ugly face would be circulating on every cell phone within minutes. And don't you forget we're travelling in a JBP branded vehicle." Rajat knew that they were out on a job. His handler had been very clear about what he wanted. Nothing more and nothing less. He had no patience for mental cases like Gowli. Especially when he didn't know much about Gowli, a last-minute addition to the team. He missed his trusted regular driver.

"That's the idea. This vehicle is like a moving JBP promotion. Look at all party flags, slogans and stickers on it. It fucking feels as if I'm going to attend a JBP wedding." He pulled the window down and spat, "Nobody dare touch us. Neither police nor the traffic 'pandu', nobody I say." Gowli guffawed loudly and turned his stiff body to reach into his pocket for a handkerchief. As he wiped his greasy face, Rajat stiffened as he noticed the end of a black handle tucked into Gowli' belt. It was unmistakably a gun, probably a .32 revolver.

"You're carrying a gun?" Rajat asked sternly.

A look of confusion passed over Gowli's face before he answered. "Oh this?" he pointed at his side, "It's just a back-up. I always carry it, don't worry," he said casually.

"You stupid man! Why the hell are you carrying a gun? This is supposed to be a party vehicle carrying party workers. What if we get searched at a *nakabandi?* You know that guns can be traced back to real people. And, you think I couldn't have got a gun with me today?" Rajat was going to lash out further, but he felt a restraining hand on his shoulder, with a whisper, "Not now Rajat bhai, we're almost at the toll plaza."

Gowli glanced at Rajat, who was riding shotgun with him. "Don't get so worked up. And stop abusing me. I've already tolerated enough," he growled.

As the green flange of the toll plaza appeared at a distance, Rajat spoke in a firm low tone. "Let me do the talking. You will keep your dirty mouth shut." Gowli responded with an angry snarl. Temporarily silenced, they all concentrated on the serpentine queue of cars waiting to get out of the city.

The atmosphere in the vehicle tensed as they entered the lane of the toll booth. As their turn came, the attendant bent and peered impatiently from his iron mesh-protected cubicle at Gowli, who in turn looked at Rajat.

Rajat spoke authoritatively, "Lift the barrier now. This is a JBP party car."

The attendant looked confused for a moment and then spoke hurriedly, "Oh no, no sir. Political party cars are not exempt and only office bearers and government vehicles can pass without toll."

This time Rajat's voice was loud and stern, "I said lift the barrier. Don't waste our time."

"Sir, I cannot do that. You can speak to the supervisor, if you want," whined the skinny fellow.

"Do you want me to handle this?" smirked Gowli.

"You stay in the car." Rajat gestured at his comrades to follow, and got off the SUV. He went over to the toll booth and looked at the attendant in the eye, "Can't you see this is a party car? If you don't open the barrier now I'll kick your ass so hard, you will regret being born." He shouted over the loud honking of cars behind them. Suddenly, one of the guys with Rajat reached through the opening in the booth and grabbed the attendant's collar loudly threatening him to open the door.

This created the ruckus their group desired, as they now had the undivided attention of all motorists and others present, though in a true big-city spirit, nobody wanted to intervene.

By then, the supervisor had reached the scene ready to accost Rajat and his group. He spoke in an appeasing tone, "Sir, please ask your men to not threaten or manhandle our people. This toll plaza is under CCTV coverage. We need an identity proof declaring you as a government official for me to give you a free pass on this toll. A car decorated with party emblems and flags won't work. Or else everyone would drive around in cars decorated like this, no?" The supervisor cast a glance in Gowli's direction, seated in the driver's seat and his good-humoured chuckle died in his throat. Something evil in the bloodshot eyes of the driver made him reconsider his decision, purely out of fear. He had to let them go.

As he was about to turn towards the toll booth, he saw the driver pull something long and black out. A loud bang followed. He felt a sharp jerk in his shoulder and stumbled as if he had been bodily pushed back, all in slow motion. He touched his shoulder and felt something warm and sticky. But he couldn't see his hands as everything started to blur around him. He sank, unable to understand why his legs felt so rubbery. In a failed attempt to stay upright, he clutched on to the front of Rajat's shirt, smearing it with his own blood.

It all happened within a span of six seconds, but to those involved, it seemed like an eternity. The crowd screamed and scattered. Rajat was the first to recover as he registered some flashlights and dreaded the presence of media. He eased the bleeding supervisor on to the floor and got into the car, almost running. He knew that they had to get out of there before the shocked crowd recovered and mob mentality kicked in. Once he was inside, he screamed, "Get the hell out of here, now." It didn't take Gowli any more encouragement to drive right into the barrier, uprooting it from its stand. He did it with a mad grin on his face. As the car sped up, they sat in silence. Soon, after a few smart turns, they found themselves on a lonely stretch of road, heading out of the city.

Rajat cast a disgusted look at the front of his shirt, smeared in blood, and then silently stared ahead. All they had set out to do was rough up a few workers at the toll plaza in full public and media view, while ensuring that the 'janata' witnessed the JBP hooliganism. It was a perfect stage, set to blacken JBP's image. But, he hadn't been prepared for what had happened. Finally, he pulled out his mobile.

He spoke in a sombre tone, "There's been a problem. We have to ditch the car. It will be best if we're not seen in public for a while." He then disconnected the call and threw the phone out of the moving vehicle.

Jaiswal sat on the edge of his seat and nervously drummed his fingers on the table, while Thapar was focussed on the toll plaza's CCTV footage on television. A smile appeared on his face as he watched the grim scene. All the scenes of the scuffle – manhandling the toll booth attendant, the gun's flash from the driver's window, the supervisor collapsing and finally the vehicle escaping, were being played on loop.

Jaiswal and Thapar had locked themselves up in their conference room; all calls and meetings were to be put on hold with strict instructions to not disturb them.

Thapar's phone vibrated but he ignored it and sat back in his seat with a satisfied grin. "Who's that? Is it Vir again?" Jaiswal glanced nervously at Thapar's cell phone. Ever since the news broke, Vir had tried to contact him and Thapar both. And where Thapar had studiously avoided his calls, Jaiswal was just, plain and simple, scared to pick up the phone.

"Stop worrying about it," he shot Jaiswal an irritated look. "See what we achieved. It's bloody national news. Armed killers in JBP party van? I would like to see them explain this one," he laughed.

"But Dindayal, I wasn't aware that there will be blood on our hands. That supervisor is in the ICU and we don't know if he will survive. This has gone way out of control." He shook his head hopelessly.

"Yes, I agree. It has gone out of control, but not for us, for JBP. They're the ones who will have to explain that blood."

Just then, the door burst open and Vir walked in. He roared at the duo, "No Thapar, it's not that easy. *You* will have to explain the blood to *me* first." Vir's booming voice vibrated off the walls of the conference room. He couldn't remember when he had last been so angry. Jaiswal turned into stone, unable to move even an inch, and Thapar looked back at him defiantly. "Manek sahab, you're here? I thought we were supposed to keep our association a secret," he said coolly.

"You scheming, low-life scumbags. You are avoiding my calls? Do you really think that your pricey receptionist can stop me from walking in here and kicking your ass?" He banged his fist on the table and both Jaiswal and the flower vase on the table shivered.

"Calm down Manek sahab, we had nothing to do with this. After all, these are goons you know. Things can get out of hand in the heat of the moment." Although appearing outwardly cool, Thapar was tempted to pick up the phone and call security, but that would mean losing whatever little association they still had with their main operative. And he wasn't done with him yet.

"Shut up Thapar," roared Vir, "I've had enough of your nonsense. I've been in this game for very long. Your man fired the shot. Why the hell was he even carrying a gun? For the last time I'm telling you, that you step out of line one more time and I'll pull the plug on this project. Not only that, I'll personally ensure that you're sorry you ever met me." Vir knew he had to leave before he ended up hurting either of the two.

"No more unnecessary deviations from our plans. Remember, blood is precious. You spill it only if it's absolutely required. You understand?" he asked and both men nodded.

"And Thapar, you pray to God that the toll supervisor lives." With that parting shot, he looked directly at the CCTV camera mounted right above the conference table. Then he was gone and a lull descended on the room. Thapar and Jaiswal sat quietly, assessing the threat Vir had left in his wake.

Arunabh Roy pulled out a tissue and wiped the sweat off his face. The tissue was completely soaked and he grumbled. The news channel's set was exceedingly hot. He glared at the lights hanging from the grid above and shouted at the production guy, "Put out the fucking lights if we aren't rolling, damn it." One of the production guys ran towards the camera assistant who was setting up his equipment, and the lights were out in an instant.

Arunabh turned to the production assistant holding a cup of freshly brewed black coffee and asked in a low, cold voice, "What's this?" The assistant hesitated nervously and said, "Sir, your coffee." He asked in the same low tone, "Seriously, is this the weather for coffee?" The assistant shook his head nervously.

Arunabh roared, "Then get the hell out of here and get me a chilled diet coke!" The assistant quickly stumbled away from him, tripping on the equipment cables on the floor and spilling coffee in the process.

With TRPs of News Today skyrocketing, editor-in-chief Arunabh Roy, the blue-eyed boy of the channel got whatever he wished, just like that. People loved his fire-brand attitude and he was allowed to be irreverent on his debates and features. He often got away with grilling his subjects and panellists mercilessly, at times even rudely. He had become a self-appointed representative for both, the intellectuals and the common man.

But all this adoration came at a price. Keeping up with constant expectations was exhausting and it left him moody, irritable and egoistic. His mind worked at a superhuman pace and slow people had no right to be around him. Right then, he was pissed about the delayed schedules. He had a hot date waiting for him over dinner for which he didn't want to be late. Another setback popularity and public life brought was, that although he had a large female fan base, there was simply not enough time. He was a fairly attractive guy with a razor-sharp mind and women found him irresistible.

As he sat referring to his notes, his long-time friend and favourite cameraman, Raghu Balan, took a chair next to him. Raghu was probably the only person around the sets who could handle Roy.

"What's that ruckus outside Arunabh? I didn't know your fan base extended till JBP." Raghu chuckled, referring to the bunch of JBP workers shouting anti-Arunabh Roy slogans outside the studio. Recently, *News Today's* reporting angles had been clearly unfavourable for JBP.

"Bloody hyenas!" Arunabh was disgusted. "I've got the footage of that too. It's going on-air in my next segment. Let people know what JBP has come to."

"Yeah, but have you seen the crowd? It's huge and they're threatening to enter the set and ransack it."

"Oh, they won't dare do that," he smirked. "Remember, we have NPP in power here. Police will be here soon to round up these JBP goons," he smiled at Raghu.

"On second thoughts, aren't you planning to cover the other side of the story? I mean JBP has officially stated that the vehicle didn't belong to them. This is a serious incident and we shouldn't come to conclusions so quickly."

"Come on Raghu, I'm here to report, not to build a crime case. That's the police's job, not mine. If JBP is full of erring nincompoops then I can't help it."

"You know what Arunabh, I heard a couple of people discussing that you've been fairly lucky recently," Raghu eyed his friend intently.

"Meaning?" Arunabh shot back.

"They feel that you have a source who is supplying you with all the information beforehand. Also... that you're unfairly targeting JBP," Raghu paused to see Arunabh's reaction before asking. "Are you?"

"Wait a second, Raghu," he said, enraged by the insinuation, "I'll target anyone who is wrong. But I'll not target wrongly. There is a difference. Nobody can question me about my facts. People should know the truth at any cost," huffed Arunabh. "And yeah, as far as sources go, who doesn't have those in the world of media? What we do is actually way more than reporting now. It's investigative journalism, and it requires sources. Viewers want every interesting detail. And we have got to give it to them."

Raghu stared at his colleague and smiled. He had no reason to question Arunabh's intentions. He got up and stretched his back. "Let me get back to the camera." He started moving, then suddenly stopped and turned. "By the way, Arunabh," he paused, his eyebrows knit as if trying to remember something. "You remember I spoke to you about that cousin of mine studying at MIT? She's visiting Mumbai and is a huge fan of yours. Is it okay if I bring her in tomorrow?"

"Yeah sure, buddy. Anything for you." Arunabh laughed and then winked adding, "How old is she?" In response,

Raghu narrowed his eyes and walked away laughing.

Arunabh stared after his friend for a long time. Was it becoming that obvious? He always took pride in his objective reporting, but this time he knew there were other motives. After all, J&T had committed to invest in his channel as soon as all formalities from the information and broadcasting ministry were in place. Although J&T had made him train his gun on JBP, the party too had it coming with their casual and callous attitude towards political conduct. If they were slipping so often, then they were not taking their public image seriously.

After the toll plaza shoot-out, he had aggressively demanded resignations from key JBP office bearers on his channel. In his scheme of things, only facts mattered. He had no intention of questioning the unique circumstances under which the news always exclusively reached him first. Feeling justified in his actions, Arunabh breathed deeply and called out to the makeup assistant for a touch-up. He was ready for the camera, once again.

Kunaal pulled the thick curtains aside and peered out of his hotel room in Davos. There were at least eight to ten inches of snow on the ground. Cars parked outside were covered in white. He thought of his rented Audi and grimaced at the prospect of scraping snow off of it in the biting cold. Kunaal loved driving in Davos. The roads were mostly devoid of traffic considering the measly population of eleven thousand permanent residents. Summers were lively in this town, but in the winter months, it bore a deserted look. He had managed to get through yesterday, but had missed his jog by the lake because of the harsh cold. At least it had been sunny, up until 4pm.

Today, however, was a bleak, grey day, right from the start. And, from his heated room, he could sense the bone-chilling cold in the stillness outside. Even at half past seven in the morning, lights were on in most houses across the street. He cursed the International Commerce Council's organizers for choosing this time of the year for holding the convention. Even the lake was close to frozen. It wasn't as if Kunaal didn't like the cold weather. He loved skiing on the Alps. Just this time, he wanted to be back in India soon. He had decided to come only because he couldn't afford to miss the opportunity to network with the elite crowd of the international business and political community. He sighed, as today was his last day in Davos and tomorrow he would be back in Mumbai.

Once again, his thoughts strayed towards Reeva and he dialled her number. As expected, she didn't answer and he felt a stab of pain. He hadn't been able to get through to her since the day of the press conference, which was over a week ago. By now, he knew that she was deliberately avoiding his calls, making him even more desperate. He knew he shouldn't have abruptly walked out that day without proper explanation. But he couldn't help it. He simply wasn't used to explaining his actions. He needed to work on that. *Maybe with time*, he mused.

Pushing the distracting thoughts aside, he quickly showered and dressed in a smart, high-neck, black sweater and a tan trench coat, and finished his breakfast. Finally, not wanting to be delayed for his presentation, he picked up his leather satchel and stepped out of the hotel, and was instantly assaulted by the chill. A tiny, chubby Swiss boy, dressed in winter clothing, was struggling to build a miniature snowman. As Kunaal passed the kid, he smiled broadly at him. Impulsively, Kunaal bent down, helped the kid place the snowman's nose, speaking to him in fluent German. The boy looked delighted and Kunaal resumed his walk, somehow feeling better.

As expected, the car's roof and wind screen were laden with snow and it took Kunaal ten minutes to scrape it off, before he could get on the road. Despite the gloves, his fingers felt numb as he got into the car shivering, and turned on the heater to full blast. He made it to the Convention Hall in the city centre just in time. The parking lot was surprisingly occupied for a town that looked dormant. Just as he switched off the engine, his mobile rang. He frantically searched for the phone in his satchel hoping that it was Reeva. But it was Uttur and his voice sounded strained.

"Kunaal, there has been a serious problem."

"What's happened Mr. Uttur?" Kunaal was immediately worried. He had been fire-fighting for JBP in terms of PR just before coming to Davos. He wondered what else could have cropped up so quickly to warrant this urgent call from Uttur.

"Kunaal, you need to get here now." Uttur gave him a brief account of what had happened at the toll plaza. Finally, he added, "Kunaal, I have personally cross-checked. That car did not belong to us or any of our associates. But media is baying for our blood. Get back here soon please." He sounded frantic.

"Please wait, I'm getting back now." Kunaal assured the leader as he disconnected the call. Lost in thought, he stared ahead, slowly tapping the edge of his phone on his forehead. Then, he dialled his local travel agent. She answered promptly in her regular cheery manner, instantly recognizing his number.

"Guten morgen, Marie Ann. I need you to prepone my tickets," said Kunaal.

"Sure, Herr Kabi. But aren't you already on tomorrow evening's flight?" she replied.

"Yeah I know. But I need to board a flight today."

"Oh! Let me see what I can find for you. Please hold." The classical hold music failed to soothe Kunaal.

"Great, Herr Kabi. We have a Swissair non-stop flight to Mumbai out of Zurich airport this evening. Should I book a business class seat as usual for you?"

"Yes please," Kunaal answered hurriedly.

"Okay done. Would you need a drop to the airport or would you prefer to drive?"

"Vielen danke Marie Ann." He thanked her for her efficiency and added, "Please organize for an airport drop." Kunaal no longer wished to drive. He needed time to think. He sat there and took one long look at the Convention Hall. He then started the engine and drove out of the parking lot. It had started to snow again and large flakes the size of cotton balls kissed the windscreen.

Kunaal walked into his office briskly, looking great for someone who had just gotten off a transcontinental flight. Within eighteen hours of Uttur's call in Davos, he was already in the MVPR office. He could feel the adrenaline kicking in. During his flight, he had also decided what he was going to do about Reeva. He needed her in his life, firmly and completely. If this required rituals and legalities, so be it. There would be no more indirect suggestions or hints.

As he entered his cabin, he was surprised to see a large grey box on his desk. He opened it slowly. The sapphire brooch shined brightly, placed primly on top of the dress he had gifted Reeva.

A note lay next to it, which simply said, *Thanks, but no thanks*, in Reeva's handwriting. He sank back in his chair, enraged and frustrated at the same time. He needed to straighten things out with her once and for all. With the note in his hand, he walked resolutely to her cabin and entered without knocking. Reeva jumped in her seat.

"What is this?" he placed the note in front of her.

Reeva concentrated on her computer's screen and said coolly, "What do you think?"

"Damn it Reeva! Stop playing games and tell me what's on your mind." He forcefully turned her chair in his direction to make her look at him.

Reeva shifted in her chair looking straight at him. "That's it Kunaal. That's what you're about, isn't it? You get angry and frustrated when you don't get what you want. I don't even know who you are. Hell, I don't even know where you live," Reeva said spitefully. "And you say I'm playing games. Why don't we discuss what's on *your* mind Kunaal, like how and why Malini died?" Reeva's tirade had left her breathing heavily and her face was flush with anger.

Kunaal's face changed from indignant to shocked and deflated, as he sank into the chair opposite her. His elbows rested on his knees and his fingers entwined as he sat leaning forward. He finally rubbed his face with both hands and then said, as if addressing a third person in the room. "So this is what it's all about? Shalini talked to you, of course."

"Kunaal, it's over. I'm done with you now. Please leave," she said quietly.

Kunaal made no attempt to leave. Instead, he sat back in his chair and fished out his mobile. He then punched in a number.

"What are you doing?" Reeva protested and he held up his index finger to quieten her.

Kunaal's call was answered promptly and he spoke into the phone in a dead-pan manner. "I'm with Reeva. You need to explain my situation in reference to the Kolkata incident. Right now, please." He extended the phone towards her. Stupefied, she took the phone and stared at it as if it was an unknown object; a faint 'hello' emanating from it.

"Go on, speak," nodded Kunaal.

She slowly put the phone to her ear and spoke, "Hello."

Kunaal sat back and watched her passively. The male voice on the other end sounded decidedly authoritative and vaguely familiar to her.

"Hello Reeva. Please excuse Kunaal for putting you on this abrupt phone call. I know you're feeling uncomfortable, but if he has done it then I'm sure he has a good reason to do so." The voice was cheerful.

"Who is this, please?" Reeva asked softly.

"Oh yes, I'm sorry." The voice was instantly apologetic. "Actually, we have met before Reeva. I'm Dr. Harsh Wardhaan, from that charity event. Remember now?"

She understood why the voice had sounded familiar, as she recalled Kunaal's friend who had conducted the charity bid.

"Oh, yes." Her voice was strained.

"Reeva, I can hear distrust in your voice." Dr. Harsh's voice was devoid of any infliction. It was completely neutral.

He paused for a moment before continuing, "Yes, I'm Kunaal's friend, but first I'm his doctor."

"What do you mean?" She asked pointedly.

"I'm a psychiatrist Reeva, and Kunaal has been in my care for over ten years now. And, if you need to see my credentials then you will have to come to my office." Reeva's eyes instantly darted towards the passive Kunaal. Dr. Harsh continued after giving Reeva enough time to absorb the news. "Now, I don't know the reasons behind your distrust, but I request you to listen very carefully to what I'm about to say." Reeva could only manage to whisper "okay".

"This is his most guarded secret, so if he has chosen to tell you about it then he really trusts you," said Dr. Wardhaan. "But let me first start with the Kolkata incident. Malini, the girl to whom Kunaal was supposed to get engaged, was a manic-depressive personality. After her death, I spoke with her doctor. She had attempted to commit suicide twice, even before she met Kunaal. She couldn't handle the insecurities, which being associated with a guy like Kunaal brought to her. I mean Kunaal is handsome, rich and highly educated. How often do you find all of these qualities in one guy?" He paused and then asked, "Reeva, are you with me?"

"Yes," she said.

"Having said this, I must also add that Kunaal had all the right intentions for Malini. He wanted a life with her. But, the fear of losing him finally pushed her over the edge." He cleared his throat before continuing, "In fact, I had to put Kunaal on an alarmingly high dosage of anti-depressants after her suicide, and it took me more than a year to get him off them."

With every bit of information Dr. Wardhaan delivered, Reeva's anger and bitterness vanished, replaced by a raw tenderness. It was as if the clouds had shifted and the golden rays of sun had found their way. She cast another glance in Kunaal's direction and her heart felt full. Sitting there absolutely still, looking handsome even in a simple white shirt, Kunaal was irresistible to her. She sputtered into the phone her eyes refusing to meet Kunaal's, "Is he alright now?"

Dr. Wardhaan sighed, "Reeva, as you might know by now, Kunaal is a type A personality. He's also a victim of borderline paranoia and obsessive compulsive disorder. His is not an aggressive case, but he needs to be under constant evaluation."

"Will he be alright?" Reeva asked, her lips quivering.

"Yes, of course, with some time, patience and care. But, he needs constant monitoring." He added after a pause, "Reeva, I don't know your circumstances, but I can assure you, that whatever else he might be, Kunaal is not the bad guy."

"Thank you Dr. Wardhaan," replied Reeva.

"No worries! And I must add, Kunaal is a happier man after meeting you. Also, please remember that by telling you all this, I've effectively violated the doctor-patient confidentiality clause," he chuckled, "So you better be careful with the information I've given you. If you ever need to talk to me then feel free to call or visit. Kunaal will give you the details."

Dr. Wardhaan disconnected and Reeva sat holding the phone limply in her hand. She looked up at Kunaal, "Why didn't you tell me?" She got up and stood close to him. He looked up at her. She embraced him for the first time, feeling the silken touch of his hair between her fingers and the power of his well-toned shoulders. She swooned as Kunaal's arms tightened around her slender waist. His after-shave was heady. And then, in one swift move, Kunaal had her sitting on his lap. She gasped and the fact that they were in office made their proximity even more intoxicating.

Their faces were close, too close, their eyes locked as if in a trance. Finally, she could take it no more as blood coursed through her and she closed her eyes, leaning in towards Kunaal. She moaned, sensing the soft brush of his lips on her parted mouth, loving his minty breath mixed with desire. With primal urgency, he claimed her mouth fully, his fingers entwined deeply in her thick hair. Time existed in another dimension as they held each other, drinking passion from their lips, losing sense of their physical presence, living purely in sensations.

Finally, Kunaal reluctantly withdrew, placing feathery light kisses on her neck and throat, making her moan softly. He had withdrawn only because they were in her office. Kunaal gazed at her lovingly, holding her close until her breathing slowed. She rested her head on his shoulder, and murmured, "You know Kunaal, you mean the world to me."

He smiled and kissed the top of her head. "I've a lot to say to you, but I need to prove it to you first."

"How?" Reeva smiled, extricating herself from his lap awkwardly.

"Would you like to attend a party with me tonight?" he looked at her expectantly.

"Sure," she smiled.

"So, can I pick you up from your house at seven?" he suggested and Reeva nodded.

"Okay then. I have got to run now. Have to meet Uttur at JBP office, this aftrenoon. Need to sort out some issues," he spoke grimly. He had consciously made it a point to inform Reeva about his schedule. He needed to get used to telling her everything about himself. Reeva smiled, as she knew that Kunaal was making an effort for her sake.

She now had a thread in her hand that would help her unravel the mystery named Kunaal Kabi. But she had to set a few things straight first, both within and around her. She did not need the burden of negativity anymore, not even from Shalini.

CHAPTER 12

Rishi Uttur firmly shook his head, "No Kunaal. I'll not cut any deals with either Arunabh Roy or those creeps Jaiswal and Thapar." They were alone in the conference room.

"Please understand. I have reasons to believe that they're out to damage JBP's reputation and public image. And I don't mean cutting any real deal, only a peace-keeping treaty. Just meet them once." Kunaal said. He was aware through his sources that JBP was being deliberately targeted by a certain business faction, although he had no proof.

"You know what that would mean. I did not like those two even when they came to me regarding their Galactic Studios project. My taking a soft stand now means giving in to their demand for that piece of reserved land. You know that's not possible, Kunaal." For the first time, Uttur wasn't agreeing to Kunaal's suggestions.

"No deals and no soft stands. We can drop just a hint, to keep them off our backs till elections. And I'm speaking purely from the public relations' perspective Mr. Uttur,"

Kunaal persisted. JBP's current situation was dicey, with some or the other negative issue cropping up regularly, in last few months. He didn't wish to spend any more time cleaning up the dirty mess, as he would rather focus on constructive PR for JBP

"No, Kunaal, I'll not do it for two reasons. First, our detractors will think that they have an advantage and I'm not going to give them the satisfaction. And second, JBP doesn't resort to such low-level tactics. We have the support of the public and well-wishers. Besides, we haven't done anything wrong." Uttur smiled and leaned onto the table adding, "So, if you have any other suggestions then please tell me."

Kunaal realized that it was a lost cause and sighed.

He finally changed tack, "Alright then, this leaves us only with the fire-fighting option. I'll get my hands on the police investigation report and also have them issue a statement immediately, that there's no proof that the car or its occupants belonged to JBP. This will give us some room. We will make sure that this statement is covered in the media with equal veracity," Kunaal looked at Uttur for an approval.

"Yeah, sounds good I think." Uttur nodded and then added as an afterthought, "Uh... Kunaal, how do you intend to get that statement from the police while the investigation is still on?" he narrowed his eyes.

Kunaal played with his sunglasses before answering, without looking at Uttur. "Let's just leave that to me. Like you said, we haven't done anything wrong, have we?" He smiled at Uttur.

Uttur nodded slowly and asked, "By the way Kunaal, how's Reeva?" Kunaal looked at him, mildly surprised. "She's fine, busy working on the strategy to enhance JBP's positive coverage."

"Hmm... what's happening with you two? Are you together now?" The politician hadn't failed to notice the sudden and subtle change in Kunaal's demeanour as he heard Reeva's name.

Kunaal looked at Uttur quizzically before answering, "Yes, we're together. Come to think of it, that status actually applies as of today." Kunaal's face flushed.

"Congratulations! I'm happy for both of you. So, when are you making it official?" he asked cheerfully, extending his hand towards Kunaal.

"I'm not sure." He was still getting used to the news himself.

"Hmm... you must do that quickly then. Girls like her come along once in a while, Kunaal. She's a gem. Don't let this one get away," smiled Uttur.

By the time he wound up at JBP's office, it was late afternoon. He needed an hour's sleep before the evening began. He had been up on sheer adrenaline for close to twenty four hours and he was not going to last much longer. That evening was a special one, since it was his first proper date with Reeva. Strangely, he found himself excited and nervous too. He shook his head disdainfully. No woman had ever had this effect on him before.

As the clock's hands neared the deadline, Reeva's anxiety rose a notch. Kunaal had promised to pick her up at seven. She glanced at her phone casually, checking for any notifications. She was dressed in a black shirt dress and suede shoes, knowing that it wasn't a formal event.

Precisely at seven, the doorbell rang. She tossed aside the magazine that she was reading, and opened the door. Kunaal wore a dark blue, fitted shirt and a smart jacket. He was holding exquisite white orchids and Godiva chocolates. Reeva stared at him and he laughed, "What? Am I not allowed in your house?" He asked cheekily.

She apologized and moved aside for him. Mrs. Rai entered the hall, and was happily surprised to see Kunaal walk past Reeva and handover the bouquet and chocolates to her, "Hello Mrs. Rai, these are for you."

Mrs. Rai gushed, "Thank you Kunaal, please sit. What would you like to have, something to drink?"

He replied, "Mrs. Rai, all I need is your permission to take your daughter out this evening." She looked nonplussed and then said hurriedly, "Of course, I know she will be safe with you. Reeva's dad is unfortunately not home. He would have loved to meet you." She smiled at Reeva.

Kunaal turned towards Reeva and asked, "Shall we leave?" She nodded.

As soon as they were in the lift, his fingers wrapped around hers. "Don't look at me like that. Couldn't pass the romantic opportunity to ask for your parent's permission to take you out," he smiled.

Soon they were in the car, driving towards a plush Juhu locality. Finally, they turned into a quiet lane off the busy road, and stopped before a tall gate. The gatekeeper immediately opened it as Kunaal honked. Seeing Kunaal, he saluted crisply with a smile.

Reeva asked him curiously, "Whose party is this, one of your friends?"

Kunaal smiled enigmatically at her, "This party is in honour of someone special. You will know." He held her hand and led her towards the house. Reeva could hear music. It appeared that the party was well underway.

As they entered, Reeva was amazed to see a crowd of close to forty people, with butler service. There was a DJ console at the end of the hall. The lights were dim and the soft music set a relaxed mood for the evening. Seeing Kunaal, the crowd turned and cheered him. Then Reeva's eyes stopped at a life-sized black and white portrait of him on a wall. She turned towards him in surprise, and he smiled, "Welcome home." He softly kissed her hand.

The rounds of introductions began. Reeva realized that everyone close to Kunaal was present. They stopped by Dr. Harsh Wardhaan, who was engrossed in an animated discussion with a group. Seeing them, he excused himself.

He hugged Kunaal tightly. "Congratulations, my dear friend, for finding yourself such a wonderful woman. Reeva, my dear!" He exclaimed, "Good to meet you again in person." He hugged her too. Reeva was relieved that there was no residual awkwardness from their previous conversation. They chatted for a while and then Kunaal held her hand signalling at her to come with him. "Let me show you the house," he said, handing her a glass of white wine.

The house was a sprawling two-storey, seven-bedroom bungalow, done up in an antique Victorian look. The glitzy glamour of his mother's apartment was absent and the colours were muted and earthy. The chandeliers too were missing, replaced instead by cosy ambient lighting, giving the place more character. Reeva instantly loved the house, convinced that Kunaal and she had very similar tastes in décor. They returned to the party and refilled their wine glasses.

Reeva whispered, "Kunaal, I love your house." Pulling her closer Kunaal corrected her firmly, "Our house." Then he whispered, "You haven't seen the best part yet, come." He led her towards a large door at the end of the hall. Kunaal stepped up and opened the door for her, and she was instantly mesmerized by the view as the sea breeze blew at her hair. The inconspicuous door had opened up into a mid-sized garden and at the far end of the lawn was a small, ornate, wrought-iron gate leading to the beach.

"Come." He removed his shoes and folded up his jeans. On a cue, Reeva too removed her shoes. Picking up their glasses, they walked across the grass patch to the gate, Reeva loving the feel of soft grass on her soles.

The beach, although a common one, was quiet, apart from occasional strollers. The moon and the tide were both high. They walked towards the crashing waves in the moonlight. Reeva leaned onto Kunaal as he held her protectively.

They settled on a small sand dune and sipped their wine.

Reeva turned towards him consciously, as she sesnsed Kunaal gazing at her intensely, "What?"

He looked at her for a long time and then bent over to kiss her on the lips, without bodily touching her. It was teasingly erotic. He then spoke, "Reeva, do you know what time can do to us?"

She shook her head.

"It can change us."

Suddenly, he took the wine glass out of her hand and balanced it next to him in the sand, careful not to spill it.

He said to her, "Reeva, could you close your eyes and hold

out your hands for me." She smiled playfully and cupped her hands before him, her eyes closed. He placed a handful of sand in her cupped hands and asked, "What do you think is going to happen?"

Reeva opened her eyes and looked at him, "It's sand Kunaal! It's going to slip out of my hands soon."

"Consider this sand as time, slipping away." He looked at her with soulful eyes.

Reeva looked at her hands. As the last remnants of the sand slipped away, something glittered in her palm. It was a large diamond shimmering under the moonlight. She looked at Kunaal, astonished, but he said, "This is my promise to you, Reeva. While time may slip away, my love will always be there for you. Now and forever." He picked up the ring from her palm and slipped in it on her finger. Reeva was speechless with emotions. She felt the tears escape her eyes but Kunaal softly kissed them away. She murmured his name repeatedly, leaning into his arms.

They kissed intensely, as Reeva sobbed, tasting her own tears on Kunaal's mouth. She felt pure and blessed. At that moment, she believed that she could die for him.

Nandita rubbed her tired eyes and closed the manuscript of the children's book she was editing. Like many of her additional ventures, this too was charitable in nature, but not any less demanding. The publisher had called last evening to politely remind her of the deadline. Often, Nandita felt that she had a tendency to take on more than she could handle. After a long day of campaign work, she had arrived home tired and had started editing with just a quick tea break.

Finally, done for the day, Nandita stretched, feeling the stiffness in her neck. She glanced at the clock, it was half past eight in the evening, and she realized belatedly that the gnawing headache she had for the past half an hour was her body telling her that she was hungry.

She opened the fridge doubting that there would be anything edible. As expected, there was nothing in there apart from some tomatoes and other vegetables. She was too tired to cook and sorely missed her mother's meals. Her mind played the memories like a film reel, the way she would call out to her every evening, "Nimmi, food is ready." She could almost smell her *khichri*. Suddenly, the jarring sound of a passing truck brought her back to the present.

Pushing back the memories, she was relieved to see some leftover bread from yesterday on the shelf, along with an old bottle of jam and some butter. She switched on the television and watched the news distractedly as she prepared the cold sandwiches.

She took a large bite of the sandwich when her mobile rang. She swallowed quickly, and wiped her mouth with the back of her hand. She made a face as the call was disconnected as soon as she answered.

As she was about to take another bite, the phone rang again. This time, she kept the plate aside and frowned at the screen. The same number was calling. She got up to turn down the sound of television and answered the phone, "Hello, who is this?" For a moment, there was no answer, but then Nandita's ear picked up a faint rhythmic breathing; there was somebody on the other end.

Losing her patience, Nandita asked again, "Who is

calling?"

"Nandita madam?" A gruff voice finally asked. Wherever the call was being made from, it was a dead silent place. Nandita caught nothing in the background apart from the male voice. Even though the voice had referred to her as madam, she knew with certainity that there had been no respect in the address.

"Yes," she answered.

"What madam? This doesn't suit you. Running around government offices and asking questions. Young ladies like you should be careful. Anything bad can happen." He was mocking her.

A chill ran through Nandita's body. "What do you mean?" She asked firmly, gambling on her instincts that this was a mere warning of what would come next.

"Madam, don't talk too much. Or we will break your legs. Maybe do something worse."

Nandita shivered as the voice continued, "You better stay in your limits, Nandita madam. Don't act smart. Or we have many ways to fix women like you." The voice chuckled lewdly and then the line went dead.

Nandita sat still, feeling violated and sullied. Even though it was just a voice talking over the phone, the impact was almost physical. She was gripped with fear and helplessness, struggling to hold back the tears welling up in her eyes.

After a few minutes, she gathered enough courage to dial Reeva's number, but her call went unanswered as the phone kept ringing. She tried several times, unsuccessfully, before dialling Nihaal. He answered on the second ring sounding a bit alarmed.

"Nandita? Is everything okay?"

"No Nihaal, not really." Her voice quivered, "Are you busy?"

"No, just making dinner. What happened?" he answered quickly.

"Can you come over to my house please, now?" She was almost on the verge of a breakdown.

He paused for a beat before answering. "Yeah, sure, but please tell me Nandita, what has happened?"

Nandita sobbed as she told Nihaal about the call verbatim. He listened to her quietly and then asked, "How far is Sunder Nagar Police Station from your house?"

"About ten minutes by auto. You think I should go there now?" she asked eagerly.

"No Nandita. You stay home and lock the door from inside. I'm reaching there soon. Call your neighbours and ask them to come over now. We will go to the police station together. We need to report this immediately. Maybe they can track the caller. As a future election candidate, they will have to take you seriously, even provide security." He spoke hurriedly, shutting the gas stove and covering the pan of stir fried vegetables. He wasn't sure if the police would help Nandita, but he wanted to take the right steps for her.

"I don't believe this," Reeva looked at Nihaal, uneasily. When Reeva had finally returned Nandita's call on Sunday morning, she had been evasive and casual about the whole thing, giving Reeva only skeletal details. Nandita almost dismissed it as a prank call just to make Reeva feel better about not responding to her that night. Only after Nihaal gave her the complete details, she fully comprehended the sinister nature of the event.

"You should have called me Nihaal, however late it was." It pained her that while she was busy with Kunaal, Nandita had been facing a nerve-wrecking situation.

"It's alright Reeva, don't beat yourself up. The situation was handled alright." Nihaal tried to placate her.

"I promised her that I would be by her side." Reeva looked regretful.

"And who says you're not?"

"What did the police say?"

"They have registered a non-cognizable offence report, as no arrests can be made without a court order in a case like this. The only proof that the call was made to Nandita, is the incoming number on her phone's call log at precisely 8:45pm for thirty five seconds. The caller's phone has been switched off since, so tracking is not an option." He paused and then added as he remembered another piece of information, "And yes, they're verifying the address given by the network provider, but my hunch is that the address will be bogus."

"So are you saying we're back to square one?"

"Yes, she's possibly in danger, but only till the election campaigns begin. Then she will be too much in the public eye to be targeted so easily. Besides, this call was obviously to warn her about the Navdeep Complex case."

"Nihaal, you know she will never let go that case. In fact, I now fear that she will double her efforts to unearth the truth," Reeva shook her head hopelessly.

"Yes. Looks as if Navdeep Complex is a dirty deal between the construction industry and politicians. And she could get in serious trouble, if she continues." Nihaal didn't have the heart to ask Nandita to abandon her crusade. It would be against all her principles. If she compromised, she wouldn't be the same person. Just when he was beginning to sense a dead end, an idea struck him.

"What the heck!" He exclaimed, "We're in media and public relations. It should have come to us earlier." He sounded excited.

Reeva looked at him questioningly, "Care to explain?"

"Actually, if we get some of the media to cover Nandita's statement that she's being threatened then it will work like a safety net for her. Then, if anything happens to her it will become a matter of public scrutiny. Nobody will dare touch her then," Nihaal beamed.

"Yeah, you're right. Especially now that she's a candidate for assembly elections."

"I think we need to discuss this with Shalini. But I didn't see her around in office today," said Nihaal.

"Let me check." Reeva dialled the reception and asked to be put through to her, but was promptly informed that she had called in sick.

"I think it's time for me to talk to Shalini. And if she's not here, then I'll go wherever she is."

Nihaal looked at her strangely, aware of the rocky relationship between the two women. Reeva picked up her purse and then paused to turn towards Nihaal. "Maybe this visit will fix things, for Nandita," she paused, "And maybe for Shalini and me too."

Nihaal nodded. If Reeva wanted to end her on-going battle with Shalini, then it was a good thing.

As she left, Nihaal was left alone in Reeva's office. He got up and noticed a collage on her desk. In one of the many small frames, a much younger Reeva was laughing carelessly, throwing back her hair. He knew he would do anything to see her laugh like that again. Today, although he hadn't failed to notice the big diamond on Reeva's ring finger, he had decided to wait until Reeva chose to speak about it. He exited her cabin, shutting the door quietly behind him.

Reeva parked her car under the shady copper-pod tree, and looked up at the sturdy and charming three-storeyed building. Shalini's apartment was on the top floor and it was obvious that the vintage-looking building had no elevators. Reeva climbed the three floors with a food parcel she had brought along, and was slightly out of breath when she rang the bell. There was no answer. She was questioning her decision to arrive unannounced when the door opened. Shalini stared at Reeva, adjusting a light flannel jacket she had hurriedly pulled over her casual, knee-length housedress. Reeva smiled, noticing that Shalini looked prettier and remarkably younger with her hair tied in a topknot.

"Reeva? Come on in," Shalini finally smiled warmly. Her puffy eyes and nasal voice indicated severe cold and flu.

Reeva entered the cosy house that held a distinct ethnic touch with Bengali music, art and literature, in abundance. Most of the furniture pieces were wooden, and very well preserved reminders of the nineteenth century.

"How are you feeling now Shalini? I heard you called in sick."

"I'm alright. Every now and then this unpredictable weather brings me down."

"Oh, are you taking anything for it?" asked Reeva, placing the food packet on the dining table.

"Just some Ayurvedic stuff and Vitamin C," she laughed and then looked at the parcel, "What's that?"

"Chicken soup and sandwiches, thought it would be good for you. Should I heat them up?" asked Reeva enthusiastically.

"No, it's alright Reeva, maybe later. Thanks," replied Shalini hesitantly.

"Don't tell me!" She exclaimed, "You're a vegetarian." Reeva smacked her forehead and both women burst out laughing.

"I'm sorry for my assuming just because you're a Bengali."

"It's okay, I understand. I'm a vegetarian by choice. Anyway, what will you have, some tea?" Shalini offered as they walked into the kitchen. She turned the kettle on and asked, "So Reeva, what brings you here today? I'm supposed to join back tomorrow. What couldn't wait till then?"

"Shalini, actually Nihaal and I are trying to help out a social worker, who is also an election candidate. But now, she seems to have gotten into some trouble." Reeva narrated Nandita's entire story, from Navdeep Complex to her being followed, and from deciding to contest in the elections as an independent candidate to receiving a threatening phone call. Shalini listened in rapt attention, not interrupting even once.

"Bloody hyenas!" bellowed Shalini, "They think they can scare a lone woman into submission with threats? Don't worry I'll immediately line up a few interviews for her. Let her story come out in public." Shalini's confident assurance gave Reeva a sense of triumph.

As they sipped their teas in companionable silence, Reeva

eyed Shalini surreptitiously, thinking how to broach the subject that had been nagging her all this while. Just then, casually turning to place her teacup in the sink, she said, "You want to talk about Kunaal, right? And yes, I do know that you two are together now." She faced Reeva and smiled ruefully.

"How did you know?" asked Reeva.

"That," she pointed at the diamond on Reeva's finger, "And, a common friend who attended Kunaal's party on Saturday. The rest of it – your face told me." Shalini's lips were pursed and she didn't say anymore, facing Reeva squarely.

"Actually Shalini, I don't know what to say." Reeva's face was full of chagrin. Shalini's direct and open approach had left her flustered. "I'm really sorry about your sister. And, I can understand your anger. But I spoke to Kunaal's family doctor." She blurted out the words.

"And of course, he convinced you that Malini was a manic depressive with suicidal tendencies and that Kunaal too was depressed afterwards," Shalini sighed bitterly. She sounded cold but in control. Reeva wanted to defend Kunaal, but something in Shalini's face told her that this wasn't the time or place.

"You know Reeva, these are just hard technicalities. But only the heart can sense the real truth beneath the facade. I've sensed that pain in Malini." Shalini turned away, and after a brief pause, she spoke again, "And I know that somehow Kunaal was the cause of that pain. He can have that effect on people, even though he may not know it himself. He's like a dark shadow and nothing can grow beneath its coldness." Shalini shivered, as she pulled the flannel jacket closer around her body.

"And you know why I hated the idea of Kunaal and you together?" She moved towards an old antique drawer nearby, pulled a snapshot out of it and handed it over to Reeva, "This is why." She spoke with finality.

Reeva's heart skipped a beat as she looked at Malini's photograph. She was standing on the edge of a stone boulder looking down at the person who had clicked the photo. She was smiling, but her eyes weren't. From the picture, it was apparent that Reeva and Malini shared the same height, body structure, skin colour and even hair. Their facial features were remarkably similar and the only marked difference was in their eyes. While Malini's wide eyes were dark, deep and brooding, Reeva's were light, almond-shaped and lively.

As Reeva looked at her with an incredulous expression, Shalini spoke bitterly, "Yes Reeva, now you know. In you, I always saw my younger sister, right from the day when you walked into my office. I couldn't bear the fact that you were so warmly alive, while my little sister was cold and dead." Shalini wiped away a tear. "But I'm not willing to lose one more beautiful soul like my sister to darkness. I'll fight this time. And remember Reeva, if Kunaal hurts even a strand of hair on your head, he will have me to answer to."

Before coming to Shalini's house, Reeva had expected arguments, accusations and drama, but Shalini's cool acceptance and the revelations about her sister had changed their equation completely. Then suddenly, an onslaught of deep emotions wrecked Reeva's composure. On an impulse, she hugged Shalini, as finally the thick layer of misunderstanding and animosity thawed away.

Reeva finally understood Shalini's hostility and recognized her love. She knew it would take time for Shalini to come around, but with little patience and work she could help her let go of the bitterness within. Reeva wasn't going to let this flame of hatred burn in Shalini. She had to extinguish it for the sake of her man, and also for her own catharsis.

The dining area of the Jaiswal residence overflowed with happy, glowing people. They were immediate family members of the Jaiswal and Thapar clan. Women chatted and laughed in groups, while the men discussed an on-going cricket match. The youngsters, having formed their own little group, made hushed plans about which nightclub to hit post dinner. After all, it was Dussera and a celebration was in order.

Jaiswal contently gazed at his guests. His daughter-in-law looked radiant by his son's side. She was expecting her first child soon, rendering this year's Dussera celebrations very special.

Jaiswal sipped his martini and turned towards Thapar, "Don't they all look so happy? It's perfect."

They were seated on the terrace that extended from the dining hall, separated by a glass partition. It had been converted into a rainforest style garden with charming sitting areas.

"Yes Jaiswal, after all, this Dussera is special. We have received such good news!" Thapar's face was joyous with pride, "Can't believe we're going to be grandparents. How time flies." Thapar smiled, and Jaiswal thought he saw a glimpse of his lost friend in those brief moments. Just then, Thapar's phone rang and his expression changed instantly.

"Hello Maneji, happy Dussera." Thapar wished Mane with an artificially concocted enthusiasm, while sending a meaningful glance at Jaiswal, who was immediately attentive, placing his martini on the table. They both knew Mane wasn't calling to exchange pleasantries.

"By the way, the Navdeep Complex issue has been managed. I've gotten the file cleared from the town planning department with a new commercial-cum-residential status. But of course, we can announce it only after the demolition of the complex." Mane's tone was casually confident, "Once it is cleared for development, the ball is in your court."

"That's great news," Thapar beamed, "But, what about the residents? They need to leave first. Will they vacate the premises easily?" He asked in a tone that challenged Mane's authority.

"Oh, you don't worry about that. The evacuation order based upon the complex being a 'green-zone' land is already underway. They will receive it sometime next week. They will have to vacate in forty five days' time."

"Uh… by the way Maneji, there's this social activist living in Sunder Nagar who is supporting the complex's residents. I heard she's also intending to stand for assembly elections as an independent candidate. I hope she won't be a problem."

"Oh yeah, I know that girl. She was offered a seat by JBP and she refused. But Thapar sahab, we can't keep worrying about such youngsters that are still wet behind the ears. We can't run our politics like that," he laughed.

"Good then. I'm happy that it's all working out. I'll wait for your instructions about the bidding process then." As the call was disconnected, Jaiswal stared at Thapar.

"But Dindayal, we have no room in our planned budgets

to take up any new projects even in the next financial year, forget this year." Jaiswal looked confused.

"Don't worry. We're not taking up any new projects. That's just to dangle a carrot before Mane." Thapar casually tossed an almond in his mouth and washed it down with a gulp of vodka.

"And why are you so against Navdeep Complex and how do you know so much about it?"

"You know Ramcharan; I've played long enough with gloves on. Soon these will be coming off. I don't believe in leaving any score unsettled. I have a plan that will hit JBP real hard. Just wait and watch." Thapar's tone stripped the surroundings off its positive vibes completely.

"I must speak with Arunabh now," he said dialling a number.

"What? Now? Can it not wait for later?"

"No Ramcharan. Arunabh has to start working out the details now."

Jaiswal downed his martini, sensing that the situation would get out of his hands, very quickly.

Vir frantically searched for change in his pocket, while balancing the box of hot pizza in his other hand, as the delivery boy impatiently tapped his foot. Unable to find the exact amount, Vir handed the boy two ₹500 notes and asked him to keep the change. He shut the door hurriedly without acknowledging the boy's thankful smile and placed the box smelling of cheese, herbs and fresh bread, on the table.

The house-maid was on a three-day leave and the place

was already beginning to look like a typical bachelor pad. Prioritizing was in his blood, and food took precedence over cleaning. Cooking, however, was beyond him. He cleared up enough space on the dining table to sit down and eat. He could never eat on the couch or in bed.

He sat there munching and various thoughts flooded his mind. Lately, his instincts about the case had been on a high alert. Something wasn't right and it went beyond Thapar's cocky attitude, which could be easily attributed to him being an arrogant prick. The shootout at toll plaza had confirmed his nagging fears about this particular client. They were out to meddle in the case with their own set of sociopathic operatives. His sources had confirmed, beyond doubt, Thapar's sudden interest in Navdeep Complex and also the independent candidate Nandita Sahay.

He finished off the last piece of pizza, closed the box and left it on the table. Then he settled down on the couch with the remote control and his mobile phone. Switching on the TV on mute, he waited for the scheduled call. The phone rang at the designated time.

"Is the toll plaza case under control now?"

"My team is underground until things cool down. The vehicle has already been pulled apart and disposed. JBP has had the police make a statement that neither the vehicle nor the people belonged to them. But media and public opinion is still divided."

"So apart from the guy who got shot, this hit was a success?"

"I would not call it a success, simply because we couldn't stick to the plan and we didn't achieve the specified objective. By completely disappearing from the scene, we gave JBP an option of plausible deniability. Besides, the guy who was shot is still in a hospital bed, partially paralyzed with no recovery span specified by the doctors. Our client double-crossed us using his own asset and it led to the near-death injury of an innocent person. I feel this was a failed mission." For the first time, he had spoken for so long to the Fixer. He had deliberately left out the details about his visit to the client's office and the threats he had made. Few things he preferred to handle on his own accord.

"Do you have any suggestions?"

"I suggest we halt all future activities on this case for the time being, until I'm able to investigate a bit more into our client. There's some information I have in hand and I need to look into it before we proceed."

There was a pause on the other end and Vir waited patiently. For the first time they had decided to pause their actions midway during a project. And that's because they had blood on their hands. Until now, they had only operated in white crimes, which included manipulating people and papers, although at the highest of levels, sometimes even internationally. But blood was never involved and the Fixer had never suggested that even in the past.

"Alright, we put things on hold for now until you arrive at a conclusion. But remember, elections are not very far. We need results as we had committed to our client." His voice was calm and decisive.

Satisfied with the outcome of the call, Vir walked to the kitchen cabinet and popped two antacid tablets to fight the heartburn his dinner was giving him. He drank a glass of cold water and felt the minty chill flush his insides. His mind was already making notes on the possible angles he needed to investigate, with both Navdeep Complex and Nandita Sahay topping that list.

Kunaal brought his SUV to a smooth halt in the driveway of a SoBo hotel and glanced at Reeva. "You look stunning," he smiled. Getting out, he walked over to her side and opened the door before any attendant could. He held her hand as she stepped out. She wore a black, fitted, off-shoulder, knee-length dress. She had tied her hair up in a loose knot that highlighted her face and collar bones. With a delicate silver neckpiece and a clutch, she looked demure and sophisticated at the same time. Kunaal's eyes did not leave her even once as they walked through the doors, and he absent-mindedly nodded in response to the durban's greetings.

They sat in the most exclusive French restaurant of the city. Although Reeva had initially resisted the idea of having a formal, stuffy dinner, she was enjoying the limelight of being next to Kunaal. He treated her like a princess, and she knew that if she was going to share a life with him, then she might as well get used to it.

The maître de walked towards them with an exclusive wine list. Selecting a crisp Chardonnay of Friuli, he left the choice of appetizers to the chef.

Kunaal then focused on Reeva with an indulgent smile, "How are you feeling?"

"On top of the world," she gushed, allowing herself a small, excited giggle.

"Good. I do intend to keep you there. So, you better enjoy." He tasted the wine with a small sip and nodded to the maître de, who then happily poured the golden wine into their glasses. Finally, Reeva couldn't resist asking, "So, what are we celebrating?"

"Hmm... maybe life?" He eyed her thoughtfully. "But if you consider this a celebration, then you have no idea about my plans for you. But that's for later, when we're alone." A lop-sided smile played on his lips.

Reeva flushed at the innuendo and under his steady gaze, colour rose to her cheeks. Kunaal's hand cupped hers on the table and stayed there, sending a rush of sensations through her.

"Reeva..." suddenly his demeanour was serious, "I just need to wind up a few things in hand and then I want to go away with you for a long, long time. Some place far away... where no one will be able to reach us." He pointed his thumb at his phone and tablet.

"You intend to abduct me?" With the first glass of wine already taking effect, Reeva was not ready to get serious.

"That's an option I'm willing to consider if you refuse to come as my lawfully wedded wife." He sat back and looked at her, his body language relaxed. Reeva smiled nervously, loving the sound of being lawfully wedded to the incredibly gorgeous man sitting before her. As the maître de placed the appetizers on the table, Kunaal focused on Reeva again.

"I'm serious Reeva. I think we should get married soon."

"For a proposal, that's pretty unromantic by your standards," she smiled.

"Would you want me to go down on my knees?" He asked earnestly and Reeva looked around panicking. He sounded serious.

"No Kunaal," she hushed him. "You know that I can't

imagine my life without you."

"Good then, that's settled. How does the early summer sound to you, about six months from now? That should give you enough time to plan things. Please choose the best wedding planner and let me know," he said coolly. Reeva nodded shyly and although she hadn't expected to have this conversation so soon, she was thrilled.

Their wedding schedule was set with such casual ease that she almost could not believe it. She figured she needed Kinsy's frenzied screams and her mom's barrage of questions to actually bring home the reality.

"Good thing you agreed. I would have had a hard time waiting any longer. If work schedules permitted I would rather have us married tomorrow." He smiled and Reeva thought about how cute he looked. Kunaal ordered a second bottle of wine, this time a red Merlot to go with their main course. Reeva selected the pink Norwegian salmon and Kunaal asked for slow cooked duck breast.

"Uh... Kunaal," Reeva started hesitatingly, "You remember that Navdeep Complex case I mentioned some time back?"

"Mmm... Oh yeah, I do remember. Sorry, with all the travelling and problems with JBP cropping up, I couldn't really look into it. What about it?"

"Actually, a social activist representing Navdeep complex has received a serious threatening call, to discourage her from helping the residents. Her name is Nandita Sahay and she's also a candidate for the assembly elections. More importantly, she's a friend."

"Oh! A threatening call? Which political party does she represent?"

"She's an independent candidate. JBP offered her a ticket but she refused."

"That explains it. To survive in this world, especially politics, one either needs to have riches or a strong backing. Looks as if your friend didn't have the first and refused the second," he shook his head, "You should advise your friend to be sensible and stay out of the mess. JBP is a strong contender to form the government in the next term. In my opinion, she should accept JBP's offer."

"No Kunaal, she's my friend. I can't advise her against her principles. And your life choices can't be based on compromises." The wine's effect had emboldened and impassioned Reeva. Surprised by her intensity, Kunaal sat back and raised his brows.

"But of course, she's your friend. That's cute," he smiled and then added with a sigh, "What do you want me to do?"

"If you could please look into this Navdeep Complex and find out the benefitting parties, in case the complex is felled. I'm absolutely sure that some people want to profiteer by demolishing it, as the structure itself is sound and sturdy and can last another decade without maintenance. Nihaal's architect friend too has confirmed this."

Kunaal's face darkened for a moment at the mention of Nihaal's name, but he chose to stay quiet. Finally, he said, "Okay, I'll look into it and there's a good chance your suspicion will be proven right. But then what? You do know how big and strong the construction lobby is. There's no way your friend can fight and win this battle. And, she definitely can't do it by herself."

"We'll cross that bridge when we come to it." Reeva was determined.

"We? You two are already a team?" He looked at her questioningly. "Reeva, you better be careful in getting involved. These are murky affairs and you're very important to me." His brow was creased. Just then, the pianist started playing soothing renditions of classic love songs and they were served their desserts, a Kahlua mousse for Reeva and Calypso coffee for Kunaal. The mood lightened and Reeva smiled up at him.

"Where to now?" she asked suggestively.

"Much as I would love to take you home with me right now, I wouldn't be able to face your mom next morning, if I did that," he winked, smiling boyishly. "So, we will drive around for some time and then I'll drop you home. But I'll try to make the best use of the drive." He smiled and Reeva giggled. Right in that moment, she wanted to be cosily ensconced with him, in the warm intimacy of the car.

CHAPTER 13

Since morning, a motley group of Sunder Nagar residents had gathered outside Nandita's house. Their mood was sombre, as they stood huddled and spoke in hushed tones. They were immediately alert as she emerged from her house, accompanied by Reeva, Nihaal, and a lawyer.

Nandita's face was shadowed by worry as she faced the crowd. She cleared her throat and said, in a firm voice, "Friends, we have discussed this notice with our lawyer Satishji." She waved the notice and looked at the aging lawyer.

"As we understand, this is the final evacuation notice issued by the municipal corporation to Navdeep Complex, asking the residents to vacate their homes and hand over the keys to the ward office within forty five days." Nandita delivered the news rather flatly, not wanting to alarm them. Right now, they needed logical thinking, not chaos. But as she had anticipated, the reaction was sharp. Everyone in the group started talking, while some even protested, resulting in a cacophony of mixed voices.

Finally, Nihaal stepped up and calmed down the crowd. "Please be quiet and listen to what Nanditaji has to say. All your questions will be answered." He looked at Nandita and backed off.

She smiled thankfully and resumed, "There are two aspects however which are in our favour, first that the Municipal Corporation cannot send us a final evacuation notice before prior written intimation. And second, if we don't wish to leave our homes then we can appeal to the High Court and eventually to the Supreme Court, to stay or cancel the order. We can even write to the prime minister." Nandita was heartened to see some hope returning to the faces around her and she continued with a renewed vigour as a chorus of support went up.

"Before the deadline of forty five days, we'll also receive a response on our RTI filed for the status of this land. Once we know the real motives behind the plan to demolish this complex, our case will be stronger. Don't worry friends. Nobody can take your homes away from you. We will fight this together." The crowd cheered loudly. After a few more clarifications, the group disbanded with plans to meet soon.

Finally, Nandita was alone with Reeva and Nihaal, happy to see their old comfortable camaraderie back. She asked tentatively, "What do you think? Was it alright to give them such hope, when I myself am not sure about anything?"

"Don't worry Nandita; you only gave them the facts. What happens here onwards is something nobody can predict," Nihaal assured her with a smile.

"Besides our case is not as weak as it seems," Reeva touched Nandita's shoulder.

"By the way, don't forget that Shalini is already on the job. Few media executives will be in touch with you regarding the threat you received. Just keep the police station's NC report copy, mobile bill and call-log's screenshot handy to show them. Rest of the story, they will fill in," Nihaal reminded Nandita.

As Reeva left with Nihaal promising to catch up soon, Nandita slumped on the cot and the fear of having promised more than she could deliver, gripped her again. Even for Nandita, who thrived on battles for justice, this was a heavy payload.

Her phone rang, jolting her out of the deep thoughts. Nandita checked the screen and saw an unidentified number. Unknown numbers made her nervous now. Finally, on the fifth ring, she braced herself and answered the call with a firm, "Hello"

"Hello, is this Nandita Sahay?" The male voice was friendly and sophisticated.

"Yes." Nandita felt relieved, instantly registering the professional and polished tone.

"Hi, this is Salil calling from *News Today*. We would like to meet you for an interview."

"Sure… but when?" she asked, unsure of her schedules.

"Is it possible now?" The voice sounded eager.

"You mean right now?" Nandita was stalling. She was nervous and not prepared mentally. This was faster than she had expected.

"Look, we just need your few minutes. Our OB van is parked very close to where you stay, just around the corner."

"OB van?"

"It's the Outside Broadcasting van with a satellite link. We can telecast live from it, if need be." The executive explained patiently and finally Nandita relented. The exceutive directed her, to the van which stood out brightly against the dull, drab background of Sunder Nagar. As she approached it, she was received eagerly by the young, bespectacled executive. He pointed towards the luxury sedan parked right behind the van, "We will talk to you in there." Nandita was surprised but agreed, unaware of the ways of media.

Holding an envelope that contained evidence of the call, Nandita climbed on to the empty back seat. Just then, a distinguished looking man from the driver's seat of the Mercedes turned around and extended a hand towards her, "Hello Nandita, I'm Arunabh Roy."

He smiled congenially and Nandita was spellbound. Her confusion must have been apparent, as he chuckled and asked, "Do you mind if we talk while driving." She nodded, impressed with Reeva and Kunaal, for having gotten a celebrity to cover her story. As he drove, Nandita quietly checked his profile. Contrary to her belief, that camera made people look vastly different from what they really were, this man wasn't any different from the one she saw on TV, only a bit tired. She started to mentally frame the responses to his questions, not wanting to come across as silly or unsure.

Once they were out of the cluttered neighbourhood of Sunder Nagar, Arunabh eased the car by the curb of a relatively quiet road, leaving the engine on.

"Why don't you join me on the front seat, it will be easier

to have a conversation," he smiled politely and Nandita complied.

"So, I hear that you're following the Navdeep Complex case very closely." His query was more like a statement.

"Yes, I am. What's happening to them isn't fair."

"Mmmm... I hear an evacuation notice has been served today." His tone was surprisingly much softer than what she was used to hearing on TV.

"Yes, that's true. How did you know?" She was surprised, as the evacuation notice was delivered just this morning.

"Oh, come on Nandita, I am in the media industry. I need to keep a finger on the pulse of everything." He smiled, "The matter of concern for you is what else I know." He faced her squarely.

"Do you know something about the caller's identity too?" she asked apprehensively.

"What caller?" asked Arunabh.

"The unidentified caller... who threatened me, about my involvement with Navdeep Complex?"

"You received a telephonic threat?" he looked at her strangely.

"Oh, you didn't know? I thought that's what we were meeting about. Are you not referred by Reeva and Nihaal? From Media Vision PR?" She felt edgy.

"Hold on a second Nandita. Yes, I did come to discuss about Navdeep Complex. And no, I don't know any Reeva or Nihaal. But this threatening call has given me a whole new angle now." Arunabh was looking straight ahead, furiously calculating certain moves in his mind. Nandita was smart enough to catch the drift.

"What did you want to discuss about Navdeep Complex?'

Suddenly, the starstruck Nandita vanished, replaced by a no-nonsense person.

Arunabh smiled at her change in tack and spoke thoughtfully, “You know, whoever thought this out for you, did a fairly good job. If you speak to the media about the threat, in face of a pending RTI on Navdeep Complex, then no one will dare touch you. It’s an excellent strategy to safeguard yourself.” He paused to check Nandita’s reaction who didn’t offer anything, considering what he had said until now were merely facts.

“Now, what if I were to tell you that you can save Navdeep Complex as well?” he looked at her pointedly.

“What do you mean?”

“Nandita, I have proof that Navdeep Complex’s land status has already been changed on papers, from green zone to commercial. But it will be announced only after Navdeep Complex is demolished using the ‘green-zone’ excuse, so that a particular construction company can build a five-star commercial cum residential complex there.”

“Why are you telling me all this?” She was sensing a hidden agenda.

“Because you’re the right person Nandita. I know your background. I’m aware of your past cases. And also, that you were offered a JBP ticket but you refused and instead chose to be an independent candidate.” Finally, Nandita was reminded of the fiery Arunabh Roy she was used to seeing on TV.

“What do you want from me?” she sounded unimpressed by his theatricals.

“I want you to go on-air with me on News Today and expose JBP.”

"What? What does JBP have to do with Navdeep Complex and those threats?" She was ruffled by what he was suggesting.

"Everything," he answered in a low tone. "The construction company who stands to benefit is funded by a JBP politician. Money has been offered to the current office bearers to change the land status. Subsequently, the development contract will be awarded to the construction company funded and promoted by a JBP man, through an eyewash tender process. The plans are already in place and the only way you can stop this is by making a public appearance with the facts and proof that I provide you with. You can lend additional credibility to our case Nandita."

She sat there, her breathing shallow. This all sounded huge. The repercussions were going to be substantial and she knew it would change the game for her. However, she didn't know if she was ready for a head-on collision with JBP, for reasons very close to her heart.

"How do I believe that what you're saying is true?"

Arunabh removed a folder from the dashboard. He handed it to her and said, "Go through this. It will help you decide."

For the next ten minutes, Nandita flipped through the pages of the slim file and then looked at him.

"When do we have to do this?" she asked, snapping the folder shut. There was enough evidence in there to put all her doubts to rest. If this is what JBP had come down to, then she was ready to expose them.

"Good," beamed Arunabh, "We need to do this fast, like tomorrow. Reach the studio by 9am and we will record your statement as soon as we set you up," he handed her a card.

"By the way Nandita, don't speak about this to anyone until we go on-air and reveal the facts. The people we're dealing with have eyes and ears everywhere and they can cover their tracks pretty fast."

As they drove back towards Sunder Nagar, Nandita did not speak much. She was hurt and disappointed with JBP. It pained her even more because her mother had once been an ardent JBP worker during her youth. All through her childhood years, Nandita had seen her single mother fully dedicate herself to the party. She had continued to attend every JBP rally, even after quitting as a party worker, for personal reasons. The facts revealed by Arunabh, somehow seemed to have marred the memories of all those years with her mother. It seemed that she had lived and died with a lie. It was an insult and Nandita was in no mood to forgive.

The autorickshaw stopped before a tall and wide metal gate, painted in dull grey. The driver informed Nandita that her destination had arrived. She had expected a much more grandiose entry to the glamour world of media and wondered if she was at the right address. She got off carefully avoiding the puddle underneath. She had chosen to wear a deep maroon dupatta in raw silk, which elegantly complemented the simply cut black salwar-kameez.

The security guard manning the gate disinterestedly checked the register for her name and opened the small side-gate for 'on-foot' visitors. As she entered the building, she was struck by the grandiose beauty of the hollow building facades of the shooting sets, with doors that opened to emptiness.

Buzzing with activity, no one noticed as she entered the building mentioned on the card Arunabh had given her. The place belied a certain organized chaos. There were overhead scaffoldings everywhere to support heavy lights and the unsightly mess of cables, plywood and other props made for a poignant reminder; whatever ugliness lay beyond the camera's lens and lights, was very effectively and smartly hidden.

Nandita felt lost, not knowing where to go. She asked for directions twice and was received with strange looks. Then suddenly, someone tapped on her shoulders and she was relieved to see the bespectacled media executive from the day before. Flashing a radiant smile, he motioned at her to follow him.

Entering an enclosed studio, she immediately recognized the familiar desk, where Arunabh faced the camera every single evening with the panellists. The media executive asked her to take a seat and had a make-up assistant look at her.

Growing impatient with the make-up guy hovering over her face, she was relieved to finally see Arunabh emerge from the far end of the set. He walked briskly towards her, referring to some notes, while talking to a young research executive who breathlessly trotted along, struggling to keep up. Arunabh quickly dismissed the research executive and walked over to Nandita purposefully.

"You ready?" He smiled encouragingly, taking a seat next to her.

"Yes." Nandita felt her stomach twist.

"Good, here's the list of questions which will be asked. It will help you prepare mentally." He looked at her closely, sensing her nervousness and added, "Nandita, I'll be the one interviewing you on camera. Remember – you must not hesitate, and be firm while answering. Also, look right into the camera. Don't worry, you will do fine." He got up and took his seat on the panel. The lights and camera angles were re-adjusted with him in frame.

As she sat next to Arunabh, the countdown began. Once on air, Arunabh delivered his well-rehearsed pitch to the camera.

"Ladies and gentlemen... today our nation suffers another blow to its democratic fibre as its citizens stand to lose their homes to the profiteering construction industry and its allied political office bearers. What's more is that the people who dare to ask questions are threatened to stay quiet or face consequences. As a nation, we need to decide, how far and for how long, can this go on. Are we going to turn a blind eye towards this regular flouting of rules and corruption? Or are we going to take the necessary action before it's too late? In yet another exposé, we bring you the proof of how certain factions with financial and political clout can blatantly destroy lives and homes in their greed." He paused and then added, "In studio with us today is Miss Nandita Sahay, a social worker of many years and an independent candidate for the oncoming assembly elections. About a month ago, Nandita Sahay filed for an RTI, seeking answers on the status of Navdeep Complex, a sturdy structure, located in Central Mumbai, which houses close to four hundred people. The same complex is now scheduled to be demolished within forty five days. It is to be noted that instead of answers, Nandita received a threat to her life and her integrity as a woman. I request our viewers to stay with us as we ask Nandita some important questions to get to the bottom of it all. We'll be back."

The production assistant shouted, "Cut!" and Arunabh turned towards her. He smiled, "In the next segment I start to interview you." Nandita was amazed by the swift and instant change in his tone of voice. While it was enraged and impassioned moments ago, it now was cool and relaxed. As the cameras began rolling again, Arunabh focused on Nandita.

"Miss Sahay, how and when did you first come to know of the Navdeep Complex case?"

"I have been working with the people of Sunder Nagar for a long time. It was natural for them to come to me with their problems. I was told that they have been asked to vacate Navdeep Complex as it's going to be demolished." Nandita sounded cool and collected on camera.

"Had they received any notice or written intimation from the municipal corporation?"

"No, nothing. An officer visited Navdeep Complex and simply declared it unworthy of habitation, after mere visual inspection. No other evaluation was done."

"Miss Sahay, how were you so convinced that the building's structure wasn't actually a threat to its inhabitants." Arunabh was leading the on-camera discussion exactly where he wanted.

"We got an experienced civil engineer from an established architecture firm to review the structure. In their opinion, the structure is so sturdy that it does not require any urgent repairs or maintenance, apart from a paint job, and can last more than a decade unaided. We have the structural integrity report."

"So, what did you do, once you knew that the condition of the Navdeep Complex building is not the reason for demolishing it?"

"I, along with the residents of Navdeep Complex, visited

the town planning office in the city and was told that the land on which the complex is situated is a green zone and thus its an illegal construction. I then filed for an RTI to get a clear status of the land a month ago, to which I haven't received any response." For a first-timer, she was doing well.

At this point, Arunabh turned towards the camera, "Let me cut in at this point. Nandita Sahay was told that Navdeep Complex is an illegal structure because it stands on a green zone." Then he dramatically waved a document before the camera, and said, "But here, I hold in my hand the order with the new revised status of the land, and please note that its new status is commercial-cum-residential. This order is dated as recent as last week." Arunabh's pitch was rising now. "So somebody got the status changed while Navdeep Complex was set to be grazed to the ground soon. Ladies and gentlemen, this sounds like a well formulated conspiracy. And it doesn't end here..." He turned towards Nandita.

"Miss Sahay, you told us that you haven't yet received any response to your RTI?"

"Yes, I haven't received any response on my RTI, but instead I received a threat to my life and integrity."

"Can you elaborate?"

"I received a call late one evening, threatening me to stop following up on Navdeep Complex or else I'll be 'fixed'. It's very clear some people don't want me sniffing around. And they will go to the extent of hurting me physically."

Now, Arunabh took charge once again, "So as you know now, certain people with vested interest in this land can go to any extent. Let me inform our viewers that an NC case has been registered by Sunder Nagar Police Station regarding the threat received by Nandita. And this brings us back to the question: who wants Navdeep Complex demolished and who threatened Nandita?"

"Miss Nandita Sahay, were you offered a seat by JBP for the upcoming assembly elections?" Arunabh directed an unexpected question at her, which did not belong to the list he had provided earlier.

"Yes, I was, but I rejected the offer." Nandita began to feel a little uncomfortable.

"Do you think that JBP made that offer to bring you around and stop you from investigating on Navdeep Complex? Is it possible that the threat you received was the next step after you refused to join the party?"

"No, I'm not aware of any such intentions from their end," Nandita was clearly not in sync with this new angle Arunabh was playing with. Before she could protest, she was cut out of the frame and the camera focused on Arunabh exclusively.

Having left his suggestive question hanging mid-air for viewers to interpret, Arunabh made a show of ruffling through his papers and brought out a slim file, and faced it towards the camera. "What you see here are the documents proving that not only the status of Navdeep Complex's land has been manipulated and changed to suit certain people, but once it is demolished on false grounds, there are extensive plans to award the same land for development to a newly launched construction company promoted and funded by Mr. Ramesh Kriplani, a long-time senior leader of JBP. The nation wants to know the real role of Mr. Kriplani in this whole Navdeep Complex case. JBP, who has been in the focus for all the wrong reasons during the past year, owes an explanation to the people. How long will it continue to harbour criminals and corrupt, law-breaking individuals? More importantly, is JBP now prepared to threaten the citizens of this nation into submission?"

As they cut off the feed for a break, a production assistant walked up to Nandita and politely informed that her part was done. Nandita gathered her belongings and walked out of the set feeling unsettled. There was a disturbing question hanging in the air, "Was JBP really responsible for that threat call?" And her mind was tormented by the dangerous possibilities that lay ahead.

She absentmindedly refused the executive's polite offer of coffee and sandwiches, once again looking expectantly towards Arunabh. But he was too busy to even look up. Nandita suddenly found the charged-up atmosphere of the studio oppressive. Slightly perspiring, she walked out as fast as she could and breathed only once she was out of the main building.

Reeva breezed into Shalini's cabin, almost out of breath, "Did you see this?" She took the television remote from Shalini's desk to change the channel and pointed at the screen. She was frantic. Nihaal, who stood behind Shalini, was also confused. Nandita's face filled the screen as they watched excerpts from the Arunabh Roy's segment on the Navdeep Complex case. Arunabh had cleverly delivered a convincing soliloquy about the extent and level of corruption within JBP, openly hinting that it was responsible for the threat call to Nandita.

"Did *you* get in touch with Arunabh for Nandita's coverage?" Reeva's tone was hassled. She sincerely hoped none of them was responsible for this.

Reeva sighed as Shalini shook her head, "No, I didn't. Anyway, no one can get that arrogant son of a gun to cover anything unless he sets his mind on to it first." Shalini sounded wary, "What's his agenda here?"

"The bugger turned around the whole pitch of the interview to suit himself," Reeva almost growled. She knew that Arunabh's aim was to cause as much damage to JBP as possible, but what angered her more was that he had used Nandita to do so. If only she had gotten in touch with her beforehand, Reeva would have had the opportunity to warn her about the predatory ways of the media. And now, Nandita had led herself into a corner.

"What now?" Shalini looked at Reeva.

"Let's first talk to Nandita," said Nihaal, dialling her number. She answered on the third ring sounding extremely tired.

"Hello Nandita? Where are you?"

"At home. I'm literally locked up inside my own house. There are people from every channel waiting outside to interview me. They are like vultures." Nandita's panic rose after hearing Nihaal's sympathetic voice. "I don't know what to tell them. I had no intention of blaming JBP. I just wanted some answers. Now, they're asking me if I did it for cheap publicity for the upcoming elections." Nihaal knew she was close to tears.

"Hey, hey... slow down Nandita. Stop panicking. You don't need to explain anything to anyone." Nihaal tried to pacify her, "And there's no need to stay locked up inside. Go about doing your things. Just say 'no comments' if someone pushes you. Don't make any further statements, until we decide the strategy."

"I wouldn't have spoken to anyone from the media, but I thought he was sent by you guys. Such a well-known person talking to me, I was overwhelmed. Then he presented me with proof about the JBP politician's involvement in demolishing Navdeep Complex. He asked me to keep quiet about it and I did. But I didn't know that he was going to connect the threat call to JBP, during the interview," she lamented.

"It's okay Nandita, just relax. JBP will also issue its own statement clarifying their status. We will do what we can. It's not as bad as it looks and it will blow over. Just sit tight." With his assurance, Nandita was somewhat pacified and disconnected the call.

"You really think this will blow over?" asked Shalini.

"Nope, I don't. I think the gloves are coming off early in this fight," he said slowly. "Well, at least we managed to achieve one objective. Nobody dare target her now. The entire media is at her doorstep." He smiled ruefully at the two women in the room.

"Damn. What's Nandita's take on this?" Reeva was getting impatient.

"She stood no chance against Arunabh once she agreed to come on the show. She had no idea about the angle he was going to take. He had specifically told her not to inform anyone about her plan to appear on TV. Agreed that somebody from JBP might be involved in this case, but a threatening call is outright goon behaviour. It reflects very badly on the party, and this is something people won't forgive easily. That, clubbed with a fresh corruption charge about Navdeep Complex land, is a disaster." He wore a worried look.

"But, it isn't true, right? There's no conclusive evidence that the caller was a JBP man. This allegation is completely baseless. I mean, nothing is proven yet." Reeva looked at Nihaal hopefully.

"Proven or not proven, trial by media is far more damaging than trial by the Supreme Court. I'm just wondering who is Arunabh's source of information on Navdeep Complex."

Suddenly, the trio was interrupted by Kunaal's voice, "I know who is Arunabh's source, but that's hardly my concern. But, I'm concerned that one of our own team members, although unintentionally, is beginning to hurt our client's interest." Kunaal's presence in Shalini's cabin was overbearing as his eyes were fixed on Reeva.

"Hey Kunaal, come join us," Nihaal pointed towards an empty chair and Kunaal took it hesitatingly, his eyes never leaving Reeva. It was quite apparent that he had only come looking for her and didn't intend to stay. Shalini's hackles were immediately raised, as she leaned forward, subconsciously readying for a battle.

Reeva felt an inexplicable panic rise within her. For her, Kunaal's respect as a professional was as important as his love for her. And currently, she felt as if she had let him down. Nandita's interview had set her back, especially after her recent grandiose declaration to Kunaal about her friendly collaboration with Nandita.

"Kunaal, that Arunabh really caught Nandita unaware. She had no intentions of maligning JBP. She's neutral and has confirmed that with us," Reeva cast a beseeching glance at Nihaal, who sat with his arms crossed and legs stretched out front, visibly relaxed. He offered no comments.

"Reeva, it doesn't matter now." Kunaal impatiently raised a hand to stop Reeva from talking, by far the rudest gesture he had ever made towards her. Reeva wordlessly bristled as he continued, "The fact remains that your so-called friend decided to casually put you and your client in a bad spot. But I can't blame you for your poor judgment, even though you were warned." He sighed and continued, "I've spoken to Uttur and an official statement from JBP is on its way. The press notes should go out immediately. And, to cover the electronic media, Uttur is going to record an on-camera message." He stopped as if considering something and then looked at Reeva, "Can you please arrange for his statement to be recorded in his Mumbai office tomorrow morning?"

"Actually Kunaal, come to think of it, Reeva is right," Nihaal suddenly spoke, "Arunabh twisted the interview around. He was already holding evidence against JBP about Navdeep Complex and he would have made it public, with or without Nandita."

Kunaal stared long and hard at Nihaal before replying curtly, "Thanks for your insight Nihaal, but I like to form my own opinions about my work and my people. Anyway, if asked to choose a charge, I would any day pick corruption against a death threat to a woman. Plus, you do realize that if anything is to happen to Nandita Sahay now, JBP will be automatically held responsible. Now, if you will excuse me." He left the cabin.

Reeva was the first to speak, "He's right. I messed it up. Even if I was trying to help a friend, I should have guided her better. I'm responsible." Her voice quivered.

"Listen to yourself Reeva. What are you saying?" Nihaal

frowned. “Unlike some people who think they can control everything and everyone, you had no control over Nandita’s actions. It was a matter of bad timing. Come on, none of us knew that Arunabh Roy was going to approach Nandita. Not even Kunaal.”

As Nihaal sat back in his chair, his eyes met Shalini’s and she silently urged him to calm down. The trio sat quietly, each of them enmeshed in their own web of circumstances and possibilities.

CHAPTER 14

For the first time, in his almost three-decade-long political career, Uttur found himself seriously falling short of words. His party workers needed guidance and even though he had just delivered a motivational pep talk, he could see that their shoulders were still hunched. JBP's reputation had nosedived in the last few months and the mood within the party was volatile. Already, and despite Uttur's stern warnings to avoid such possibilities, skirmishes had broken out between JBP and NPP workers. Luckily, media hadn't been able to sniff them out. How they had managed to unearth the proof of Ramesh Kriplani, a long-time JBP veteran, being involved in Navdeep Complex was a mystery to him. He had personally questioned Kriplani, and all he could surmise from the discussion was that Thapar wanted to start a company with Kriplani as one of the directors and that Kripalani had signed a few papers to that effect. As a politician, it was at the most a case of conflict of interest, but by no stretch of imagination was it corruption.

Uttur exhaled deeply, as the last of his men moved out of his office at JBP's Mumbai headquarters. He always prided in being a self-assured man and whenever the pressure mounted, he invariably became even calmer, almost thriving on crisis. But lately, he found himself low on energy. At times like these, he missed having a family, people with whom he could let his guard down, and enjoy banal activities like watching movies and cooking. But long ago, he had consciously locked and buried that part of him, dedicating himself fully to the betterment of his nation. He often wondered if he had made the right choices and sadly, never found an answer that could justify his current life.

Finally, shaking off the growing nostalgia, he remembered that he was supposed to record an official statement. He looked at himself in the mirror and noticed the bags under his eyes and the lines creasing his forehead. Hoping that the camera would be kind to him on a bad day like this, he walked into the conference room.

He stopped at the edge of the room and noticed Reeva discussing camera placement with the crew. Sensing Uttur's presence, she looked at him and smiled awkwardly, aware that he knew about her and Kunaal's newly altered relationship. Uttur smiled and took his seat. Somehow, Reeva made him feel protective towards her. She could have been the child he would have had, if he had followed a more mundane life.

"Hello Reeva, good to see you. How are you?" The brightness in his voice came naturally, even though he was dead tired.

"I'm good sir, but you must be very busy... and tired." She narrowed her eyes.

Uttur laughed rubbing his face, "Is it that obvious or are

you guys from the media always this observant?"

Reeva had expected a tensed, edgy politician but Uttur's calmness relaxed her. "Sir, I'm really sorry about the recent incident. It wasn't supposed to be this way and I know all this is just adding to your problems," she sounded distraught.

"Oh, come on young lady; don't sound so down and out. It's just a political circus," he smiled encouragingly, "At times like these, I expect you to gather all your strength."

"But sir... at such times, how do you manage to remain so calm? I mean, doesn't all this bother you?"

"Reeva... I know that we're standing on a precipice of a great change in our country's political make up. And as the wise philosophers say, *at times of change, we need to focus all our energy not on fighting the old but on building the new*. And that's what I'm doing."

"But isn't all this mentally and emotionally corrosive? What keeps you going?" Reeva knew she could be crossing a line with the top politician of the country but her curiosity made her go on.

Uttur smiled ruefully before answering, "Couple of decades ago, I would have never thought that my life would be like this. But time unfolds us. If you're asking that do I ever wish I was not in this position, then my answer is yes, the thought does cross my mind." His eyes bore into hers as he continued, "Long ago as a young man on a mission, I felt passionate about things around me. I wanted to bring about a change, which I ultimately did in my own little way. But it would be a grave fallacy to expect to change everything and at the same time, want it all to remain the same. I have to accept change as a package and not just selectively, according to what suits me." He smiled at Reeva.

"Sir, can I ask you something?" asked Reeva nervously.

"Sure."

"Were you aware that JBP offered assembly elections' ticket to Nandita Sahay?"

"Why do you ask this now? I'm just about to issue an official statement about the party's stand on this matter." He folded his arms. Not getting any response from Reeva, he said, "Oh yes of course, you're wondering if the truth is any different from the official statement I'm about to make." He laughed, "Yes Reeva, a ticket was offered to Nandita by JBP. And this decision was based purely upon her merit as a candidate. I felt that she would be an asset to our party. But she refused it and we respect her decision. This had nothing to do with Navdeep Complex. These are two unrelated issues. We will look into the corruption charges, but I can personally vouch that such a ghastly threat would never come from any quarters of JBP." Uttur paused to observe Reeva, who was stunned by his passion. He continued, "I'll have the same message for your camera Reeva, because this is the fact. I don't ever need to lie. I know that we are being targeted by a business faction repeatedly, but I don't wish to start a blame game. It won't be a politically mature stand for JBP. Kunaal must have told you about it all," he said softly.

Checking his watch, Uttur decided it was time to change the mood. "So, by the way how is Kunaal? I heard the good news." He was back to his bright self.

"He's fine, just a little upset about the current JBP incidents."

"Well, is that the reason he didn't come with you today?" laughed Uttur, "I know, he's not used to losing, but he's a good man Reeva. You may find him to be a bit moody, but he's also somebody you can rely on. And I can see that he loves you and that's important."

She smiled self-consciously, while remembering how upset Kunaal had been about Arunabh's interview with Nandita. Relieved with her heart-to-heart chat with the senior politico, Reeva was dying to share her insight with Kunaal. Even though somewhere, at the back of her mind, there was a nagging question: "what was it about certain business factions targeting JBP?" She couldn't recall Kunaal discussing anything like that with her. If not at a personal level, she deserved to have all information about her client on professional grounds. Why was Kunaal keeping such crucial information from her?

It was past five and the sun was already weakening. Nihaal finally looked up from his computer screen and peered at the clock. The day had gone by so fast he almost felt cheated. He stretched out leisurely and decided that he needed coffee.

He casually sauntered towards the cafeteria and groaned as he saw his trusted coffee machine replaced by a new swanky one. Confused by the machine's intricacies for a while he pressed the button to get a normal Latte, realizing too late that he had forgotten to place a cup underneath the nozzle. The machine hissed out steam and hot dark coffee spewed out of the nozzle and flowed into its steel grate. Panicking, Nihaal pressed various buttons for the machine to stop.

Suddenly, a hand shot out and pressed the Stop button. An amused smile played on Shalini's lips.

"Thanks... that was a calamity averted," he smiled back.

"It's simple. Just place the cup and press the button marked latte." The smile stayed on.

"The earlier one was good enough. It's just coffee. Why do we need to make it so complicated?" He shook his head in disdain.

"Oh, come on! Don't feel so challenged; it's just a coffee machine," she giggled picking up her coffee and they walked to a table.

"So, what's keeping you in office this late?" Nihaal sipped his coffee.

"Just some assessments for J&T infrastructure to be completed for the quarter end. And needless to say, JBP is turning out to be a tougher client than anticipated. In all this chaos, certain other clients are getting side-tracked," Shalini sighed.

"Yeah, it's funny the J&T Infrastructure campaign didn't take off. Their Galactic Studios project was rather big and one-of-a-kind in the country. It would have put us prominently on the world tourism map," he said.

"Yeah that's true, although I don't care much about the Jaiswal and Thapar duo. To me, they came across as thugs. I'm not surprised Kunaal is close to them." There was a bitter taste in her mouth. She looked up when she didn't get any response from Nihaal. He looked distracted and as she followed his gaze, she saw Reeva at the far end of the hall. Reeva disappeared into her cabin but Nihaal continued to look in her direction.

"So, how are you holding up?" She decided to break his reverie.

"Hmm... What do you mean?"

"You know what I mean. You're a fairly transparent guy

and it's not difficult to see how you feel for Reeva."

"There's nothing wrong in feeling something for a friend." His tone was dismissive.

"No, nothing's wrong with that. Problem is when you're in love with that friend," she peered at him.

"Oh Shalini, please. I didn't expect you to be so restricted in your definition of love, or friendship for that matter." He refused to meet Shalini's eyes.

"Nihaal, do you know the worst part of this deal? All your life, you will be forced to watch this beloved friend, married to a man who is wrong for her in so many ways. Are you ready for that?" Shalini's words cut through Nihaal like a double-edged knife and he winced, but even then, his words came out calm.

"Yes I'm ready, as long as it makes her happy. She knows she will always have me as a friend." He sounded resolute, beyond doubt.

"Oh, Nihaal. I hope you know what you're doing," she shook her head hopelessly.

"This is not all about me Shalini. It's about Reeva too. You think she could have ever accepted me without first putting her own beliefs about love to test. She's a brave girl and she believes in meeting challenges head-on. So, she's not going to abandon her love for Kunaal just because she feels it will pose a challenge. She won't take the easy, safe way. And honestly, I would be disappointed if she did." Nihaal drained his coffee and placed the mug back on the table.

"Well, what can I say? Mr. Nihaal Kapoor, I'm honoured to know you. I wish there were more knights in shining armours like you," smiled Shalini. Nihaal gestured towards the corridor, "Shall we, my lady?" He smiled back playfully.

Jaiswal was a happy man and for once, he owed this happiness not to any lucrative business deal but to his son and daughter-in-law. The family doctor had confirmed his grandchild's arrival date within a month's time.

As he entered the lift, he caught himself humming a tune from an old song and greeted the lift operator with exuberant cheerfulness. Making a mental note of ordering sweets and gifts for the entire staff to celebrate the happy occasion, he entered his cabin and immediately dialled his secretary's extension. Pramila Gupta, an aging old-timer at the office, understood her boss's moods very well and appeared before him almost instantly.

"Pramila, please order boxes of imported Lindt chocolates for everyone in the office. And, I would like to personally sign the messages."

"Very well sir. What's the occasion?" Pramila smiled widely.

"I'm going to be a grandad, Pramila," he declared with pride.

"Congratulations sir. When is the baby due?"

"Next month… can you believe it? Someone will actually call me grandpa!"

"Oh, that's so nice," Pramila smiled consciously, but it didn't take much for the perceptive businessman to sense her hesitation.

"What is it Pramila? Something bothering you?"

"Oh no sir, I'm sorry if I gave you the wrong impression, but in our customs, distributing sweets before a baby is born is considered inauspicious. Not good for the baby, you see," her eyes didn't meet his. She hated to throw a wet blanket on the would-be grandfather's enthusiasm.

"Oh okay, I understand. But of course, our customs have an ancient wisdom behind them. Thank you for your candor Pramila. No problem, you can place the order for next month and while you're at it, get the chocolates and boxes custom-made," he beamed at her. Pramila sensed a cue for her dismissal, but she hesitated once again.

"Sir, if you have a minute, can I talk to you about something?"

"Yeah sure, go ahead. What is it?"

"Sir, Mr. Dibyendu Kumar, Vice President, New Projects, would like to have a word with you regarding Galactic Studios. If you don't mind, can he come in now?"

"But DK is already scheduled to meet me and Thapar along with the financial team this week. He can discuss all the issues there in details."

"Sir, he says he needs to speak with you alone, for the benefit of the company," she added hastily.

"Oh, okay. Call him in." Jaiswal was still unsure. He hated behind-the-back meetings, especially when the back belonged to a friend, business partner and now also a close relative. Pramila turned on her heels and vanished. Soon, there was a knock on his door. He looked up and saw the familiar and trusted face of Dibyendu Kumar with a file in his hand. DK was his star performer, who had successfully executed many prestigious projects for the company. He was next in line for joining the company's board. Sincerely hoping that DK had something significant to share, Jaiswal asked him to take a seat.

"Good morning DK. So, what is it that you wish to discuss?"

Instead of responding, DK quietly slipped the file across

the table towards him. Jaiswal opened the file and flipped through it. And with every page, his eyes widened.

"DK, what is this?" His tone was incredulous.

"I know Mr. Jaiswal; these are communications agreeing to our proposal that we find an alternative site for Galactic Studios India. The Studio understood and respected the fact that the land piece selected by them was earmarked by the Indian government for social welfare projects."

"But, these communications from Galactic Studios are more than two months old. Why didn't you discuss it with me or Mr. Thapar till now?"

"Actually, Mr. Thapar knows about it," DK looked around uncomfortably.

"What?"

"It was clearly instructed that this should not be discussed with anybody, not even you."

"By Thapar?"

"Yes," DK admitted, "In fact, the reason why I'm here today is because the fresh, ninety-day period granted to us by Galactic Studios will be up by next month. We now only have thirty days left to identify and acquire the new land parcel. Failing this, either the Studio will switch to another construction company or shelve the project in India for the time being. In both cases, our bid deposit will be forfeited. It will be a huge loss for the company."

"Thanks for the update. Please leave this file with me." Jaiswal could feel anger rising within him. He added, "And don't worry. Let me tackle this," he assured DK.

After he left, Jaiswal sat still for a long time, his mood dark and sombre, in sharp contrast with this morning. He was more shaken than angry. So, they could have abandoned this elaborate ploy against JBP and simply looked for another piece of land. Instead, Thapar had chosen to deceive him and continued on the bloody path, even if it meant putting their reputation and business at risk. He thought of various ways to confront Thapar and in the end, settled for a direct approach. He wanted to storm into Thapar's office with the file right then, but he knew he had to compose himself first. Apart from being his partner, Thapar was also the father to his pregnant daughter-in-law. Finally, he picked it up and walked over to Pramila's desk outside. "I'm going to see Mr. Thapar. Please inform him that he should be expecting me. And, please instruct the front desk to hold all calls and visitors until further instructions." Pramila nodded and busied herself without asking any questions, although her brow creased with worry. She had never seen her boss so shaken up before.

Thapar's newly recruited, young secretary jumped out of her seat as she saw Jaiswal approach. She promptly pulled the cabin door open for him.

As Jaiswal stepped in, Thapar walked around his table and hugged him warmly, "Congratulations my friend, we're going to be grandparents very soon now! I just got the call. I was about to come over to you." Thapar's exuberance quickly evaporated as he sensed Jaiswal's nervous tension.

"What's happened Jaiswal? Everything okay?"

"I didn't expect this of you Dindayal." Jaiswal placed the file on the table. Thapar picked up the file tentatively and browsed through it, his face devoid of any expression. Finally, he said, "Sit down Ramcharan. Let me explain please."

Jaiswal crossed his arms and sat down, looking pointedly at Thapar.

"It's not how it seems Ramcharan, please understand."

"What should I understand? That you cheated? Kept secrets from me? That you put our business at risk and continued to play cat and mouse with JBP for reasons beyond my comprehension? You thrive on darkness Dindayal, and you find all good, principled practices mundane and boring." Jaiswal shook with anger.

"Go ahead Ramcharan, say all you want. Yes, I'm a bad person!" roared Thapar and threw the file on the table in a fit of rage. "But, I was never going to let that Uttur get away with insulting me. The day he threw us out of his house, I decided to destroy him and everything that matters to him. If all this affects our so-called principled lives, then so be it." Thapar continued, "I didn't tell you earlier because then you would want to stop me. And nothing can stop me now Ramcharan, not even you. Because, you're only a scared, spineless man," he jabbed a finger at Jaiswal.

Jaiswal stared numbly at Thapar, "What do you plan to do Dindayal? I don't care about the money, but please think... what about our families, our reputation?"

"I don't have to do anything. The media has already done its part. Now, the girl has to die and JBP must take the fall for it."

"You're talking about Nandita Sahay?" Jaiswal's eyes widened.

"Yes, I don't care about JBP anymore, but I'll make sure Uttur's political career dies with her. I gave him a second chance and sent a message through Kunaal Kabi but he said he doesn't even wish to talk to us. As if we were some roadside goons!" The menace in Thapar's eyes sent a chill up Jaiswal's spine. He couldn't believe how the desire for vengeance had turned Thapar into this evil, obsessive man.

Thapar fished out his phone, and punching a number, he said, "Good that you're here now, you can't complain that I didn't tell you."

"Hello Arunabh," Thapar put the call on speakerphone, "It's time for the next move."

"Hello Mr. Thapar, but I'm still not through investigating Ramesh Kriplani's involvement in the land issue. The evidence against him has not been established yet."

"Forget about that story Arunabh, I've something even bigger for you."

There was a pause, "What is it Mr. Thapar?"

"I want you to go on-air with breaking news that Nandita Sahay has promised to offer you some new information about the involvement of Uttur in a multi-million dollar land scam."

"What?" Arunabh sounded confused, "What are you saying Mr. Thapar? But, Nandita hasn't offered me any such information, not yet at least. And, I can't go on-air without firm evidence."

"The information and evidence will all come to you in time. I promise you that. You know I've always given you concrete leads."

"But Mr. Thapar, this is very big news. It will cause a virtual storm in the country. I don't know if the *News Today* board will approve of me proceeding on mere hearsay."

"So convince them. Or else, I can easily take this important breaking news along with my investment in your proposed channel somewhere else." Thapar's tone was cold.

There was a pause as Arunabh weighed his options, "Okay, let me see what I can do." He disconnected. A triumphant smile slowly crept over Thapar's face.

The pieces had started to come together in Jaiswal's mind. The mere thought of getting someone murdered made him want to puke and the fact that the victim was almost the same age as his daughter-in-law didn't help either. But it didn't affect Thapar. He was going to get Nandita killed and then ensure that the needle of blame would point at Uttur in specific and JBP in general. Jaiswal instinctively knew he had to get in touch with Vir, and soon. He wasn't going to let an innocent person die, at least not on his watch.

The house was alive with the rich aroma of ginger and lemongrass tea. Nandita poured two cups and handed one to Reeva, which she held in her hands almost reverently, sighing contentedly. Between her busy schedule and Nandita's election campaign, they had been able to finally find some time together.

"Honestly, this quiet feels good, after days of being hounded by the media. But why do I sense that its just a lull before the storm?" smirked Nandita.

"Well, this is just the beginning. You better get used to being under constant media scrutiny. It's like being under the microscope all the time. If you as much as sneeze, they will try to find dubious reasons behind it." Reeva laughed, "And by the way, I did meet Mr. Uttur after your famously controversial interview."

"Oh, what did he have to say?" Nandita's discomfort was apparent.

"I thought he would be upset, but surprisingly, he was very cool about it. And if it makes you feel any better, he actually thinks very highly of you. Have you ever met him?"

"That's very nice of him. But I guess as a politician he has to put his best foot forward." Nandita was evasive.

"Reeva, I'm really sorry." Suddenly, she looked disconcerted. "Sorry for putting you in such a tight spot, with both Kunaal and your client JBP. That interview with Arunabh was a disaster."

"I agree it was a disaster Nandita," Reeva smiled kindly, "But not of your making. Don't give yourself all the credit," Reeva winked teasingly.

"I know you're only being nice about it. Anyway, how is life?" She changed tack. "Six months is not long enough to plan a wedding. Because, I know one thing for sure – a guy like Kunaal would love to spoil you." Her excitement was palpable.

"Yeah, I'm managing as best as I can." Reeva's response didn't match the enthusiasm in Nandita's voice. And the mere mention of Kunaal's name caused a searing pain in her heart. She hadn't seen or heard from him since the past week. As always, Kunaal had easily distanced himself from her. She knew he was working off his anger alone, by himself, while she would rather have him confront and argue with her, like real people did. His absence was like a dark cloud hanging over her head.

"Hmm… I can imagine." Nandita sensed her reticence. "Don't worry. Once the JBP's election campaign concludes, you will be able to get on with your life," she smiled encouragingly.

"And what about the Navdeep Complex issue? I hope all that media hoopla will at least bring a stay on the demolition order." Reeva got up and strained the remaining tea from the pot into her mug.

"No such luck. I just had a word with that friendly officer. They have yet not received any notice to revoke or stay the order. With just fifteen days to go, there's little chance of any such order coming in," Nandita pursed her lips in disappointment.

"So, what are we going to do?"

"There's only one way now. Physical resistance. The residents of Navdeep Complex will have to fight for their homes, literally. Meanwhile, our lawyer is filing an appeal with the Supreme Court to challenge the order."

"You mean they will have to *physically* stop the municipal corporation workers from demolishing the building?" Reeva stared at Nandita in disbelief, "I mean things could really get out of hand. People could get arrested or worse! We're talking about the safety of hundreds of people here, Nandita. This is way too dangerous."

"Yes, it's dangerous, but what are our options? There comes a point when one has to dig in one's heels and fight for one's rights. If all of our freedom fighters hadn't fought until the last drop of their blood had oozed away, we would have continued to be a slave nation. Navdeep Complex is these people's home. They can't just give it up." Nandita's grim determination jolted Reeva out of her cushy, sterile cocoon.

"Okay, I understand the lack of options." She sighed, "But please keep me informed about everything. I would like to be present here at the time, if possible with media. In their presence, the authorities won't get unnecessarily rough. I just want to ensure that things stay as peaceful and organized as possible," Reeva squeezed Nandita's shoulder.

"Thanks Reeva, I'm glad you understand. If you wish to be a part of this fight then it's very important for me that you believe in it."

"I believe in you Nandita and I know that you will never do any wrong. It's a privilege to stand by you."

"Oh come on, you're embarrassing me now," Nandita giggled self-consciously.

"I'm serious Nandita. You're special and most women in your place won't be able to achieve even half of what you have." She gave Nandita a one-armed hug. "Anyway, I must leave now." She checked her watch.

"You sure you don't want me to drop you to the taxi stand?" Nandita asked again. Her latest acquisition, a second-hand Bajaj scooter purchased on the modest campaign budget put together by the Sunder Nagar residents, afforded her the luxury of being able to offer a ride to Reeva.

"Thanks, but I have to walk. This is the only bit of exercise I can get nowadays. At this rate, Kunaal might not recognize me on our wedding day," Reeva made a face and both women laughed.

Reeva enjoyed the cool evening breeze, as she brisk-walked to the taxi stand. The road was empty and she mentally kicked herself for not calling an Uber. Reeva knew that the short walk to the closest bus or train station passed through certain questionable alleys. Lately, she had become extremely cautious and missed her old easy-going self.

As she stood at the curb figuring out her options, Kunaal's huge Audi Q7 pulled up next to her, its powerful engine purring softly. Reeva's heartbeats quickened, as she saw him leaning over to open the door for her.

"How did you know I was here?" She asked breathlessly.

"I went to your place first, your mom told me you were coming here," he smiled.

"You went home and then came all the way here? Why didn't you call me?" Reeva didn't know whether to feel elated or stalked by her lover's enthusiastic overture.

"Wanted to surprise you. But as always, you made me wait too long," he winked

"So, you know I was visiting Nandita." She was tentative, unsure about Kunaal's reaction to this.

"Yes, I know." Kunaal smiled and deftly guided the car through the narrow roads, without losing his cool. "I had to come. I couldn't bear the thought of you alone in this jungle. Seriously, you shouldn't do this anymore."

"Oh Kunaal, you've no idea how I've felt without you the past few days," she gushed and complained at the same time. "I never know how you will react to what I say or do. I'm tired of emotionally tip-toeing around our relationship."

"Then don't. I'm all yours Reeva. Me and all that belongs to me, is yours. You could walk all over me if you wished, but you don't. And that's just one of the reasons I love you so much. It's maddening every time I stay away from you." Kunaal spoke without taking his eyes off the road but the sincerity in his words was unmistakable.

"Next time you're upset, just yell at me, and get as angry as you want. But please don't leave me alone like this."

"I would rather not have the next time at all. But knowing

you, there's no such guarantee, my crazy little sweetheart," he smiled. "The only time I want to stay away from you is when I'm angry. I know that I'll end up hurting you."

"You hurt me more when you stay away." She touched his hand on the steering wheel and he tensed.

As Kunaal looked at her, Reeva caught her breath. His eyes were smoky and filled with desire. He wanted her right there and then. Practicing all his restraints, Kunaal parked the car at the sea-facing curb and turned towards her. He touched her face with his palm, grazing her lips with his thumb, as she shivered at his touch. Pushing his seat back, he pulled her so close that she was almost sitting on his lap. Running his fingers through her hair, he kissed her delicately on her forehead, and working downwards, kissed her eyes, nose and then neck, skipping her mouth. As she moaned in protest, he smiled and pulled her close. He claimed her mouth with an urgent frenzy, his mouth and hands hungry for her.

After what seemed like an eternity, they pulled away and he smiled coquettishly at her, "You always look the most beautiful at such times." Reeva punched him lightly. "No really, one of these days, we need to go all the way. This is like ending a five-course meal at the appetizers." He winked, a rogue smile playing on his face.

"Kunaal!" Although she blushed, his words sent a shiver of excitement through her.

"What?" he exclaimed, "You're the one who wants me to behave normally. This is also what normal people do. You've got to trust me Reeva." He wore an innocent expression and Reeva giggled.

"By the way, I've gotten one worry off your list. The Taj-

Rambagh Palace of Jaipur is available for our dates. My office just received the confirmation today. So, the wedding venue is fixed. Now we only need to charter the flights. You happy?" He removed an envelope and waved it before her nose.

Reeva grabbed the envelope and opened it in disbelief, "Yes! But Kunaal, this will get so expensive." Rambagh Palace was her dream venue.

Kunaal shrugged, "Well, it's our special day. And we will go together to invite Nandita, okay?" He smiled and Reeva hugged him. It all seemed magical, almost as if she were living a fairytale.

Jaiswal downed the glass of cold water at one go and wiped the sweat off his face. He could feel his blood pressure rise as he prepared to break the news to Vir, who appeared withdrawn and in a particularly bad mood. He had refused to meet Jaiswal unscheduled and it had taken persistent pleading to convince him otherwise. Finally, in a major breach of operational codes, Vir had agreed to meet Jaiswal at home.

Vir was still carrying a bad taste in his mouth from the toll booth incident, more so because the toll supervisor had survived, but with a permanent handicap. And in some way, Vir held himself responsible. His on-going investigations had revealed many dark secrets about the Jaiswal and Thapar duo, including their association with Arunabh. So, Jaiswal's unexpected request of wanting to meet him alone had left him wondering if it was another of those ploys.

"Manekji, I'm in trouble. And only you can help me out

of it," blurted Jaiswal, lacking his usual composure.

"Get to the point Jaiswal," growled Vir.

"It's about Thapar," Jaiswal hesitated. Vir smirked sarcastically, knowing that Thapar was the bad news between the duo.

"Manekji, he is planning to kill someone," he looked away nervously, "He wants to kill Nandita Sahay and blame it on Uttur. You know the current situation with JBP after Nandita's interview on *News Today*. He plans to falsely announce that Nandita is going to expose Uttur and then get her killed. You have to stop him." By now, he was on the edge of the sofa with hands clasped before him. Right then, he was not a business tycoon, but only a father, a family man worried about his and his family's life and reputation.

Fury filled Vir and he got up and walked to the bar to pour himself some scotch. His worst worries about this client were manifesting themselves and he could feel his neck muscles tense.

He spoke only after allowing the bitter warmth of the liquid to sear his insides, "How do you know for sure?" he asked flatly. His training kicked in instinctively – first, verify the facts.

"He told me himself. We're business partners, friends and also relatives, but he told me only because he doesn't see me as a threat. To him I'm a weak, spineless man. And now, his desire for vengeance is going to ruin us."

Vir weighed his words before speaking, "He wants to take revenge on Uttur for not granting that land in Dharampur for your studio project? He took it too personally, as an insult I guess."

"You know about it?" Jaiswal obsessively wiped his

reading glasses, an old nervous tick.

"There's very little that I don't know about you two," sighed Vir. "But it's not that simple now. This is not business anymore. This is personal for Thapar. Only, I didn't know that he would be willing to go this far." Vir downed his drink and sat down, contemplating his next moves. An innocent's life was at risk.

"Please don't let that girl die," pleaded Jaiswal.

"Funny that when it was about counting the money, you were all game with Thapar. And now, when it has come to cleaning the blood on the floor you've come running to me. Thapar is right. You are a weak, spineless man. Now, get out of here and let me think."

"And make sure you update me about every development. Keep your eyes and ears open," added Vir irritably.

Jaiswal's departure left Vir in an intense state of contemplation. He knew he had to step in to save the girl. And that would mean working against a client and the project itself. In his cold logic, he also knew that Nandita's death would deliver that one final blow required to bring both Uttur and JBP down to their knees. But that's not how he functioned.

His area of operation very often consisted of mediating power-broking deals, corporate espionage, business sabotage and even whitewashing large-scale official and political lies. It was dangerous work involving very high stakes. Yet, direct bloodshed wasn't even remotely close to their scope of work. He had to confer with the Fixer before he could proceed. Aware that he was placing an unscheduled call, he reluctantly dialled the unregistered number and heard the ring go through.

"Anything urgent?" snapped the voice, somewhat rushed.

"Yes, regarding our current project. Thapar has gone hostile and is intending to neutralize an innocent target, and blame the kill on Uttur."

There was a slight pause that any other person would have missed, but Vir was too finely attuned to the voice to miss any pitch variation. "Name of the target?"

"Nandita Sahay."

There was another pause.

"Is the information verified?"

"By his own partner Jaiswal. He's asking for help. He wants us to stop Thapar." Vir was a thorough and detailed man, but he stuck to staccato answers, because the detailed reports were already with the Fixer.

"Thapar cannot be allowed to run amok. You need to curb his actions. Use your ground resources. Figure out Thapar's moves even before he makes them."

"What about Nandita?"

"The girl is not a direct concern of ours. Watch out for her, only if it's not risking your exposure in this case. Although, I would prefer things not get bloody." The Fixer had set the priorities clearly, but Vir was surprised by his aloof response.

He had to work out a safety net for Nandita and fast. He preferred to work towards safeguarding her, instead of trying to talk things out with a bigoted, egotistical maniac like Thapar. Vir knew his crucial cue would appear on Roy's *News Today* first and that here on, any news linking Nandita and Uttur would be of critical importance.

He already had Nandita's address and phone number. But he needed to know everything about her, including the toothpaste she used every morning. If he intended to save her, then he first needed to work out the angles from which the attack could come.

CHAPTER 15

Kinsy's eyes widened at the neat row of exclusive neckpieces laid out in front of them, as the jewellery boutique's sales attendant expertly rattled off the cut, colour, clarity and carat of the diamonds used in each necklace.

She looked at Reeva surreptitiously and whispered, "Your credit card better have no limits."

The attendant heard Kinsy and smiled, "Don't worry madam. Mr. Kabi has instructed us to assist Miss Reeva in her selection. The bills will be settled by his personal accountant. Would you ladies like to have something to drink? Tea, coffee or some champagne maybe?" Both the women asked for green tea and the attendant vanished behind the door. Kinsy silently mouthed 'champagne' and raised her brows.

"Stop acting funny, Kinsy," Reeva chided her friend, "You're behaving like a kid in a candy shop."

"Funny, you say? I'm getting the collywobbles in my tummy. All my life, I never thought I could even cross the threshold of such a place. Pinch me, quick." Kinsy extended an arm towards Reeva, which she chose to ignore.

"Are you going to help me choose or what?" Reeva was getting impatient, but she understood. Kinsy was finding herself unable to place her closest friend in this glamorous new role.

Reeva had always been a very modest shopper, but Kunaal had insisted that she buy nothing off the rack and get it all custom-made. So Reeva had called Kinsy. Thankfully they were at their last stop for the day.

"You know what, I have an idea," chirped Kinsy. "Let's take a break and come back after an hour. Even if your loaded fiancé is footing the bill, these are big-ticket purchases. Any expensive piece of jewellery that you pick up now and end up not liking later will become a pain in the neck… literally."

Reeva agreed, "The Marriott nearby has a lovely coffee-shop. What do you say?"

Kinsy nodded and the attendant eagerly offered to keep the showroom open for extended hours. Clearly, Kunaal Kabi was a very important client for them

At the Marriott coffee shop, Reeva chose the familiar corner table and placed their order of chamomile tea with scones. Kinsy excused herself to use the ladies' room and Reeva settled down to reply all her pending text messages and emails.

"Come on girl; let me make your day." Reeva was surprised to see Kinsy back so soon.

"What is it?" Reeva was nonplussed, but allowed her friend to tug her away.

"There, you see." Kinsy pointed towards the lower level of the lobby, interspersed with luxurious sofas and tables. It took a moment for Reeva to spot the object of Kinsy's interest and she gasped as she saw Kunaal, deep in discussion, with another man.

"Come on, let's go bomb him," Kinsy suggested excitedly.

"Not now, he seems busy with serious business, Kinsy."

"So what? You're his fiancée. Come on, you guys are getting married," Kinsy was getting adamant.

"That's exactly my point. What's our marriage got to do with his work?"

"You're so boring," Kinsy pouted.

"Nope, just practical… and mature," smiled Reeva.

"Who's that guy sitting with Kunaal? He looks familiar but I can't place him." Kinsy's brow creased.

"Don't know, I didn't notice." Reeva was non-committal, although she knew that man very well. And in fact, it was bothering her. What was Kunaal doing with him? Just then, her phone rang and seeing Kunaal's number, she jumped. Had he spotted her? She answered the phone as Kinsy shifted in her chair with glee, knowing it was him.

"Hello Reeva, where are you? If you're done I could pick you up?" He was cool as ever and Reeva relaxed.

"Yeah, almost done. I'm with Kinsy. We're just having tea at the Marriott coffee shop."

Kinsy raised her eyebrows. In Reeva's place, Kinsy would have been jumping up and down telling her fiancé that by some twist of fate, they were present at the same venue at the same time, unplanned. But Reeva had chosen to stay quiet.

"Great, I'm nearby. Can I drop by to catch up with you girls?" He sounded genuinely happy and Reeva said yes, even though it bothered her that he hadn't disclosed his location.

"So, this is when I finally get to formally meet your Mr. Big Shot," Kinsy smiled warmly.

"I'm serious Kinsy, no more wisecracks." Reeva warned her and the bantering continued. Soon enough, Reeva spotted Kunaal standing in a corner, scanning the room. His face lit up as their eyes met. Reeva was keenly aware of some pretty heads turning, immediately registering his presence. She heard Kinsy whistle quietly. "Wow, what a dish Reeva," she whispered.

"Hello girls, may I?" He pointed at the spare chair and sat down as the girls approved. "Hope you had a good day shopping, sweetheart?" He kissed Reeva's forehead and turned to Kinsy, "And you must be Kinnari, or do I have the liberty to call you Kinsy?"

"Reevs dear," Kinsy ignored Kunaal and spoke earnestly, "Are the wedding invites printed already?"

"Why?" Reeva was confused and Kunaal eyed her curiously.

"I mean is there a way I could steal this gorgeous man from you? Your clothes will fit me fine and I'm ready to marry him tomorrow." They laughed, and the atmosphere turned light and easy.

"When did you get here?" Kunaal asked finally.

"Just a little while ago," answered Reeva and Kinsy registered her friend's cautious tone. Reeva was still not telling Kunaal that she had spotted him earlier. It made Kinsy wonder about their relationship.

"So, can I take you ladies out for a nice dinner tonight? I know of a lovely Italian joint nearby," offered Kunaal, but Kinsy beat Reeva to reply,

"Actually, Kunaal if you don't mind can I have your pretty fiancée to myself for the evening. I'm seeing her after a long time. We have a lot of catching up to do."

Kunaal hesitated before responding. "Yeah, sure. As long as it's only for one evening," he smiled. "You girls have a good time. So I guess we will catch up tomorrow Reeva. Call me if you need anything." He got up and hugged Kinsy, and kissed Reeva on her cheek. Once he was gone, Reeva finally asked, "So what do you think?"

"I think that guy is obsessed with you. He won't share you with anyone and I seriously mean *no one*." Kinsy watched Kunaal exit the cafe. "Oh, and I remembered the name of the guy he was sitting with; Arunabh Roy of *News Today*, isn't it?"

"Yes," said Reeva.

"But isn't he the guy who's constantly been damaging your client JBP's image?" Kinsy folded her arms, but Reeva looked away.

"Damn," Kinsy shook her head in dismay, "Girl, we need to talk... about your cosy little arrangement with prince charming. What's this? Some kind of a 'non-disclosure' clause in your relationship. Why the hell didn't you ask what he was doing in the enemy camp? Why didn't you confront him?"

Reeva wanted to tell her friend everything, but felt bound by her loyalties to Kunaal. She wanted to bare the complexities of her relationship with Kunaal. But it would also mean divulging the secrets Dr. Wardhaan had revealed about Kunaal and that felt like outright betrayal. She believed if Kunaal had met Arunabh, he must have had a darned good reason. But that wasn't the thing bothering her. Her problem was that he had deliberately chosen to hide it. Kinsy's questions were valid and she wondered if she was slowly turning into Kunaal's mirror image.

She knew that she owed Kinsy an explanation, but it

would have to wait until a more appropriate time. Although it was a tough task, Reeva decided to stick to 'distract and divert' strategy with Kinsy. For a good part of the evening Kinsy was reluctant to let go of her issues about Kunaal, but ultimately Reeva was able to coax her out of her combative mood with a promise of a proper woman-to-woman talk later. The rest of the evening flew by as they chatted, ate, drank and danced as if tomorrow did not exist.

Arunabh was driving almost as if on auto-pilot, when he suddenly swerved to avoid a biker by an inch. He swore loudly and tried to concentrate on the road again. He was not accustomed to being challenged, and was fuming after his meeting with the channel's principle directors.

They had been very clear. If he wanted to go ahead with declaring a statement by Nandita on-air, without any real backup evidence, then it was purely his call. It was a sensitive matter and in case of any controversy or backlash, the channel would not be held responsible or back him. Translated, it meant that he would be fired. How dare they? After all that he had contributed towards building the channel's brand. He felt let down and his anger further fuelled his determination to go ahead with the announcement. His defiant mood lasted all through the drive to the studio.

Although he was early for the evening slot, Raghu was already in the studio, concentrating hard on the camera monitor. Arunabh flung his jacket on the chair and settled next to him.

"What's the matter? You're radiating a certain angry

vibe," chuckled Raghu.

"They say that the channel won't own up to any statement I make on-air about Nandita, without proof," he said, grabbing a chilled Diet Coke from the cooler.

"Well, they are simply safeguarding the company's interest in case of a legal liability. It makes business sense," Raghu shrugged.

"Their business sense is what made them put the channel in my hands. Why make me the chief editor when I don't have a say in what we cover!"

"Hmm... but they could have stopped you, instead they are just saying that they won't support it."

"It's the same thing. They are letting me do it because they know the TRPs will sky-rocket." He swallowed half the Coke, hoping to calm down.

"But honestly, don't you think it's a bit risky? You announcing that Nandita has offered you critical information, without any back-up evidence, is outright lying, Arunabh."

"Evidence will come. I'm confident of my source."

"If your source is so sure then why can't he wait to lay his hands on the evidence before expecting you to announce anything publicly?"

"My job is not to analyze my source. My job is to analyze news and information and make it profitable for the channel." Arunabh was getting angry again.

"I agree. All I'm saying is that don't form a theory before you have proof or twist facts to suit your theory. For once, think it over. Hope you're not on a wild goose chase. Because, this could cost you heavily." Raghu put on his spectacles and went back to his monitor, leaving Arunabh with his own thoughts.

Arunabh's mind was screaming red alerts as he saw reason in what his friend was suggesting. But in the end, his ego and anger got the better of him. Asking the regular camera man to record a small capsule, he readied himself. As he faced the camera, he felt the familiar rush of confidence coursing through him. His trademark aggression was in its full form.

"Dear viewers, once again we're here with a shocking piece of news. Social worker and upcoming election candidate Nandita Sahay, who helped us expose the corruption in the Navdeep Complex case, has once again come forward with a revelation that will shake up the political fibre of our nation." He continued, impassioned by his own belief, "Nandita, who was earlier too threatened with dire consequences, allegedly by JBP henchmen, has now promised to reveal substantial evidence about the large-scale corrupt practices of a top national leader from JBP. And if I were to take a guess about who the leader is, then only one name comes to my mind. And that name is Rishi Uttur. I urge our viewers to stand by for more information and evidence. Because, we will not stop until we have seen the truth behind every political face." Arunabh paused for a couple of seconds before taking a deep breath and calling for a cut.

As the camera stopped rolling, he called in the programming head and instructed him to plug in the capsule, on an hourly basis, starting at prime time the same evening. He wanted the hype generated to a crescendo before his final exposé. With this done, Arunabh relaxed. Now, he just had to wait for the evidence from Thapar. However, the nagging feeling of not closing the loop continued to bother his journalistic instincts. He knew that he had put his career on stake but there was no way he was getting bullied by management. Content of reporting was always going to be his decision alone.

He had no idea about how his announcement would affect Nandita. At worst, she would need to issue a clarification backtracking from the statement and at best, she would be sitting in a negotiation meeting with JBP, working out a substantial deal for retracting her statement. In both cases, he knew that he was going to turn Nandita into a celebrity overnight. And this would be a much-needed boost for her election campaign as an independent candidate. People were willing to pay an obscene amount of money for what he was going to do for her.

What he didn't know in his distorted world view was that, he had unwittingly condemned Nandita to a punishment she neither deserved nor expected. And that it would be very difficult for him to escape the consequences of his own action or lack thereof.

Nandita was surrounded by a pile of documents in her small, congested, makeshift office dedicated for the campaign work. Although fatigue was already overpowering her, she didn't want to drag the work till the next day. Originally a garage, the office was windowless and the used tables, chairs, and benches had been donated by the locals. It certainly was not a charming space, but it was functional. The late evening mood in the office was tired and dull, as most people volunteering for the campaign had already left for the day. Only Raju, a young, enthusiastic teenager, had stayed back to print the campaign posters.

Nandita stifled a yawn and got up from her desk. She walked over to Raju, who looked up and smiled.

"It's quite late now Raju, you can finish the rest tomorrow. If you stay late again today, your mom won't allow you to come here tomorrow," she smiled and patted his head.

"Didi, it's alright, I've told Mom that I'm helping you and that I would be late for dinner. I'll leave after I've finished this lot," he promised enthusiastically. As she was about to start an argument with him, there was a tap on the wooden door. Nandita looked up startled.

"Reeva, what are you doing here?" Nandita was glad to see her friend although somewhat alarmed by the unexpected timing of the visit. Reeva didn't respond and dumped her bag on the table.

"Are you alright Reeva?"

"Nandita, why are you doing this?" Reeva asked flatly.

"Doing what, Reeva?"

"You should have been straight with me. As a friend that's the least I expected of you." Her tone was defeated. "If you were planning to team up with that wily Arunabh to malign JBP and Uttur, then why did you do all that drama with me? Is this for money or power?"

"What drama Reeva? What are you talking about?" Nandita grew impatient of Reeva's insinuations.

"Oh come on stop it! As if you don't know of your announcement on TV via Arunabh about another JBP exposé." Reeva was bitter now.

"What? I haven't spoken to Arunabh since that interview. What announcement are you talking about?" Nandita forced herself to remain calm.

"Didn't you see it on TV?"

"I haven't watched TV in the last two days. My cable connection isn't working and the cable guy hasn't visited yet. And anyway, I was too busy for TV. Reeva, please tell me what's this about?" Nandita's forehead was creased with worry. Reeva too had a concerned look on her face. Raju was eyeing the two arguing women curiously.

"Raju, I think you should leave for the day. It's quite late already," Nandita said firmly. Raju quickly gathered his things and walked out of the office without any further protest. Nandita looked at Reeva quizzically, expecting her to resume their conversation.

"So, you don't know that Arunabh has announced that you've promised him some key information to expose high-level corruption in JBP, possibly involving Rishi Uttur?" Reeva said slowly, as if trying to figure out something.

Nandita did not speak for a long time. She didn't have the spirit to respond to Reeva's question. Her instincts were screaming that she was in a very dangerous situation. And, the sinister plan to frame her, was way bigger than Arunabh Roy's race for viewership and TRPs. The dark motive behind this announcement was slowly firming up in her mind.

Reeva slowly walked up to her and touched her shoulder.

"Reeva, I haven't offered any information to anyone. In fact, I don't know what information they're talking about. But I do know that I'm a target now." The panic and fear was evident in Nandita's eyes.

"What do you mean?" she asked softly, burdened with the guilt of doubting Nandita.

"It's simple Reeva. After my last interview, I have already been labelled anti-JBP. I'm now someone who can cause serious damage to the party. After Arunabh's last announcement, if anything happens to me, it's an easy guess who will be held accountable. My death can, and will be, easily blamed on JBP."

"Don't be crazy Nandita, this is not a Bollywood movie. There's law, police, security and systems in place. Nothing will happen to you. I won't let anything happen to you. Besides we can approach other channels too. We will issue your statement clarifying your stand."

"Yeah, and then they will say I have been bought over by JBP, to keep my mouth shut," smirked Nandita. "Either way I'm doomed."

"Okay, then you just sit it out. If you haven't given any information to Arunabh then he will soon fall on his face with his own false claims."

"Not if they kill me first and the so-called proof dies with me. They have established a very strong motive for JBP to kill me, even if falsely. But I know, JBP is not the one targeting me. Although I feel that I'm somehow missing a crucial link here," said Nandita, and silence followed.

"Enough." Finally, Reeva spoke, "You're coming with me right now. Pack your bags. Till this is sorted, you will stay with me at my place."

"Calm down Reeva. You know I can't come with you."

"Alright, then I won't leave without you."

"Please understand Reeva, I can't leave Sunder Nagar now. Elections are just a couple of months away and we may get news on Navdeep Complex soon. These people need me here."

"But you can't live here with this threat hanging on your head. This is madness."

"I am and will always be a soldier Reeva. This is my battlefield and I cannot abandon it. My enemy wants me to retreat, but there's no way that's going to happen. And yes, I'm a little mad that way."

Reeva hugged Nandita tightly and her eyes were moist when she let go of her. "Okay. You go ahead and fight your battle, but I'll draw up the rules. Now onwards, we will be in constant touch. I want to know where you are all the time. And you will not go anywhere alone. Am I clear?" Reeva took Nandita's hand in her own and looked deep into her eyes.

"And once all this is over, we will take a long holiday together," added Reeva, and Nandita fought back the tears, unable to speak. In absence of a family, Reeva was the only real relationship she cherished.

"Why don't you come with me to office tomorrow morning? I'll pick you up. We can assess the situation and plan ahead. Shalini and Nihaal will also be there." Reeva wanted to keep her as close as possible. Nandita agreed to the proposal quickly.

Nandita had always put up a brave front, but fighting alone was beginning to get to her. Despite the bravado, deep down she was just a vulnerable young woman. The recent threats to her existence had left a chink in her armour and it was corroding her very soul. She was really looking forward to some healing, feel-good companionship the next day.

For the umpteenth time, the call went unanswered and Reeva threw a worried glance at Nihaal. She had been repeatedly calling Nandita since morning.

"No response again?" Nihaal sat on the edge of his seat.

"Nope, she hasn't responded to any of my text messages either," said Reeva, feeling tendrils of fear beginning to creep up, "She was supposed to be here over two hours ago. Nandita is very particular about timings." Reeva regretted agreeing to Nandita's change of plans. "I wanted to pick her up on the way, but she said she would come later on her own."

"I think we should check her house. Maybe she's unwell or something," suggested Shalini.

"You're right Shalini." Nihaal got up, "I think one of you should come along." He looked at both women expectantly and Reeva offered to come.

Just then the office intercom on Reeva's desk buzzed loudly. In their current mood, it sounded ominously urgent to them. Reeva grabbed the phone and heard the cheery voice of the receptionist on the other side.

"Ma'am, Miss Nandita Sahay is here to see you. Should I send her in now?"

"Yes please, right away." Reeva sighed with relief and sank back into her chair. "She's here." She announced and finally, Nandita entered looking hassled, as if she had lost something important.

"Where have you been Nandita?" began Reeva and then stopped as she noticed Nandita's dishevelled state of mind. "What happened?"

"Raju has had a serious accident this morning. I'm coming straight from the hospital." She didn't meet anyone's eyes.

"That young boy from your office? Oh my god! How?" Reeva recalled the handsome, youthful face from her last visit to Nandita's campaign office.

"He took my scooter to deliver some documents to the

local election office in the morning. The brakes failed and he drove straight into an oncoming dumper. He's suffered multiple fractures and severe head trauma. He's lucky to have survived." There were tears in Nandita's eyes and a stunned silence descended upon the room.

Before Reeva could say anything, Nandita continued, "And you know what he said to me while being wheeled away for the surgery? That he was sorry he won't be able to help me in my campaign."

They all stood silently, allowing Nandita to regain control of herself.

"That scooter was yours… the one with failed brakes…" asked Nihaal finally.

"Yes," Nandita looked up at him, "It was serviced just two days ago. And I hadn't used it since then. There was no way I would have known, until this morning," she sobbed. "The scooter was tampered with; the garage confirmed that the brake wires were cut. It was meant for me and I should have been in the hospital. Not Raju."

"Damn, this is too much. Whoever is doing this certainly has a link with Arunabh. I say, we confront him. He has the answers we need," suggested Shalini.

"Yes, I agree," said Nihaal.

"Wait, I think I know where to begin with the questions," Reeva said firmly. "You stay here Nandita, I'll be back soon," And then, with a determined look, she walked out of the room.

Nihaal looked at Shalini and an understanding passed between them. Nihaal understood where Reeva was headed, right this minute. Without a word, he too exited the room and Shalini offered Nandita a hot cup of tea to settle her.

Reeva barged into Kunaal's cabin expecting to see him at his desk, but his cabin was empty. But his Mac was there in sleep mode, which confirmed that he was in the office somewhere. Reeva looked around, her anger elevated by his absence. Just then, she heard a mobile vibrate. Kunaal had left his cell phone on his desk, right next to a framed shot of him and Reeva. They were laughing carelessly in the picture, but Reeva couldn't remember the occasion or place.

After a morose glance at the photo, she picked up the buzzing phone, but the call was from an unregistered number. As she stood debating whether she should answer it, Kunaal walked into the room absorbed in an open file. He looked up and brightened to see her. But then his eyes fell on his buzzing cell phone in her hands and his smile froze.

"Can I have that back please?" He took the phone from her and disconnected the call before slipping it into his pocket.

"We need to discuss about JBP as professionals, Kunaal."

"What? Oh yes, about that friend of yours who has landed herself and our esteemed client in a soup," he chuckled dourly, "I told you to stay away from her. She has shown her true colours, hasn't she? I wanted to trust her just because of you, but now she has crossed the line. She wants to malign JBP and Uttur." Kunaal paused to sip some water before continuing his tirade. "Honestly, I would love to see some hard evidence from her soon. Or I'll shred that lying woman to pieces in the media and she can forget about a political career forever." Reeva was unprepared for the onslaught of Kunaal's bitter anger.

"Kunaal, she hasn't promised Arunabh any information. He's lying. She's the one who has had attempts made on her life." Reeva's voice was just as sharp. "And you have to tell your friend Arunabh to back off and retract his statement now."

"How dare you call him my friend?" Kunaal lowered his voice and almost growled, a single nerve on his forehead bulging with temper. "Unlike you, I choose my friends carefully."

"Yes, you're a very careful man Kunaal. Careful enough to hide things from your own life partner. You keep mundane secrets from her such as, which business factions are attacking JBP politically or the clandestine meeting with Arunabh Roy at the Marriott." Reeva paused for effect and was satisfied with Kunaal's shock.

She continued, "Yes Kunaal, I saw you with Arunabh the evening we met at Marriott. He's the very guy who has been continually attacking JBP, *all this while*. Why don't you tell me what your meeting with him was all about? Were you discussing the successful execution of JBP's campaign strategy with him?" Reeva's tone dripped with sarcasm.

"Is that the reason you had my cell phone, to check it when I am not around? It was just an official meeting. We were discussing another project." He looked away dismissively.

"Oh, of course you were, very conveniently. How many more skeletons can I expect to tumble out of your closet Kunaal? Or are you going to get Dr. Wardhaan to call me again, with another story to pacify this silly little girl."

"Shut up Reeva," Kunaal banged his fist on the table.

"Why? So that you don't have to explain your lies to me? Is it that simple for you? I'm not Malini!" Reeva was shaking with anger. Kunaal didn't respond, but the twitch in his facial muscles gave him away.

He moved swiftly across the table and gripped Reeva's shoulders, his fingers digging into them painfully. It was that moment in which Reeva didn't know what to expect, as her eyes held Kunaal's. "Reeva I…" he started, but just then, there was a knock. Nihaal stood at the door, his feet slightly apart and arms folded. His posture was openly confrontational.

Kunaal let go off Reeva's shoulders and she adjusted her slightly askew shirt collar, rubbing the collarbone where his thumb had dug in.

"Nihaal, we're having a conversation here. Could you please excuse us?" Kunaal spoke icily.

"Since when did a conversation start requiring physical contact, Kunaal?" he said looking at Reeva. "And Reeva, if you're done here then you're required for an urgent meeting in the conference room, *now*."

Reeva shot an irate look at Kunaal and walked past Nihaal, who held his stand for a beat, and said, "I don't know the issue between the two of you. Neither am I interested. But if you lay a hand on Reeva one more time…" Nihaal left the words unsaid and walked away.

Kunaal sat down slowly in his chair. That day, he had finally gathered up the courage to explain everything to Reeva. He knew he would never be able to do it under normal circumstances. He had to be really angry for it and today he had been that. But it had all gone horribly wrong. He never wanted to hurt her, although emotionally he had ended up hurting her every single time. Once again, he had forgotten to draw the lines. Somehow, it was starting to become the story of his life.

CHAPTER 16

Window shopping neither suited nor complemented Vir's way of life, but pretending to shop was better than aimlessly roaming the streets. He hated doing anything without an objective. Burdened by the collateral damage he had witnessed in the on-going case, he sought solace in Bandra's burgeoning crowds. This was the first time that he hadn't been able to control a case. He had finally received the instruction he had been waiting for, from the Fixer. A simple text message had come in asking him to abort and withdraw from the Jaiswal-Thapar case, with immediate effect. It was a good decision, but a tad too late.

As expected, the first clue had come from Arunabh's announcement about Nandita and Vir had been on alert ever since. But what was eating away at him was that an innocent bystander had been hit. He had seen the boy being taken to the hospital by Nandita. His asset had already briefed him on the 'so-called' accident in details. The first attack had already come and Nandita had survived with a close shave.

This was the second casualty under Vir's watch and he knew Thapar was somehow responsible, once again.

He felt his temper flare, as he clutched his phone tighter in his palm. The only reason he hadn't openly threatened Thapar was because it would expose Jaiswal. And he didn't want to lose his inside mole as he needed quick first-hand information about Thapar's next moves. Yet somehow, Raju's accident had rattled him. He was ex-military and had witnessed enough loss of life but he hated innocent blood on his hands.

Weary of walking, he stopped by the cosy little pub, to grab a drink. The cool, dark ambience felt good after the noisy, humid outdoors. The attendant showed him to a table that gave him a good view of the entrance. He felt a little settled only after he took his first sip of the scotch, on the rocks. He fished out his phone and stared at it for a long time before punching in Thapar's number. As a habit, he never saved any client numbers on his phone, preferring to memorize them instead.

"Hello," said Thapar.

"Thapar, this is Manek Vir."

"Oh hello, what made you think of us Manek sahab?" The sarcasm in his voice was unmistakable.

"Thapar, I'm warning you. Stay away from that girl." Vir got to the point.

"What girl? What are you talking about Manekji? I don't understand." The feigned ignorance was outright artificial.

"Thapar, I'm shadowing that girl and I know your every move. I'm telling you nicely, one last time. Back off now."

"Manekji, I haven't come this far in life by backing off when asked to."

"If you make another move on that girl's life, I will destroy you," Vir matched Thapar's tone.

"Are you threatening me?"

"Yes, consider it an open threat. And just for the record, we're no longer working on your case." Vir disconnected the call and got back to his drink.

On the other end, Thapar shook with rage as he played with his Zippo lighter. Taking deep breaths, he pressed the lighter's switch and held the flame under a pink rose from a small flower arrangement on his desk. The pretty flower instantly singed, and filled the room with an acrid smell. He tossed the lighter aside as if bored with the game and dialled a number.

"Maneji, you're taking too long," said Thapar, as soon as the call was answered by the chief minister.

"Mr. Thapar, there are procedures to follow. I cannot jump a process. But we're almost done."

"Great. Can we now prepone the demolition of Navdeep complex?"

"It's already scheduled for next week. Plus, don't worry about the demolition. It will be done. You should be more concerned about getting the tender contract to acquire the land."

"Listen to me carefully without interrupting. I want the demolition to be scheduled at the earliest. And by earliest, I mean within a couple of days, not a week. Can you do that at least?"

"Alright, I'll get the schedule preponed" Mane answered quietly. He hadn't missed the insult but knew that in the current circumstances, he couldn't rub Thapar the wrong way. Contrary to his initial doubts, the businessmen duo had been true to their word. JBP's name being dragged through the mud, had led to their popularity to nosedive. For the first time in the past couple of years, Sathya Raj Mane had a real shot at retaining his seat. It was as good as it would get for him.

The receptionist at *News Today* looked strangely at the trio crowding her workstation. She was not used to receiving visitors hoping for a walk-in interview with Arunabh Roy. But she had run out of all her reasoning skills to convince them that Arunabh didn't meet people randomly, even if they belonged to the media industry.

"Okay, just tell him it's about Nandita Sahay. We're representing her," Nihaal finally fired the last salvo. He knew that Nandita's name would draw Arunabh out. The receptionist was clearly familiar with the name, but she continued to stall. "Alright, Mr. Roy is in a meeting now. I'll tell him as soon as he's free. Now, if you could please wait there." She pointed at the chairs.

"I said call him *now*," snarled Nihaal. Both Reeva and Shalini were surprised by his aggression. Something in his tone also prompted the receptionist to call Arunabh's extension right away.

"Sir, there are some people here to meet you without an appointment. They say they're representing Nandita Sahay. Should I..." The girl stopped short, and continued to listen to the instructions in rapt attention, nodding along. She disconnected the call and looked up at them, once again strangely.

"Mr. Roy has asked you to wait here. He's coming out

to meet you soon." In her experience, this was the first time Arunabh had agreed to meet unscheduled visitors.

True to his word, Arunabh breezed in within minutes. He was dressed in a crisp, dark suit.

"Hello, I'm Arunabh." He introduced himself in a perfunctory manner, and shook hands with all three. "Let's get ourselves a place so that we can talk." He ushered them into one of the visitors' rooms.

As soon as they were settled, Arunabh quickly got to business. "I'm sorry, but I'm a little tight on time. So, what brings you guys here?"

"Nandita Sahay is what brings us here. And your blatant lies," said Reeva.

"Look, can we have a civilized discussion? You've come here to talk, haven't you?" Arunabh raised his hands and shrugged.

"Yes, we need to talk. Actually, we need to know why you announced that Nandita has offered you information for an exposé on JBP, when she hasn't even *spoken* to you," Nihaal intervened.

"Well, I have my own sources and I can lay my hands on any information, as and when I need to." He remained nonchalant.

"But that source is not Nandita, so I'm beginning to wonder why you named her?" asked Nihaal. "Is there a motive here I need to figure out?"

"Yes, my motive is to expose JBP and its top-level corruption. I'm sure Nandita knows something, which makes her answerable to people."

"How can you be so sure, when she hasn't even spoken to you?" questioned Shalini.

"Because, I rely on facts and information." He fished out a memory stick from his pocket and inserted it in the wall-mounted TV's USB slot. The TV displayed grainy long distance footage of a road and Reeva was the first to recognize the location. It was outside JBP's Mumbai office, late in the evening or night. Arunabh forwarded the video to the time where a lone figure briskly exited the office. As he paused and zoomed in on the person, there was pin-drop silence in the room.

"That's your Nandita Sahay exiting the JBP office. My sources confirm that she visited the party office to meet Uttur, who was in Mumbai that night. Now, you answer me – what was her business meeting him even after the huge controversy she had raked up with JBP recently. Or did she go there to negotiate a heavy deal for herself? Did she go asking for a price to keep her mouth shut?" Arunabh was a powerful orator, but Nihaal was unimpressed.

"Don't go about baselessly accusing people Mr. Roy, her visit doesn't prove anything."

"Well, if you think I'm baseless in assuming that Uttur is involved in a humongous land scam for Galactic Studios' entry in India, then that's your naïve prerogative. Likewise, if you believe that Nandita Sahay is not holding back information…"

"That's impossible," Reeva cut in, "I know both Nandita and Utturji. They cannot be involved in such a thing. You're stooping to such levels only for TRPs and viewership. Retract your statement now. There are attempts being made on her life, for God's sake," she huffed.

"Oh, come on Miss Reeva. When you swim with sharks, what else can you expect? I think you hold rather emotional views about politics. But I guess they're about to change into a more sceptical nature soon, as I lay my hands on real proof and verifiable information. I'm in the business of dispersing information and I know how to do it well. You should be thankful I haven't released this footage yet. Just give me forty eight hours. The truth will be out soon," Arunabh smiled politely.

"Mr. Roy, you do know that Nandita can approach another news channel to release a statement clarifying her position. You also know that falsely framing someone publicly, without any evidence is a punishable offense and can bring a defamation lawsuit so huge to you and your channel, that it may force you to down your shutters for good," Nihaal pointed at the footage playing on TV. "And about this footage, it is illegally acquired and hence, not admissible in court. So, whatever happens with Nandita is another question altogether. I think you need to worry more about your own reputation. And, you sure don't have forty eight hours." Nihaal got up and walked out, with Reeva and Shalini at his heels.

The meeting was over. But the three of them had only one question bothering them. Why did Nandita visit JBP's office in the thick of a controversy? And even if she did, why did she keep it a secret?

As Thapar scanned through the first draft of the quarterly financial report, that was to be presented to the investors' board, his face darkened as quickly as the winter evening outside. Effective from the current month, J&T Infrastructure had officially gone into negative profitability and this was not a good sign for the key investors. This wasn't a totally unexpected development, as he had directed all his attention into bringing down JBP for the sake of Galactic Studios. Even when JBP had become an irrelevant issue after the studio had relented on the Dharampur land, his obsession with JBP and Uttur's defeat had continued. But he was unwilling to recognize this judgement error now. It was too late anyway. But he had not expected Vir to know about Nandita. He already regretted speaking to Jaiswal, wondering if he was the leak.

The soft chiming of his phone brought him back to the present. It was Arunabh, calling him again. He finally answered it. He did not want his game to be disturbed at this stage, by any panicked reactions of Arunabh Roy on TV.

"I told you give me some time. Calling me repeatedly won't help. Trust me, I need that proof against Uttur and JBP as much as you do." Thapar was impatient and irritable.

"That's not why I'm calling." Arunabh was offended by the tone. "Nandita Sahay's so-called representatives came to meet me today. Actually, you know them. They're with Media Vision PR and are threatening to approach other news channels to challenge me. Now, it won't be easy for them to do so and I also have that footage you gave me to counter them. But even then, if I don't come up with concrete proof soon, I'll be forced to retract my statement. And that won't go down well with the channel owners. Needless to say, your purpose won't be served either." Arunabh paused and then continued, "And if this flares up and I get questioned regarding the source of all my anti JBP information, then you know where that thread will lead."

"Don't worry, I'm on it." Thapar hadn't missed the veiled threat, but he also knew he couldn't mess with Arunabh.

"Mr. Thapar, I sincerely hope you're not planning anything stupid." Arunabh disconnected the call without any parting courtesies.

Rage surged through Thapar. This was the second threat he had received – first Vir and now Arunabh. He sat unmoving, letting the wave of anger pass. Then he dialled a number from his cell phone. The call was answered after several rings.

"Where are you?" Thapar barked into the phone, "Why haven't you answered my calls since the morning."

"I'm busy doing what you've asked me to do, Thapar sahab." The rough and vulgar male voice answered with a chuckle, "After the toll plaza incident you made me stay underground for so long, that I feel a bit rusty now."

"I've taken very good care of you Gowli. Hope you're not wasting my money and time. Your last attempt was a joke."

"That woman got lucky. She should have been in the hospital now instead of the boy. That feisty bitch has a real mouth. Can you believe she even talked over me when I called to threaten her?"

"Stop fooling around. I want you to kill her. I'm not paying you to put her in a hospital," Thapar gritted his teeth.

"Thapar sahab, just get me my gun. One shot and she will be taken care of." Madhukar Gowli's casual approach was getting to Thapar.

"You will do no such thing. Now listen to me carefully. Navdeep Complex is due for demolition in the next forty eight hours. You will finish her then."

"That's great Thapar sahab! You've even selected an auspicious timing for the job," Gowli roared with laughter.

"It will be an accident, so no guns. But, it should look like a planned accident with an intent to kill. And, I want some witnesses who can tell the police later that it was a murder," said Thapar, ignoring his morbid humour.

"You need witnesses? Why do you want to put me into trouble?" Gowli's tone was far from troubled.

"Don't worry. You will head straight to the airport from Navdeep Complex and leave the country within hours. Your tickets and long-stay visa for Indonesia have already been organized. The money will reach you there directly."

"Alright. But please keep me in mind for such jobs in future as well Thapar sahab." His tone was cheaply flattering.

"Remember all my instructions. I want it done just the way I said." Disconnecting the call, he leaned back and rubbed his eyes. He had stopped worrying as he was now at the point of no return.

Outside Thapar's office, Pramila stumbled away from his door horrified, completely forgetting about the important documents she had come to hand over. All that her shocked brain had managed to retain was that Mr. Thapar had instructed someone over the phone, to kill an innocent woman. For the first time, the quiet and peaceful office she enjoyed working in, appeared ominously threatening to her. She had to get to Mr. Jaiswal immediately. Ignoring the empty lift that had just arrived on their floor, she took the staircase, as fear completely gripped her.

Nandita disconnected the call and turned to the small crowd of Navdeep Complex residents crammed into her tiny office. She had to tell them and she had to tell them right now. She was bracing herself to deliver the bad news when there was a knock at the door. Reeva entered, followed by Nihaal and Shalini.

"Hey guys, anything positive?" Nandita looked at the trio hopefully, knowing they had gone to see Arunabh.

Nihaal shook his head, "For now he's sticking to his track. He says he will have the proof in forty eight hours." He studied Nandita closely for any reaction but there was none. She looked deflated.

"I have nothing good to tell either. Just got a call from the town planning office. They have confirmed that a fresh order is out. The municipality workers will be here to demolish Navdeep Complex within the next two days." There were disgruntled and scared protests from the residents. Nandita, realizing the sensitivity of the matter, quickly turned to them.

"Listen up. This does not change our plans. We will take turns to maintain a 24x7 vigil at Navdeep Complex. As per my information, the demolition squad may come late night or even early morning. So, we're not going to sleep until we get an assurance from court that our houses will not be touched. Now go home, organize refreshments and tea, coffee etc., for those who are going to be on the night shift. One member from each family will be on vigil at all times. They may come tonight or tomorrow or day after. So, from here onwards, we will be on high alert." Nandita had not given them the time to get emotional. She wanted them to act instead. With that, the group dispersed quickly.

"Nandita, let us know if you need us to bring anything for the evening. I mean stuff like torches, medicines, or food etc. I think we too will be back here tonight after resting a bit," said Nihaal.

"Thanks guys. You being here is all I need for now."

"Nandita, in the current circumstances, I mean with the threat to you and all, is it a good idea to expose yourself like this?" asked Reeva.

"Didn't *you* say that nobody would dare touch me when I'm amidst a crowd? They're my strength. Besides, why should I worry when I have you guys?" Nandita flashed her smile, which left every argument invalid.

As they discussed the evening's plan, Reeva quietly stared at Nandita for a long time. She wanted to ask her about her visit to JBP office, but could not bring herself to. Not that Reeva doubted her, but it was that one piece of the puzzle that did not fit in. Nihaal and Shalini too had not brought it up.

Reeva attempted to focus on her screen, but sleep came to her in waves. She had to approve the report of latest findings on Jagrut Bharat Party's brand image survey, but all she wanted to do was crawl into a bed and drift off. Sleep deprived from the previous night's vigil at Navdeep Complex, she was feeling drained. The demolition squad had not come last night but if Nandita's lead was correct, they were definitely expecting some action tonight.

She sipped some more diet cola, just to keep her eyes open. Suddenly, there was a knock at the door and she saw Mr. Sehgal peek into her cabin.

"Hey Reeva, I know you're busy but can we talk?"

"Yeah sure Mr. Sehgal, please," Reeva gestured towards the empty chair.

"Uh Reeva, don't mind my doing so but I'll get to the point quickly. This is about Nandita Sahay. I'm aware that you're helping her with Navdeep Complex, which is a good thing. But, I believe that it's a conflict-of-interest scenario for our client JBP. Nandita is out to *literally* damage their image. And your association with her will be interpreted wrongly by both the media and JBP, especially after the last statement by Arunabh," he said.

Reeva bristled with anger. Ajay Sehgal was never a conceited or presumptious man, so she didn't expect this from him. She was ready to defend Nandita, but before she could say anything, she heard Kunaal's voice. He was cheery as he spoke, "Mr. Sehgal, don't worry about JBP. I've updated Mr. Uttur about everything, including the fact that Reeva is associated with Navdeep Complex only in its fight against the demolition, that too in her personal capacity. Media Vision PR has nothing to do with it. As far as the media is concerned, you can leave it to me to handle," Kunaal smiled.

Mr. Sehgal smiled back, recognizing the diplomatic save.

"Alright, Kunaal. That's good enough for me. I'll leave you two with your busy schedules."

As he left the room, Kunaal said, "Reeva, I came to say sorry."

"Sorry? You don't get to apologize for what you are Kunaal," Reeva's tone was bitter.

"You're tired, Reeva. Go home and get some rest. I'll look into this," he pointed at the screen, ignoring her vile mood. "And I'm getting a few chairs delivered to Navdeep Complex now for the protestors. You don't need to spend another night sitting on the floor."

"How do you know?" Surprised, Reeva turned to face him.

"Well, although it's infinitely better than the floor, spending a night in the car is not very comfortable either," he smiled.

"You were there?" Her eyes widened.

"Yes, I was. And I will be there tonight as well. As long as you're there, I'll watch over you. But you know that I cannot come out there in the open due to my allegiance with JBP. It just won't look right." He shook his head. Once again, he had touched a chord within Reeva.

"Oh Kunaal, Nandita is in danger and I know you can help her. Please talk to Arunabh. It's just a matter of setting the record straight. She didn't offer any information to him."

"Why don't you understand? I have no control over what he says or doesn't say," Kunaal mumbled apologetically.

"But you know him, don't you?" She looked at him beseechingly.

"Reeva, in our profession, we work with a lot of people. It doesn't necessarily mean that we *know* all of them. I don't know him. Heck, I don't even know myself."

"The question is whether I'll ever know you Kunaal, like a woman is supposed to know her man." Reeva sounded defeated. Kunaal sighed deeply and said, "You need to rest. You won't last another night in your current state. Come, let me drop you home." He got up and Reeva slowly gathered her things. Neither of them said a word throughout the drive. The silence felt soothing after the jagged edges of words they were getting used to.

Vir flipped from one news channel to another, and was not surprised to see each one of them dealing with the JBP-Nandita Sahay controversy. The coverage was not only repetitive but also tiresome. And the content was either pure speculation or mundane details from Nandita's day-to-day life. But every single channel claimed the so-called 'fresh perspective'. In reality, the channels were clueless until Arunabh Roy came up with the proof of Rishi Uttur's corruption to support his claims. Vir's sources had confirmed that the previous night at Navdeep Complex was peaceful, as the demolition squad had not arrived.

He stifled a yawn and thought about grabbing a snack. Although it was already dark outside, it was still too early for dinner. Just as he selected a piece of apple pie from the fridge, his phone rang. He quickly fished it out and answered the call, balancing the plate in the other hand. The caller was distraught and speaking rapidly. It took Vir a few seconds to identify him.

"Jaiswal, slow down. Take a deep breath. Tell me what happened," he said, unable to understand Jaiswal's gibberish.

"He's going to kill her tonight Manek sahab, during the Navdeep Complex demolition. Help her please." Jaiswal broke down. Vir went cold, feeling the pressure built up at his temples.

"How do you know?"

Vir patiently listened to his account of Pramila overhearing Thapar conversation and said coolly, "Listen to me carefully. Nobody should know what you know, not even your family. Instruct your secretary too. Let me handle this. Now stay calm and keep your mouth shut. Nothing has happened. Go home and have dinner with your family." Vir disconnected the call. His mind was swiftly working out various possible scenarios.

Vir knew that the danger to Nandita was real. The only advantage was that he knew the venue, time frame and the profile of the attacker. But it would complicate matters with a large crowd involved. He knew there would be close to two hundred people at Navdeep Complex that night. He couldn't do this alone. He needed reinforcements, but there was radio silence from the Fixer's end. Understandably so, because his last instruction had been very specific. *Stay clear.*

Vir's investigations had revealed certain unexpected things about Nandita, which had surprised even a jaded soul like him. On a personal level, he couldn't care less, but he had to save this girl, especially after knowing her involvement with JBP.

He finally decided to call the one person who he knew would help him. He walked to his cupboard and flung a heavy windbreaker over his T-shirt. He then opened the locker and pulled out his gun. After checking its chamber and safety-lock, Vir slipped it into an inner pocket of his windbreaker.

And then, he dialled an important and personal mobile number from his memory. After a few rings, a dignified voice answered the call. He could hear a news channel in the background. Knowing that there was no turning back from here, Vir spoke crisply, "Hello this is Manek Vir."

There was a pause and then, "Yes?" The response was staccato and uncomfortable.

"We need to meet. I have crucial information about Nandita and the situation surrounding her. There's going to be an attempt on her life tonight."

"I'm not at the party office now. Come straight to my

residence at the state guest house." With that, Rishi Uttur disconnected the call.

Reeva got off the cab on the deserted main road and walked briskly towards Navdeep Complex. The day's rest had done her good and the late evening breeze felt refreshing on her face. As expected, Kunaal had been incommunicado, but both Nihaal and Shalini had promised to meet her there after dinner. She sensed a buzz in the air as she reached Navdeep Complex and broke into an open smile at the sight that awaited her.

It was a transformed scene from the previous night. The crowd had doubled and the complex was aglow with halogen lamps, lighting up the venue like a stadium for a day and night cricket match. True to his promise, Kunaal had managed to deliver chairs for the protestors. There were cars parked with open doors and karaoke mics plugged into their systems. The local grocery shop owner served water, tea and cold drinks to the participants. Banners and flags with 'Save Navdeep Complex' written all over were visible everywhere. Youngsters wore black T-shirts and black bands around their arms.

Reeva spotted Nandita walking towards her, "Thank you for the chairs. I was wondering if I could organize it, but budget restrictions, you see." Nandita gushed apologetically.

"Nah not me, that was Kunaal," said Reeva.

"Really? He seems like a nice guy..." Nandita said, and then added, "in a strange sort of way." She narrowed her eyes and they laughed.

"Wow. This appears professionally managed," Reeva smiled, glancing around.

"Oh yes, leave anything to the youngsters these days and rest assured, it will be well packaged, at the least. But, they have turned this into some kind of a celebration," she shook her head in exasperation.

"Well, whatever works to keep the mood upbeat," Reeva shrugged.

"Come on, let's sit down. We have a long night ahead of us." Nandita scanned the crowd once and they took the chairs placed in a corner, away from the glaring lights.

"Hey guys!" Nihaal and Shalini chorused, as they too pulled chairs for themselves.

"Hey, when did you guys get here?" asked Reeva.

"Just about now." Shalini was dressed in casual jeans and T-shirt and looked quite cute.

"And by the way Nandita, one of your guys wants to start an online campaign. He wants us to put together a database of everyone who is present today." She wore an amused smile.

"That must be Sukesh. He wants to get into software engineering. And the guy organizing tea for the event wants to get into hospitality," Nandita sighed and Reeva giggled.

"Anyway, you've a good thing going here Nandita," chuckled Nihaal, "By the way, me and Shalini are thinking of preparing the older residents of Navdeep Complex for their media statements. I guess the media hounds will be here sooner or later." Nihaal wore a white kurta over blue jeans, brandishing his effortless good looks.

"Thanks Nihaal, although I could never thank you guys enough." In response, Nihaal winked at Nandita and left with Shalini to meet the older residents. Reeva and Nandita settled in quietly, knowing that their watch had to last all night. Reeva kept stealing glances at Nandita, only one thing playing on her mind. And finally, she could no longer resist.

"Hey, can I ask you something?"

"Sure." Nandita looked up from the newspaper article she was reading.

"Did you visit JBP office after that interview with Arunabh?" she had to ask.

Nandita looked into Reeva's eyes and smiled. Then she carefully folded the newspaper and put it away with a sigh.

"Look... if you don't want to answer, I can understand."

"That's very sweet of you Reeva, but you should never trust anyone so blindly." Nandita looked at her. "I'm not going to question the source of your information, because that's not the point here. And yes, I did visit their office. But let me give you my word, that it wasn't for the reasons media and Arunabh are speculating. I didn't go there to cut any deal with JBP." Nandita continued, "And once all this is over and when we take that long holiday you mentioned, I'll tell you my reasons. I promise."

"I don't need any promises from you Nandita. Your answer is good enough," Reeva smiled. Just then, a couple of youngsters came rushing towards them and engaged Nandita in a rather impassioned discussion. Reeva smiled indulgently at her, who rolled her eyes dramatically and rushed away with the boys.

Left alone, Reeva scanned the crowd for Nihaal and Shalini, when her phone buzzed to announce an incoming message. It was from Kunaal, simply saying: *At the main road now. Can you meet me for a bit?* Reeva's heart danced. She grabbed her bag and left through the alley, leading to the main road.

Unknown to Reeva, Manek Vir emerged from behind a group of men in intense discussion and eyed her curiously. Tonight, he intended to keep a close watch on everyone. But he already knew where Reeva was going and that wasn't his concern anymore. What was worrying him was that even after a thorough scan, he had been unable to spot Madhukar Gowli in the crowds. Where the hell was he?

Reeva arrived at the main road but it was deserted. Kunaal's Audi Q7 was nowhere to be seen. She fished out her phone and rechecked the sender. The message was from Kunaal, but he wasn't here. Panicking, she started to walk back while speed-dialling him. Maybe he had not arrived yet. But it wasn't like him to ever keep her waiting. In her rush, she had completely missed out the black van parked at the curb. As she passed by, the van's door slid open and powerful hands grabbed Reeva, pulling her in. A hand covered her mouth to keep her from screaming.

It all happened in the fraction of a second and Reeva found herself on a cushy leather seat inside the van. As she finally breathed Kunaal's face came out of the shadows and hushed her. She stared at him in disbelief. Kunaal sat back and flashed a cocky smile at her.

"See, how easy it is to kidnap you? This is why I tell you not to visit such places alone," he goaded her.

"How dare you?" She punched him all over, but it hardly affected him. He laughed uncontrollably.

"Why didn't you bring the Audi?" Reeva asked, as she finally caught her breath.

"Well, I thought that it would be better if I'm not noticed while I'm on surveillance. Plus, this had more legroom, in case you visited," he said suggestively. They looked at each other for a moment before he pulled her into his arms and kissed her passionately. Urgency emanated from Kunaal, as if he needed that kiss to survive. But its intensity left Reeva's lips feeling raw.

As they sat quietly in the after-rush of the kiss, Kunaal touched Reeva's face delicately, "Was I too rough?"

Reeva shook her head and he pulled her closer. This time tenderly, as if she would break. Her head found a cosy spot on his shoulder, inhaling his scent. After a few minutes of peaceful silence, Kunaal murmured, "Reeva, I need to explain something to you."

"Yeah, explain to me how you manage to turn me on every time, with just a touch," she looked up at him naughtily.

"I'm serious..." He began, but was cut off as Reeva's cellphone buzzed loudly. The call was from Shalini.

"Listen, I should go. They will worry unnecessarily. And it would be embarrassing to tell them that I was necking my boyfriend in a car, like a sneaky teenager." She hurriedly adjusted her clothes and made for the door handle.

"Can you not stay for a little bit longer?" pleaded Kunaal and something in his eyes made her stop.

"Kunaal, once this is settled, we will have a nice, long dinner and a proper chat. I know we need to do that. Tomorrow, maybe. And who knows, it could be the night we end up going, as you say, *all the way*." She smiled teasingly and got out of the van, leaving Kunaal alone in the dark confines of the van.

Reeva was relieved to notice that the atmosphere at the venue had not changed while she had been away. She felt acutely conscious and repeatedly adjusted her clothes and re-applied the gloss to her lips as she walked towards the crowd, trying to be inconspicuous. As she was about to take a seat, she was accosted by Shalini, "Where have you been?"

"Oh, just had to use the toilet," Reeva said pointing towards the alley.

"But the toilets are that way." Shalini pointed the other way with a questioning look, "Never mind. Come quickly, you've got to see this." Her face brightened as she pulled Reeva's arm.

They approached a small crowd huddled around Nihaal and a few children, as they danced completely out of rhythm to old Bollywood songs. Reeva giggled, and then joined in cheering them.

Suddenly, Nihaal pulled Reeva in their dancing troupe and another cheer went up in the air. Swept by the mood, Reeva matched Nihaal's steps until the medley ended and they were all tired and breathless. With the performance ending, the crowd dissipated slowly, their mood decidedly elevated. Shalini received a call and quickly moved away from the din. Reeva was alarmed by the odd timing of the call and wanted to follow her, but she saw Nihaal approaching her.

"I thought you didn't dance. Where did you learn to dance like that?" Reeva gushed.

"Was born with it, you don't acquire this kind of talent," replied Nihaal. Reeva laughed carelessly, stopping only after she felt Nihaal's eyes on her. His unwavering eyes openly admired her. After a beat, Reeva felt too hot under his intense gaze. This was the first time that she had felt so conscious in Nihaal's company.

"What is it?" She hoped to break the awkwardness of the moment.

"You look beautiful when you laugh," Nihaal didn't take his eyes off her, "Actually, even more beautiful."

There was another awkward silence and Nihaal continued, "Well, my mom thinks so too." He hesitated for a moment, "You do know Reeva that I would do anything to see you laugh like this forever." Something sparked inside him and he felt that he had to speak up. He needed to uncork the bottled-up emotions he had held within for too long.

Reeva did not know how to react; even though this hadn't come as a surprise. But, she had already made her choice. And Nihaal knew it. That Reeva still cared for Nihaal made the situation very difficult for her. She shivered and hugged herself in the winter morning chill.

"Don't worry, this is just for the record. Just file it away somewhere in the back of your mind," he smiled and changed tack as he sensed Reeva's discomfort. He had not intended to put her in an odd spot. Reeva was struggling to formulate an appropriate response when she spotted Nandita and Shalini rushing towards them, their faces shadowed with worry.

"They're almost here. I just received a call from the officer. Right this minute they must be approaching the main road," huffed Nandita.

"Let's get everybody organized quickly. Come on." Nihaal checked his watch and looked up at the sky. It was past five in the morning and there was a faint hint of light on the horizon. They briskly walked towards the group of senior citizens and youngsters to brief them once again about the dos and don'ts. They could not afford to take chances. It was almost daybreak and people were sprawled on chairs with their feet up, almost dozing. Few others were huddled around small bonfires. Most kids had arranged the chairs into makeshift couches using their mothers' shawls and were fast asleep. The lethargy of an entire sleepless night had already caught up with Navdeep Complex.

The core group gathered around Nandita, listened to her in rapt attention. "Remember, as I said earlier, we're not here to fight. We're here to resist. None of us will touch any officer from the department. We will only block them physically. None of us will carry any weapon, not even a stick." She searched the faces for any challenge, but there was none. These were regular people, not warriors.

Nihaal hurriedly added to Nandita's instructions, "Don't panic when they start pushing. Just stay calm. Lie down on the ground if need be. And make sure that all the younger kids are sent back home with a small watch group right now." He wanted to continue, but the sound of metallic clanging of the wrought iron gate made them all turn.

The demolition squad was here.

CHAPTER 17

The four officers listlessly stared at Navdeep Complex from across its rickety gate, whose sole purpose was to mark the territory, not provide security. It was apparent that they were in a dour mood for being forced out of their beds at such an ungodly hour. A few paces behind them stood the demolition squad members, alert and ready, next to a couple of yellow earthmovers. Hidden away in the shadows, were the police officers, inconspicuous yet threatening. Nandita couldn't fail to notice that they wore a uniform different from the Mumbai police.

As she and the group approached the officers, suddenly the lights brightened, almost blinding them. They were the camera lights focused on where the action was unfolding. Along with the demolition squad, the media too had arrived quietly. They had been waiting to pounce at the right moment. Ignoring the media, she and her group approached the officers.

"Who is in charge here?" One of the officers, apparently

a senior, asked gruffly. He eyed Nandita sceptically as she stepped up and continued, "Madam, you must have received the demolition notice. The notice period is over. We're here with the demolition squad."

"But we haven't accepted the order. We have appealed to the court against this order," she replied.

"You haven't accepted? Is this some kind of a joke?" The officer looked at his colleagues sourly. "Madam, I haven't come here with an invitation to attend my son's wedding. We're government officers to serve you this final warning and demolish an illegal structure. The notice period is over."

"And I'm telling you that we will not allow you to demolish Navdeep Complex," Nandita crossed her arms. Nihaal watched the police force becoming restless at the back. He recognized them as Riot Control Police, a special faction of Mumbai police, trained to control large protesting groups. The bulletproof vests they wore meant they were ready for any major action.

"You're wasting our time, madam. You planned all this? You think this can stop us?" He pointed towards the group of media reporters. "Instead of all this drama, you should have worked towards finding alternate homes for these people. I'm going to tell you nicely one more time. Ask your people to clear the area and let the demolition squad move in. I'll even give you an extra hour to let your people move out from their flats."

"Sorry officer, that's not going to happen."

"Alright, suit yourself. It will only be messier now." The senior officer let out a deep breath and ordered his subordinate, "Get to work." The subordinate barked a few quick orders to the demolition squad and the Riot Control

Police moved immediately to approach the gate, the front-line officers leading the formation.

The RCP unit was armed with large wooden shields in one hand and wooden batons in the other. From their waist hung tear-gas guns and grenades, an effective tool to dissipate large crowds. The unit moved towards the gate silently like a wave and with just a little pressure, the gate gave in and swung open. It was the first move to breach the territorial sanctity of Navdeep Complex and despite Nandita and Nihaal's repeated assurance, the crowd panicked.

A large part of the crowd scattered, causing a mini stampede. Another group of protestors held hands to form a human chain against the RCP. One of the officers warned repeatedly through a blow horn, "This is a warning. Step away and let the demolition squad do their job. Otherwise, we will have to use force."

Nandita and Reeva exchanged panicked glances as Nihaal pulled them away from a large group of people forming a human chain, one after another. It was becoming apparent by the minute that things were not going to proceed the way they had planned.

"Get the kids out of here Nandita." Nihaal shouted over the din, "Reeva and Shalini, make sure that people stay calm. No one should even touch any officer. We can't give them a reason to use aggressive force."

Even before Nihaal had stopped speaking, the RCP started pushing inwards, forcing people back with their trained, brute strength. Suddenly, all four of them were swept up by the crowd. Reeva panicked on losing sight of the others. She could only spot Nandita hurrying away to round up all the kids and get them to safety. She suddenly thought of Kunaal and the warmth of his arms. This place had suddenly gotten way too dangerous for everybody and Kunaal was so far away from her.

Suddenly, she heard multiple screams and turned to see that few people were now on the ground, being hit by the RCP officers with the baton. By now, the crowd mentality had taken charge, with people pushing officers. In retaliation, nobody was being spared the lathi-charge. A fresh wave of panic washed over her as she saw Nihaal trying to break up a small mob of protestors, which had cornered a single officer with an intention of hurting him. From the looks of it, he was losing ground.

Reeva looked away helplessly. It was a battlefield and there was nothing she could do. Shalini was already positioned in one corner, providing whatever little first-aid she could offer to protestors coming in with bruises and cuts. The idea was to keep as many people as possible on the ground. If RCP managed to clear the courtyard of people then nothing would stand between the demolition squad and Navdeep Complex.

Suddenly, there were loud bursts like the sound of a firecracker, followed by incessant screaming. RCP had now started firing tear-gas grenades onto the crowd and the result was complete pandemonium. The thick, bitter smoke spread slowly. Scores of people started to retreat, coughing and gagging, their eyes blinded by the irritation. The more they breathed, the more the gas burned their throats and lungs.

But some of the youngsters with swimming goggles and masks decided to stay put. The RCP slowly and steadily pushed inwards. Reeva decided to help Nandita with the kids and seeing her kneeling on the ground, rushed towards her. In her arms was a young girl, barely seven or eight years of age. The kid's forehead had an open cut and blood from it seeped into Nandita's blue kurta.

"Sia, baby, are you okay?" Nandita tapped the child's cheek lightly. "She is in her senses, but in shock. She's not talking. It all happened when they started firing the tear gas. She got caught up in a stampede, I think." Nandita looked up at Reeva, her voice tight with tension. Reeva knelt beside the child and felt her breath with her finger. It was steady and strong but the little girl was growing colder by the minute.

"Yes, she seems to be in a shock. But, it's a deep cut and will need stitches. She needs to be taken to a hospital, before she loses any more blood." Reeva's brow knitted in concern and she could sense that her own legendary headache was going to invade her soon.

"Where do we find transport? You can see what's happening around here. Who do I ask?" Nandita was unable to think clearly.

"Wait, I think we can find a ride. Just get her to the start of the alley leading to the main road. I'll meet you there in ten minutes," said Reeva. She got up and ran towards the road. If she ran fast enough, she could reach Kunaal's van within five minutes.

Reeva expertly avoided the parked handcarts and unexpected potholes. The adrenaline from the kick of actually doing something had made the run easy. Even then, the icy morning air formed pins and needles in her lungs, which were already sore from the tear-gas exposure. Hitting the main road in record time, she bent over to catch her breath and saw that the spot where Kunaal's van was parked, was empty. She felt panic and frustration swell within her as she scanned the deserted road. Where was Kunaal? Had he left already? She took a deep breath to calm herself and checked her watch. She had promised to meet Nandita and the little child with a ride in ten minutes. She now had only four minutes left.

She speed-dialled Kunaal's number and started to run back to the building. His phone was unreachable. As she ran back to the complex, she spotted Nihaal carrying Sia with Nandita beside him. She knew Nihaal hadn't brought his bike either. She eyed her phone again, attempting to reach Kunaal.

In that distracted moment, Reeva's foot was caught in a loose pavement tile and she went toppling forward. Just before Reeva's face hit the road, she saw Nandita already moving towards her.

Reeva tried to get up, wincing from the burning pain from her grazed elbows and chin. She could see Nandita running to cross the road and made an awkward attempt to get up.

Just then, a speeding vehicle suddenly appeared out of the alley and hit Nandita without stopping. A loud shriek went up in the air and with a sickening crunch, Nandita flew a few feet away and landed on the side of the road.

Reeva was up on her feet immediately although her mind had gone numb. Everything was a blur as she ran to reach Nandita, who lay completely still. She looked oddly shrunk, like a child curled up on the bare asphalt road. Just as she sat down next to Nandita, the SUV came to a screeching halt about fifteen feet away and a face peered out of its window. It had a certain evil madness about it and the smile on it proclaimed a proud and satisfied responsibility. The face was familiar, but Reeva couldn't recall where she had seen it. To her, it all seemed to be happening in slow motion. She tried to register the vehicle's make or number, but her fuddled mind was like a sleek, oiled wall and nothing stuck. Then, with a few menacing growls of the engine, as if to challenge Reeva, the monster sped away, leaving behind black clouds of fume.

As the first light of dawn filtered through, Reeva sank beside Nandita and slowly, very slowly, shifted her bloodied head on to her lap. She couldn't hear the panicked voices of the crowd that was beginning to form around them.

"Nandita? Can you hear me?" Reeva whispered to her, lightly touching her cold, smooth cheek. There was no response. Reeva looked around, her vision blurred with adamant tears refusing to leave her eyes. She could see Nihaal run towards them. "Nandita, please talk to me," she sobbed. With a sudden convulsion, Nandita opened her eyes into small horizontal slits. She couldn't focus, but looked peaceful even then. Nandita's lips moved in an attempt to speak and Reeva lowered her ear, close to her lips, "Nandita?" She called out softly once again.

Finally, for a precious moment, Nandita focused on Reeva. And as if using all her remaining life essence for that one last word, her lips moved again to repeat something. And then Reeva heard it, "Rishi Uttur."

Nandita stared at Reeva beseechingly and then with a hiccup, a streak of blood left her mouth, moving across her cheek in a straight line. Nandita had gone still. Reeva sat there holding Nandita rocking her gently. She stared at the blurred version of Nihaal saying something to her urgently, but she could not hear him. Sounds and visions were faded and a ravaging headache took over her.

At a distance, Vir shrunk away from the fast approaching

crowd of residents, media and police. He felt tired, defeated and pointless. The first rays of sun were already kissing the top of the tall trees and birds were chirping as they always did every morning. But to him, they didn't sound the same. He sat down at the roadside curb and pulled out his cell phone to make that one last call, to report one final time.

Reeva woke up with a start and almost slid off the narrow cot. The air smelled of an unknown disinfectant; she felt sore all over. Everything around her was a shade of green. She saw Nihaal dozing on a sofa nearby. And then it all came to her. She was in a hospital and the green light was from the curtains. She tried to get up once again and her head swayed. Nihaal was instantly by her side steadying her.

"Take it easy," he said softly.

"How is she?" Reeva asked sharply, ignoring him.

"Reeva, relax. I've called your home. Your folks are on their way to pick you up," he gently pushed her to lie back.

"I asked you something. How is she?" Reeva's tone was little short of a scream. She frantically checked her watch. It was close to mid-morning. She had been out for more than three hours.

"How long have I been sleeping Nihaal? And where is Nandita?"

"Reeva, you weren't sleeping. The doctors gave you a sedative to calm you down. Actually, you were supposed to be asleep for another couple of hours." Nihaal sounded tired and heavy.

"And Nandita?" Reeva's voice was distraught.

"Nandita didn't make it, Reeva." He looked deeply into her confused eyes. "She was gone even before the ambulance arrived. We came here only for her to be declared 'dead on arrival'," said Nihaal and looked away. "It was severe internal bleeding due to a blunt force trauma to the head. You were refusing to let go of her so the doctors had to sedate you." Nihaal sank back into the sofa and eyed her doubtfully, unsure of her reaction.

But Reeva had gone rigid. She did not react, as at a deep subconscious level she already knew. Nandita's final moments came rushing back to her, along with the last name on her lips. She got off the gurney and faced Nihaal.

"What are you doing?" protested Nihaal.

"I have to see someone urgently." Grabbing her bag, she slipped her moccasins on.

"But your parents will be here any minute. Wait for them. You can leave after you've met them. I promise I'll take you wherever you wish to go."

"Nihaal, who is taking care of Nandita's last rites?" She ignored his suggestion.

"Shalini is coordinating it. Post mortem is already done, now they're awaiting a formal report for the morgue to release the body." Nihaal felt miserable referring to Nandita as merely a 'body'. "Anyway, just a week ago she had left instructions with her lawyer that in case of her death, she should be cremated in an incinerator. Maybe she knew." Sighing, Nihaal closed his eyes.

Reeva walked over to him and held his hand. An absolute calm had descended over her. "Nihaal, I want you to do two things for me. First, ask the hospital authorities to hold on to Nandita until you hear from me. And second, please explain to my parents that I'll come home to them soon." Before Nihaal could protest, Reeva was already out of the door, and for once, he had no idea where she was headed.

Rishi Uttur finally closed the old photo album and placed it back carefully into the drawer. He walked over to the window of his office and stood there without opening the blinds. He knew what lay beyond. After an entire sleepless night, he was still not ready for the dark questions facing him.

He had switched off the television almost an hour ago to avoid the news channels' cold and clinical analyses of Nandita's death. On the other hand, Arunabh Roy and *News Today* were surprisingly quiet. They were airing some inane news about an international business meet.

Finally, he slid open the blinds and was met with an overwhelming scene at the main gates of JBP's office. There was a large gathering of reporters outside the gates and the crowd surged like waves. Rows of OB vans were parked on both sides of the road, ready to transmit live. They all wanted to talk to him. They wanted to talk about Nandita. They wanted to know if he had her killed. He sighed, knowing that they would wait indefinitely to do so. Eventually, he would talk to them, but first he had to make some important choices.

Just as he was about to shut the blinds again, he spotted Reeva at the gate. She seemed to be in an argument with the head of the security for not being allowed in. Uttur returned to his desk quickly and punched in the extension number of his personal secretary, "Ask them to let Miss Reeva Rai in, right now. I need to see her, but remember, only her alone." He disconnected the call. And then, he sat still. Within minutes, there was a knock and the door to his office cracked open. Reeva hesitated, as if coming into his room was like a bridge she considered crossing over.

"Come Reeva, sit." Uttur's voice was low and soft. She took the chair opposite him without a word. They sat silently for a few moments.

"You look as if you haven't slept in a long time." He proffered to break the silence.

"So do you." Reeva looked straight into Uttur's eyes.

"Good you came. I really needed to meet you."

"And I really need to ask you just one question." There was certain sharpness in her voice.

"Today, you will get all the answers Reeva. Whether you will like them or not, I can't say," he sighed.

"Just tell me if you're responsible for what happened to her, Mr. Uttur."

"I'm glad you're asking me instead of simply assuming… like them." He pointed towards the window "It gives me hope."

"Come to the point Mr. Uttur. Did you get her killed, to cover something up?"

"No, I did not. I couldn't have," he answered simply.

"Then, why the hell was your name on her lips while she was dying?" Reeva stood up and glared at him.

Suddenly, Uttur's face changed. He looked away and blinked a few times. Without responding, he opened the side drawer of his desk, brought out the photo album, and placed it on the table between them. "Because of this…" He pointed at the album, "Go ahead and open it." There was a terrible sadness in his voice. Reeva stared at the album for a few seconds and then pulled it towards her. It was heavy and old, with black and white photos stuck on a thick, black paper.

There were photos, lots of them, of a very young Rishi Uttur with a spirited looking, beautiful woman. Turning the pages, Reeva felt as if she had seen this woman before, but also knew it was not possible. The grainy quality of the pictures told her that they were easily three decades old. Reeva looked up at Uttur confused, "What's this?"

"I was in love with that woman. Actually I still am. Her name is Nirmala Sahay." He stared at the photos fondly. "She's Nandita's mother."

"What?" Reeva was stunned.

"Reeva, Nandita was my love child with Nirmala. Or as they say, she was my illegitimate daughter." He choked on his own emotions, "There you go. A powerful politician like me didn't have the courage to own up to his own doing and give his child the life she deserved. I sacrificed our love and relationship to work for the society, thinking that I was being a real man. I was so wrong."

Reeva sat still, remembering Nandita's response about her visit to Uttur's office. This is what she was going to tell her once everything had settled. That's why Uttur's name was on her lips even at a time she could barely speak. Tears streamed down Reeva's cheek, but she didn't have the will to wipe them.

"She was a very principled girl, just like her mother. Unlike me, she had the courage to do what she believed in. She refused my offer to join JBP, saying she didn't want it easy just because she was my daughter. She accepted nothing from me, not even my help when she knew she was in danger." His hollow eyes were of a man who had run out of tears but was still crying.

"That night she came to see me here. I knew she was in danger and offered her security. She told me that the only security she wanted was that of a father, nothing else. I asked her to give me some more time and she just nodded and smiled."

"Who killed Nandita then?" Reeva's voice quivered.

"Reeva, my dear I'm so sorry in so many ways today." He slid a small note towards her. It had an address on it, of somewhere in the outskirts of the city. "All your questions will be answered here. But go only if you're ready to face the answers. Later, let me know if you need help dealing with any of them." He looked at her meaningfully. She had a million questions, but the look on Uttur's face told her that he wanted her to find the answers and not just hear it from him.

Reeva slowly picked up the slip and asked him, "What are you going to do now?"

"I'm going to do what I should have done long ago. I'm going to give my daughter in death what I couldn't give her in life. The love and recognition she should have gotten from this unfortunate father. I'm going to the hospital to claim her body as a father should. I need to spend time with her before she's gone forever," he smiled sadly.

A father had finally found the courage, but as a friend, Reeva still had to seek many answers. She looked at the piece of paper in her palm as if it were a dark omen, the address on it beckoning her. And even though she had a very bad feeling about it, she knew she had to go.

The compact and square media-monitoring room was dark, bathed only in the eerie glow of the white lights emitted by the rows of LED screens. All the screens were hooked to live feed from various news channels. And, even though on mute, it was obvious they were covering the same news.

Arunabh sat in a corner chair, passively watching the screens. He had ousted the monitoring executives from the room as soon as he had arrived, almost two hours ago. He sat still and tense as he watched his long-standing career slowly, yet decidedly unravel before him. He realized then how a chronic, over-confident gambler feels after he puts everything at stake, believing that he could never lose. And then, a single roll of the dice takes everything away from him. How and when did he, the intelligent and prudent Arunabh, reach this place in life?

Although he did not know how, he sensed that he had unwittingly become a part of the chain that had led to Nandita's death. His repeated calls to Thapar had gone unanswered. For the first time ever, he believed that his choices had gone unforgivably wrong. He was so deep in his thoughts that he completely missed the persistent knock on the door until Raghu peeked in and called out his name.

"Hey buddy, how long do you think you want to stay here? The faster you get on with things, the better it is." Raghu meant facing the board of directors and more importantly, his fans and followers.

"I know. I just need to work things out in my head first." Arunabh knew he had to get back on air soon; he owed it to his fans.

"Hmm... you're blaming yourself." Raghu raised his brows. "Well, at least one good thing has come of it.

The demolishing of Navdeep Complex has been stayed indefinitely, subject to fresh assessments. So, her death wasn't for nothing." Raghu switched on the master light of the room and Arunabh squinted as his eyes adjusted to the sudden brightness. Raghu studied him with narrowed eyes, "Do you still believe that Uttur did it?" Raghu made a conscious effort not to sound hard, knowing that his friend was already beating himself up.

As Arunabh hesitated to form his response, his phone buzzed in silent mode. His brow creased at the unknown number as he answered the call reluctantly. The voice on the other end was cool, calm and collected, but definitely authoritative. Arunabh glanced at Raghu meaningfully as he listened to it intently. Then he frantically gestured to him for a pen and paper. Hurriedly scribbling something down, he opened his mouth to form a question, but the call was disconnected. The owner of the voice was done talking. Arunabh sat still, staring at the paper, his mind frantically processing the new development.

"What is it Arunabh? Who was it?"

Arunabh smiled sadly. He then punched in the programming head's extension number and spoke urgently, "Get the team ready now, we need to be doing a segment on Nandita Sahay and Rishi Uttur. And make it quick, we should be on air within thirty minutes. And also despatch an OB van with a senior crime correspondent to Airport Road, *right away*." He paused to hear and responded impatiently, "No, not to Navdeep Complex or the hospital. I want the team to leave for Airport Road immediately. I'm texting you the exact location now."

He texted furiously and looked at Raghu, "It's time to

make amends. Come let's go." He stood up a renewed man. "It's not always that one gets a chance to redeem oneself." He walked out of the room with Raghu in tow.

The production team was caught off guard by his sudden appearance on the sets and the atmosphere was instantly charged. As Arunabh composed his thoughts, Raghu was beside him again, "Want to tell me what's this all about?"

"Nandita Sahay was Rishi Uttur's daughter. And we have a tip-off about the SUV that killed Nandita. It's been found at the Airport Road. I was wrong this time Raghu. Uttur did not kill his daughter," he stared at his hands, regret apparent on his face.

Raghu shook his head in disbelief and sat back in his chair, sensing the weight this was putting on his friend. Once again, Arunabh's phone rang and this time it was the crime correspondent calling from the Airport Road. He spoke incessantly and Arunabh heard him out till the end.

Finally, as the camera got ready for him, he positioned himself on the chair. He looked deep into the camera and spoke as if he owed an explanation, "Dear viewers... today, we're here to talk about Nandita Sahay, a courageous soul that fought until the end for others. And she achieved what she had set out for, which is an indefinite stay on the demolishing order of Navdeep Complex. Although now she's no longer here to talk for herself, I, Arunabh Roy, as a responsible and aware journalist, want to bring to your knowledge a certain personal aspect of her life that will clear the dust of misinformation surrounding her death.

For once, I wish to settle the misdirected speculations about the involvement of a certain politician in her death." He paused and looked down to refer to his notes. "I would like to publicly apologize to Nandita Sahay and Shri Rishi Uttur for the baseless insinuations that were made about them. I personally apologize for even suggesting that a father was responsible for the death of his own daughter. Yes, this is true that Rishi Uttur is Nandita Sahay's father. And right now, he is on his way to claim his daughter's body from City Hospital. I appeal to all the viewers and all my colleagues from other channels to respect this moment and give Mr. Uttur the space and privacy to grieve. You will have all the time later, to seek your answers." Arunabh called for a cut.

He did not know how the media world would react to this revelation, but his own studio had gone completely silent. He had deliberately decided not to go into details, wanting to stick to the main agenda. To him, it was most important to clear Uttur's name. This was the least he owed to that honest and true young woman, whom he had refused to help, in his blind rush for success.

Soon, the programmer gestured that he was ready with live input from Airport Road and Arunabh faced the camera again, "The witnesses from this morning clearly saw a beat-up SUV emerge out of the darkness and hit Nandita deliberately with its full force. It was evident that it wasn't an accident, but murder. *News Today* has successfully tracked and identified the SUV and the driver, responsible for Nandita's death. The SUV has been found in a badly mangled condition after being in a severe accident. It looks like it suffered a massive sideways impact from another large vehicle, on its way to the airport. Over to our senior crime correspondent Neil, who is at the accident scene right now." With that Arunabh sat back, having done his bit. He knew that the law enforcement system would take over from here. Any other day, he would have wanted to control everything, but today, he felt a strange disconnect from it all.

The live feed kicked in and the worried looking correspondent filled the screen with a mangled SUV in the background. He spoke animatedly, "As you can see behind me, the SUV is damaged almost beyond recognition. The driver of the SUV has been identified as the same person involved in the toll plaza shooting incident few months ago. The police have taken him into custody, but the chances of his survival are remote and he has been rushed to the emergency medical centre. But, the first-hand information from the police has confirmed that in his semi-conscious state he was naming a top industrialist, who had hired him for this job. The officers have refused to divulge the name yet, as the case is under investigation. The police have also confirmed that the perpetrator had a passport with a ticket and visa to an overseas destination and he was on his way to board an international flight. We will continue to report the developments in this case as we get more information. With cameraman Ketan, this is senior correspondent Niel Datta, reporting live for *News Today*."

The live feed was cut and the channel's logo and signature tune played on. Arunabh sat back satisfied and called his assistant, "Get someone to cover the rest of the segment. I'm going home."

"You're going, *now*? When can we expect you back?"

"I'll be back only when I'm ready," he smiled and patted

her shoulder, "Don't worry, you will do fine." Picking up his jacket, he saluted to a visibly confused Raghu. And then, for the first time in his career, Arunabh walked out of the studio, in the middle of a 'Breaking News'.

Reeva, still fuzzy from the heavy sedatives, took longer to find her car, although it was parked in its usual spot. Her head hurt and she was in no mood for human interaction. So, she was irked when her phone buzzed. It was Kinsy calling once again. She was tempted to disconnect as she was in no state of mind to explain things. But there were numerous missed calls from home too. Not wanting to worsen the situation she decided to answer.

"Hello Reeva, why aren't you answering your phone? I've been worried sick. Your parents are worried sick. You left the hospital even before we reached. Where the hell are you right now?" Kinsy was breathless and angry.

"Kinsy, I'm fine. I just need to go somewhere and then I'll be back."

"What? Is this the time to go around paying visits? One of your close friends died and you were sedated in a hospital, this very morning." Kinsy was frantic.

"I know."

"Do you know what's happening? Rish Uttur has announced that Nandita was his daughter… and, oh God… just tell me where you are, I'll come… you shouldn't be alone."

"Kinsy, I promise you I'll be back soon. And don't worry, I am taking someone with me. Okay?" With that false assurance, she disconnected the call. Reeva understood Kinsy's concern but she was growing impatient.

"So, who are you planning to take with you?" Shalini's voice startled Reeva. "Really, the person on the other side of the phone has given you good advice."

"How did you know I was here?" Reeva was relieved and edgy at the same time.

"I spotted you on TV outside the JBP office and called Mr. Uttur's assistant. He told me that you met him and then later were dropped here. It's pretty obvious your family doesn't know you're here," Shalini crossed her arms.

Reeva leaned back against the car and sighed tiredly, "I need to do something. And I need to do it now."

"Hmm... And from the looks of it, this thing you want to do is clandestine and not so safe." Shalini's eyes bore into Reeva's. "Let me come with you. I promise I won't interfere. But just let me drive, okay?" Reeva gave in, simply because Shalini had not tried to deter her from going. Within minutes, they were driving out of the parking lot, with Shalini behind the wheel.

"Mind telling me where we're going?" She asked and Reeva fished out the paper and handed it over to her. Shalini studied the address and made a mental note, "This is at least an hour and a half's drive. Why don't you take a nap? It will help clear your mind. I'll wake you up when we're about to reach."

Reeva nodded gratefully. Comfortably snuggled against the seat, she passed out even before the car hit the highway.

The car jerked as it left the smooth, tar road and turned onto a dirt road, leading towards the sea. Reeva opened her eyes and tried to focus. The narrow trail lined with coconut trees was barely wide enough for their car.

"I think we're almost there," Shalini sounded tense.

Reeva sat up, her senses alert now. She noticed a wooden board mentioning a single bungalow number. For a seemingly unvisited and deserted place, the board was in a good condition.

Finally, the trail led to a sandy clearing with a mesmerizing view of the sea in glorious high tide. They got out of the car and walked towards the gate of the large, sea-facing villa. There was no security and the heavy gate swung inwards gently, with a single push.

They walked slowly to the driveway, almost stealthily, as if expecting someone or something to pounce on them. Reeva reminded herself that she had come to confront whatever or whoever she found there and suddenly, her confidence returned. She looked at Shalini who was edgy but in control, eyeing the quiet surroundings suspiciously.

The house was a beautiful, Mediterranean style villa with arches and open alcoves. The front porch extended towards a well-tended grassy lawn and to the far side was a huge amoeboid-shaped swimming pool, with crystal clear water. Both seemed unused for a long time. The villa itself was quiet, devoid of any life. But with the quickly falling dusk, Reeva could see a couple of lights on, in the back of the house.

Suddenly, Reeva froze as she instantly recognized something. She blinked twice to confirm what she saw and her instincts told her that from here on she had to proceed alone.

"Shalini, I think you should leave now," she said flatly.

"What? Are you out of your mind? I can't leave you here."

"You had promised you would not interfere." Reeva's tone was cold.

"And I'm not interfering. But leaving you here alone, is something I'll not do."

"I know what I'm doing. Let's just say this is personal and I need to do this alone." Reeva waited for Shalini to respond, but she stayed quiet. "Shalini, please leave. You know where I am and I'll call you if I need help."

Shalini sighed, "Okay, you stay safe and call me if you need anything. I'll be waiting." She turned around and slowly walked away. Reeva stayed rooted to her spot, until she saw her drive away. Then she slowly walked over and closed the wooden gate, bolting it from inside.

Reeva turned towards the house, nervously eyeing the reason why she had wanted Shalini to leave. The large, black van, in which she had spent those intimate moments with Kunaal the previous night was parked in the garage. Only now, the front of the vehicle looked as if it had been in a head-on collision. Although, the sturdy van still looked operational, the damage was substantial. This was undoubtedly Kunaal's house.

As expected, the main door was open too. She walked through the beautiful house in a state of déjà vu, checking and touching things, as if she knew them from before. The taste in décor too was unmistakably Kunaal's. Finally, she arrived at a huge hall with French windows on one side opening to the sea and on the other side, was a massive fireplace with an ornate mantle above it. On top of the mantle was Kunaal's favourite happy picture of them together that Reeva had always seen on his office desk. She was automatically drawn towards it, but as she reached out to pick it up, she noticed a stack of files kept primly next to it. These files had names on it.

Right on top of the stack was a file named Nandita Sahay, followed by many other names she knew, including those of some high-ranking politicians, leading industrialists and media personnel. There were files for J&T Infrastructure, Dindayal Thapar, Ramcharan Jaiswal, Arunabh Roy, Rishi Uttur, even Madhukar Gowli – the man identified as Nandita's killer. Each file's inner pocket carried a sleek memory drive with the corresponding name etched on it.

Reeva's mind was reeling. How was Kunaal connected to all this? Nothing was adding up. She tentatively picked up Nandita's file and was just about to open it, when Kunaal's voice made her jump.

"You came. I knew you would. You are only one who could have reached me." Kunaal stared at Reeva calmly. He wore folded khaki pants with an open white shirt, his hair windswept. He had just returned from the beach. The sombreness of his face and a half-empty bottle of Grey Goose in his hand confirmed Reeva's worst nightmare.

She shivered involuntarily and sat down on the nearest couch. Then, gripped by an inner turmoil, she cried without restrain, hoping her own tears would cleanse her. When she finally looked up, she saw that Kunaal had not moved an inch. For all her doubts and questions, she could only form one word: *why?*

CHAPTER 18

Kunaal wanted to explain everything to Reeva; he wanted to hold her and protect her. He wanted to kiss away those tears once again. But instead, he stood still, and watched her passively. He knew it wasn't about what he could do now, but what had already been done. Her simple question, 'why?' had hit him squarely.

Kunaal slowly walked over and sat down next to her. Taking the files from her hands, he kept them on the coffee table and placed his arm lightly around her shoulder. He relaxed when she did not protest. Reeva looked deep into his sun-crinkled, tired eyes. She could smell the alcohol on him, mixed with his aftershave.

"Reeva, I should have told you long ago. And believe me I tried." Kunaal paused and pointed towards the files, "I tried telling you about the real me. I wanted to tell you everything, even things no one knows about me."

"Tell me now," Reeva whispered without looking at him.

Kunaal sat back on the couch. He sighed, "Reeva, I am a

power broker… of the highest order and of the worst kind. I'm also known as the Fixer. I control people and make them do what I want them to do. I twist things around to gain advantage over them, even if it means manipulating or blackmailing them. I do whatever it takes to turn circumstances to my advantage." Kunaal shook his head and continued, "The worst part is, I enjoyed doing it. I never needed the money. I had enough already. I can't remember when or why it all began. But with time, it became my favourite game, where I got to play God."

"Did *playing God* include killing Nandita?" Reeva asked, her voice devoid of emotion.

"No!" He had a pained expression on his face. "I agree that I was working against JBP, behind the scenes for Jaiswal and Thapar. And, I masterminded every single act against JBP, even though I knew I was working against my friend and mentor. It was just a project to me and I had accepted it, even before Uttur involved me in the JBP campaign. But I kept saving the game for Rishi Uttur, partly because he was my friend and also because I loved the challenge," he sighed, "It was like playing a game of chess, with myself. Finally, I called off the project, but I guess it was too late already. Last night, after my man Vir met Uttur to talk about Nandita, I came clean with him about Thapar's plans. He knows all about me now and I told him to give you this address. He left it to you and me, to sort out this mess I've created."

"Tell me Kunaal… are you responsible for Nandita's death?"

"There never was any plan to ever harm Nandita. She was nowhere on the radar, until Thapar got a whiff of her. She got caught up in this mess just because she was Uttur's daughter. Thapar hired Gowli to kill Nandita, to get even with Uttur for not cooperating and instead, insulting him. He wanted to get a daughter murdered and blame it on to her own father. This was his ultimate punishment for Uttur." Kunaal paused and rubbed his tired eyes, "It's a long story and it's all there in those files. The fact is that I called off the project when I learned that Nandita was Uttur's daughter and under threat. I instructed Vir to look out for her. He too was present at Navdeep Complex last night to keep an eye on Gowli, but I guess we didn't think it through." Kunaal sat quietly, waiting for it all to sink in. But with the burden of lies lifting, talking was becoming easier for him.

"Where were you when I came looking for you this morning, when the demolition squad arrived?"

Kunaal said, "You know what Reeva, I've done a lot of things in my life that could easily fall in the grey area, but I never hurt an innocent person. Yes, I was ruthless with the wealthy and the powerful. But, your coming into my life changed everything. I was scared at first and I didn't know what to do with you. I was worried that my dark past would hurt you in some way. Nandita symbolized all the fears I had about you and that's why I wanted you to stay away from her," he sighed and walked over to the windows. The sun was already halfway underwater, bathing the horizon in its fading orange and grey hues. The sight was beautiful yet sad.

"I knew I couldn't let anything happen to Nandita, for your sake. But things got worse and I lost control for the first time. This morning, as the demolition squad arrived, I spotted Gowli in his car, entering the main road. I followed him, but he managed to hoodwink me and parked himself in a dark alley. That's why you didn't find me on the main road.

When Vir called me after the accident, I chased Gowli and finally caught up with him at Airport Road. I was the one to inform Arunabh Roy about Gowli's accident site, so that the police and media could get their facts about Thapar's involvement from Gowli. I told Arunabh to clear up Uttur's name in an honourable manner. Honest to God, I wanted to kill Gowli right then, but his staying alive was important to clear Rishi Uttur's name."

"Was Arunabh Roy involved too?"

"He was associated with Thapar and Jaiswal. In fact, they very effectively manipulated him too. He was just being an over-ambitious journalist, blinded by the thrills of success and power. That day at the Marriott, I tried convincing him to withdraw his campaign against JBP and Uttur. But he refused. He saw the truth of Thapar's agenda a little late I guess. But today, he was happy to publicly apologize to Uttur and Nandita, in a late but fair attempt to clean up the mess."

"What about me Kunaal? Did you even once think about what this would do to us? Even with all your reasoning, you are still involved. You might not be responsible for Nandita's death, but now, I don't know how many other collateral deaths you are responsible for," sobbed Reeva.

Kunaal looked at her and slowly kneeled before her. He held both her hands in his palms and said, "Reeva, I will not justify anything to you. I do not ask for your forgiveness and I do not ask for your love. Not now at least. But, I do ask for your trust. Will you trust me, one last time?" He kissed her open palms and buried his face in them. She sobbed like a child and relented into his strong shoulders, sinking into his embrace.

They held each other for a long time, Reeva's sobs turning

into soft hiccups as Kunaal rubbed her back slowly, his face still buried in her neck. Finlly, she looked into his eyes and smiled through her tears, "Last night, I promised you tonight would be special." She paused to wipe a tear. "I'm not hungry and we already had a long chat. I guess that leaves us with just one more thing to do."

Kunaal's face was blank. This was the last thing on his mind. He knew that she felt raw with emotions and wasn't sure if this was just her way of dealing with it. But he didn't want their first time to be a result of her emotional vulnerability. He had taken advantage of a lot of people and situations, but he wasn't going to do it again, ever. "I don't know Reeva, if this is the right time," he hesitated.

Slowly, Reeva got up and looked at him, who was still on his knees. She held his hand and whispered, "I need you Kunaal, now. I need to feel that rush of love with you for real. I need to heal." Kunaal got up and faced her, and knew, that right then nothing else mattered.

They were quiet as they walked through the house, Kunaal holding her hand and leading the way towards the master bedroom. Together, hand in hand, they moved like small kids lost in the big, bad world. Finally, they were in Kunaal's bedroom. He switched on the light and the brightness filled the dark room. From the balcony, the starry indigo sky was visible and the white translucent curtains fluttered delicately as a light breeze blew from the Arabian Sea.

Kunaal slowly sat Reeva down on the sofa. Even though they had been intimate before, there was a raw tenderness in their movements: conscious and a little unsure. Kunaal removed his shirt and dropped it on the floor. Reeva's eyes caressed his sculpted form rippling with muscles. He looked irresistible and Reeva extended her hand.

He took it and sat down, his eyes smoky with desire. Her breath was caught in her throat as he pulled her closer, till their lips almost touched. He gazed deep into her eyes and she sensed that familiar, heady feeling surface within her, making her skin exquisitely sensitive to his touch. His lips caressed her face and neck before they claimed her mouth. His hands were all over her. She moaned softly, as his hand slipped into her shirt and moved over her body, feverish with desire. Kunaal effortlessly lifted her off the sofa and carried her to the bed. He eased himself next to her, holding her almost protectively in his arms. She shivered as he removed her shirt, the cool, evening breeze touching her bare skin. Kunaal pulled the light duvet over them, slipping his hand underneath to unbutton her jeans. His hungry mouth and hands explored her body. Breathlessly, looking into her eyes, he whispered, "You're so beautiful." Then, in one fluid motion, he claimed her body, her core, as if he needed it to live. Reeva gasped as she felt him within her, opening up to him, letting him take her. He moved slowly and sensuously. Reeva moaned, her pleasure so intense that it was unbearable. In a fit of uncontrolled desire, she bit his shoulder, tasting salt on his bare skin, igniting him further. Finally pushed to the brink, Kunaal gave in to pure sensation and no more able to control his body, he allowed the natural rhythm to take over.

Later, as they lay together in the afterglow of their lovemaking, their breathing heavy and bodies warm, Kunaal pulled Reeva closer and kissed the top of her head, "I was right, you're the most beautiful like this." He smiled – the same smile that had brought butterflies to Reeva's stomach while parking that fateful day. Reeva looked up at him and then her gaze travelled to the balcony, "The sky looks so gorgeous." She mumbled against his bare chest, every fibre of her body relaxed. She felt cosy, protected, like she always did with him. Kunaal sighed contentedly, "Yes they do, but not more than you. You're my shining star forever. I love you." She snuggled against him comfortably and they lapsed into a silken silence. Kunaal gazed longingly at her, as she peacefully drifted off to sleep. A sad smile played on his lips and he wondered if he would ever be able to heal this beautiful, loving woman he had almost broken with his own hands.

Reeva woke up disoriented and registered the bedside alarm clock's incessant chimes as the cause of her interrupted sleep. She sat up in the bed, still groggy. The clock said half past six, but it took her a few seconds to figure out that it was morning. Then the memories of the previous day came rushing back to her. Kunaal was not in the room and the house had an empty, unoccupied aura about it. She sensed something wasn't right. Just as she was about to fling off the duvet, her eyes spotted the red rose next to her pillow. Beneath it was a folded piece of exclusive, handmade paper and a sealed envelope.

Reeva unfolded the note impatiently. It was in Kunaal's impeccable handwriting. The note was addressed to her.

Dear sweet Reeva,

Hope you slept well. Yes, I set up the alarm so that you don't over-sleep. Today is an important day. And no, I haven't gone anywhere. I've just removed myself from the scene temporarily. Why? Because Reeva, you have to take some important decisions by yourself. And I thought that my being around may take away your ability to make balanced decisions. If after you have made your decisions, we're still together, then at least I'll know that you weren't blindsided by my love.

I'm going away for now, but I have left my contact co-ordinates in the sealed envelope along with this note. I'm also leaving behind all the files as evidence of my dark businesses. If you're not able to trust or forgive me, then you can hand over all the evidence and my new address details to the authorities. Don't worry, they will know what to do with it. If you think we have a chance together in the future, then simply burn the files and reach out to me on the address provided in the envelope. We can go somewhere far away and start a new life, away from all this.

So here on, what happens to our relationship depends on what you do with the evidence and information I'm leaving behind. And remember, no matter what you do, it won't change my love for you.

I made mistakes and I'm sorry.

Hopelessly yours,

K.K.

P.S. – There are cookies in the kitchen and your favourite tea, too. Eat something or you will get a headache.

Reeva sat numb with shock. Kunaal had gone away, leaving the burden of the decision completely on her. She had expected arguments, clarifications and discussions with him before she decided what she wanted to do. But he was simply gone. With her mind starting to clear, the weight of what she had learned yesterday became heavier. The daylight was now amply spread over the sea and it looked serene, calm and withdrawn in low tide.

Finally, as she sat at the kitchen counter sipping tea, she glanced at Kunaal's note and the sealed envelope. She missed him. She still felt the tenderness of their lovemaking and longed for him. The words from his letter tugged at her heart and tears formed in her eyes. Panicking, she picked up the sealed envelope and fought the desire to rip it open and reach out to him at that very moment.

And then suddenly, it was all clear to her. The reason Kunaal was gone and the reason she needed to take this decision alone, lay right before her in the envelope. How could she have taken an important decision level-headedly, while Kunaal was around, when she was barely managing to control her desire to run to him? Deep in her heart, she had wanted him to convince her to stay with him, to absolve her from the decision making. But, she knew herself, and so did Kunaal. They both knew that once the tide of emotions receded, she would see the dark, jagged rocks of all the wrongs that were committed in the past. And she didn't know if she loved him enough to look beyond.

She fished out her mobile from her purse to order an Uber but there was no network coverage. Deciding it was time to go anyway, she gathered the files and picked up the note and the sealed envelope and walked out. Kunaal's damaged van was gone too. As she shut the gate, she instantly spotted the sedan parked across the house. A tall figure leaned on the car, facing the sea, lost in thoughts. Then, as if sensing her presence, the figure turned. It was Nihaal and he looked as if he had not slept all night. He made no move to approach her. Instead, he opened the passenger door and she got in without a word. Reeva recognized the unused luxury sedan from his garage. She cast one last, forlorn look at the villa as the car moved away.

Soon, the car was moving smoothly in the sparse, early morning traffic, both its occupants stoically silent. Reeva was the first to break the quietude.

"How did you know I was here?" Reeva's tone was almost apologetic even in enquiry.

"Shalini called me as soon as she left. She thought you weren't safe. So, she waited in your car on the main road, until I came over." He said matter-of-factly. Nihaal, never made a fuss about anything.

"You've been here all night? Why didn't you call me?" Reeva's voice quivered.

"Because, unlike Shalini, I didn't think you were in any danger once I knew you were with Kunaal. I also knew that you had to tackle a few things by yourself. I just hung around in case you needed help," he shrugged.

"How did you know I was with him?" She whispered.

"I wasn't going to let you stay inside alone, unless I was sure you were safe. So I did some snooping around the house. The main hall of the villa is clearly visible from the beach and I was surprised to see Kunaal there. By the way, Kunaal's van was caught on a CCTV camera, driving away after hitting Gowli's SUV and the footage is all over the media. But the number wasn't visible and hence the owner's details were unavailable. I knew the van the moment I saw it parked. He left in it, during the wee hours of the morning."

"You saw him leave?" Reeva's body tensed at the prospect that Nihaal knew the identity of the van's driver, but was willing to overlook.

"Yes, I did. But he better be back soon. It's a media circus out there. Thapar has been named as the person who masterminded Nandita's accident. Gowli confirmed it last night at the hospital, in his dying declaration. By the way, where has Kunaal gone?"

"Somewhere far away, I guess," Reeva didn't know how long she would be able to avoid the inevitable questions. For now, Nihaal only knew a small part of the mystery Kunaal was.

"What do you mean?"

"Nihaal, how does one judge a person, who is neither all good nor all bad?" She looked at him, her eyes moist.

"You don't judge; you make a choice based on whether you can live with it. Hey, what's up Reeva?" He asked urgently as she sobbed. "Tell me Reeva, what's wrong?" He parked the car in an empty spot.

She looked at her friend and then with a deep sigh, started talking. She told Nihaal about each bitter fact she had learned the previous night.

For a very long time, Nihaal quietly listened without interrupting her. He knew that in telling him the truth, she was herself coming to accept it. In the end, she handed over Kunaal's last note to him. Nihaal read it. To him, that note was a cruel thing to do to Reeva, but then what other option did Kunaal have? Of all the people, Nihaal knew what it was like to be in love with Reeva. He held her as she wept against his shoulders, her tears soaking his shirt.

Nihaal returned the note to her and pointed towards the envelope in her hand, "Are those Kunaal's new coordinates?" Reeva nodded a yes. They drove quietly for a few minutes before he asked, "So, where to now?"

"Please take me to the office. I need to prepare a media statement." She turned visibly calm. Nihaal drove towards the city silently, hoping that Reeva would finally choose to do what needed to be done. Once again, he did not know what was on her mind.

Reeva smiled at the framed photos of Nandita and Nirmala Sahay, which finally had their rightful place on Rishi Uttur's desk. She looked at him and fought the tears blurring her vision. In less than forty eight hours, her life as she had known it, had been turned around completely. But she had the clarity she needed, for what she had to do.

"You know what Reeva? I've decided to start a charitable organization for women and children. It will be named after Nandita's mother," Uttur smiled, picking up the frame. "They couldn't be with me when they were alive, and now even if I want them to, they can't." He paused, and then added, "But then I have always lived alone with their memories. So, I guess that's how it will be here on too. These two, they were the first and final loves of my life."

"That's a lovely thought Utturji. I'm glad you're doing this," Reeva smiled warmly and suddenly Uttur's demeanour changed.

"Reeva, are you sure about this?" He pointed towards the file that lay before him. "You know that after this, it will be very difficult for him to set foot in the country. He will have to vanish," he added cautiously.

"Yes, I'm sure." Reeva looked down and sipped her tea. "Everything's in the file, the facts about how the anti-JBP campaign was executed and the people involved in it. From the staged 'slap-gate' incident to the toll plaza incident, and from Thapar's mastermind plan about Navdeep Complex to Sathya Raj Mane's role, everything is in it. There's also evidence about the Fixer," Reeva pursed her lips as she continued, "My role with MVPR is over and I'm moving back to Creative AdZone. But, the evidence in the file is substantial and I suggest that a PR and legal team from within JBP be deputed to tackle it. I thought that it's only fair I bring all this to you. You had the most at stake."

"What about your stakes, Reeva?" He looked into her eyes. "Do you really want the Fixer to be exposed?"

"According to this evidence file and the press statement that I've prepared, I only know that the Fixer exists. Nobody has ever seen him apart from a conduit who exeuted his plans, and he's no more traceable. As far as I'm concerned, I don't know him and I never will. And that's my stand." Reeva smiled with a hint of forlorn sadness on her face.

"Hmm... So, no one will ever know his true identity. I still believe he was a good guy. A little misplaced in his judgement, but not altogether bad. You do know you can still reach him," Uttur regarded her unsurely.

"I know. The question is, should I?" She stood up and extended her hand.

"Okay then, Reeva," he smiled, "And remember, that you can reach out to me for anything, anytime." He shook her hand firmly, "And I say this selfishly because you're my only link to Nandita now. I see her in you." Then he walked her to the door of his cabin and instructed the secretary to organize a drop for her.

"So, where do you want to go?" He asked meaningfully.

"I know where I don't want to go." She smiled and Uttur patted her head lightly before turning back and vanishing into his office. Reeva couldn't be sure, but she thought she saw tears in his eyes.

As she sat in the car, she placed the sealed envelope on her lap and covered it with both hands. This was it. This was where she knew she had to keep moving.

She had always known that it would be tough for her to be with Kunaal and she had walked into his world with open eyes. Now she stood at a difficult crossroad. She could easily take the road that would lead her to the man who she knew loved her so much, that he was willing to undo himself for her. And, she could live basking in his love forever. The other road moved away from him, a possibility she had never considered. A possibility that would shatter her heart and make her lonely. She knew she had to choose ultimately. But, she didn't know if she would have the strength to live with any of the choice she makes. She sat looking at the envelope and sobbed.

Reeva lifted the envelope and pressed it against her lips and kissed it, the thick handmade paper soaking her tears. Then slowly and decidedly, she tore the envelope into two, and then four. She continued until she could tear it no more and it was just a small heap of paper in her palms.

The car glided smoothly on Bandra Reclamation road. It was the same road where Kunaal had first told her how he felt about her. Lowering the window, Reeva held her palm up, feeling the strong wind outside the moving car. The envelope's pieces gracefully lifted into the air and instantly dispersed. Reeva felt the sharp jab of loss as she turned in her seat and looked at the paper pieces fluttering in the wind. She kept looking back, until she could see them no more.

The view of the French Riviera from the terrace of a top floor duplex in Monte Carlo would have been mesmerizing during summer months. But right then, even in the mildly cold winters the clear, azure waters of the Mediterranean Sea were a beauty to behold.

Although the crème-de-la-crème tourists invading the designer boutiques enlivened the shopping streets twenty floors below, the duplex apartment and its sole occupant were quiet. The only sound emanating was from its living room where the large TV was playing a live telecast from India.

The news anchor was excitedly reporting the turn-around in the image of JPB and Rishi Uttur, after the facts about the systematically planned anti-JBP campaign by Thapar and Jaiswal were bared in the media. Speculations were rife about the identity of a mysterious power broker, known as the Fixer, who had aided them in this endeavour. The subsequent sympathy wave had now ensured that nothing could stop JBP from getting elected into power unequivocally. Mega industrialist Dindayal Thapar was under police custody and being charged with the murder of Nandita Sahay. The Fixer was wanted for serious financial and political offences. However, for lack of information and recordable proof, the identity of the so-called Fixer could not be established. But, the police investigation was still underway.

Kunaal sighed and shook his head. Switching off the TV, he tossed the remote aside and ran his fingers through his hair. He sat silently for a few minutes and then smiled sadly. He knew Reeva had made her choice. It had been seventy two hours since he had left her sleeping in his bed. The news had made it clear that all evidence was with the relevant personnel already. Apart from his identity and current whereabouts, she had released all the information to the police. But she hadn't contacted him.

He got up and walked out to the terrace of his duplex. He gazed forlornly at the Circuit de Monaco's F-1 racetrack, which ran through Monte Carlo and the beautiful marina beyond. The memories of his budding love for Reeva during his last trip to Monte Carlo were as fresh as if it were just yesterday. The boutique where he had laid his eyes on that fated Christian Dior dress for her was just a street away from his apartment. Suddenly, he felt alone and vulnerable. He knew that the sealed envelope he had left for Reeva didn't exist anymore, because he also knew her. She loved him, but not blindly enough to move over to the grey area. And grey was the colour that shaded his entire life.

Then, as if snapping out of a reverie, he fished out his cell phone, with a new sim card, and dialled a local number. After a couple of rings, the phone was answered with a crisp French greeting.

"Bonjour, Jean-Luc. When do you think you can fix a meeting with the state minister of Monaco? I need to decide on my investment plans quickly, without wasting time." After listening to the urgent, eager explanations in a mix of

English and French for a while, he disconnected with a polite "Merci beaucoup."

Kunaal was ready to start his journey, once again, all alone. He had everything in life apart from the one person who could complete it.

Epilogue

In contradiction to the famous adage – well begun is half-done – Media Vision PR wound up rather unceremoniously and folded back into its parent company Creative AdZone. With Reeva's inability to want to continue at MVPR, due to personal reasons and Kunaal Kabi's extended absence on health grounds, it didn't take much for Ajay Sehgal to arrive at the decision, once he received a resignation by email from Kunaal. His repeated attempts to contact his mother were stonewalled; she had simply informed him that Kunaal was at an undisclosed location for treatment, and would not be back anytime soon. This was also confirmed publicly by their family friend and physician Dr. Harsh Wardhaan. Mrs. Kabi continued to live a glamorous life of a socialite, unaffected by the absence of a son, who had never been around that much in the first place.

In due course, JBP's popularity ratings indicated a clear majority in all the states that were up for polls. Strong backup from the business groups, who conformed to

Uttur's ideologies and sheer goodwill, helped him fund and inaugurate the Nirmala Foundation for Women and Child Welfare, on schedule. He had carefully selected the location to be Sunder Nagar, amidst the people with whom Nandita had belonged. He did not forget to invite Reeva and she sat next to him on the dais. When she addressed the crowd emotionally, a cheer went up among those who knew and remembered her as their dear Nandita didi's close friend.

Navdeep Complex was demolished, so that a spanking new residential building could come up in its place. This time, however, with fully approved papers and clear titles for its residents. There were talks among the members to rename it as 'Nandita Nivas', but as per the last known status, the matter was still on the table.

Having been exposed of his criminal plans, Dindayal Thapar was convicted for the murder of Nandita Sahay. Vowing to challenge the conviction in a higher court, he continued to serve his sentence, embroiled in an on-going legal battle. Thapar's claims that it was not his doing, but of a mysterious identity called the Fixer, went unheeded by the officials. Sathya Raj Mane's name too was dragged into the investigation, but nothing could be established against him. By then, he had already become an expendable asset for NPP. Not wanting to carry the deadwood any longer, the party's high command asked him to resign. He was left with no option but to retire from active politics and join his wife and son in California.

Expectedly, stock values of J&T Infrastructure had nosedived, but not before Ramcharan Jaiswal smartly exited the company, selling all his shares. His full retirement from the corporate world came as a surprise to all his friends and business associates, but his family loved him for it. Slowly, people stopped hearing about him.

Manek Vir permanently removed himself from the heart of action, retreating into the serene Himalayas. He never considered it retirement because to him, what he had done all these years was strictly off the record. He was simply ex-military. But this time, he had decided to start afresh and on-record, of course under a changed identity. His obscurely named adventure sports academy in peaceful Narendra Nagar gave him the advantage of both, reclusive living and flexible timing. It suited him fine, mainly because most of his clients were tourists and they never asked too many questions. Vir never attempted to trace or contact the Fixer. The day he exposed himself and the Fixer to Uttur, in the hope to save an innocent life, was the day he knew he needed to walk away from all of it. He could not save the girl, but he had saved the father in Rishi Uttur and that was his partial redemption.

Arunabh Roy remained on the fringes of police investigation regarding the anti-JBP campaign, being called in repeatedly for questioning even after clearing his stand on all matters. Finally, Rishi Uttur's intervention managed to get him off the hook. After a brief sabbatical from news reporting, he started his own news channel with overseas funding. Since it was a matter of dollars coming into the country, nobody asked questions. Not of the elaborate nature anyway. He continued to be at the top of the TRP ladder, although with a milder attitude.

Three Years Later

Reeva sipped her steaming Earl Grey and looked out contentedly at the busy Park Street, a famous thoroughfare in Kolkata. She sat with Shalini, at a corner table in Flurys, the famous patisserie. It was her idea, as she believed that their trip to Kolkata would be incomplete without visiting this place. But Reeva knew, it was more about Shalini's need to touch base with the city and her memories, having returned there after almost eight years.

"So, how does it feel, being back here after so long?" asked Reeva.

"Well, a lot has changed, but in a way, it still feels the same. We continue to be the food-loving Bongs." She made a face.

"Hmm... a week in town and you're already getting touchy," giggled Reeva. "But honestly, I preferred Calcutta. It had that old-world charm about it."

"My mom will absolutely love you for saying this." Shalini paused and looked at Reeva meaningfully, "Thanks for convincing me to come back." Before Reeva could respond, Nihaal walked up to them, "Okay, while you girls were chatting, I placed the order for the pastries."

"I hope you remembered the ones Mom asked for?" Shalini smiled at him.

"Of course, sweetheart! How could I dare forget my mother-in-law's favourites?" He winked and kissed her cheek before settling next to her.

Reeva stared adoringly at the pair, the two people in her life who had seamlessly metamorphosed from colleagues to friends and finally, to family. The next day would be their first wedding anniversary and Reeva had suggested they spend it with Shalini's mother. In the end, she too had agreed to join them in Kolkata, but only after the couple's continuous insistence.

"I can't believe we will be leaving the day after. It's too soon," Nihaal's expression was morose.

"Oh, come on, you can come back anytime you want." Reeva laughed and got up, "Let me go check whether our pastries are ready. I don't want to be late for the feast aunty is preparing."

As she left, Shalini turned to Nihaal, "What do you think? Sometimes I wonder if she's alright."

"Yes, she is. She's way stronger than you can imagine," Nihaal smiled, taking his wife's hand in his.

Reeva stood at the takeaway counter and impatiently eyed the attendant packing the pastries in a box, slowly and meticulously. Finally, he placed it before her with a polite smile. She grabbed it and turned around, only to stop in her tracks again. The man dressed in a classy black suit, briskly walking out of the café right that second, looked uncannily familiar. *How is this possible?* thought Reeva anxiously.

It was the structure, profile and the way he moved as if he owned the world that Reeva could never mistake. Even the way the wind blew at that rogue mop of hair on his forehead, reminded her of just one name. *Kunaal*.

Reeva rushed to the door. As she walked right into the crisp, winter evening her frantic eyes spotted him across the street, already getting into a car. She knew he was too far to reach then. And the next second, the car swiftly blended amid the heavy evening traffic. It had all happened within seconds, but to Reeva, it was in slow motion.

Confused, she looked back at the table and saw Shalini and Nihaal engrossed in each other. Reeva slowly walked towards them with the box of pastries. Nihaal looked up quizzically, "What took you so long? The waiter brought the pastries as soon as you left."

"Huh?" Reeva's face turned pale as she saw the other box on the table. Nihaal and Shalini eyed her curiously. She carefully opened the mysterious box and saw a silk-lined, exquisite-looking ring case inside. Her heart skipped a beat as she saw what was placed within. It was the designer sapphire brooch.

"Hey, that's beautiful," murmured Shalini, as she leaned in. "Who is it from? A secret admirer?" She smiled.

Reeva slowly picked up the glittering brooch. It brought back all the memories she had safely stored away. She didn't know the future back then and she didn't know it now. Yet, not knowing the future seemed like a blessing.

Reeva whispered, "Maybe."

Acknowledgements

Gratitude. This is something that I feel immensely, in every fibre of my being. I don't know where to begin, yet I write because feeling gratitude without expressing it, is like buying a gift for someone and not giving it. Although there is no way I can thank enough the people associated with this book, directly or indirectly, I will make a humble attempt.

To begin with the beginning, I would like to thank Joydeep Datta, my sounding board, critic and advisor, and the first person to tell me that I am wasting my time, if not writing. Thanks JD, for having faith, when my own faltered. You made me see with clarity, when self-doubt clouded my thoughts.

Sometimes, we feel motivated to do something but finish it only because it will make someone else very happy. My mom, the simplest person I know, has given me the purest form of love I could ever receive. If my book's existence puts a smile on her face, then it was all worth it. Mom, I always want to see you smiling.

I don't know if I should consider myself fortunate or whether destiny was being kind, for Jaico Publishing House was the only publishing house I approached with my manuscript. Thank you Sandhya Iyer, Managing Editor, for believing in the potential of this book and asking me to be patient. You did say that the process will be a learning experience for me. And it certainly was. Thank you Jaico, for all the professional hand-holding.

Often in this imperfect world, we come across diamonds. Sanjana Parikh, you are one of such shining diamond. I thank you for correcting every single error and sweetly arguing everything back and forth with me, even when I was wearing you down. As my editor, you stood your ground and that made the final product come out as it has. Looking at you, I can say that angels do come without wings.

There are a number of people, places and events, from the past and present that inspired me to write this book. For all of them, I look up to the sky and say, "Thanks."

To the reader, who will pick up this book and choose to spend time with it, I express my deepest gratitude and sincerely hope that you like it. After all, this book is meant for you.

JAICO PUBLISHING HOUSE

Elevate Your Life. Transform Your World.

ESTABLISHED IN 1946, Jaico Publishing House is home to world-transforming authors such as Sri Sri Paramahansa Yogananda, Osho, The Dalai Lama, Sri Sri Ravi Shankar, Sadhguru, Robin Sharma, Deepak Chopra, Jack Canfield, Eknath Easwaran, Devdutt Pattanaik, Khushwant Singh, John Maxwell, Brian Tracy and Stephen Hawking.

Our late founder Mr. Jaman Shah first established Jaico as a book distribution company. Sensing that independence was around the corner, he aptly named his company Jaico ('Jai' means victory in Hindi). In order to service the significant demand for affordable books in a developing nation, Mr. Shah initiated Jaico's own publications. Jaico was India's first publisher of paperback books in the English language.

While self-help, religion and philosophy, mind/body/spirit, and business titles form the cornerstone of our non-fiction list, we publish an exciting range of travel, current affairs, biography, and popular science books as well. Our renewed focus on popular fiction is evident in our new titles by a host of fresh young talent from India and abroad. Jaico's recently established Translations Division translates selected English content into nine regional languages.

Jaico's Higher Education Division (HED) is recognized for its student-friendly textbooks in Business Management and Engineering which are in use countrywide.

In addition to being a publisher and distributor of its own titles, Jaico is a major national distributor of books of leading international and Indian publishers. With its headquarters in Mumbai, Jaico has branches and sales offices in Ahmedabad, Bangalore, Bhopal, Bhubaneswar, Chennai, Delhi, Hyderabad, Kolkata and Lucknow.

SINCE 1946